AUGMENT NATION

AUGMENT NATION

SCOTT OVERTON

No Walls Publishing

SUDBURY, ONTARIO, CANADA

Copyright © 2022 by **S.G. Overton**

All rights reserved. No part of this publication may be reproduced, distributed or transmitted in any form or by any means, without prior written permission.

Scott Overton/No Walls Publishing
Sudbury, Ontario, Canada
www.scottoverton.ca

Publisher's Note: This is a work of fiction. Names, characters, places, and incidents are a product of the author's imagination. Locales and public names are sometimes used for atmospheric purposes. Any resemblance to actual people, living or dead, or to businesses, companies, events, institutions, or locales is completely coincidental.

Book Layout © 2017 BookDesignTemplates.com

Augment Nation/ Scott Overton -- 1st ed.
ISBN 978-1-7774308-8-7

To my children.
I've tried to teach you to live your dreams. Thanks for taking that message to heart, and for respecting mine.

Man is not going to wait passively for millions of years before evolution offers him a better brain.
— CORNELIU E. GIURGEA

The mind is its own place and in itself, can make a Heaven of Hell, a Hell of Heaven.

—JOHN MILTON

RECOVERY AND REHABILITATION *September 3, 2040*
Memorial Hospital Trauma Center, Surgical Critical Care Unit—Fifth Floor:

Damon Leiter looked down over his broken body and understood that the course of his life had become defined by two things:
 The computer implants in his head had undergone a hard reset.
 And he was going to have to rely on his organic brain to figure out who'd tried to kill him.
 The implants were still functioning—he could feel them—unless it was an illusion, like *phantom limbs* after an amputation. Data from the past forty-eight hours should have flowed back into his conscious awareness a few minutes after such a reset. That's what he'd been told—but it had never happened before, should never have happened. He checked for the presence of long-stored data, like a tongue probing a tooth. Yes, older data was still there. He took a mental sniff: there was lots of wifi and white-fi in the area—the stale, rusty smell of older, slower frequencies probably installed five years ago, but also the ozone-sharp scent of the newest vintage. That made sense. He was in a hospital

room, and there was probably a well-connected nursing station nearby.

Like a human brain, his implants had a buffer to hold new data for a time before it was sorted by importance for long-term storage. Maybe the buffer had been damaged; although a strong power flux from a hard impact could have wiped it. A basic diagnostic scan didn't show any lasting malfunction, just a blank where the past forty-eight hours should be. No digital memory of those two days at all. That was a problem.

He turned his eyes to the far wall with its flat, pastel-green paint. *Shouldn't there be a mirror there? A window to the left? Vid screen hanging in the high corner to the right?* No. That was another hospital room, fifteen years ago. Strange that the old memory was so vivid. He relaxed and let his eyes lose focus. He didn't want old memories—he needed the fresh stuff of the past two days, and plenty of it. *Real* memory was a capricious thing, like the still surface of a pond—touch it wrong and the ripples would distort the image it reflected beyond recognition. It was doubtful that he'd actually find the details he needed there or be able to fully trust the ones that did arise, but it might give him a place to start.

At first nothing came. Then he felt the room lurch into a spin and his muscles jerked and snapped like a string of firecrackers tossed on the ground. He groaned and arched with a bright swell of agony, and dimly heard an alarm go off from some equipment behind him. Nurses would soon come running.

No good. Pushed to revisit the moment of near-death, his brain relived only the trauma without revealing peripheral details. Or, fear and confusion had simply never allowed those elements to register in his mind in the first place.

He was badly broken, but he'd survived. To stay alive, he'd need to know who had tried to kill him, and how urgently they would try again.

There was no way to determine that with the information from his biological neurons alone, but it was clear that he wouldn't be leaving the hospital bed any time soon. He might as well use the time to search his digital archives.

How far back should he look? Through nine years of data? To those early days he'd rather forget, when he was the boy *David* and not yet the man who'd become *Damon*? Could he even be sure the identity of his would-be murderer was there to be found, in the sensate library of his life?

It had to be. He had to trust that there'd be a clue somewhere in the shades of his past.

He closed his eyes and pictured an accordion string of images: a photo album stretching far off to an obscure horizon. And then he sent his mind hurtling along it.

BOOK ONE

1

August 12, 2031

Patient Name: David Allen Leiter

Age: 14 Sex: M

Next of Kin: Astrid Leiter (mother)

Medical History: No relevant history

Preoperative Diagnosis: Broad-spectrum agnosia secondary to severe cerebral trauma incurred in a vehicular collision.

Investigations: Functional Magnetic Resonance Imaging (fMRI) scan of head. Right-parietal craniotomy, left-parietal craniotomy, and occipital craniotomy for purpose of implanting electrodes for a brain-computer interface (BCI), and for implantation of a combination BCI and digital storage device known as the *Taggart BCID*. Intra-operative assessment of functioning of the BCID.

Anaesthesia: Monitored anaesthesia care with local anaesthesia (Marcaine and lidocaine). IV sedative.

Complications: None

Detailed Procedure Description: The scalp was shaved and scrubbed; sterile sheets placed. The patient was prepped with Betadine and a Leksell frame was mounted. Incisions were made and burr holes drilled along the parietal bossings, the sagittal suture, and the lambdoid suture. The skull was opened, and three large contiguous sections removed. The dura was cauterized. For each electrode array implantation, microelectrode recording was done, target cells identified, then a deep brain electrode (DBE) connected to the BCID was planted on target in the cortex and tested. Multiple high-density microelectrode arrays were implanted (see attached appendix A for type, number, and detailed placement). The BCID unit was attached to the underside of the parietal bone flaps using titanium screws. External ventricular drainage (EVD) and a brain pressure monitor system were positioned. Saline irrigation was used, and the dura sutured closed with Vicryl mesh. Parietal and occipital bone flaps were replaced and secured with plates and screws. The skin was closed with common poliglecaprone sutures.

Cerebral pressure was monitored to note any increased pressure from either surgical manipulation or the BCID, but

```
the device is very thin (see appendix B
for device specifications).
    Leksell frame was removed and patient
was transferred to the post-operative
area in stable condition. His vital signs
were monitored and within normal
parameters. The patient reported no pain
or discomfort.

    V. A. Klug, MD
    per Emery R. Taggart, MD
```

Image: *A thick vertical line with a shorter horizontal line across it about three-quarters of the way to the top. Something in David's mind supplies the word "cross". He doesn't hear the word, or truly see it, but he becomes aware of it somehow. Then a shape is in front of the cross: a human shape, a man shape. David's eyes look at the top of the figure and his brain says the word "face". As David tries to make sense of the image, there comes a sound. The man on the cross is speaking to him. He says:*

"Hello David. I'm Doctor Taggart, the surgeon who installed your implant. How are you feeling?"

David's eyes began to focus. An impression of lifeless green paint and sterility. A hospital room, then—he could see the corner where the far wall met the ceiling. Halfway down the wall was a big rectangular ...something like a window that reflected stuff. [A mirror.] The cross was a reflection in the mirror.

That was it. He was lying in a hospital bed with a mirror on the opposite wall. The cross must be above the bed, and he could see its reflection. There were strange shapes on either side of it, with blinking lights and screens. But the man wasn't in the reflection. He was standing in front of it, at the end of the bed, obscuring most of the cross.

David's voice didn't work right away—his throat felt tight and dry. Sore, too. He tried to clear it, but someone placed a container with a drinking straw in his hand and he took a few sips. Just water. He tried to speak again and managed to say, "I'm OK."

"Great. That's good to hear. Don't worry that you don't remember me. You had *agnosia*—do you remember what that is? Including *prosopagnosia*. So, we've met—lots of times—but you haven't been able to recognize my face from one time to the next. You remember my voice, though, right?"

David nodded. He groggily tried to concentrate on the man's features and more words appeared in his awareness: [Emery Rueld Taggart, MD]. He was pretty sure he'd never known Dr. Taggart's other names before. He liked the face, though. What he could see of it above a blue cloth mask. It was a strong face with bushy eyebrows and blue eyes alive with interest. "Dr. Taggart," he said.

"That's right, David. Your surgery's over and it went really well. You should heal without any problems, just like I promised, although it'll take a while for your hair to grow back." Smile wrinkles above his mask showed Dr. Taggart was trying to be chummy, but he wasn't very good at it. "And if everything's working the way it's supposed to, your implant should already be helping you identify the things you see. Faces too. Is that happening?"

David nodded and sipped more water. "Yes," he said. "There are words. They just...they just...."

"Just come to you? That's right. That's the way it's supposed to work. Signals from the implant are actually sent right to the vision centers of your brain and in a form your brain can recognize, but they're not images exactly. We're pretty sure you'll be able to learn how to store whole images in your implant's memory, but that could take some time and it's not critical right now. The

most important thing is that your implant identifies what you're seeing and tells you what it is. OK?" David grunted agreement. "Great. So, are you ready to look at some pictures?" The doctor took silence as consent and held up a square of paper in his gloved hands.
[Paper. Picture.]
"It's paper," David said. "A picture on paper."
"Yes, but what's it a picture of?"
No new words came to David's mind.
"OK, I knew this might happen. Not a problem." Taggart gave a half nod to someone else in the room. David tried to turn his head to see who it was but found he couldn't, and that it hurt to try. He moved his eyes instead and ignored the ache from that. He could just barely see two other man-shapes a few feet away. He looked at their faces, but his mind said [unknown—unknown].
"The implant is analysing the object too literally. David. Now, here are some pictures of things. I need you to look at the pictures and try to imagine the real things they represent—make a kind of new image in your mind of the *real* objects. Can you do that?" He waited for David's shrug and then held up the page again. "OK, what's this a picture of?"

There were straight lines and some of the spaces between the lines were shaded. It looked like something he knew. There was a word for it.

"Box. It's a box."

"Very good. How about this one?"

"A ... pyramid?" Was that right? It looked like two triangles pushed together. Pyramids were in Egypt. With sand, and mummies, and burning sun.

"That's right. Good, good. OK, let's try something a little more complicated."

Green and brown. Thick line below, wide convoluted shape on top.

"A tree."

"Good. This one?

Rectangular. Red. Round shapes underneath.

"A car."

"Excell...."

"2025 Honda Accord."

Taggart laughed. "Even better. We weren't sure how much orientation would be required for the implant to provide more detail. Apparently not much." He held up another picture.

"It's a dog. A Labrador retriever. Dr. Taggart, my brain already told me your name when I looked at your face. Do we have to look at kindergarten pictures?"

"Fair enough. We can let it go for now. You're probably still tired." He gave a little shrug to the other men, but the show of sympathy didn't disguise his impatience.

"How come I know your name, but not these other people?"

"Well, we put my face into your implant's database as a reference, along with thousands of other well-known and historical people, and tens of thousands of objects. But your implant is supposed to learn new faces and objects you encounter by storing new images and their identifying data *as you learn it*. This is Dr. Robert Burke, and Mark Phelps, a graduate student. I guess you can't actually see much of our faces with our masks on, but they're for your protection."

"My implant takes pictures? Through my eyes?"

"No. It records the signals that pass from your retina along the optic nerve and encodes those signals for storage so they can be faithfully reproduced. That way, when that data is recalled from the implant, your brain processes it the same way it would process fresh data from your eyes. That requires much less storage space, and your brain accepts the information more readily. But maybe that's enough questions for now. You should rest again, David."

Just then someone else came into the room. A woman. Long, straight black hair around a small face with large eyes and long eyelashes (but his head didn't supply a name). About the same age as David's grade-eight teacher, Miss Simon. This woman was on the skinny side, but she had an attractive sway to her walk; and David's teenaged eyes locked onto her large breasts. She was pretty. Very pretty.

Suddenly the men were laughing.

"Look at that reaction!" Mark Phelps was watching something going on behind David's head. "Look at the EEG. And the blood flow from the thalamus across the cortex. I'd say you're a hit with this young fella, Doc." He turned to the woman, who blushed, started to say something, then just looked down at the clipboard in her hands.

David was mortified. *How did they know what he was thinking? How could he make it stop?* He screwed his eyes tightly shut and gave an involuntary shudder.

"I think perhaps we should all leave David alone to get some more rest." Taggart sounded annoyed. "Especially you, Doctor."

David listened to them walk from the room and felt wetness on his cheek.

#

Image: *Same reflective surface [mirror] but with a different shape in front of it. Round, but with a short, thick trunk below, spreading into a broader box-like shape. The top part [face] has features: two beside each other [eyes], two others below [nose and mouth], two others, one on each side [ears]. Familiar features [identified in database: David Allen Leiter, features reversed].*

David was glad that he was now allowed out of bed for short periods, even if he couldn't leave the ICU room yet. He stood looking into the mirror, that he now knew to be the mirrored side of an observation window and wondered if anyone was looking back.

There was reason to believe that the reflection he saw was his own face, but he couldn't really sense that. There was no ultimate recognition, only the data readout from his implant, and the fact that the eyes in the reflection winked when he commanded his own to do so. That could be a trick, but he knew it was pretty unlikely.

His reflected face was very different from the faces of Dr. Taggart and the other men. It took him a moment to realize the difference had to do with the top of the head. Something missing. [Hair]. Yes. The head in the mirror was bald. Of course. They would have shaved his head to perform the surgery. He tipped his head forward a little and looked at the ragged tracery of dark pink lines over the top of it [stitches]. Was there a pattern to them? Were they shaped like continents? A simple map of the mind beneath? He had a vague recollection of continents, though he wouldn't have been able to identify any without assistance.

What about the brain under that mapwork of lines? How had it changed? It had been probed and prodded, punctured and poked. It also had artificial electrical leads imitating neuronic pathways, and a wafer-thin computer laid overtop, but not separate—not anymore. The implant was wired right in with dozens of connections, some to receive input, some to give output. Did that make his brain an *alien* thing?

Was he even still human?

He tried to picture the head with hair—could his implant supply that by superimposing a stored image of himself with the current one coming from his eyes? The implant was supposed to act automatically, but it was a kind of computer. Maybe there was a way to give it commands. For this, he would need to picture a mirror image, like the one he was looking at, maybe from brushing his teeth at bedtime or something like that. He tried thinking the command, then saying it out loud, but neither produced any effect. Then he simply concentrated on his name and tried to evoke a sense of the past. A shadow flitted over the reflection—features flickered slightly—but the changes wouldn't stay. That would take practice, apparently. Well, he had nothing else to do.

He pulled his head back and rocked it, raising his arms in the beginning of a yawning stretch, and then a combination of images tweaked at his brain. He was seeing the reflection of his head and arms, he knew, but there were straight lines extending beyond them, upward and to the left and right.

The cross. He was standing in front of its reflection. Something about the montage made him shiver.

#

There came a time when David was finally allowed to return home. Yet his home's familiarity was tainted somehow, as if overlaid with a new reality. Every token of the past was, at the same time, a reminder of how much his life had changed.

Whenever he tried to remember his accident or the months after it, David could only retrieve bits and pieces. Fragments. Isolated moments. That was *wet* memory. Neuron memory. Only strong impressions were moved into storage, along with some of the facts he was told after the event.

His mother had been driving. David had missed the bus and was going to be late for school. Mother was cursing under her breath at a traffic light, and when she saw the signal for the cross-street turn red, she started forward without waiting for her green. A furniture truck from the other direction ran the red light. David only had time to register a looming shadow and a howl of brakes before the world crashed in on him.

Their Toyota rolled. He remembered his head banging against something hard, more than once. Other noises didn't catch up until the crumpled car came to a stop. Then he was assaulted by sound: screams, sirens, saws. Odors that he vaguely associated with animals. He could never remember any pain, only a detached sense that this was what it was like to die.

He'd spent months in the hospital, and only a few weeks at home before they got the call from Dr. Taggart's clinic. Those had been frightening months; he remembered that much. Every so often someone would walk into his view with his mother's soft voice, or his aunt Jenny's cackle, or the bored drone of Dr. Strong, the doctor assigned to him in the hospital. But it wasn't them, so he didn't respond, waiting for the real people to show up. The impostor-doctor told him his brain was just tricking him—it had been hurt in the accident and it couldn't connect faces he saw with the memories of the people he'd known. Or objects either. A nurse would tell him she'd put a glass of water on the bedside table, but David could never find it on his own. He couldn't remember what a table looked like.

He learned to recognize his mother's smell and touch, and that would make it OK for a while. But each time a stranger would come into his room and smell like his mother, he was surprised and suspicious.

It was just as hopeless for him when he was able to go home. He couldn't accomplish anything. Everything he wanted to do required some *thing* that he could never find on his own. One day, they got a call from Dr. Taggart's office, and were told about radical experimental surgery that might cure the agnosia. The doctors warned his mother time and again that the surgery was risky, but her response was always to ask another question, as if she couldn't recognize words of caution, like David couldn't recognize faces.

Yet, after all, that surgery had worked.

It had left him altered; something new had been added to his original body, to his very brain. That made him a new person, didn't it? David Leiter *reborn*?

At fourteen, like most people, he couldn't remember his early childhood struggles with language such as pre-school efforts to read: painstakingly learning each letter one-at-a-time, then words, then sentences. Heck, babies had to learn a name for each new object they discovered—every single thing in their world. Did they get frustrated? Now, feeling like a baby in a teenaged body, David certainly did. His implant supplied the names, but there was always a slight lag—perhaps only microseconds, but surely more than his real brain had needed. It was the interface: one brain (computer) needing to pass information to another brain (flesh). He could only trust Taggart's promise that the process would get faster, until he wouldn't notice it.

During the long weeks of rehabilitation in the hospital, Taggart also promised that David would discover lots of other benefits from the implant over time; but for the first few months back home, the terrible drawbacks of the surgery outweighed everything else.

He'd always loved sports and was gifted at hockey—had even dreamed of an NHL career. No longer. Contact sports involved too much risk to his implant and his now-more-vulnerable brain.

His coach suggested he try cycling. David found he liked the speed, the freedom of the open road, and the wind in his face. Competing in the sport would be too risky, and he constantly had to remind himself to slow down; but thanks to a special, oversized helmet, he was able to convince his mother to let him ride for fun.

Then the world threw another block into the road.

His mother had always been a shopper, compulsively acquisitive. She blamed it on a deprived youth. Never able to have the things she wanted then, she was determined to make up for it as an adult. Maybe that was part of the reason his father had left them when David was just five. A bargain, to her, was like a rabbit to an eagle; but when she found a great deal, she always bought too much. Their small home was a warehouse of the unnecessary, everything largely bought on credit, since his mother's desires were far greater than the income from the housekeeping and retail jobs that were the only kind she could get.

If David's brain-implant surgery hadn't been part of a fully funded research study, he would never have been able to receive treatment for his condition. Even the hospital stay afterward would have been far beyond his mother's means. He was grateful that his affliction and its cure were not the cause of her financial troubles.

Even so, she wasn't the only architect of her downfall.

When hackers looted the database of the Treasure Trove rewards program, they stole Astrid Leiter's identity. Long before the company saw fit to alert their members, her meager savings had been cleaned out and her credit rating trashed. Though she went to court to clear her name and her credit record, the case dragged on for years, and the last of David's time at home was spent dirt-poor. There was no money for a decent bicycle. No money for dreams.

David overheard his mother's lawyer say that he half-suspected the ad company behind the rewards program of engineering the identity thefts themselves with a fake computer attack for cover. David never forgot that.

Lack of money was only one of the reasons that the teenage years of David Allen Leiter were a time spent longing to escape. So, four years later, when his enhanced abilities helped him earn a lucrative scholarship to university, and the move gave him an opportunity for a new identity, he wasted no time shedding his old name and the painful shell it had come to describe. *Daemon* was a term from programming class; in a broad definition it described an agent that was part of a greater undertaking but worked in the background. Under the radar. David liked that. There was something attractively subversive about it. But to use Demon or even Daemon as a name would only have invited a new ostracism, so he became *Damon*. Close enough.

His mother still called him David, not understanding that his "David" years were years of loneliness and exclusion, of ridicule and sometimes even torment. Who wouldn't want to leave that behind?

#

Image: A wide-open space populated by figures moving chaotically through it. At first glance they seem to be evenly, if randomly, distributed. Then, as time passes, it becomes clear that almost all the figures are linked somehow, part of a nearly cohesive whole. But they are seen from the outside, from the perspective of one who is not part of that whole. Isolated. Isolated and alone.

When he first got his implant, David fantasized that it made him like a superhero, with special powers beyond those of ordinary people. Dr. Taggart had been right: it did much more than just help him identify objects and faces. Nearly every week he learned a new trick, especially once Taggart's team began to provide firmware updates that he could download on his computer and transfer to his implant via Bluetooth. The implant's combination of flesh and graphene circuitry produced some brilliant results. He would need that advantage.

The day he entered high school was a month after the term had started. His mother cooked scrambled eggs, sausages, and hash-brown patties for breakfast—his favourites. That confirmed his fears: he was *screwed*.

In high school, "special" was not something you wanted to be. To his new classmates, he was a target: a shrimp who started classes a month late and was nearly bald, with only a layer of fuzz covering a quiltwork of pink scars over his head. Dismayed at their reaction, David tried wearing a wig—only once. It was cuffed from his head and trampled into the schoolyard dirt within minutes of his arrival. He didn't even pick it up.

Before three more days passed, he was beaten up for the first time. A big kid named Thorne and his circle of sycophants chose David for "special" attention and would corner him whenever the chance presented itself. He quickly learned to avoid wandering off on his own in the schoolyard, but that didn't help much, and the beatings continued every second day for more than a week, until Thorne grew bored with David's refusal to resist. The younger boy never hit back since he was forced to keep his head covered with his arms to protect his fragile skull. His mother threatened to take him out of school, but she never did.

The other kids noticed how his eyes went blank when he was consulting his implant. They began to call him "Spacey", and the name stuck. He took to "spacing out" more and more in class, choosing to retreat into his head and revisit the few good memories his implant had filed for safekeeping. TV shows and movies he watched once could be rerun as often as he wanted in the privacy of his mind. He could even get away with that in class sometimes because his eyes moved with the action, nearly camouflaging the blankness of his other features. Eventually, though, his teachers caught on.

After that, they called on him often to see if he was paying attention. David began to hate his teachers.

Except Ms. Brooks. She was kind to him, and she was pretty. He hardly ever zoned out in her class because she made things interesting; and once in a while, she gave a smile just for him that made his breath stop. He paid close attention to her, waiting for those magic moments.

He couldn't get up the nerve to say much to her in grade nine. But when he found himself in her English class again in grade ten, he thought it must be destiny. It wasn't too difficult to arrange to be the last to leave her classroom, and sometimes she spoke to him then. She'd ask him what class he had next, or if he had any brothers or sisters at home. One time, she even walked with him to his next class.

That had to mean something. David began to think about a plan.

The very next day he found himself alone with Ms. Brooks. He had a study period and she asked him to help her sort some papers. He quickly agreed, then nearly spoiled everything by getting the papers mixed up, all of his attention focused on finding something clever to say.

His chance came when Ms. Brooks asked him if he had a favourite author. He knew that she loved Shakespeare, and his implant was fully supplied. He called forth the words and let them roll from his mouth.

"Shall I compare thee to a summer's day?
Thou art more lovely and more temperate.
Rough winds do shake the darling buds of May,
And summer's lease hath all too short a date...
But thy eternal summer shall not fade
Nor lose possession of that fair thou ow'st"

"David, I'm very flattered, especially that you would have memorized that sonnet for me," she said, her face shading pink. "But, you know, that's probably not something you really want to say to your teacher."

Not want to say? True, it only *hinted* at what he really wanted to say. Maybe a sonnet wasn't enough. Perhaps something more impressive, from *Venus and Adonis*....

"'Fondling,' she saith, 'since I have hemm'd thee here
Within the circuit of this ivory pale,
I'll be a park, and thou shalt be my deer;
Feed where thou wilt, on mountain or in dale:
Graze on my lips; and if those hills be dry,
Stray lower, where the pleasant fountains lie."

Ms. Brooks' eyes grew wide, and the pink in her cheeks had turned to red. He felt his stomach turn over.

"*Good God!* David. That's...more than inappropriate! What do you think I am?" Flustered, she snatched at his sleeve and yanked on it. "Come on, David. You need to explain your choice of Shakespeare to Mr. Sharp."

David tried to protest his innocence on the way to the vice-principal's office, but no words came to his rescue. His implant was obstinately silent.

If Mr. Sharp, a pinch-faced little man in a steel-grey suit that belied his name, had ever owned a sense of humour, he'd had it excised like an appendix for its lack of purpose. He had a thorough arsenal of outrage, though; and simple words served him as bamboo shoots under fingernails. He'd been waiting for an opportunity to cross-examine David Leiter, the boy with the marvellous implant that let him maintain a passing grade without paying attention to the material in class.

"Tell me about it," he said. "That thing in your head."

"What about it?"

"Where is it? How big is it?"

"It's...like a thin cap under the top of my skull."

AUGMENT NATION

"And you need it because you're brain-damaged."

"I...I...was hurt in a few places, including the [*fusiform gyrus*] ...a part called the fusiform gyrus. So I couldn't recognize objects. Especially faces."

"And now you can."

"Yes."

"And what else can you do, thanks to your implant? Cheat on tests?"

"No, sir."

"C'mon, David. Does your implant store other information? Dictionary definitions? Encyclopaedia entries? Math equations?"

"Yes, sir. All of those."

The BCID had come with an extensive database built in. but had also been programmed to learn. When David encountered someone new, he'd supply an auditory tag for their image by speaking the person's name. With practice, he learned to say the names silently in his head. Many concepts beyond nouns and names could be stored that way. Optical character recognition allowed him to read text and numbers on a page or screen and store the data in perfect detail. Then the implant was upgraded to be able to recognize *ascii*, *ansi*, and other character codes including some international codes like UTF-8, which meant that he could upload almost any kind of text directly from his computer to his implant, without even having to read it first.

"So, you have whole books stuffed into your head. From where?" Sharp's questions indicated interest, but the tone of his voice projected anything but.

"Project Gutenberg, sir. A few other places."

"Textbooks from your courses, too?"

David sensed that there was no safe response.

"Once I've read them," he ventured.

"So, you don't really *learn* anything in class. You just store the answers in that plate in your head and pull them out when you need them?"

29

David didn't answer. He was no longer sure he could see the distinction.

"So how come you don't get a hundred percent on every test?" Sharp growled.

The boy didn't dare admit that he'd begun to deliberately give wrong answers, just to avoid persecution by his classmates. There was another reason, but he knew it wouldn't be welcomed either. "Some of the test answers are outdated," he said in a soft voice.

"*What* did you say?"

"Some of the textbooks are out of date, sir. If I know the right answer I give it, but sometimes the teacher marks it wrong." He knew that he was treading on dangerous ground, but the injustice of the situation made his ears hot.

"So, you just decide that you're right and the *teacher's* wrong, is that it?"

David looked out the office window. There was sunshine out there, but the glass hadn't been properly cleaned in years, so the outside world had acquired a tint of distance and irrelevance. Sharp's office resolutely depended on artificial light.

"And now your cocksure attitude includes spouting pornography at your teachers. Do you somehow think you're untouchable, boy? Do you think you're beyond punishment?"

"No, sir." *Pornography?* David associated the word with lurid internet sites his friend Raj had shown him when they were eleven. How could those possibly have any connection to Shakespeare? Was that what Ms. Brooks thought, too? Maybe it was. Otherwise, why would he have been brought to Mr. Sharp in disgrace? In that case, his life was over. Maybe he could run in front of a bus.

"Consider yourself lucky that I can't wash your mouth out with soap, Leiter. Lucky that I can't use the *strap* anymore. But you will serve two weeks of detentions after school, beginning tonight. I'll be there—I'll come up with some things that the computer chips in your head won't be able to do for you. And I'll be watching you from now on. Watching to make sure you don't use that thing to cheat."

But how can it be cheating, David thought, *if you just know?*

#

He left Sharp's office stunned, unable to think clearly. The world had collapsed on him again.

Which was why he made the mistake of taking the stairwell at the far south end of the school, the end that contained the automotive shops and a few empty classrooms.

"Well, look who it is." Thorne gave an ugly smile as he and his friends stepped from under the stairs. "And Danny says he saw the little weasel bein' taken to Sharp's office by Brooks. I wonder why? Whaddya say, Spacey? Whadja do to piss off Miss Hottie?"

David's throat had turned to a pen barrel lined with broken glass. He couldn't have spoken if he'd wanted to.

"Ya think ya can get away without answerin'?" a flunky named Ball asked with a laugh.

"Yeah, Spacey. Give your head a shake," Thorne sneered. "No. Let me do it for ya."

July 14, 2033

Patient Name: David Allen Leiter

Age: 16   Sex: M

Next of Kin: Astrid Leiter (mother)

Case History: Recipient of *Taggart* model Brain-computer Interface Device.

Physical Examination: Surgery from two years ago has healed well, the scars unnoticeable under thick hair. There is evidence of a recently mended dislocation of the nasal cartilage that the subject attributes to a fall. No connection to BCID implant. Other physical indications are normal.

Neurological Examination: Scans reveal increased activity in several areas of the brain since the last examination, especially the thalamus, the visual cortex (specifically Brodmann area 17) and the postcentral gyrus. Activity of this type has increased with each subsequent examination and can be attributed to increased and more wide-ranging use of the BCID.

Case Progress: The subject's agnosia has been entirely overcome by use of the BCID, and the subject reports that he is seldom consciously aware of the implant's prompting with object labels and related information. He just "thinks" of the object's name. In a similar way, he has fully integrated the device's data storage and recall functions for text and numerical values. The subject has also shown remarkable ingenuity in training the device to provide other functions. He has stored nearly every mathematical formula available to him and is able to access them for computational purposes as soon as appropriate data are recognized by his visual centre. He has uploaded very detailed maps of his home neighborhood and uses them for precise navigation. However, the subject has complained of occasional interference from recalled visual data with incoming signals from his eyes (*generated* images sometimes obscuring portions of his *real-world* visual field). This was one of the justifications for device upgrades performed two weeks ago. Hardware updates were attached only subcutaneously rather than intercranially to the posterior occipital sector of the device. Other upgrades were accomplished through firmware updates.

List of Upgrades: 1) Auditory functions have been enhanced with text-to-speech capability in order to provide data recall aurally as well as visually. This enhancement is linked to character-code recognition internally, and optical-character recognition externally, enabling the BCID to "read" to the subject in a data form interpreted by the brain as heard speech.

2) Bluetooth functions have now been supplemented with wifi capability of the most recent standards, plus a tuneable white-fi transceiver, including a frequency and signal strength detector.

3) The device's original rechargeable battery has been supplemented, and largely replaced by, a piezoelectric generator implanted in the patient's chest which generates electricity from the motions of the patient's breathing.

Additional Observations: In order to facilitate future upgrades, dozens of high-density microelectrode arrays were implanted during the original surgery with the knowledge that they would not immediately be used. As the patient's use of the BCID has diversified, dormant electrodes have been activated as needed with 100% success. A secondary feature has also become activated that functions upon demand: the EEG and functional Near-Infrared (fNIR) sensors have allowed the brain-computer interface to self-adjust to the subject's brain workload and other mental states such as frustration or elation and to alter its data recall rate accordingly.

Assessment/Recommendations: The subject adapts very rapidly to upgrades of the BCID and newly discovered hybrid applications of the device, showing remarkable neural plasticity. It is the team's recommendation that the schedule of future firmware updates can be accelerated.

Private Note: Due to the involvement of *Imaging Capital International* as primary funder of the research, Dr. Taggart has reluctantly added some additional protocols incorporated at a very deep level of the subject's implant. *Imagicap* did not reveal details about these protocols, but it is believed by me and by others that these protocols could be used to create artificial imperatives within the subject's brain that would function like subliminal suggestions. If so, the ethics involved are problematic.
    V. A. Klug, MD
    per Emery R. Taggart, MD

Image: *Tunnels...caves.... No. Empty hallways, like a maze or a rabbit's warren—a warren that's been invaded by a predator about to appear from behind the nearest corner. Overlaid on the image are numbers and letters, graphics, scrolling text, block diagrams. It is another world: a world of information. This second world offers potential power. If only it could offer escape.*

On the first day of grade eleven, Thorne was waiting. David tried to avoid the nearly abandoned section of the building, but the interval between two of his classes was just too tight for him to take the long way around. He nearly tiptoed down the stairs, imagining the sound of each breath echoing through the stairwell. Then there were other breaths. The enemy appeared out of latticed shadow as he reached the bottom floor.

David's hand went to his chest, to the spot where the new power source for his BCID had been implanted. The site of the incision was still sore to the touch, but more than that, it gave him a new point of vulnerability. He didn't know if he could effectively protect both his head and his chest from the beating that was coming.

"I'm surprised you got the nerve to come back here, year after year, Spacey," Thorne said. His face was fatter than it had been before the summer and was now shaded with sparse black growth over his chin. "Or maybe you're just stupid. That's no surprise. That plate in your head don't make you smart where it counts, I guess, huh?" The bully stepped forward slowly.

Over the summer, David had changed, too. His BCID could now feed him information by his auditory nerve, as if he were hearing it, so his vision didn't have to be compromised by overlaid data. He'd already learned how to corral the visual display into a corner of his field of view and alter its brightness. So he didn't need to "space out" to consult his implant—he could call on it anytime. Even access the internet directly, through wifi or white-fi.

He used it now, trying to calculate the distance to the door, the likelihood of a teacher nearby, his own top running speed versus the speed of four converging opponents. The results weren't encouraging.

"Your toy calculator ain't gonna help you, weasel." Thorne smiled. "You can't escape that way."

If only he could. Just transport himself into the internet and vanish among bits and bytes, metadata and memes. But maybe there was a lifeline.

Knowledge—he needed to know more about his enemies. He sent a mental call over the internet: Google, Yahoo, Bing...US government pages, state government pages, news archives.

"I don't have to escape, Thorne. I know things," David stalled. "Things about you. Things you don't want other people to know." *Was it true?* Almost. He could feel it—there was some bit of information nearly within reach that just might save him.

Thorne hesitated. "Sure you do, weasel. Like what?" The voice was cocky, but there was a new look in his eyes.

Fear. Thorne was afraid of something and trying to bluff. What was worrying him? What was it?

There! *Pay dirt.*

"Like maybe why your father hasn't been around for three years," David breathed, the paragraphs from the Department of Corrections scrolling across the upper left corner of his view. They were detailed—how much did he dare use?

"You fucking little prick!" Thorne started forward again. David took a step back. Wrong choice. The threat had only made Thorne mad.

"Or maybe what your mother's been doing to pay the bills while he's gone," David blurted, getting his arms ready to protect his head from a rain of blows.

The face of his enemy blanched, a film of frost grown over the irises. His fists reflexively clenched and unclenched. The standoff lasted an eternity of ten seconds or more. Then Thorne hissed, "You're dead, Spacey. You're a dead man walking."

"I don't think so." David swallowed. "If I don't go online for twenty-four hours, the whole story shows up on my JoinSpace page. And yours, and the pages of these losers, too." It was a lie, but Thorne couldn't know that. Was he going too far? *The best defence is a good* offence. Had von Clausewitz ever had to deal with mental defectives like these?

Thorne's face was like stone as he stepped to the side and gave a quick flick of a hand to signal his crew to do the same. But as David hesitantly stepped past, Thorne shouldered him hard into the frame of the door. David whirled around, eyes blazing.

"For that, you get to see an interesting tidbit about your juvie record posted online. And if you *still* don't learn, there's a lot more that the whole school will love to read!" He spun around and walked away, the nerves of his back crawling with the anticipation of another attack. But it didn't come—the bluff worked.

Even so, he didn't make it to his class. He spent the next twenty minutes in the washroom, throwing up.

#

Image: *A desktop of blond wood, veneer chipped away in the top left corner. Scars from a knife blade in the bottom right, in the form of crude, angular letters: a girl's name, but not the name of the engraver. Roughly centered on the desktop is a piece of paper covered with runes. They are mathematical symbols, but decipherable only with unaccustomed effort. More daunting are the blank spaces. The blank spaces demand to be filled with answers.*

David stared at the test page, fighting an inner struggle that no-one else would understand. The previous spring, after his terrifying interview with Vice-Principal Sharp, he'd asked Mr. Foster, his former cycling coach, about cheating. David never meant to cheat, in the sense that he understood it. He received information from his implant without effort, sometimes without deliberate intent. Mr. Foster had said that the point of tests was to show how much the mind had learned, of both facts and *processes*. The *how* was at least as important as the *what*, and if David relied on his implant to do everything, his own brain would never be wired with the skills he'd need to function in adult life.

David trusted Mr. Foster. He didn't fully understand the man's answer, but he accepted it, and he tried hard to make a distinction between mere facts that could be left to secondary recall (consulting his implant was no worse than looking up a definition in a dictionary) and the procedures that he needed to learn with his wet brain. And he tried hard not to use his implant for school tests.

But it was damned difficult. His brain and the BCID had learned to communicate at a level that wasn't palpably conscious. The device responded almost as soon as a desire for information began to form, and its responses were incredibly difficult to ignore. The implant hadn't been created with an "off" switch—no-one had foreseen the need. So, the greatest effort David faced when writing a test involved shunting the feed from his implant out of his conscious focus. The problem was compounded because the device adjusted itself to his state of mind. It could sense his building frustration, and David's vexation made it try to be even more helpful!

The result was a stabbing headache. His math teacher, Mr. Ford, noticed the sweat on the young man's face and smiled.

David gave up long before the rest of the class had finished. He kept his head down over the paper and moved his hand from time to time as if he were still writing, but it was only for show. He could do no more on the test. The accusatory minutes left on the clock passed so slowly he couldn't stand it. He needed a distraction to kill the time.

Idly, he turned his attention inward and scanned the area for wifi. His signal detector was almost like one of his body senses. There was a node nearby: Mr. Ford's laptop computer. Would he have biometrics enabled on it? Probably not—Ford was old. On a whim, David began to try out different passwords to log in to the machine. A math teacher would probably amuse himself with something complicated.

At its most basic level, the operating system of David's BCID was built on Linux. That allowed him to experiment with a lot of programs he found online, although creative measures were sometimes needed to read the output. As he felt Mr. Ford's eyes on him, he tried a simple password-hacking application.

His login succeeded just as the bell rang to end the period. The password was the value of *pi* to ten digits—he should have guessed that! His face creased with a smile.

"Satisfied with your answers, David?" Mr. Ford asked. "Or just glad the test is over?"

"Yes, sir. Both, sir." With a little more time, he probably could have found the answers to the test on Ford's laptop, but that was only another way to cheat. He was glad not to have faced the temptation.

During a free period later that day, he found himself in the hallway outside Ms. Brooks classroom. He didn't have classes with her anymore—a rumor on JoinSpace claimed that she'd wanted it that way. He slouched against the wall a few meters from her door and *sniffed around* for her laptop's wifi signature. He was sure he had the right one when he solved the password: *rubaiyat*. It also gave him an idea.

At the end of the class, Ms. Brooks found a passage from Fitzgerald's translation of *The Rubaiyat of Omar Khayyam:*

> A book of Verses underneath the Bough,
> A Jug of Wine, A Loaf of Bread—and Thou
> Beside me singing in the Wilderness—
> Oh, Wilderness were Paradise enow!

AUGMENT NATION

Mr. Sharp's office looked exactly the same as the last time. So did his suit.

"I don't know how you did it, Leiter, but try it again and you'll be out on your ass in the street. I won't have students in my school hacking teachers' computers. What were you doing—looking for test answers?"

"I don't know what..."

"Shut up, Leiter. You think I can't prove you've been using that calculator in your head to cheat, but you just slipped up. I know that you just wrote a math test, and all I have to do is compare your answers with the teacher's copy of the test answers. I don't think you're smart enough to disguise them. Who did you have last— Mr. Ford? Let's just see how you did." He reached for a button on his intercom and called the math teacher to his office. "Now just sit there, Leiter, and imagine all the ways I'm going to make you sorry."

David didn't waste his time imagining anything. He probed for wifi and found Sharp's desktop computer. The second password he tried was *4discipline*. It worked.

But Sharp's files were a disappointment. The man had a small mind, and his documents reflected that. David didn't want to read other students' school records, or Sharp's assessment of them. His comments made for teacher evaluations might be interesting, but probably predictable. Financial records and school-board documents would be deadly dull. Yet there was a folder named 'Supplemental' that caught his attention. It looked large, but its directory was empty. No. Wait. Not empty—*hidden*.

David glanced up at Sharp. The man was leafing through some papers. Would he notice the flicker of a few windows on his computer screen?

It was easy to command the machine to display the hidden files. A nest of other untitled folders was revealed, one within another within another. When he

41

opened the inmost folder, he gasped out loud. He had to turn the sound into a sneeze.

They were picture files: jpegs, with anonymous titles made of numbers, but he thought he could guess why they were hidden.

Just then Mr. Ford knocked on the office door. David quickly copied one jpeg to his implant, returned the *file view* settings, and logged out, breathing hard.

"Don't sit down yet, Mr. Ford," Sharp said with a tight smile. "I'd like you to bring me a copy of the test young Leiter just wrote in your class. I have reason to believe that he cheated—that he got a copy of your test answers. Just look at the boy—he's practically shaking."

"Well, I can save myself the trip," Ford answered. "I've already taken a quick look at Leiter's paper. He didn't copy my answers, or anybody else's answers, I hope. Because that would mean I have at least *two* washouts in the class." The man frowned at David. "Your test was a mess. Didn't you pay *any* attention in class? Didn't you study? I've always thought you were smarter than that."

David's stomach was already churning. The news could scarcely make him feel worse. He stayed numbly silent and kept his head down when Sharp snarled at him to leave.

At home, he transferred the file he'd lifted from Sharp's desktop machine onto his own tablet computer and, after a last hesitation, opened it. The image it contained nearly made him vomit.

He'd seen disgusting sexual positions like that before, online. But never involving a young boy. The kid couldn't be more than six.

Sharp had a collection of child pornography on his office computer.

David quickly deleted the file and then spent the next hour backing up his own files so he could reformat his tablet and make sure the vile image was truly, irretrievably gone. He'd never been told how to erase data deliberately in his implant. It was an autonomous function for the purpose of regulating storage space—no other need had been anticipated. He finally concentrated on a mental image of a bottomless pit and sent the file tumbling down to vanish into the darkness. Hopefully that worked.

By the time he'd finished, he was icily calm. Sharp was even worse than he'd always thought. Far worse. The question was, what could David do about it? What *should* he do?

Blackmail occurred to him—a higher-stakes version of what he'd done to Thorne. It would be heaven if he could force Sharp to leave him alone for the rest of his high-school time, maybe even erase the black marks on his record. But that would make him a party to what Sharp did, what Sharp *was*. He'd have to think of something else. He'd have to think hard.

He rose from the chair and went to have a long shower.

#

Image: *A gathering of teenaged boys in a low-ceilinged basement. The lights are dim, the better to see the glowing wall lit with simulated explosions and animated gore. The game players wear 3D goggles, earbuds, and accelerogloves to enhance the simulation. Three pairs of hands are making wild gestures in the air. One pair is fluttering in hesitant spasms, as if handcuffed. Surely there must be handcuffs.*

David's implant wasn't a help with video games. Far from it. Distraction was the worst. The game only required him to spot things, track them, and shoot them as quickly as possible. It wasn't necessary to *identify* the objects by name, and it seriously tied up the processing power of his meat brain.

He suspected that Rand Coburn had only invited him over so Rand and his crew could show they were better gamers than the kid with the computer in his head. And they were.

David's wet brain was many times better on its own with games that called for spatial orientation and pattern recognition, like the Tetris derivatives. The other kids weren't laughing at him, not yet, but he could feel himself subtly pushed out of the circle. It was only a matter of time before they not-so-subtly uninvited him.

He needed an edge. His mind drifted out onto the net and found a possible answer: a hack for the game they were playing. A key code that provided a major weapons upgrade along with an aimbot, stronger shielding, and glitching to see through walls and obstacles. Was there a way for him to enter the code and use the hack for himself? The others would be sure to notice.

"Hey, Spacey," Rand called, "you in this game or not?"

David's throat was dry. He had a powerful thirst for a Chinotto, but Rand wouldn't have an Italian soft drink in the house. David didn't even know how he'd developed a taste for it himself—his mother got irritated when he asked her to put it on her shopping list.

"Dudes...." He cleared his throat. "I found this hack. Wanna try it?"

"What's it do?"

He told them. Robby Parker was outvoted by the other three, and they entered the code.

It didn't help David play any better, but at least he was still in the game.

#

Ashley Good wasn't the class hottie, but she had nice hair and a pretty smile. David sat next to her in three classes and thought about her a lot the rest of the time.

The debacle with Ms. Brooks was never far from his mind, either. Maybe it would help that Ashley was David's age. Or maybe not—he tried posting the *Rubaiyat* passage on her JoinSpace page anonymously, but the next day he overheard her tell her friends that it must have come from a nerd or a geek. David wasn't a geek. He liked sports and could even tolerate hip hop in small doses. He searched through the lyrics of the hottest current songs on iTunes, but most of them were too sexual and even demeaning. He found a pop-song lyric and posted that. Ashley complained that the mysterious poster was lame if he couldn't come up with anything original.

In the meantime, she was paying a lot of attention to Rik Morrison, a senior who'd always been a jerk to David. He heard that Rik had asked Ashley to hang with some of his crew at Boston Pizza and maybe go for a movie. The news made his stomach do a slow burn.

A few days ago, during History class, with Ashley beside him (and Rik off on his lunch period), he'd posted a crude sexual verse from a rap song on Ashley's page and signed it "Rik". He'd learned how to disguise the message's origin while keeping its real time stamp, but apparently, he hadn't learned much about young women. Ashley went on the date, and apparently had agreed to another.

Now, with his chin resting limply on fingers linked across his desktop, David watched Ashley give a presentation to the Literature Studies class. Surfing Google images at home, he'd found a picture of a naked woman who looked a lot like Ashley, with the same long strawberry-blonde hair. He imagined Ashley's face with the naked woman's body.

Except he could do better than *imagine*—he could superimpose the stored image from his implant over the real-world Ashley in his vision. It worked surprisingly well, but it made him feel dirty. He looked out the window instead. If anybody were going to see Ashley naked it would probably be Rik Morrison, and maybe soon.

The idea that came to him was disgraceful. But it might work.

It took most of the evening to produce a jpeg that looked authentic, and then another hour to learn how to upload the file to his implant and place it where he wanted it in cyberspace. He had History class again the next day. Rik was on a spare. The new JoinSpace message simply read, "Can't wait to see you like this." The picture said it all.

Jabber texts were flying before classes even ended. In spite of Rik's denials, Ashley's date with him was definitely off. Ashley didn't come to school the next day. She looked on the verge of tears the day after that. Unexpectedly, David found himself nearly alone with her in the hallway at the end of classes Friday.

"Ashley...." He swallowed hard. "Sorry about...about what happened with your JoinSpace page."

She turned to him with a look of horror. "You saw it too? Fuck, Spacey, that's all I need. Just leave me alone! Migod! You're...you're *creepy*."

David stumbled awkwardly to his locker and stood looking into it for so long that he missed the bus and had to walk home. It gave him a lot of time to think.

He didn't blame Ashley. She was right. He was a freak with a machine in his head.

Why couldn't he meet a girl with an implant? Maybe there were some. They could send secret messages to each other—be closer than any couple before them.

What good were all of his abilities anyway? Useful if he wanted to become a criminal, maybe—hack into bank accounts or automated cash machines. He was a whiz at destroying people's reputations. Sure. Bound to big money in a line of work like that.

One thing his abilities did not do was make him a hero. They couldn't even make his own life better. He wished he could just close his eyes and shut out the whole world.

But with no "off" switch, even that didn't work.

There was an open white-fi node at a café he'd just passed. Without conscious bidding, his implant accessed the internet, and a Google map image of his neighbourhood slowly blossomed in his mind.

He gasped out loud. He'd never been able to picture online graphics with anything approaching that kind of detail before. Maybe it was a spinoff from learning how to picture Ashley with another woman's body. That was how a lot of his abilities manifested themselves: as unintended side effects of something he'd deliberately tried to create.

This one had potential. If only he had a GPS in his head, he could walk home with his eyes closed.

What if he could use the new version of Google Street View? Wouldn't that be almost like seeing?

The alley probably wouldn't have been covered by Google vans, so he walked to the street and then tried to call up the Street View image in his head.

No good. The resolution was too low, and the feed stuttered—probably too much data to be processed and then translated into a form his brain could use. He selected the simple map view again and set off, eyes closed.

Even with his ears on full alert, he nearly ran into someone within the first block; so he looked around for a long stick, and then swept that back and forth in front of him like a blind person's cane, hoping it would warn people to steer clear. Sounds of traffic from his left bounced off the buildings to his right, and that kept him fairly well centered on the sidewalk. He had no choice but to open his eyes every now and then to reorient himself within the map, usually when he felt a curb underfoot—he wouldn't risk crossing a street blind—and whenever he had a premonition that he was about to run into a streetlamp or a mailbox. His wet brain took into account every piece of sensory input available to it, from the changes in light through his eyelids, to sounds altered by objects, to the different textures beneath his feet. That was cool—his two brains working together, each doing what it did best.

He only ran into one wall—a jutting half wall that marked the edge of the outdoor patio at the Dutch Mill restaurant where David had bought packets of salty licorice that he'd developed a taste for over the summer. He should have remembered the patio, but instead, the doctored image of a naked Ashley Good had popped into his head

3

January 5, 2034

Patient Name: David Allen Leiter

Age: 17 Sex: M

Case History: Recipient of *Taggart* model Brain-computer Interface Device (2031). The BCID has undergone several firmware upgrades (Appendix A). The subject also received a hardware upgrade at the age of 16 via an additional subcutaneous implant (Taggert A4) to provide wireless transmission and reception.

Physical Examination: Physically healthy, good weight of 70 kilograms (154 lb) and body-mass index (20.3) normal for a teenage male. He has experienced a significant growth-spurt in the past year, and now measures 185 centimetres (6'1").

Neurological Examination: The subject continues to show activity in the right side of the cerebral cortex that is significantly above-average, and that can be attributed to spatial integration of BCID data. Notably, there is not much difference between response to exogenous stimuli (as measured by the P300 response) and stimuli generated endogenously, showing that the subject's internal visualization has nearly the same priority as external vision. This is surprising. Alpha-wave measurements during a variety of both physical and cognitive activities show relaxed alertness indicative of fully integrated control of the BCID functions. There is still no indication of degradation of the implanted high-density microelectrode arrays.

Case Progress: The subject has shown remarkable ingenuity in deriving novel and unexpected benefits from interplay between the BCID and his own brain abilities. Since he is able-bodied, additional functions of the device were not designed to respond to imagined muscular movements (which would produce a conflict) but to visualized combinations of symbols, unlikely to occur in normal cognition. The subject has consistently incorporated these commands into his normal mental protocols to the extent that to him they have become indistinguishable from other trained skills or conditioned reflexes. His further ability to imagine new combinations of skills and correctly "map" the desired function of the BCID to the appropriate neurons in his brain is astonishing. Such a level of adaptability was not anticipated.

Additional Observations: David has begun to show signs of mental stress not related to physical use of the BCID, but more likely produced by a combination of hormonal and cultural teenage pressures and angst coupled with a perception of being 'different' from his classmates. Extra abilities provided by his implant do not yet seem to compensate for his feeling of being an outsider, a feeling common among many gifted teens. It is hoped that the compensatory benefits of the device will become more evident to him in adult life.

(Note: These progress reports are somewhat limited by Dr. Taggart's protocols (Appendix B) that require that all interactions with David be from behind a one-way mirror and that there be no direct contact with him.)

Assessment/Recommendations:
Psychological counselling should be offered to David and his mother. Also, it should be recognized that David Leiter has become an invaluable resource as a case study in the development of brain-computer interfaces, and every effort should be made to acquire and utilize the special knowledge he has developed and continues to refine.

Private Note: David has mentioned a desire to pursue a career in the field of marketing. Given the increasing involvement of ImagiCap in this research project, the career interest is probably not coincidental. ImagiCap's liaison requested that we question David about his favorite treats. The boy mentioned salted licorice and an Italian soda — both rather unusual choices. The liaison seemed pleased, but the significance of such a request is unknown.

Also, since David is a minor, his mother asked for and was given access to the ongoing 'live' feed from David's implant which now provides more than simple telemetry due to David's increased capabilities.

In my opinion, continuing to monitor this expanded feed, and especially providing this access to David's mother, is unwise.

V. A. Klug, MD
per Emery R. Taggart, MD

Image: Clutter. A room full of clutter. Every object can be identified by name, type—a myriad of classifications—but not by relevance. Not by meaning, or emotional significance. Not by personal connection. It is the room inhabited by David A. Leiter, but not "home" in any special sense. Most of the objects are mere purchases: bargains or bribes, from a mother with little else to offer. The few nostalgic ties that once existed have been lost, excised by the knife of misfortune. The old life has been cut and cauterized; the new, simply categorized.

For David, his senior year was an exercise in numbness. He wished he could slip into semi-consciousness while his implant handled the daily

AUGMENT NATION

procession of dull routines, and then, like Rip Van Winkle, reawaken in June. His BCID had no programming for that. The prosaic and the mundane were the purview of his flesh brain and its burdensome sense of the passing of time.

He had no real friends. Friendship as he experienced it was based on an equation of mutual benefit: if the guys he hung with stayed interested in the game hacks and arcane knowledge he could provide, they let him stick around. If not, he had to find somewhere else to be. He didn't mind being alone. What he really yearned for were two things his classmates couldn't provide: a shared experience of someone with a cortical implant like his, and someone who needed him as he needed them.

His brain and its graphene-circuited augment were powerful tools badly underused. He needed to be done with school. He needed to get into the working world, where his abilities could be channelled into productive areas. Like marketing. He was fascinated with the idea of crafting a created desire for something for which no natural desire existed. There is magic in making people *like* something, *want* something, even believe they truly *need* it. That is true power.

The downside was that a marketing career would require more years of school—at least a BA, maybe even an MBA at university. The end of all that seemed an eternity away.

Most of his free time was spent surfing the web on his computer. It was still easier than using his BCID for browsing certain kinds of sites, especially if they involved lots of graphics and dense data.

One Friday, after school, he surfed to the website of the university at the top of his prospect list, as if looking at entrance requirements would make his enrolment real. There was a link to a fraternity page that offered reams of links to recreational facilities, and random fun stuff. A link called "Engineering co-eds" looked like the results of a JoinSpace search with lots of pretty faces, but when he clicked on one of the images, he got more than he bargained for.

Dozens of naked and semi-naked women in provocative poses, inviting, promising. He hesitated, then selected one. It opened a page that was full-on hard-core. Couples, threesomes, foursomes...all entangled in improbable acrobatics and awkward forms of penetration. Sex toys. Leather. Lesbians.

His hand moved to close the browser window, but he couldn't tear his eyes away.

He had his pants undone when his mother burst through the bedroom door.

"*David!* Oh my God. *What are you doing?*"

Astrid was nearly hysterical. David was thunderstruck.

He fumbled with his pants and tried to knock the tablet out of his mother's view. It skidded off the desk and thudded to the floor with an electrical pop.

It was one of the worst moments of his life, as bad as when his father left, as bad as when he woke up after the accident.

It was only much later that he began to wonder how she had *known*.

#

The following Saturday he spent two hours searching his room for a hidden camera, even dismantling a heater vent and going over the wallpaper with a magnifying glass. He found nothing.

It was possible that she'd had someone install a remote control program on his computer, or even just one that would mirror his screen onto another machine. He spent more hours hunting for new programs, hidden files, malware, or even hard-wired siphons from his modem and router installation. There was nothing he could find.

It finally occurred to him: there was an open wifi receiver/transmitter that could conceivably reveal every action he took.

His own implant.

As soon as the idea came to him, he was sickeningly sure that was the answer. Someone—almost certainly the Taggart research team—was getting a data feed from his BCID. Was it like screen mirroring? Probably. It would be easy for them to do. The internet was a two-way street, involving constant back-and-forth communication by computers. But *why* in God's name had they given access to his *mother?*

His wifi sensor didn't reveal any outgoing signal. That wasn't surprising. If the Taggart team had installed it (who else could have?) they wouldn't want David to be able to switch it off.

He didn't know what to do. He only knew that he couldn't allow someone to watch his every move, eavesdrop on every conversation, even detect certain kinds of thoughts. His ears burned with the shame.

Lying awake that night, his mind finally hit on a solution.

He went on strike.

From that moment on, he used every means possible to cut his implant out of his life.

He refused to go to school. He kept his eyes closed. He used none of the symbols that activated his BCID. It was like pretending his arms were paralysed—difficult, but not impossible, and he improved with practice. After years of learning mental shortcuts to coordinate his implant with his native mental processes, he taught himself how to do without them. It was a surreal experience: painful, but also exhilarating because he was pushing back—standing up for himself. Doing *that* was long overdue.

His mother had never apologized for bursting in on him. Now she disingenuously asked if he was sick. He didn't answer. He pushed a dresser against the door, knowing she wasn't strong enough to dislodge it. She asked if she should call a doctor, then threatened to do so if he didn't answer her. By the end of the second day, she was pounding on his door. He removed the dresser, calmly opened the door, and looked into her face.

"Stop the spying," he said, then barricaded the door again. His room had its own entrance to the bathroom, so his biggest challenge was hunger. His anger helped there. His stomach soured whenever he thought about all the private experiences of his life that had been so flagrantly put on display.

The next morning, one of Taggart's young researchers was at the bedroom door.

"David? David let's work this out. Come on, talk to me, OK?"

David went to the door, but he didn't open it. "I know you've been getting a feed from my BCID. Now you're going to shut it off."

"There isn't any feed like that, David."

David returned to bed and closed his eyes.

The man was back by late afternoon.

"OK, David, I admit we were monitoring a few of the data readouts from your implant for safety's sake. This kind of thing is new territory, you know, and it can be risky. So, we were just keeping an eye on things to make sure the implant didn't get you into any trouble."

"Is that why you let my mother watch, too?" He heard his mother's gasp, and a sound as if the man was hushing her.

"Listen, David. If you're really set on having us stop the data readouts, which are for your own safety...we can do that. We'll shut it off if that's really the way you feel."

"I already said it—shut it off."

"Well, it might take some time...."

"No. It won't. Shut it off now." David closed his eyes and lay on his bed, making a cocoon for his mind from which the noise of their pleas simply bounced off.

Early the next morning the man was back at the door. "It's done, David. The feed has been shut off."

"You're a liar."

David had come to realize that since Taggart and Co. were getting a feed via the internet, he should be able to detect the pinging from Taggart's end. So, he'd sent his consciousness sifting through the grey spaces, using sensory analogs. *Listening* for interference like whispers in the dark. *Sniffing* for traces of a foreign presence. *Tasting* for the bitterness of betrayal. He knew the familiar feeling of Bluetooth, the wifi frequencies of the various 802.11 standards, and the white-fi bands. He couldn't sense anything out of the ordinary about any of them. After all, the traitorous data stream had likely been there since the beginning—part of the background.

The only solution he could think of was to find a way to shut down all the feeds he knew and see if anything remained. That called for reverse thinking. He'd always demanded more and more of his implant's capabilities—it was counterintuitive to try to disable them, and it took him most of two days to figure out how.

He'd already had some control over selection, able to choose whichever channel provided the best signal at any given time. This time, he concentrated on *de*-selecting, dismissing one option after another. The final mental leap to disable all transceiver capability was like jumping from the last of a line of steppingstones into a pond. Dark water closed over his head.

He felt deaf, blind, and mute: a drifting mote in a great void.

It was astonishing to realize how much he'd come to rely on the presence of those signals. Could he really give them up for good, in spite of his protests?

But he'd been right—the leak hadn't stopped. He could still feel it, though he couldn't yet say how. He had to dig still deeper. Peel back *all* the layers. Hold his mental breath until the faintest stir of air gave itself away.

And he found it. On a frequency buried deep in the white-fi bands, the television "white noise" that had been freed up when analog TV was abandoned in favor of digital transmissions. He knew there were wireless standards in that frequency range intended to operate over sixty miles. Maybe more. This frequency was in an area that the FCC had never released for public use. So, who was using it? The government? Some interesting implications there, but that wasn't his concern for now—he just wanted to make the signal stop.

The output from the spy transmitter *smelled* older than the product of his other transceivers. That would put it inside his original implant, the one under his skull, not the second device stitched under the scalp at the back of his head a couple of summers ago. No doubt they'd wanted telemetry from his original implant for their research. Fair enough, he supposed, but that didn't excuse their continued snooping when the transmission began to include so much more. And letting his mother access the readouts on their servers.... Even though he was still technically a minor, that was inexcusable.

He wasn't used to sensing individual hardware components. He'd have to find a physical analog for his mind to work with.

His sense of smell was already taken, mapped to the electromagnetic spectrum; and his eyes and ears were involved with a lot of double functions. What about touch? Could he *feel* his new skin growth and distinguish it from older layers? No. He tried running his fingertips over his scalp, but there were too many sensations from the real nerve endings. He didn't think he could filter them out well enough to discover any phantom perceptions underneath.

He hadn't brushed his teeth that morning. He ran his tongue over them. His face split into a smile.

The old transmitter gave off the barest trace of electrical vibration—like accidentally touching a fork to a metal dental filling, but far weaker. He tried to picture cutting off power to it or shorting it out. Nothing happened. Instead, he imagined wrapping it in some dense material, thicker and thicker, deadening the vibration. After a time, the fiction was complete. He prodded at the bundle with an imaginary tongue tip but felt no tingle. Gradually he relaxed and realized that he was wearing a big grin.

He was free.

Not forever—the Taggart group would find other ways to tap into his other transceiver signals, if they hadn't already, so he'd have to encrypt them somehow. It could be done, he was confident.

The man at the door never came back. David's mother gave him a sheepish look when he emerged from his room but didn't mention the subject again—and neither did David.

The taste of victory was one of the sweetest feelings he'd ever had.

#

Image: *Shifting waves of navy blue, like a choppy sea on a cold day. The peaks are mortarboard caps, the shoulders belong to fabric gowns. High school graduation. An image of restlessness, of trite banners and soon-to-be-neglected scrolls of paper. An overall atmosphere of desperation.*

David could hardly believe that he'd graduated. His marks were terrible, and he was sure most of his teachers hated him. Yet there he was, shoulder-to-shoulder with his gowned classmates listening to boring speeches. He'd only come to the grad because his mother insisted on being there, and it was easier to give in than to pay the price in recrimination for years to come. Even the news that he'd been awarded a scholarship to a respected out-of-state university seemed so unlikely that he kept waiting for someone to admit that it was a joke.

His skin still crawled whenever he looked at Vice-Principal Sharp. When the man got up to give a speech about bright minds and bright futures, David thought he would puke. But he had a plan to remedy that revulsion.

Tuning out Sharp's banal words, he probed for wifi, found it, submitted a MAC address and the familiar username and password. He accessed the email account, sorted through the address book, formulated the message, pasted the link. But he didn't send it—not yet. That would wait until Sharp was done with the ceremony and had returned to his office. The timing wasn't critical, but it was a nice touch. There. All ready to go.

David relaxed and began to pay attention to the ceremony again. He moved his head and found Brad Lindsay looking at him.

"You must really like this shit, huh Spacey?" Lindsay said.

David just shrugged. Some shit he liked a lot.

Later that evening one hundred and sixty-seven people—teachers, parents, and others—received an email from Mr. Edward Sharp. It contained nothing but a weblink that came from Sharp's office computer—a link to a child pornography site.

David heard later that the cops had sent two squad cars.

RECOVERY AND REHABILITATION September 8, 2040
Memorial Hospital Trauma Center, Step Down Unit—Fifth Floor:

Reporters were driving him crazy.

Word of Damon's improbable survival after a possible murder attempt had leaked out and become a big story in the blogosphere. Mainstream media had swamped the hospital with requests for interviews and drowned even his best attempts to charm the nurses who now gave him sour looks.

Bloggers were the worst. He had to keep the window opaque after one nutcase rappelled down from the rooftop. Another had impersonated a nurse and made it all the way to his room before being caught. David had been about to file charges against that one until he realized how much information about himself would be included in the police file, and therefore available to anyone with halfway-decent hacking skills. Fortunately, the police had treated the matter as a freak accident, and he'd had the sense not to contradict that when he awoke. It would only have increased attention tenfold, and he had no confidence that the police would learn the identity of whoever had set the trap.

Just as frustrating was his lack of an internet connection offering any hope of privacy. The hospital's wifi security was as thin as their bathroom tissue—there was no way he'd risk using it—and he was too high and too far from neighboring buildings to tap into any other networks with his implant. There was one white-fi source that was pretty strong, but he suspected it belonged to the police or the municipal government, and that meant leaks. He flirted with the idea of searching on the frequency that Taggart's people had used to spy on him—it would be secure from the public, but there was a chance they were still monitoring it.

So, he was on his own and would be for weeks to come as his body healed. Disconnected. The sensation was unnerving, as if he'd lost the use of his hands.

He had a powerful craving for salty licorice to offset the bland hospital food, but the commissary didn't carry it.

He still didn't know who wanted him dead. His search of archival data from his past hadn't provided any answers so far. It was possible that Larry Thorne had graduated from schoolyard bully to would-be murderer. Even more likely was that Edward Sharp was out of jail and looking for payback. The man wouldn't have needed proof to know who'd been responsible for his exposure and arrest. Neither bully had the technical ability to arrange Damon's near-fatal "accident" on their own. They could have hired help, but he was sure both would prefer their revenge up close and personal.

What about after high school—his university years and later? Had he made a deadly enemy without knowing it?

He suddenly became conscious of a strange hum at the edge of hearing and realized it had been going on for a few minutes. Then a voice startled him.

"Mr. Leiter. Damon Leiter. I'd like to speak with you. My listeners all over the world are dying to hear your story. You don't have to do anything—just talk and we'll hear you."

Really? Had someone been able to get into the room and plant a bug?

The voice had come from the direction of his window. He touched a remote to make the glass transparent.

Good God! *A drone!* Someone had brought a drone to a hover about two meters from the glass, its nose twinkling ruby-red. Its speaker was loud enough to hear through the double-paned window, and the bastard was probably using a laser to eavesdrop on the room through vibrations in the glass.

Damon thought about a profane reply. Instead, he made a hand gesture, then darkened the pane again. A nurse had provided him with earplugs. He used them and lay back on the pillow.

An ugly thought came to him: if somebody could get away with buzzing his window with a drone and a communication laser, why not a drone with a gun? The hospital wouldn't have bullet-proof glass.

True, but whoever had tried to end his life had taken pains to make it look like an accident. A flying gun-platform wouldn't be their style.

The nerves in the back of his neck weren't convinced.

Relax. He had to relax. Focus on his memory archives again: his university years—maybe his answers lay there. Fortunately, his implant's data storage capability hadn't required him to be sober.

4

September 4, 2035

Patient Name: David Allen Leiter, now calling himself Damon Leiter

Age: 18   Sex: M

Case History: Recipient of *Taggart* model Brain-computer Interface Device with subsequent hardware and firmware upgrades.

Physical Examination: Subject in very good physical health. Appears to have attained adult height of 188 centimetres (6'2"). The expandable mesh framework of the original BCID has adjusted with the patient's brain growth and its cranial anchors of the same mesh have flexed as required to accommodate skull plate movements. The device remains optimally positioned as cranial sutures have fused.

Neurological Examination: Somewhat difficult to assess. Subject frequently alters his brain readouts by imagining various tasks while data is being recorded. This is evidently deliberate. However, previously recorded correlations between certain BCID functions and activity within parts of the ventral intraparietal area have become stronger, as if some elements of the interface are being processed as somatosensory input.

Case Progress: The subject has learned an awareness of his native neurological processes that is totally absent in the average person, attributable to his increasing awareness of his BCID processes. This awareness is likely a result of his need to create new neural control pathways and mental protocols in order to activate BCID functions and hybrid neuron/BCI functionality. The microelectrode arrays of both his devices are still unimpaired.

Additional Observations: David/Damon has decided to become a different person (as his new name suggests) having left high school to enter university. This personality change will bear watching. Also, since the research team has lost full-time access to Damon's implant, following an unfortunate incident with his mother, and since he is clearly trying to assert his control during neurological monitoring, future data from this subject may become increasingly unreliable.

Assessment/Recommendations: Although it will compromise the quality of certain data, it may be necessary to use sedative drugs to reduce this subject's conscious control during future neurological assessments. Also, he and his mother have consistently refused psychotherapy, so it may be useful to have these progress reports reviewed by a psychology professional to detect and forestall any tendencies toward schizophrenia or such other mental disturbances as have recently been discovered in another patient in the Taggart-implant program.

Private Note: Dr. Taggart has offered to provide me with an implant of my own, for research purposes. The offer is very tempting, but the involvement of ImagiCap is of concern to me. Whatever agenda they have, I am already a part of it, but I fear that an implant might be an irreversible compromise.

V. A. Klug, MD
per Emery R. Taggart, MD

Image: *Long, flowing hair framing an oval face with plucked eyebrows, full sculpted lips, aquiline nose. Not one face: a succession of faces, all remarkably similar. Their eyes reflect yet another face: a male face that is both familiar and unfamiliar, it has changed so much.*

Damon Leiter entered university as a virgin, but that undesirable condition didn't last long.

None of his high school graduating class had followed him out of state to this campus—he'd checked. No-one at this school knew anything about his implant. So, he created a new identity for himself: no-longer-meek victim David Leiter. Now he was *Damon* Leiter: confident, capable, and charming. His hair had grown back full and wavy, and his mother said he was a "looker." Freshman girls seemed to agree. Or they were just equally eager to lose their own virginity. He didn't even need to seduce them with poetry pilfered from the Bard.

He had three trysts within the first two weeks. None of his partners was experienced, so his own shortcomings in technique weren't noticed, and he was a quick learner. After getting basic learning in that course of studies, he was able to give a little more of his attention to his regular classes.

He was amazed to be in university at all. His high-school grades had been no more than average, and there was no way his mother could afford the tuition. For years, she'd deluded herself that Damon's father would suddenly reappear with an offer to pay for his son's higher education. But as the end of high school loomed, they learned that the man had died six months earlier in some kind of botched convenience-store robbery, flat broke.

That news caused Damon far more pain than he ever would have thought. He had only wet-brain memories of his father, and those were few; yet he'd sculpted them into a composite of an ideal male parent, despite all evidence to the contrary. When his fabrication was shattered and the pieces swept away, it felt as if the last trace of his own innocence vanished with it.

After that, the most he'd hoped for was that a job as a retail clerk might pay for a few online courses once in a while. Then he'd been surprised by a call to the guidance counsellor's office. A private benefactor had provided a new scholarship for the underprivileged: one student per school, and somehow his name had been chosen. He'd been stunned that anyone had applied on his behalf. He'd thought he was invisible.

The escape from his old neighborhood and its smothering vapors kindled a new flame in him. He was determined to pay attention in class and win over his professors as well as his classmates. That didn't seem impossible—he'd been well-liked in primary school. It was the "otherness" that radiated from him after his implant surgery that had killed his chances of a normal high-school life. In university, he left the name Spacey behind with the name David.

Hoping for a career in marketing, he knew an MBA would help him climb the corporate ladder. He'd start with a humanities BA and include economics and an introductory course in business law.

Accommodations in the student residence were designed for double occupancy. Damon's roommate was Jeff Conway, known only as "Con", who was already settled in when Damon arrived. Con ushered him into the room like a real-estate agent at an open house. A tall, frizzy-haired computer fanatic from Buffalo, he would have been the stereotypical hacker/geek, except he didn't live with or sponge off his parents, and actually made out with women instead of just fantasizing about it. He also drank beer instead of Red Bull and had sporadic programming jobs that paid his bills and then some. He rarely talked about his freelance contracts except to say they inevitably "made the world a better place." That was his pet phrase. He forgave the college food-court kiosks for their fat-laden fare because their leathery French fries *made the world a better place*. His well-worn sweatshirts had pouches in the front from which he would occasionally pull a fry of uncertain vintage and pop it into his mouth. Damon hadn't thought anyone even *made* sweatshirts like that anymore.

Con was in Damon's economics class. He was a natural with computers. But he couldn't get the hang of economics.

By mid-term, it became clear that even late nights of tutoring before exams wouldn't be enough. Damon tried to help his friend find ways to "level the playing field"—they were both careful to avoid the word *cheat*.

Con made enough cash to be a classic first-adopter and he had a brand-new Apple Cortico. The commercial brain augment couldn't do as many things as Damon's implant, but it didn't require years of practice either, and it had the advantage of being completely external. It attached with surgical glue just behind the left ear, like a flatter version of the old Bluetooth phone earpieces and interfaced with the brain mainly through the primary auditory cortex. It could also feed sound through cranial bones near the inner ear. That made it almost exclusively focused on sound and language—a serious flaw in Damon's opinion, but it was designed to be an entertainment device more than a tool.

Conveniently, it was completely hidden by Con's frizzy curls.

"Maybe we could get a miniature radio microphone, and you could whisper the answers to me from across the room," Con said. "I'm sunk here, man."

Damon knew a mic wouldn't work. He'd be overheard, or seen moving his lips. But there was another way, though it meant revealing the existence of his own implant to Con.

The computer buff was suitably impressed. Especially when Damon's BCID read the answers to his own test paper and sent them as audible packets by Bluetooth to Con's Cortico. Con did Damon's household chores for a week as a reward.

Damon was pleased for the sake of his friend, but he wasn't able to rationalize why, after working so hard to keep from using his own implant to cheat, he'd been willing to do so for somebody else.

Con became mildly obsessive about Damon's implant after that, wasting precious drinking time speculating about the potential of the technology to "make the world a better place." Most of his ideas were puerile:

sending spoof messages over the campus public address system, planting porn images into a prof's projected lecture notes, or implanting his cell phone number into address books of attractive co-eds under the name "Dreamlover." Damon laughed such tricks off, even as his brain figured out ways to make them work better. While Damon didn't follow through with any, he did take note of new techniques they inspired him to discover.

In the meantime, Con taught Damon a whole new level of computer hacking. He had a sophisticated collection of password-cracking techniques and programs, and was willing to share. All of the university's systems had succumbed to his attentions within his first week on campus, but he was smart enough to get good grades on his own in everything except economics; and he knew that if he simply changed his marks in the computer files, he'd be caught. It would be too easy to miss an entry, and grade software was thoroughly cross-referenced to identify hacking attempts.

Instead, Con used his skills to plant testimony about his sexual prowess on the JoinSpace pages of the hottest women he encountered, making the entries invisible to the owner of the page, but obvious to everyone else. For fun, he'd sometimes collect secret data from low-level government sites, but he never did anything with it, and made sure it was even more secure on his own computers than it had been on the original servers.

One of the first things he'd done with his Apple Cortico had been to learn how to defeat its security measures. After that, he got a kick out of infiltrating other Corticos and Nike Neuro augments for minor mischief, messing with daily reminder settings or planting Rick Astley songs into iTunes folders. He taught all these skills to Damon in return for occasional help in economics.

No-one would have been the wiser, if Con hadn't become greedy.

They didn't know about a grad student who sat in the back of the economics lecture hall to monitor tests. The guy used the time to do work on his own digital scroll, enabled with Bluetooth.

Damon and Con both aced the economics final. So did seven other students. Four of them had answers that were uncannily similar to Damon's. The grad student had detected the Bluetooth activity, though he couldn't track the source. The prof didn't need that—he'd known that only Damon knew the subject well enough to have supplied the original.

Damon was furious. Con offered to split the money he'd earned from the other cheaters—he wasn't about to give them refunds just because they'd been too stupid to disguise their answers. Damon refused and spent a sleepless night trying to decide whether or not to reveal his roommate's moneymaking venture, in hopes of a lighter punishment for himself.

All four students were given a failing grade for the course. Two were expelled because of previous infractions. The others were put on probation, and that included Con. Unexpectedly, Damon was given a chance to redeem the lost credit and his good standing.

All he had to do was help the university catch other cheaters.

#

Image: *Faces. Twisted, distorted...not by a trick of funhouse mirrors but by anger. Strobe-frozen expressions of outrage: storm-cloud eyebrows over orbs full of lightning; chins outthrust like swords; lips pulled back from bared teeth into rictuses of aggression. A defensive show, like the arched back of a cat.*

Damon couldn't believe that he'd been given such a break. He was even put on the payroll as a teaching assistant—an opportunity to earn spending money for the first time. The associate dean he reported to was a cynical man named Bower who was told about Damon's implant and wasn't impressed. Bower believed all cheaters should be kicked out for the first offence. He was especially disgusted with those who chose to cheat when they were intelligent enough to succeed without it, and he left no doubt that he placed Damon in that category. It didn't matter that Damon hadn't done it for his own benefit.

Relief at his reprieve was short-lived. The secret assignment was like an invisible wall that built itself between Damon and his fellow students. He was the "other" again. He still made friends, but he knew the friendships were fragile. A careless word could shatter them. Yet, even as guilt gnawed at him, he enjoyed the challenge of trying to outsmart cheaters. Many showed a real genius for deception. He wondered if the CIA searched for recruits among them.

Since it was obviously better to prevent cheating than to have to catch the perpetrators after the fact, the first security measure Damon instituted was powerful jamming of Bluetooth and wifi signals in exam halls. He left it to Bower to fend off complaints from faculty and others nearby. The jamming worked, but not for long. Students turned to laser beaming to share information between digital devices. Damon countered that with an adaptation of dry-ice "smoke machines" to lightly fog the air so that lasers were easy to spot.

Paper exams were archaic, and since no way had been found to make students' personal electronic devices cheat-proof, the university had purchased hundreds of reusable digiscrolls whose rollable paper-thin screens could be written on with special styluses. They were expensive, but they could be connected to analysers that measured how long the student took to provide a response. Cheaters filled in answers faster than it should have taken them to thoroughly read the questions—clear evidence of copying.

Screening machines looked for traces of electrical activity from hidden devices. Pockets were emptied; wrist-phone implants taped over. Corticos and Neuros had to be disabled before an exam. Damon and Bower accumulated quite a collection of button and pen cameras.

Low-tech methods were even more amusing: chewing gum wrappers with notes carefully printed inside; oversized sunglasses with answers lightly inscribed on the lenses. One student had course notes printed all over the sleeves of her blouse, only visible with the special polarizing contact lenses she wore. In an empty hallway a small distance from the exam room, she couldn't wait any longer to remove the irritating lenses, and Damon was watching.

Though the university was pleased with his efforts, the number of cheaters kept rising. He began to interview the ones he caught. Almost all of them said the same thing: they hadn't had enough time to study for the test.

One young woman who'd tried to cheat with her Nike Neuro was typical. As Damon questioned her, her face occasionally blanked for a few seconds and her right forefinger twitched. She'd ask Damon to repeat the question. Or if she was talking, she'd pause in mid-sentence, then continue as if nothing had happened. He finally asked her about it. The look she gave him made him think he'd suddenly switched to baby talk.

"Jabber," she said.

"Jabber? You mean you're Jabbering while we're talking?"

"Of course. I have to catch up for the time I was in the exam hall."

Although Jabber had started out as text-bursts, augments like the Neuro rendered its messages into speech heard through cranial bones. He'd thought that sending a response required a dermal touch-pad on the wrist, but obviously he was out-of-date. Nerve impulses to a finger appeared to be enough.

He estimated that the woman was receiving and replying to a "Jab" every thirty-seven seconds, on average. No time to study? Heck, she didn't have time to *think*.

Her case turned out to be the rule, rather than the exception. Whether it was Jabber, or JoinSpace, or a legion of online forums that stole their time, the cheaters had none left to spare for schoolwork, and couldn't understand why. What they did understand was that the accumulation of good test-grades was the prescribed path to their university degree, so they'd get them by whatever means were available.

That's why their puzzlement always turned to anger.

They were genuinely indignant at being treated as if they'd done something wrong. As far as they were concerned, they'd purchased their university degree when they paid their tuition. They needed it to get a job, and they'd paid for it up front. The rest was just window dressing.

The news that they could be expelled from the school and lose their tuition was always met with unfeigned disbelief despite it having been made clear in university calendars and orientation guides.

The worst were the entitled ones from wealthy families. They could easily buy their way out of trouble, and Damon didn't bother to pretend otherwise. He rarely left one of those sessions without being compared to a bug on a sidewalk.

Image: *Buildings made generic by motion blur. Streaks of taillights, strobes of traffic signals, flares of gaudy neon. A frenetic urban landscape smeared across the awareness by the desire to affirm immortality through speed.*

Con was the only one of Damon's close acquaintances who'd learned to drive. A big slice of his earnings from coding went to automotive taxes, road tolls, emissions levies, and insurance, but he'd inherited his car: a candy-apple-red, low-slung, electric model modified for speed with a so-called 'voltage amplifier.' Con used the amplifier all the time. What was the point of taking a car if it didn't get you where you were going faster than mass transit, with a fiery shot of adrenaline as a bonus?

Maybe the car was part of the reason Damon and Con stayed friends, even after the debacle of economics class. The transit system was decent, and privacy screens with wifi access meant you never had to endure face time with a stranger, but it wasn't free. Damon's only spending money came from his irregular hours as a "teaching assistant."

Even by their third year, Con and Damon spent weekdays studying and weekends partying, racing around the city in the Con's rolling sex salon. Traffic Central predicted heavy traffic areas more than an hour in advance, and Con relied on the predictions constantly to find routes that would let him "goose his wheels" for a few seconds at a time.

Damon's popularity had a different source. The commercial augments of his friends told them where to find available restaurant tables, short movie line-ups, and alternate routes around traffic jams or police presence. But Damon always knew where disguised celebrities were hanging out, where bands were giving surprise concerts, even where to find a safe viewing-spot when poverty riots flared. He wouldn't stand for stealing, but he could disable most security and surveillance systems to allow the gang to go places they weren't supposed to go and make love without fear of bureaucratic voyeurs. He didn't even have to tell them how he did it—they just knew he could.

Even so, Damon knew that his bag of tricks had limited shelf-life. Sales of the Cortico and the Neuro had caught fire, despite their outrageous price tags. Kids with rich parents could afford the augments with full real-time connectivity, and a whole digital infrastructure was being built up around them. Damon would have to work to stay ahead.

"Pretty soon everybody'll be like you," Con said to him, as the car seats wrapped around them for another race against boredom.

"Yeah. I guess." Damon realised that he'd come to think of himself not only as special, but superior. He wasn't sure what to make of that.

"S'okay, bro. It ain't the size that matters, it's what you do with it." Con laughed and sent the car screeching through the gates of the campus.

From the beginning, Con had taught Damon how to hack into the commercial BCI's. First it had been to impress girls by scanning their iTunes libraries to know their favorite music and movies. Then he searched for things like sports-score apps, blog subscriptions, club memberships, all in the interest of making conversation and anticipating favors he could use to surprise people. As the novelty of that paled, snooping began to give way to little practical jokes. He changed minor settings in people's augments, planted gag tunes or images, or even altered internal passwords just to watch somebody squirm for a bit. It was all harmless—he didn't damage anything. He was particularly proud of the time he made love to a girl and triggered her Cortico to softly play Ravel's *Bolero* to her. The look in her wide eyes was very satisfying.

Damon never messed with Con's Cortico.. Undoubtedly equipped with the most impenetrable security screen it could handle, it would have made an interesting challenge. But Damon didn't try. They were friends. Lifelong buddies. There was trust there, and trust had to be preserved.

On all other fronts, the temptations he faced every day were mind-boggling. Resisting them was like wading against a current that grew stronger with each step. There was a buffer in the process that helped a little. Even though a lot of his implant's functions had become so reflexive as to be virtually automatic, he still had to exercise conscious choice to access external devices.

But that all changed when he got his second implant.

5

March 16, 2039

Patient Name: Damon Leiter (formerly David Allen Leiter)

Age: 22 Sex: M

Case History: Received original *Taggart* model Brain-computer Interface Device (BCID) at the age of 14. Received *Taggart Opus* BCID one month prior to this examination. No other relevant medical history.

Physical Examination: Subject is in excellent physical health. The seven burr holes drilled into his scalp for the implantation of new BCID components are healing well. A bone flap was removed during the surgery to allow integration of the new device and two coin-sized sub-processors with the main processor of the original implant. These incisions are also healing well, and hair growth is returning to normal. The subject reports no lasting side effects from the surgery.

Neurological Examination: One month after the activation of the second BCID, total integration with the first device can already be observed. As with the original device, there is significant extra EEG activity in the visual cortex, as well as higher-level activity in the seven brain-areas where electrodes of new subsidiary sensors were placed. This activity was expected; however, it is also apparent that there is increased connectivity among these seven locations in ways not observed in a typical brain. This phenomenon was confirmed by a fiberoptic visual examination of one site, which revealed substantial glial production of myelin along axons of new neural pathways. The significance of these connections is uncertain.

Case Progress: The subject reports improvement in functions related to his brain-computer interfaces by what he refers to as an "order of magnitude." Certainly, there appears to be a wide-ranging set of brain-computer interactions that operate below the level of conscious thought and with great rapidity. Also, for the first time, he has been given a home control-system: software on his home computer that allows him to tweak certain settings of his BCID in relation to neural potentials. This new system has allowed him to greatly

AUGMENT NATION

refine command thresholds and simplify command sequences.

Additional Observations: Damon Leiter appears mentally healthy and, indeed, uncharacteristically cheerful, excited by the potential of his new BCID. He is no longer uneasy about his shaved head or concerned about being "different" from other people. His new attitude must be taken as a good sign; however, it is unfortunate that he still refuses to allow even the most basic ongoing monitoring of data from his implants. Such data could be very helpful to further development of the BCID program.

Recommendation: If Damon's mental capabilities have in fact increased by the degree he reports, it is recommended that he be kept under close observation because of the opportunity it would provide to continue refinement of brain-computer interfaces. It is also an opportunity to learn how such previously unknown abilities might affect the human psyche.

Private Note: The liaison from ImagiCap asked to observe this examination with me from behind the one-way glass. He was accompanied by a rather short man, clearly an executive, and two large men whom he described as assistants. These visitors were not introduced to me; but I learned from the clinic's security log that the executive was Reinhardt Janus, director of the company division that funds our research. I don't know the reason for this visit, but I am disturbed by its implications. With Damon Leiter developing new capabilities never before recorded, the consequences cannot readily be predicted.

   Since I too now have a cortical implant, a *Taggart Quartus* model, I've observed Damon with extra personal interest. I admit that I might not be completely unbiased.

   V. A. Klug, MD
   per Emery R. Taggart, MD

Image: *A pervasive white glow. It is radiant, and nearly tangible, but does not last. Almost without notice, fine cracks appear and begin to spread across the luminous vista. Its radiance begins, ever so slowly, to dim, and soon the field of vision is a flat eggshell vandalised by hairline fractures and blemishes. An expectation of perfection, marred by reality.*

"What do you mean *a new implant?*"

"I mean we're offering you a replacement for your original BCID. It's what, eight years old now? Wouldn't you like a new one?"

The voice on the phone had identified itself as Mark Phelps, a member of Dr. Taggart's research team. Damon remembered Phelps as a cocky young guy. He didn't sound cocky anymore, but the voice was familiar. It was the content of the conversation that he was finding hard to credit.

"Let me get this straight," Damon said, "I haven't cooperated with you people for...five years—my last examination was just after I stopped your *spying* on me—and now you're offering me a new implant? Why?"

"A fair question," Phelps replied. "I won't say we aren't disappointed that you've ignored our requests for an examination. There were certainly some who said that ruled you out as a candidate for Dr. Taggart's new device." Phelps didn't say if he was one of those.

"Then why approach me now?"

"Dr. Taggart. He has the final say. And his arguments were convincing. There is no one in the program who's had a Taggart device longer than you have. And frankly there's no one who has done as much with it as you have. Maybe that's because you got it at an early age—the other recipients have all been adults. Or maybe you just have a *gift*." The last words carried the hint of a smile, but Phelps hadn't offered a video connection, so Damon couldn't tell if the smile was sincere or sarcastic.

"What do you get out of this? There must be strings attached."

"No strings. But we'd like it if you'd allow some ongoing monitoring of certain telemetry."

"No deal."

"It would only be minimal data collection...."

"No."

Phelps sighed. "All right. I was instructed to try to get your permission for that, but Dr. Taggart doesn't want it to stand in the way of reaching an arrangement. However, he'd have to insist on occasional verbal interviews, so you could at least tell us how the device is working and what you're experiencing. You have to give us something."

Damon thought about it. Of course, it would have to be worth their while, and if he didn't cooperate at all they'd just have extra motivation to sneak something past him. But did he really want a new implant that badly?

The answer was a resounding Yes!

#

When they rolled him into the operating room, he was surprised at how little he remembered from his first surgery. His perceptions this time would be more lasting, no doubt.

The first impression was of pristine whiteness. Optimism, perhaps, because after a moment he noticed a water stain in one of the ceiling tiles above him. The tile next to it was whiter than all the others in the room. So, a leaky pipe had forced the replacement of the worst of the tiles, but only one. A heating duct had a grey smudge over it. There was a lightning-bolt ink-mark on the green scrubs of one of the nurses. Dark specks formed a short exclamation point on the wall to his left. Blood? Maybe sprayed from a cranial saw?

Most disturbing was a hand-printed sign above two gas connectors that protruded from the right-hand wall to make sure staff didn't confuse oxygen feed with nitrous oxide.

It was a relief to succumb to the anesthetic.

His awakening was surreal: nearly psychedelic, and frightening. His first blurry image through teary eyes had no sooner resolved into the contours of a room than it began to be overlaid by glowing lines and squiggles, and then replaced by images of buildings and a streetscape that expanded, shifted, and shrank of its own volition. The new vision was detailed, but betrayed a faint graininess that marked it as an artifact: a photographic reproduction from somewhere. He closed his eyes, but the flow of imagery continued, eventually coalescing into a still image dotted with what he recognized as text.

The words identified it as a graphic representation of the hospital he was in. There was even a slowly flashing red outline around one of the windows on the sixth floor, and a number superimposed beside it—presumably the room he occupied. He mouthed the name "Dr. Taggart" and the right side of his field of vision was filled with more text about *Taggart, Emery Rueld MD*. A pretty thorough biography, from the look of it. His mind focused on a header about brain augments, and the header inflated into a full article on the subject, from an online encyclopedia.

The movement of the aerial street view combined with shifting textboxes and graphics gave him some vertigo before he could get control. He'd learned to keep data feeds from his old implant from interfering with input from his physical senses—he tried the same techniques now, but with only partial success. Obviously, a lot of neuronal pathways had changed. The alterations would have to be identified and incorporated into his system of mental protocols. That would take practice. More startling was the way the new BCID was already obeying commands he wasn't conscious of having given it, so some protocols must have been natively transferable. Or, more likely, the new device had already *learned* the old protocols from the older implant, adapting and adopting them where appropriate. That was fascinating in its implications.

He kept his eyes closed and probed for the new device, eager to unlock its mysteries. Hopefully, the nursing staff would think he was still asleep, so he wouldn't be disturbed.

The next morning, he was drowsing when he became aware of music playing somewhere. It was a multilayered pop arrangement, but his ears couldn't place it in space—that meant that it was internal. Had his implant responded to a subconscious desire to hear music? No, he didn't recognize the song—it couldn't be coming from his music library. Would the BCID just reach out into the cloud for some random melody?

He opened his eyes. There was a young nurse in the room, moving to check the readouts above his bed to compare them to a tablet-like device in her hand. She hadn't noticed that he was awake, and was humming unselfconsciously, her finger tapping on her tablet case.

The rhythm of her taps matched the beat of the song. Her lips twitched along with the words in his head.

The music was coming from her.

When she saw his open eyes, she gave him a smile and moved to the end of the bed to adjust the blankets for him. She bent slightly and brushed hair back from her face. Damon caught the tell-tale edge of a Nike Neuro behind her ear. It must be wide open, with no security protocols at all. Some people never got the hang of securing their home wifi networks, but it had never occurred to him that brain augments could suffer the same neglect.

"Is there anything I can bring you?" she asked.

He took a moment to register the question—actual sound transmitted through the air—then made a noise of refusal and shook his head slightly. Her eyebrows knit with puzzlement.

"OK. Just buzz if you need us." She left the room and he let his head drop back onto the pillow, eyes staring into space. At some point, the music stopped.

Good God. He'd always had to follow a complicated process of mental commands to tap into another person's augment.

Now, apparently, it would require a deliberate effort not to.

#

Image: *A face and a name, inseparable: Valerie. A delicate oval framed by flowing red hair. China-plate skin; cornflower eyes; folded-poppy lips. A face of simple beauty. A face that held the mystery of a hundred secrets and the promise of a thousand kisses.*

Phelps interviewed Damon a couple of days after the surgery. Damon's mother had visited the hospital often and wanted to be included in the interview, but Phelps politely asked her to excuse them, and a young intern took her to the lunch area.

Phelps led Damon to the room where his regular checkups and progress assessments had taken place. They went through some timeworn psychological and neurological tests, followed by general questions, while Damon nonchalantly used his BCID to read everything on public record about Phelps. An impaired driving charge when he was twenty dismissed for some reason. Faultless academic grades despite comments from professors about his untidiness and lack of ambition. An application for a marriage license withdrawn a week later. A warning from police only a month ago about cruising slowly through a neighbourhood known for its prostitutes.

"Have you felt any unusual urges...like sexual urges?" Phelps asked.

"No. Have you?" Damon smiled.

"It's a common question when there's potential for neurological damage." The other man frowned. "We're just trying to be thorough."

"I feel fine. Terrific. As I told you, the two implants are interfacing with my brain and each other better than I could ever have hoped. I would have lost so much if I'd just let you deactivate the old one and replace it with the new."

"All of the data would have been copied over to the new device, including your modifications to the operating system, and the BCID's own learned adaptations."

"Maybe. But since you couldn't risk removing the original electrodes anyway, I'd rather have the old chunk of metal and rare earths actually doing something instead of just sitting there like scalp underwear."

Phelps shrugged. "It was your choice and we honored it." He glanced up at the mirror on one wall. "I hope you'll remember that as I ask you this question one more time: will you give your permission for the Taggart Clinic to activate a feed of real-time telemetry from your implant back to the clinic?"

Damon felt a groan begin, but then the annoyance was replaced by a warm feeling of well-being.

"You can trust us," Phelps said. "We don't have any interest in doing you harm. Look at all we've done for you already. We're your friends." He tried hard for a genuine smile, and despite Damon's scepticism, he couldn't help but give the man the benefit of the doubt. After all, life was good. Taggart and his boys really had given Damon a great gift—he couldn't argue that. He'd been angry about them spying on him, but it was understandable, given their investment. They'd never done anything to hurt him. And now, thanks to their newest contribution, he felt invincible.

"Why not?" he said. "Just as long as it's the bare minimum this time. Brain wave readings and cerebral blood flow are OK. Video and audio aren't."

"Sure, OK. No problem." Phelps said, his head nodding vigorously as if in a hurry to seal the deal.

When they stood to leave the room, Damon gave Phelps a friendly punch on the shoulder.

He just felt so damn good.

#

The cheerful mood evaporated as he drove his mother home, and was gone by the time he got back to the apartment he shared with Con. He cursed at himself for giving in to Phelps. Lying on his bed, he probed his mind-space for tell-tale signals that smelled unfamiliar. It took a while, but he found the new outgoing datastream. As he'd feared, it was using more bandwidth than simple telemetry would require. That was enough justification to put a stop to it. He visualized turning off a valve. Afterward, he waited for his phone to ring, but Phelps didn't call. Hopefully the man knew it wasn't worth the bother.

Later that week, in one of those defining moments that go unrecognized at the time, he met Valerie.

While he'd been on medical leave from the university, his anti-fraud tasks had piled up. One case was intriguing: a mature student, a woman suspected of cheating despite a total lack of evidence. He went to talk with the English lit professor named Swanson who'd requested his involvement.

"Have you found any text that she's plagiarized?" Damon asked.

"No, but the anti-cheating services aren't a hundred per cent, you know." Swanson shrugged. "Just have a look at this paper."

Damon could tell that the sentences were well-written, but the document on the screen told him no more than that.

"It's the sophistication," Swanson persisted. "She's an undergraduate student, a mature student. She says she works as a store clerk."

"She references Joyce, Faulkner, and Fitzgerald. Everybody does that."

"Yes, but she does it right. And she doesn't just use the worn-out quotes you can get on the internet. It looks like she's actually read the stuff."

Damon rubbed the smooth patch under his lower lip, where a refusal to grow hair kept him from trying a beard. "Maybe she's just smart. But I'll have a look."

The woman had an assignment scheduled in an intermediate poetry class two days later. He set up his gear in the back of the exam hall, including an electromag detector and a digiscroll that showed feed from two overhead cameras. The rollable screens of digital scrolls didn't stand up to much punishment, but digiscrolls were convenient for his purposes. During the class, the woman tapped the screen of her exam-issued digiscroll at a steady pace, occasionally brushing red hair back with one hand or another. There was no sign of an augment behind her ears. Damon spared a few glances for the other students, but not many. His target was worth his exclusive attention, with long hair just a shade redder than auburn, and a fine-featured profile. When she was finished and rose to leave, he saw that her light sweater and mid-length skirt showed off a strikingly attractive figure.

But he hadn't spent all the time admiring her looks. He'd done his job. And he'd come up empty. There was no sign that she'd cheated. With his high-level clearance, he was able to access her assignment file almost immediately and used every digital tool he knew to find a match between her words and thousands of other similar papers in digital archives. There were a few low-bit hits—that would happen even with a monkey typing—but no high-confidence content matches, or even any red flags from style analysis. This woman was an original, and obviously intelligent. Damon would have bet money that she was actually some kind of professional, not a retail worker; but that wasn't the university's concern. He reported to Swanson that she was clean and left the office feeling relieved.

He didn't see her again for two months. He'd gone to the Taggart clinic for one of the checkups he'd promised. Phelps made a fuss over the telemetry feed, and Damon began to relent again, but his resolve hardened almost as soon as he left the building.

He was starving after the checkup and stopped for a corned beef on rye at an auto-deli across the street. Then he walked toward the rail station. Just next to it was a combination art gallery and bookstore, with real books on paper. The next car wasn't due for twenty minutes. On a whim, he went into the store.

With nothing particular in mind, he stood just inside the entrance, looking around, then had to make way for a guy with big shoulders who entered just behind him. A short, dark-haired man in an expensive suit came in soon after, and Damon thought he might be with the big guy, but they went in different directions.

Discolored signs hung from the ceiling—painted signs, not electronic—that indicated the arrangement of books by topic. Damon wandered toward the Literature section, and as he turned into the aisle, he was startled to see long, red hair that looked familiar. He couldn't see a face. She was concentrating on a book in her hand. He sidled along the shelves, pretending to read titles, then gave a cough.

She turned to him, and her eyes sprang wide. Had she recognized him? The university was a big campus but a small world. They probably travelled the same corridors all the time. He hoped her surprise wasn't because she was guilty after all.

"Hi, I've seen you on campus, haven't I?" he said.
"Have we met?"

"No. I mean, you do look familiar, but I don't think we've met." She hesitated, then held out a hand. "I'm Valerie...Wise."

"I think you'd have to be," he said, nodding at the book she was holding, "to read Dostoyevsky for fun. Wise, I mean."

She gave a small smile. "He's actually very readable. And human."

"Always a good start, as far as I'm concerned." He returned her smile and looked more carefully at her face. Close up, he could tell that she was older than most of the undergrads. Probably in her thirties. But it was a maturity in her eyes that said so, rather than any signs of age. Her skin seemed flawless.

He'd found her physically attractive when he first saw her in the poetry class, but now there was something deeper: a flush of warmth rose from his stomach, and a tingle of heightened awareness dried his mouth. Her eyes grew large, and they held his gaze with a new light.

"Would you like to...."

"...go somewhere?" He finished the sentence she'd begun, and they both laughed.

When he remembered the moment later, he was sure that they were in love before they left the store.

6

August 8, 2039

Patient Name: Damon Leiter

Age: 22   Sex: M

Case History: Recipient of *Taggart* original plus *Taggart Opus* models of Brain-computer Interface Device.

Physical Examination: Subject remains in excellent physical health.

Neurological Examination: Minimal cooperation from the subject prevents anything more than minimal assessment. Both implants and all electrodes appear to be functioning without degradation.

Case Progress: The activities of both BCIDs appear to have been fully integrated with the subject's normal cognitive functions. His use of their capabilities could be compared to using fingers to touch-type, rarely requiring conscious thought.

Additional Observations: Damon has become secretive about the extent of his abilities involving the implants. This is an unfortunate loss of information of great value for future progress in the field, especially since Dr. Taggart himself has decided not to do any more of this work. Of more concern is that Damon's secrecy might also be a sign of incipient paranoia or other psychological maladjustment.

Recommendations: Damon continues to resist professional counselling. No further recommendations.

Private Note: Personal observations of Damon are both enlightening and worrisome. I've been very sensitive to any sign of ImagiCap influence in my own cortical implant and have detected none. I would have said the same about Damon, until he suddenly announced that he was going to work for them! This development and its future ramifications are alarming.
V. A. Klug, MD
per Emery R. Taggart, MD

Image: *Perfectly-symmetrical blue netting over crystal clear water—that's the overriding impression, except stretched into a giant edifice towering into the sky. Row upon row upon interlinked row of elongated octagonal eggs of glass, fitted together with wonderful precision.*

AUGMENT NATION

What did it represent? Ultimate wisdom? Implacable strength? Or simply unbridled vanity?

The offices of Dyna-Mantech BCI caught only a little of the morning sun or they might have been impossible to look at. Damon's neck quickly grew stiff gazing up the gleaming face of the building. It was a far cry from the university's aged architecture of world-weary brick that he'd always associated with esoteric learning. His wonder at the soaring construction in front of him was very like his amazement at being here to look at it.

The university had to be losing patience with him. His MBA thesis just never got done. Yet the administration itself was largely to blame. The number of cheating cases they wanted him to look into had exploded—where was he supposed to get time to research his subject and write a book about it? Then, out of the blue, he got an extension on his thesis *and* a job offer on the same day. As on so many other occasions, Con fulfilled the time-honored duty of a university roommate by looking after Damon while he got totally blasted.

Confronted by his new workplace, his stomach was still a bit delicate.

The new job represented validation of his research work—personal validation, too—but it also promised a solid income. That was a first. He sometimes wondered how much of his isolation in high school had been due to his implant and how much had been because of his clothes. Self-cleaning fabrics had just come out, but his mother couldn't afford them. His clothes were never in style, all too often smelled of dampness, and were worn until they began to fall apart. University hadn't been a lot better. His job there was a concession to save his career—it paid little more than meal money. The thought of having some serious disposable income was dazzling. He decided that most of his first pay would go to new clothes and shoes—a pure status display, of course, but necessary if he were to fit in at a place like D-M. He'd need Valerie's help to know what the hell was in fashion that week.

The recruiter had said he was just the man they needed, with a combination of rare personal experience and unique knowledge. Dyna-Mantech BCI was a subsidiary of a giant international conglomerate called Imaging Capital International—ImagiCap for short. He had no idea what business ImagiCap was in—probably most of its employees didn't either—but Dyna-Mantech specialized in brain augments and related peripherals. His qualifications in that field were certainly more than academic, but he wasn't technically trained in the hardware, and told them so. It turned out that the subject of his unfinished marketing thesis made him attractive for a special project.

They were hoping to exploit the vast new potential for marketing to people with digital brain augments.

A man named Jaden Black had interviewed him. The HR guy had video-star looks, and his tightly curled hair gleamed as if it were waxed.

"Your thesis compares marketing to hypnosis, I understand."

"I wouldn't put it that way." Damon shifted in his chair. "Several studies have noted that older people are less susceptible to hypnotism—the power of suggestion—while children are very open to it. There must be a neurological reason for that, and since marketing certainly involves suggestion, I thought there could be a correlation worth exploring."

"Have you made progress?"

"Uh...not as much as I'd like. I've had to catch up on a lot of neuroscience. Studies on magnetic stimulation have suggested that the right hemisphere of the brain might be the place to look. It's also known that certain kinds of brain damage—especially to centers like the anterior cingulate gyrus and areas of the prefrontal cortex—can make people more susceptible to suggestion. I'm drawing up a protocol for a meta-study of data on the subject, and I've had some preliminary agreement from my university to do some testing with volunteers." It sounded lame as he said it, but Black only smiled.

"How'd you like to have the resources of a big company at your disposal as well? You could even use some of the brain-augment data from our projected marketing study for your thesis, subject to our approval, of course."

Damon felt his eyes grow wide and struggled to keep a professional face. "Wow, yeah, that would really help! To pin down the best way to reach *all* the various commercial augment users we might need some pretty big sample sizes, though."

Black smiled. "We can access lots of research about marketing from our parent company, but it's the neurological basis of it that we're hoping you can help with. Especially since you have a brain augment of your own—you know how it feels, how it works." He went into details about work hours, salary, and benefits, but Damon only nodded his head. He was afraid that if he said too much, it might all vanish like a sweet dream at the shrill of a wake-up alarm.

And now here he was, standing in front of a glass monolith with huge revolving doors that waited expectantly. He pushed his legs into motion.

The main lobby was seven stories high, dominated by a huge geodesic dome with neon struts connecting it to the walls on either side, like electrodes attached to a brain. Of course. It would be so cool to work in that, but as he wandered compulsively into the dome the signage revealed that it was partly a museum of brain-computer innovation and partly a showcase of the company's products. Shiny and irresistible, the area was for clients and the general public, not for staff. The largest amount of display space was dedicated to a new cortical augment the company was developing that they claimed would render products like the Nike Neuro and the Apple Cortico obsolete.

Damon reluctantly made his way out of the Plexiglas maze and over to the reception desk for the special ID badge he'd need to access staff areas of the building. He was stoked about the thought of working in one of the offices on the upper floors with a view of the not-too-distant waterfront. Then the receptionist pointed to the office listing on the wall behind her and his face fell. Research Lab C was on sub-floor 3. The only lower location was a parking level for maintenance vehicles. So much for a view.

There was no receptionist at the lab. He'd shuffled a few yards to his right then doubled back toward a line of cubicles, when his new boss Ram Khouri came around a corner. Khouri was nearly a foot shorter than Damon with unruly white hair and eyes that seemed to bulge a little, an effect exaggerated by contact lenses. He showed no sign of being glad to see his new underling. As Damon would discover, the man wasn't capable of it. Not because of resentment, as Damon first feared, but only a simple, universal and consistent ambivalence to other human beings.

With a minimum of words, Khouri led him deeper into the meandering complex until they encountered Layla Goring, the sociologist who handled most of the department's direct human studies. Goring was rake-thin and fortyish, with dull brown hair as devoid of curves as a prairie road. She had a tattoo of a six-pointed star on the inside of her left forearm. One of the star's points was a luminous green while another shifted shades from blue through purple to red and back again. An *alert-tat* showing one voice mail and three text messages waiting. Old tech. Obsolete now that she had an augment, but she hadn't bothered to have it removed. Damon wondered how long the message notifications had been lit.

Khouri directed Goring to "show Damon around" then followed them at a distance, engrossed in the readout of a larger-than-usual digiscroll. Every so often, he'd roll up the flimsy screen into a tube and tap it against his leg. Before long, they were joined by Greg Welsh, a thirty-something snappy dresser with the pale, freckled skin of a natural redhead and more meticulous grooming than his ordinary looks deserved. Welsh was assigned to the project for marketing only and apparently had other duties that he clearly considered more important.

"So... we're trying to figure out how to access brain augments with marketing messages?" Damon asked.

"Not the way you make it sound," Welsh said. "We could spam them with email or jabs right now, but how effective would that be? We want something meaningful—impossible to ignore."

"Hopefully organic to the device itself," Goring added.

"Don't the Neuro and the Cortico already include advertising?"

Welsh gave a snort. "It's not much more than a database the user can access that lists a company's products and their specifications. Updatable, and linked to occasional discounts, but that's about it. Besides, we don't just want access to our own customers, we want to be able to reach those misguided Nike and Apple buyers, too. And not just to sell them Dyna-Mantech products—this will be a whole new marketing stream for every business out there."

"Like how billboards ID your cellphone when you walk past them and tailor their pitch to your interests." Goring said. "That's the kind of thing we're shooting for right now: to have hubs around the city that would detect an augment, learn from it, and provide a message right there in mindspace that's worth something, and useful to the customer right away."

"You think you can do that?"

"If you don't think so, you shouldn't be on the team." Welsh looked asshole-smug. Damon glanced down the hallway at Ram Khouri, who was shaking his head without looking up.

"No... I'm sure there's a way. Devices like that—the commercial ones—are easy to hack, but the user would be ticked off at you. Better if you give them a choice about allowing the message, then make it irresistible. I can think of a few ways that might work."

"Yeah, well, just don't get us sued." The corner of Goring's mouth twisted downward. "For some reason people get sensitive about things in their heads."

#

Damon stopped at Valerie's on the way home to tell her about his first day. She tried to be enthusiastic, but something seemed to be holding her back. When he'd first told her about getting the job, she was clearly shocked—an undeniable blow to his self-esteem. She'd insisted that his ability wasn't in question, but when he'd pressed for an explanation, she'd changed the subject.

A few weeks later, his first pay disappeared almost as quickly as it had come. Valerie's own fashion sense had always seemed effortless, but she had a bemused look as Damon led her through clothing stores, always to the racks featuring the top brand-names. They might be clients, he insisted. She quickly gave up offering advice and merely nodded or shook her head at questions of color or fit.

He was more in love with her every day. He was pretty sure she felt the same way, though she refused to move in with him—she insisted on her own space and areas of her life that she kept for herself. As a justification she'd point to her dog, a chocolate lab named Mud, which not only described his colour but his far-from-purebred genetic mix. Mud was a leftover from a former love affair. He'd belonged to the guy, but developed a stronger bond with Valerie; so, when the relationship crashed, Mud ended up with her. The constant reminder of love gone sour had cooled her feelings for the big mutt. He instantly took to Damon in a big way which, paradoxically, returned him to Valerie's affections, too.

They made it a rule to keep their work separate from their life together. Valerie stayed away from Dyna-Mantech, and Damon never returned to the bookstore. He often felt guilty for having to spend so much time at the university, but Valerie claimed she didn't mind because it gave her a chance to catch up on her reading: everything from Dickens to Sparks, Milton to Rushdie. Once, when she was absorbed in something by W.B. Yeats, Damon asked her to read it to him. After some persuasion, she gave in and found that speaking the words aloud brought the rhythm of the lines to life and heightened her own understanding and enjoyment of the piece. After that, she often read to him from a comfy chair while he sat on the floor at her feet. Most of the time he listened with full attention. Sometimes his mind wandered elsewhere through the world with the help of his implant, but he always loved the sound of her voice.

Damon's mother kept asking to meet his new girl. She'd never known him to stay with anyone for longer than a week, so this one must be special, she said. But it never happened. His initial insistence that he had no need of his mother's approval didn't last. It wasn't true. He wanted to show Valerie off. He just didn't get the chance. Three times, the plans they made to meet were scuttled by last-minute calls for Valerie to go in to work.

Thanksgiving came, but she was committed to seeing her parents, because her work schedule would keep her in the city over Christmas. Damon's mother was disappointed, but happy to spend the time fawning over her university son, all grown up.

The Wednesday after Thanksgiving the police came to Damon's door to tell him his mother was dead.

A car accident. Probably her fault. She'd always been a terrible driver—had never improved, even after the collision that had nearly derailed Damon's life. But at least her death had been quick. One minute alive and vital, the next...only a collection of assorted stark images in his BCID and random scraps of wet memory that must be considered unreliable, tainted with emotion.

It came to Damon that night that he had no family left. They'd never kept in contact with his father's relatives. His maternal grandparents were long gone, both taken by a killer storm in Louisiana, and his only aunt had died of lung cancer two years earlier. He realised, with a terrible pang of guilt, how lonely his mother must have been. Always, but especially since he'd left home. He'd rarely made time for her even though she was only a few hours away by train, visiting only every couple of months when she sounded particularly needy. Thanksgiving had been a gift, but he and his mother had squandered it as usual, watching video or socializing with near-strangers online instead of focusing on each other.

God, what a little shit he was. Had he ever thanked her for putting up with him? Ever praised her or given her a compliment? Ever told her that he *loved her* with words from the heart?

When he'd been a kid, sure. After that, he'd only been dismayed by her unabashed lust for material things and humiliated by their poverty. Where she'd offered a cloak of love and protection, he'd seen only chains. He wouldn't have had his implants without her faith—she'd steadfastly refused to acknowledge that anything could go wrong. And though he couldn't see it at the time, she'd been a lifeline, time after time, when waves of despair had threatened to drown him.

Valerie went with him to his mother's funeral that was dutifully attended by a few neighbours. Then she let him cry on her shoulder long into the night in the barren living room of a home now derelict.

For weeks afterward, remorse and sorrow would ambush him in the blind canyons of his inner solitude; emotional aftershocks, they threatened the foundation of his psyche, forcing him to hide until he could regain his self-control.

The legal wrangle from the Treasure Trove hacking had finally been settled in the year gone by, and he'd insisted that his mother use the money to pay down the mortgage on her house. Now, from its sale, Damon inherited nearly three-quarters of a million dollars, after taxes. Con thought he should blow a good wad of it on a round-the-world tour, but Damon insisted that he'd just started at Dyna-Mantech and couldn't take time off so soon. The truth was that he didn't want to leave the best thing in his life, even for a few weeks. There were other riches to be enjoyed: quiet hours in humble surroundings. He vowed never to take Valerie for granted as he'd done with his mother.

On a Sunday in mid-December, while Valerie was reading Emily Dickinson to him, she confessed that she wrote poetry, too. She'd never shown it to anyone, not her doctor-father, her tax-lawyer mother, nor to any previous lovers. Damon understood that she wouldn't have brought it up unless she secretly wanted him to read it. He asked—she refused. He'd expected that, too.

A few weeks later she asked him what he wanted for Christmas. His answer was a copy of her poems. She refused again, blushing, but come Christmas Eve, a soft, red-wrapped parcel under the miniature Christmas-tree in her apartment contained thirty hand-written pages in ornate script. His delight was genuine. He'd bought her some fresh calligraphy supplies and some rare facsimiles of John Donne sonnets in manuscript, along with a quirky piece by Thomas Gray. They looked nearly illegible to him, but she was thrilled.

They made love, slowly and attentively. Then he prepared some hot chocolate and she read five of her poems to him. Though his literary tastes had been molded by the Stephen King and Elmore Leonard novels his father had left behind, he'd heard enough poetry by then to tell that she had real talent and said so. They made love again, with lots of laughter and energy. He stayed the entire night for the first time.

They spent Christmas Day together, the first Christmas Damon had ever spent away from his mother's home, and he talked too much about his old family traditions. Like how his mother had roasted the turkey, but always complained that it should have been deep-fried. She'd given up her southern cooking when she married a northerner and somehow never returned to it after he'd left. There were always pecans, though, both on the table and in Damon's Christmas stocking. And she'd insisted on setting off firecrackers to ward off evil spirits.

That made Valerie laugh. Their day was filled with a lot of laughter, and the times she caught him staring into space, she left him with his thoughts. They went out for a mid-day walk for cappuccino and some hot roasted chestnuts from a street vendor. In the evening they watched sappy Christmas movies until they couldn't stay awake any longer. Then Damon went home, over Valerie's protests, to preserve the magic of those occasional times when he would stay.

The day after Christmas, he awoke alone in his apartment. Con had gone home to Boston for the holidays. Damon listened to the quiet, pulled the covers around him like a mother's arms, and stared into the silent darkness of pre-dawn. Eventually, he got up and made some bad coffee for himself, yearning to call Valerie but unwilling to wake her up.

Sipping the bitter liquid, he skipped through his implant's stored memories of his teen years, and especially of his mother. He made a selection of his favourites and set up a protocol to provide easy access to them. He flagged the bad ones and buried them deep. When he was finished, he reached for the phone.

The university was close to Damon's place, so he and Valerie often took Mud for walks around the campus. The dog became a minor celebrity and gained eight pounds thanks to Con's endless supply of pizza pockets. Damon would show off, identifying all the trees and most of the plants, then adding their scientific names, even though Valerie knew about his BCIDs.

She had remarkable tolerance for the state of Damon and Con's apartment, only commenting that Con left a trail like a slug: remnants of fast food and snacks that were inevitably greasy, and items of clothing that weren't much better. She was more interested in Damon's room, with its shelves of esoteric gadgets she'd never seen him use.

"Too many cheesy ads with the videos I watch. But they work, I guess," he said, his face coloring a little.

"You hear about a new product and have to get it?"

"I don't stand in line at midnight to get the newest iScroll or anything," he said. She raised an eyebrow. "OK, I've done that a couple of times. But mostly with Con—he loves that shit."

"Uh huh. And when did you decide you wanted to go into marketing for a career?"

"I always have. Well, since I first started thinking about jobs. About the beginning of high school, I guess."

Valerie nodded, looking at the floor. When he wanted to know why she'd asked she said, "Mud's looking bored. I think he wants his walk now."

#

Image: *A tall ceramic mug, porcelain-white and glazed-shiny, seen from above: the contents a rich liquid black topped with creamy swirls like perfect clouds, and two ruddy cinnamon sticks thrusting up through them like a ladder to a magic land. Homey wisps of steam rise. Yet, faint in the background, is a picture puzzle of pending catastrophe.*

Valerie was an excellent cook and quickly learned to cook Damon's comfort foods: scrambled eggs, sausage, and hash browns on weekends. Corned beef on rye. Seafood gumbo. Or even real fried chicken for a special dinner. They were things his mother had cooked, before she went on a health kick and insisted that all those foods were bad for him. Was it a coincidence that his deserter father's favourites were declared to be the unhealthiest? It wasn't as easy to explain his fondness for chinotto drinks and salted licorice—probably he just wanted to be different. Valerie didn't indulge those tastes—he had to buy them for himself.

In late January he got a powerful craving for barbecued steak. They went out for dinner at a steakhouse, but it wasn't enough. He had to borrow a barbecue from a friend and cook in a snowstorm. Next it was a yearning for a fine red wine. He didn't normally care much for wine, but a bemused Valerie gave him a quick lesson in proper tasting, and they sampled a couple of older vintages. They were surprisingly good.

He tried to persuade her to go on vacation with him to the Mexican Riviera for Valentine's Day— somewhere with a good beach so he could swim. He'd had dreams about swimming. The result was one of their first arguments: Valerie reminded him that he'd just started a new job. She'd get in trouble with her boss, too. And it would be a waste of good money. She snapped that he should take a bottle of sunblock to the public swimming pool, then was astonished when he tried it.

She hung up on him when he brought up the idea of getting a fast car.

Of course, it wasn't practical or necessary—that wasn't the point. What was the good of having lots of money if you didn't do something to enjoy it?

Maybe they didn't have so much in common after all.

He was deep in thought on the walk from the light-rail stop to the Dyna-Mantech BCI building when his view of the street ahead was suddenly obscured by a giant shape that made him flinch, a huge cylinder of some kind that just landed in front of him. Except it wasn't *real*—he could see street details around its edges. It was a projection in the air. No, not even that—he turned his face and the shape stayed centered in his field of vision. *An image in his head.* A huge coffee mug. Starbucks. *Where in goddamned hell had that come from?* And how could he get rid of it? He couldn't *see!*

It was like when his first implant had superimposed text over his field of vision. He tried the same mental exercise to clear it. The image faded, but it was still there.

Get out of my head! he commanded.

The blast of a truck horn came just as he felt his foot plunge off a curb. Reflexively, he twisted to the side and something tugged hard at his coat. Then the coffee mug was gone, and he was lying in the street, watching a big furniture truck shudder to a stop. Its side mirror must have clipped him.

He staggered to his feet and muttered apologies to the angry truck driver, who read the shock in Damon's face and returned to the cab with muttered curses. Damon slowly brushed himself off. The building facades and street signs he'd passed so often felt suddenly unfamiliar. He carefully scanned the traffic, crossed the street, pushed through a door, and collapsed on the nearest seat. As his wits regrouped, he saw that he was in a Starbucks with a big poster of a cinnamon cappuccino hung on the wall.

Good God. Was that where the image in his head had come from? No, he couldn't have seen it—he'd been staring down at the sidewalk. And anyway, the poster would have been hidden from the street. Had someone hacked into his implant? Or somehow placed a self-triggering file in it? That seemed too goddamn close to some of the things they were playing with at Dyna-Mantech.

He pushed off the chair and hurried down the street.

He found Ram Khouri in a far corner of the research floor, head bent over the digiscroll that seemed attached to his hand. When irritated, the man had a habit of rolling and unrolling the filmy screen constantly. Khouri had an office, but was never in it.

Face-to-face with his boss, it wasn't so easy to voice his suspicions.

"Mr. Khouri? Sir? You, uh... I mean... the marketing team wouldn't be trying out some of our new projects on *me*, would it? Using me as some kind of guinea pig? I mean, I know I work here... and maybe I'd agree to it if I was told ahead of time...."

"What are you talking about, Darren?"

"Uh, Damon, sir. Could the marketing people be trying out some of their image-projection hardware out on me? Sending stuff to my implant?"

Khouri looked blankly ahead, as if waiting for Damon to start speaking a language he knew.

"On the street, I suddenly was overwhelmed by an image. It was a Starbucks cup, sir. I overheard somebody say Starbucks was one of our test accounts. And my implant has never just projected an image into my visual field at random before." His voice trailed off.

Khouri looked down at his oversized digiscroll as if it might offer advice on how to deal with a sudden pain in the ass.

"I'll look into it, Leiter," he said.

Damon waited for more, then simply nodded and backed away slowly toward his small workstation. Khouri's answer hadn't told him anything, but it wasn't a denial either. Would the team really try something like that without warning him? Maybe that asshole Welsh thought it up, and the rest of them thought it was a joke. Or maybe a sub-group of the department had decided to do a little guerrilla-testing on a small sample of the public and he'd been caught in the net by accident. How could he find out?

There was a custom search tool Con had once given him. He took remote control of a workstation that wasn't currently assigned to anyone, disguised his own workstation's address, and began to search.

It wasn't easy. The department's network held a huge number of files in layers and sub-layers and a profusion of security protocols that seemed deliberately inconsistent. Filenames were obscure. A lot of folders were empty. But after nearly an hour of refining his parameters, he stumbled onto a list hidden behind a partition of its own.

He sat back with a quick breath and looked around him to make sure he was alone.

It was a list of people implanted with Taggart BCID's. His name was right at the top.

RECOVERY AND REHABILITATION October 1, 2040
Memorial Hospital Med-Surg Unit—Sixth Floor:

Damon reflected on the healing process.

He'd been confined to a hospital room three times before: after the car crash that had left him with a traumatic brain-injury, and then following the surgeries that provided his implants. Each time he'd recovered rapidly, though far from quickly enough for his liking. With the two surgeries, the risk of death had been counterbalanced by the promise of great rewards. He'd chafed at any delay in being able to enjoy them.

This time was different. Death had come to grapple with him without warning and had very nearly triumphed. This time it had been no accident and no calculated medical procedure, but a cold-blooded attempt on his life. It was pure luck that there was anything left of his bones to heal, and luckier still that his skull had been spared serious trauma. His brain remained intact, his neural augments nearly so. They'd gone into an emergency reset but were otherwise undamaged.

He was healing. The process had taken four weeks already and would require many more, but he would get better.

Why didn't he feel lucky? Why didn't he exult in having cheated death?

Such an experience was supposed to give you a new appreciation of life. A fresh start. Instead, the road ahead was obscured in a shroud.

While his cranial bones had stitched and stretched and sealed after his earlier surgeries, his mind had ranged ahead, eager to seek out new possibilities. Now, as his shattered skeleton strove to mend itself, he cast his psyche into the past, adding pain that was nonphysical to the physical, scraping away at the very foundations of his life.

Then: a hopeful naïveté. Now: a brooding paranoia.

Someone had tried to end his life, and although the direct act might have involved no more than one or two key players, he hadn't been able to rule anyone out as a possible conspirator. He felt as if his heart were wrapped in a clammy compress of soiled linen that sucked away its warmth and its joy.

The police presence at the hospital was another mystery. Even as they assured him he was the victim of an accident, their questions probed for possible assailants and motives. The guards they provided against the intrusion of the media and the public made him feel imprisoned rather than protected. He was far from sure that all the uniformed bodies that took turns outside his door were even real members of the police. Having poked at the sleeping giants of government and international industrialism, he had to expect the attention of their minions. The galling question was, were they merely taking advantage of the opportunity to watch him? Or had they put him there in the first place?

Valerie visited morning and night. Con came a few times. No-one came from work, or the university. Was that significant? Probably not. No-one likes to be near illness, and more than ever before, society riveted its focus on bright perfection. Anything less, even temporarily, was a reminder of mortality, to be avoided if at all possible.

In truth, he was glad to be alone with his thoughts. And his memories, although his search through the archives of his implants had still borne no fruit.

No-one was a suspect. And everyone.

That was the most painful part. The loss of certainty, of trust. Even though the doctors predicted he'd be released within weeks, he knew that part of him would never heal.

The past might not hold the answers, but his gut told him that it was still a better bet than a potentially endless search over the internet, especially without any clear place to start looking. Closing his eyes, he once again set himself to sift the ore of implant memories for the nuggets of information he so badly needed.

7

March 25, 2040

Project: Minotaur
File: Janus 1
Progress report: The Taggart BCID program has provided invaluable insights into cognitive processes that can be co-opted for marketing and other communication purposes we have planned. Leuschen's subliminal directives have produced desired behaviors in 97% of the subjects. One subject became schizophrenic and obsessive-compulsive, traits likely latent before surgery. Suggestibility was increased in 55% of subjects, resulting in still-greater success with behavior modification, and revealed indications for improvement.

A broader application of these techniques to exterior brain augments such as those made by Nike and Apple remains a significant challenge. As well,

Taggart implants include many enhanced capabilities that we consider undesirable in the general population because they could potentially be used to impede marketing efforts. These features are not included in commercial augments currently available and will not be provided with the forthcoming Dyna-Mantech BCID models.

A drawback to not including such features is that non-implanted BCID's will not allow us the same level of access into subconscious thought-processes.

Damon Leiter continues to be a key figure in our plans. While his full capabilities are not known, he has responded well to subtle direction and will remain a valuable asset.

A recent (unauthorized) test of projected Starbucks marketing provided a strong lesson about the need for caution in our endeavors. We deal with living, breathing, but unpredictable human beings. The loss of any individual means an unfortunate reduction in the already-small size of our test sample, and could lead to detrimental publicity and potentially damaging litigation.

H. Reinhardt Janus

Image: *An apartment building hallway, brightly lit, but with lights of a harsh blue color. Anonymous doors signify the presence of dwellings, but within the apartments, there are no signs of residents: no sounds, no smells, no personalized touches. Residents may share a location, but apparently nothing else.*

Jace and Naya Robbins met Damon at the door and invited him into the apartment. He guessed that they were in their mid-thirties. Both were good-looking, and well-dressed. Jace's welcoming tones reminded Damon of those of an insurance salesman; but on the phone he'd said that he was a talent manager, handling a few Jozi-jam and tok-hop acts whose names Damon didn't recognize, as well as his own wife's singing career.

Naya's voice was husky and warm. She wore a red print silk-scarf over a black V-neck in some kind of stretch fabric. It clung to an athletic figure that would suit a dancer. Her makeup wasn't garish enough for X-dreem—possibly soul or jazz. That guess was all but confirmed by posters of Sarah Vaughan and Nina Simone that faced each other from opposite ends of the main room.

Jace wore crisply pressed slacks and a good-quality dress shirt. As Damon accepted the invitation to sit on a cream-colored leather sofa, he asked Jace, "You're in X-dreem music?"

The other man laughed. "I was in meetings with record company execs today. When I hang with my clients I put on the T's and bling."

"Puts on the slang, too." Naya rested a hand on her hip. "Sometimes even I don't know what the hell he's sayin'." Her husband kissed her cheek and sat in a heavily padded armchair. Naya perched on an ottoman.

"Yeah. Feel like a horse's ass when I do that, but it's expected. Gotta talk the talk, flaunt the look, y'know?" He turned to look up at the wall behind his right shoulder, and his face lit up with real pride. Several rows of framed publicity shots had been hung together, showing at least a dozen different acts. "But it works. Some of my acts gonna be superstars soon."

"Are all of them making it?"

"Well, not yet...."

"That's my man—a little too soft for his own good, sometimes," Naya said with a smile. "Some of those acts—they got real talent. I mean big talent. Others, well...Jace ain't always good at sayin' no." She laughed and her husband joined her.

"We're talkin' about dreams," he said. "Sometimes you just can't kill somebody's dreams, y'know? It ain't right. Besides, what do I know—they might just make it."

"Better you than me," Damon smiled, "Musical talent skipped over my crib." He looked at Jace's leg. "I didn't notice any limp. You must be healing well."

"Yeah. Like I said on the phone, nothing was broken. Just bruises all over my body and I twisted my knee bad. Nearly lost a finger, too." He held up his left hand. The ring finger was bandaged. "Naya wasn't too happy they had to cut off my wedding ring, but they were able to save the finger and we got the ring repaired. Got caught between the escalator step and the side panel for a few seconds."

"How far did you fall?"

"Probably thirty feet or more. Then I ran into a fat guy who fell on me." He laughed again. "Lucky I did. Coulda gone all the way to the bottom. Damnedest thing—just as I go to step on the escalator, all this...jewellery...appears in front of me, and I miss the step. Start to tumble. Don't see anything but sparkling necklaces and bracelets all the way down. When I finally stop falling, I realize they're gone. Then all I see is a big ol' white ass-crack—honest to God. Plumber's smile the size of that sofa cushion." He broke into another belly laugh and Damon couldn't help joining in. Naya only shook her head.

"Was there a jewellery store near the escalator?" Damon asked.

"Now you mention it, yeah, there's that diamond place. Dazz-L? Just passed it before I went for my tumble."

"Naya, you didn't see anything?"

"She wasn't with me. She was home in bed with the flu."

"Maybe that was a lucky thing. I can't believe you both have brain implants," Damon said.

"Well, that's how we met," Naya answered. "Bumped into each other near Dr. Taggart's surgery after we'd both had checkups. There's a little art gallery down the street—part gallery-part bookstore."

"I thought she was looking at the *Kama Sutra*. Turns out it was just Tagore's poetry," Jace said, making a sour face. His wife swatted him with a throw cushion.

"Like you got anything to complain about. So, as I was sayin', we were both at the Taggart clinic. Both of us got his third model of BCID, the Taggart *Tertius*. I had a stutterin' problem ever since I had epilepsy when I was little. Epilepsy went away—stutterin' stayed, but Doc Taggart said his gadget could fix it, and it did. Never stuttered when singin', but doin' interviews and such, you know."

"And my problem was like yours: agnosia," Jace said. "Motorcycle accident. BCID solved it, though. Been good for a few years. Don't know why there'd suddenly be a glitch."

"I...don't think it *was* a glitch, exactly." Damon looked at his hands, uncertain how much to say, now that he was really with them. What if they were angry? What if they sued? "I think...I think it might have been advertising."

"What do you mean, advertising?" Naya leaned forward.

Damon explained about sending advertising pitches to brain augments. "I think they might have chosen Taggart implants because they're directly connected to the visual cortex. But I'm sure they weren't planning to hijack people's vision completely."

"Shit. I coulda been killed!" Jace narrowed his eyes. "Who do you mean by 'they' anyhow? Your people?"

"My boss denies it. I haven't seen any evidence in our company files, either. Could be a bunch of companies are looking into the same thing—there's huge money riding on it."

"And you're involved in this kind of thing yourself?" Naya asked, her eyes wide.

"No, no. The system I'm working on would give you a choice. As you walk by a store maybe a small icon appears in the corner of your eye, promoting a discount or a special offer. If you want to know more, you mentally grab the icon, or maybe just say yes or no. Anyway, if you're not interested, the icon goes away." He shrugged.

"And you're OK with that." Jace frowned. "Businesses just putting pictures in your head."

"No, well...people should be able to turn their reception function on or off. If they want to know about deals offered at the places they pass, they leave it on. But if they don't want to be bothered, they can hang up the 'Do Not Disturb' sign." Damon smiled, but the Robbins didn't join him.

"Why would anybody subject themselves to that?" Naya asked.

"Obviously you'd have to make it worthwhile for people. Kind of like those rewards programs—the benefits of membership, and all that." His ears felt warm. How had they put him on the defensive? "Anyway, what I came for is...I found out that you both have Taggart implants and figured you might have had the same problem with those images popping up. I've had some practice controlling stuff like that, so I thought I might...offer a few pointers. So you don't get hurt if it happens again."

Their faces said they suspected there was more he wasn't telling, but they allowed him to continue. It took about forty-five minutes to run them through the techniques he'd developed for himself, and he found some pictures on the internet they could use for practice. After a little more small-talk, he finally made his way to the door and said goodbye.

He liked the Robbins. They were good people. When he left them, Naya was on her way to perform a benefit concert for seniors who were at risk of becoming homeless. She did a lot of that kind of thing, making Damon feel thoroughly selfish in comparison.

Didn't they deserve the full truth? Should he have told them about the others? The names he'd found in the Dyna-Mantech files and then matched to news stories on the internet? There was the man who rode his bike through a red light and into the path of a bus. A couple killed when their car collided with a train. An elderly woman who fell over the railing of the second-floor loft in her home. And a teenaged girl who'd stumbled off a platform in front of a subway train. None of them had survived, but the bike rider had said something to bystanders about a milkshake before he died. A giant milkshake.

All of them had died the same day. All were recipients of Taggart implants. All lived in the city. A localized test, then.

Three others had somehow been spared like Naya: a midwife, a surgeon, and a history teacher. He'd visit them next.

He'd told the Robbins there was no evidence that the Dyna-Mantech team was behind the intrusions, but that wasn't strictly true. The D-M network was where he'd found the list of Taggart BCID recipients. If D-M was involved, that could make him guilty by association—certainly an accomplice after the fact if he didn't go to the police with what he knew.

No. With what he *suspected*. Accidents happen every day. He had no proof whatsoever that these people had died because they'd been blinded by an advertising message to their implants. Certainly, there was no evidence he could take to the police. All he could think to do on his own was to pass on some of his protective techniques to people who were likely targets. Implantees.

Whoever had produced those images, it was a clumsy first effort, and the deaths ensured that they'd never admit to what they'd done. But neither would they stop. The company was sure to be looking to expand to the external commercial models next. And there were already hundreds of thousands of those.

#

Image: *A glass pitcher filled with an amber liquid. Faces reflect from its curved surfaces, distorted, not quite human, vaguely disquieting. Bubbles rise eagerly through the liquid, but when they reach the surface, they vanish. Freed? Or simply gone?*

The Horse and Paddock Pub was awash with noise and superfluous motion that filled it to its fake-antique rafters. The half-hearted attempts at Olde English décor were sabotaged by 3-D video screens in the corners showing an English football match. But the simple chunky tables were real wood, scarred and stained from a decade of inebriated customers. So were the booth benches—Valerie had swept theirs off before sitting down, but still complained about feeling grit through her cotton skirt. Damon pressed close to her to make room for Rosa Ferraro on his left side. Jace and Naya Robbins sat across from them, with Helayne West beside Jace.

Ebon Parrish had pulled a chair up to the end of the table—waitresses glared when they had to squeeze by with heavily-laden trays, but Ebon said he was used to far worse looks from his high-school history students when he gave them homework. He'd ordered two pitchers of beer and worked valiantly to drain them after Damon, Jace, and Valerie took their share.

Rosa drank iced tea because she had a surgery to perform first thing in the morning. Helayne over-stirred a virgin banana daiquiri while she looked enviously at the beer—as a midwife, she was on call that night. She didn't begrudge the sacrifice, though. From the joy that lit up her eyes as she described her work, she might be bragging about the progeny of her own flesh. Her few free hours were often spent making the rounds of the new mothers whose time with her had been short-changed while she was on the clock.

Damon watched his companions as he talked. He'd only met the Robbins before this. The Dyna-Mantech files offered background details about the others, but nothing about their personalities. He'd brought them together to learn what kind of people they were.

Rosa pulled a cell phone from her purse and left it on the table where she could look at it every few minutes. Checking the time? But her implant would tell her that whenever she wanted and let her know if she had any messages too. So, the handset was either a prop, or a habit she couldn't break. Whether she reached for the phone or her glass, her hands were surgeon-steady without a trace of excess motion.

"What do you mean you're jamming them?" Ebon asked Damon. A conservative blue tie was part of the teacher's uniform at the private school where he worked. He'd enthusiastically loosened it when he sat down, and now he tugged at it again.

"The Taggart clinic took an audio and video feed from my first implant for months before I discovered it, and then tried to do it again with my second one. My assumption is that they've done the same thing with all Taggart implants. The signal from mine was on a white-fi frequency, so a guy I know rigged up a jammer that puts out a signal of random noise on a range of frequencies close to the one I discovered. Hopefully it's overriding all of your outgoing signals."

"My God!" Rosa leaned over the table. "You mean they're *spying* on us? All the time? Even video?"

"All of our implants are new enough to translate signals from the optic nerve into pretty high-res streams; so, yeah...they probably see everything you see—except now, because I'm blocking it. If that TV in the corner was still using broadcast signals our fellow patrons would be getting pissed off about now."

A roar of noise made Helayne jump, as the favored football team scored a goal. Damon searched her face. She looked ill, tearing small pieces from a paper napkin in her hand.

"The bastards," Jace growled, turning to his wife, whose eyes had gone wide. Her hand went to a silver crucifix hanging over the cleavage beneath her low-cut top.

Damon squirmed and glanced at Valerie. She was staring at the table. "They might not be taking a video feed," he backtracked. "Maybe just telemetry from the implants' sensors. But that's still too intrusive for my tastes. I taught my own implant to find the leak and plug it. I think I can teach you how to do that, too."

"So you didn't need to bring that jammer for yourself," Ebon said, after an impressive pull at his beer and the resulting belch. "You didn't want the Taggart clinic eavesdropping on our little get-together through *our* implants."

Damon nodded. "After my first visit to the Robbins, my boss dropped a heavy hint about bad things that happen to people who dig into company files. Sounded like he knew I had a list of implant recipients, and that seemed to implicate Jace and Naya's BCID's."

"Wait," Naya said, "Your boss has access to our implants' spy feed?"

"Or somebody above him. It turns out that Dyna-Mantech BCI's parent company, ImagiCap has been funding the Taggart clinic for years. They wouldn't be doing it out of the goodness of their hearts. They want new ways to market to people, including right into their brains. Or the next best thing: their augments."

Jace twitched and swept his fingers through his short-cropped hair. "Teach us," he said, his face like a storm cloud. "Teach us how to block these scum. Teach us everything you know."

#

Damon leaned against the bathroom door frame watching Valerie brush her teeth. They were late getting back from the pub and the next day was Saturday, so she'd invited him to stay over. He admired the view as she stood in panties and bra concentrating on the mirror. She noticed him and gave a mock frown before spitting toothpaste into the sink.

"How am I supposed to maintain my feminine allure if you watch me spit?" she said as she dabbed at her mouth with the towel.

"Don't worry—the allure is intact. The mystery, too." His smile faded. "You closed your eyes."

"When? Just now?"

"No. At the pub. When I was teaching the others how to shut off the clinic's spy feed from their implants. You closed your eyes, too."

He caught her gaze and held it. After a moment she looked away and squeezed past him into her bedroom. She put her discarded clothes into the laundry hamper, pulled open the drawer with her underwear and pyjamas in it, and idly moved things around. After a half-minute of playacting, she dropped her hands to her side and hung her head.

"I have one," she said quietly. "I have a Taggart implant."

He sat slowly onto the edge of the bed. Her movements in the restaurant had made him suspicious, but her name hadn't been on the Taggart list he'd found. Did that mean there was another test group? Or did the list just reflect a certain subset? But none of that was important right then.

Why would she have kept such a secret from him all that time? *How* could she? He felt an impulse to reach out a hand toward her, but the gulf was too wide.

"I...I didn't tell you because...because Ron paid for it," she said. Ron was the former lover who'd left Mud the dog behind when he left, but she'd never said much more about him. A stockbroker or something like that—lots of disposable income anyway. Damon had pictured a guy with mostly grey hair, immaculately groomed and tailored.

"You thought I'd be jealous because he bought you an implant?"

"Something of him, still left inside me. Doesn't that bother you?"

"Seriously? You thought that would bother me more than your keeping it a secret from me?" He stared at his hands, slowly rubbing them together. "Shit. I can't believe it! I've told you everything about mine—talked your ears off about it. You must've had a few good laughs about that." His voice grew quieter. "What else aren't you telling me?"

She stepped closer and tried to take his hands, but he pulled them away.

"I'm sorry. I'm so sorry. I don't know what else to say. I meant to tell you, but after a while I didn't know how, and the longer I waited...well, I knew you'd react this way—anyone would. I was afraid you might not trust me anymore."

"You had that part right." He stood slowly, legs as leaden as when he'd once tried to run a marathon. "I think I'd better go."

"No. Please! Don't do this!" She raised a hand to his cheek, her eyes filling with tears. He'd never seen her cry before. Not even close. "I made a mistake. It was stupid. You have every right to be angry, but be angry with me *here*. Now. Yell at me. Swear at me. But please don't leave me. Not like this." Her voice broke, and she lifted her other hand to his face. Through her hands, he could feel silent, helpless sobs.

Standing before him nearly naked, she looked achingly vulnerable. He yearned to wrap her in the shield of his arms. Instead, he grabbed his jacket from the arm of the couch and lurched out the door.

#

Image: *Eyes, green as glass, flecked with grey and blue. Behind them, visions of sunlit lawns, library walls lined with books, a lake bordered by pines and poplars. Unfamiliar faces, some resembling Valerie, but not her. Her family. Her past.*

Damon didn't answer Valerie's calls the next day. She stopped calling, and he suffered through another day willing the phone to ring and knowing that made him a gullible asshole. For so long he'd wished for a lover with an implant—someone who could truly understand him. Now, the dream had been turned to ashes by the knowledge that even a lover like him could lie, could hide their true self.

On the third day he came out of the Dyna-Mantech building after work and found her waiting by the street.

"What can I do to make you trust me again?" she asked.

"Nothing comes to mind."

"Mind. That's it, isn't it? If you could just read my mind, you'd know how much I love you. And how much I don't want to hurt you. I never wanted to hurt you."

He started to walk. She followed.

"It's not that simple."

"Why not? If you could see into my mind, you could satisfy your doubts. And if I let you do that...how much more trust could anyone show? I give you my complete trust and you give me another chance to earn yours."

He turned away but her face was reflected in the window beside him, willing him to meet her eyes. He did. She didn't flinch.

"How would you propose to do that?"

"By letting you into my implant. All the way in—anywhere you want to go. Any time."

The skin of his face tingled. Would she really be willing to do that? Would anyone? Even the Taggart clinic's spying hadn't come close to that. He felt ashamed at the thought, and fascinated.

"It's password-protected. Highly encrypted."

"Of course it is. And I'd give you full access. I know the codes—everyone with an implant knows the codes for their own. The encrypted key-vault is separate from the main processor and memory, but every implanted brain knows the way in, so no one ever accidentally locks themselves out of their own augment."

That was information even he hadn't known.

What she was proposing was far more intimate than sex—a far greater surrender of self. A proposal of marriage would have been less surprising—trivial in comparison.

The gentlemanly thing to do would be to acknowledge her gesture but refuse it, proclaiming that her mere willingness to make such an offer was testament enough of her sincerity. He found that he couldn't do that—his own hurt was too deep, and words couldn't be trusted. But unlocked memories....

"Why would you do that?" he asked.

She said nothing. They stood on a windy corner. Her nose had dripped onto her upper lip, her cheeks were rouged with cold. Strands of auburn hair flitted over red-rimmed eyes. He thought she was radiantly beautiful.

"Let's get something to eat," he said.

#

"Should I try to think of a peaceful place or something?"

"I'm not trying to hypnotize you. Or control you. And I won't be able to read your flesh mind at all."

That might not be wholly true. When he'd hacked into other people's augments in university, they'd always been commercial BCI's. He'd pilfered a little information, toyed with a few settings, but he'd never dug deeply into their stored memories—that was a line he wouldn't cross. He'd never connected with their minds. He couldn't. But Valerie's implant had connections that ran deep into her visual cortex, temporal cortex, and much of the parietal lobe. It linked to her senses and her own memories. Maybe he wouldn't be able to tell what she was thinking, but he certainly would be able to sense significant amounts of the synaptic energy exchange that was called "the mind." He had no idea what form the experience would take.

Would it be like his teenage dreams: love as a true submersion within the identity of another?

"Just do anything you'd normally do," he continued. "Unless you'd rather I stopped."

"No, I gave you access. Use it. I'll be fine. I'll watch TV—one of the celebrity-shows you hate."

"Perfect choice, so I'll want to get back out of your head as soon as I can."

She smiled and took his chin in her hand. "I love you."

He kissed her but said nothing. Instead, he swivelled around and lay back with his head in her lap.

"Are you sure it's my head you're trying to get into?" she teased.

"That's for later," he said. He closed his eyes and told his implant to search for her BCID's IP address, use the protocols and passwords she'd given him, make the connection.

Immediately, he felt the difference from other augments he'd infiltrated: a signal that was so much stronger, richer, broader. Instead of a cold, digital interface, her BCID sparked with energy, and a presence that was unquestionably alive. His own implant was truly a part of his mind—information from it was processed using the same brain centers that processed visual signals and sensory information, so the most natural way to handle such data was by using metaphors of the body's natural actions. Snooping around in the other augments had at first been like his fingers riffling a sheaf of papers. Later, it had become smoother, more like a web search. Neither comparison fitted here.

Commercial implants had file structures borrowed from earlier operating systems. Taggart implants borrowed from them too, but weren't quite the same. Even so, it seemed a reasonable place to start. He pictured file cabinets and drawers. The metaphor was imprecise—its visual manifestation wobbly and nebulous, but it gradually solidified. One cabinet gave off a metallic cyan glow. He mentally reached for it and tugged at a drawer handle. It wouldn't open. An additional permission was needed. He sent a command through his BCID. The drawer pulled free.

He gasped. The inside of the drawer wasn't filled with papers, but a velvet blackness punctuated by sparkling whorls of color that drifted slowly, without pattern. He grasped one of the whorls and shook it out like a cloth—it fluttered open and expanded until it surrounded him.

The view was ethereal and without sharp detail, but it was recognizable: a lake, surrounded by pine trees and poplars. A few white birches. There were other dwellings around the shoreline. He tried to shift the view mentally. Nothing happened. It was a still picture. But life's instants weren't experienced in isolation, as still pictures. There would be more instants, a nearly infinite number, both before and after this scene.

He envisioned himself gripping the image and pulling at it, trying to stretch it into something three-dimensional. The tableau responded, and moved...and pulled another after it, subtly different. He pulled harder—another perspective followed. Like frames on a strip of movie film? Except those were flat and lifeless: visual snapshots. These were so much more.

Like a train, he thought: tug at one car and the others followed after. He pulled at Valerie's memories—drew the future toward himself—and it came, more and more readily. He tried to send his presence gliding forward along her train of life-moments. The first merged into the next, and the one after that, and almost before he could distinguish it happening, the scene bloomed into vibrant life and motion.

He tried again to look to one side or another, but still couldn't. Then the view lurched to the right on its own, and a modern chalet-style building wobbled into view, slowly coming into focus. Virtual reality games in arcades were like this, but sharper and patently artificial. There he had some control, but not here. He had an urge to touch things, to smell the air, but couldn't. Of course not. This wasn't real time—it was real memory, and recent enough to have been recorded by the implant in a format of data impulses that Valerie's brain—and his—could process. But the implant wasn't programmed to record olfactory signals. He wasn't as sure about haptic input, but unless Valerie had touched an object during the real event, there would have been no sensation to record anyway.

What about sound?

He concentrated on hearing. There was a gabble of voices and cheesy music—not from the recorded memory but from his real ears. Goddamn annoying, but he wasn't about to tell Valerie to turn the sound down on the TV. He needed to create a kind of artificial synesthesia, forging unnatural links between neural nodes within his brain. Real synesthetes saw colors associated with specific numbers, or experienced moods attached to different days of the week. He'd learned to produce a directed form of synesthesia years ago to *smell* the strength of wifi signals, among other things; but it wasn't always easy to map neural connections the way he wanted. The brain could do incredible things, but you had to know the right way to ask it.

Gradually the babble faded, and he could pick out a high-pitched chirrup in the background, punctuated by occasional clear, liquid notes. Crickets and birds. The sounds of a lakeside getaway. Then there was another sound, modulated and familiar. Yes. A woman's voice, calling something. A name. Valerie's name.

The view shifted again, and he saw a woman approaching from around the corner of the chalet. Red hair, slim build, pale skin. Valerie's mother, he assumed—the resemblance was unmistakable. The woman talked as she walked. He could sense the tones: a question here, an assertion there. But the words came and went like recordings out of phase. He concentrated on her lips and was able to understand more. It was only a casual conversation. Something about Val's father going into town, an aunt visiting later, the annual regatta in two weeks.

He focused his mind to withdraw. The scene held him a moment longer, then relinquished its grip and shrank into a small, shiny patchwork globe. He brushed it aside and reached for another. At a touch, it blossomed like a flower in time-lapse photography. He slowly slid into the captured scene.

Night-time. A city street. Red taillights of passing cars, neon glow of passed signs.

Valerie was walking—he had the uncomfortable impression of lurching forward in an unfamiliar way. Spike-heeled shoes? So, some body awareness had been recorded.

Her head turned; there was a man walking beside her. Not like Damon pictured Ron. This man was younger, with dark hair and a slim build. There was a dimple in his cheek when he smiled—Damon's brain was obviously getting better at interpreting detail. His implant even supplied a name: [Mark Phelps]. His own augment could interpret Valerie's stored memories well enough to match a face. The realization brought a shiver of excitement. But the name nagged at him. *Phelps?* The associate at the Taggart Clinic? Valerie would have met him there, of course, but why would they be together at night? *Was this a date?*

Watching, he felt like a voyeur in a way he hadn't felt at all while viewing her visit with her mother. There were loud traffic noises, but he could make out almost all their words: mostly small talk about work. Valerie seemed to know a lot about what Phelps did. Maybe they'd gone together for quite a while.

Damon tried again to look around, but was limited to what Valerie had seen. Though the human brain received observational data far beyond what was noticed by the conscious mind, a recording by an implant was more like the view from a camcorder, although it was possible that extra cognitive information such as emotional context might be attached like the metadata of digital photographs. If so, he'd have to learn the trick of accessing that later.

As long as Valerie didn't shut off his access. How would she feel about what he was seeing? How much should he tell her? How much would she be aware of without being told?

Was there a way to fast-forward memory? He had no interest in Phelps' attempts to be charming while they waited for a table, although it was amusing to note how often Valerie looked away from her date to check out other guys. Did she do that when she was out with Damon? He'd have to watch for it from now on.

That understanding jolted him into a mental limbo.

Access to her implant was a game-changer—a relationship-changer. He'd known that empirically, but now its implications hit with full force.

She'd hoped that it would repair his trust in her; and though it might succeed in that, it was just as likely to destroy as to heal. In a normal course of events, he'd only learn about her inner life by what she *chose* to tell him. Even being at her side as she experienced daily life would only reveal so much. That was utterly different from witnessing her experiences firsthand, from her own point of view. What he learned that way would ensure that he'd never be able to think of her in quite the same way again.

He'd yearned to abolish secrets between them. He hadn't understood the price.

With the nebulous shades of the restaurant scene still visible in his mind's eye, he admitted to himself that what he really wanted to know was whether or not Valerie and Phelps had gone to bed. And that made him feel cheap. So he pulled back—let the sights and sounds of the dining crowd slip away into the void. He backed out farther, to what had been the level of the filing cabinet—but now it looked like a pasture. A field full of rabbit holes. He knew he could dive into any one of them, but he couldn't know what not-so-wonderland lay at the bottom.

He'd had enough of that for now. So far it had only made him feel soiled.

But there was another experiment he yearned to try.

Drawing back further from the memory-pasture he found a nebulous space of shifting color and a sensation like the blind spot of the eye: something hidden behind nothingness—impressions that wouldn't solidify, couldn't be grasped. He thrust his presence forward into a grey mist and reached out with his own senses—tried to picture his arms stretching, his fingertips becoming more sensitive, his ears growing. And his eyesight—he concentrated on seeing the world with his eyelids closed, like trying to pin down a dream. There came a tantalising suggestion of light. He leaned into it.

The light developed patches of color: dimmer, muddier shades surrounding a central patch of flickering brightness. He reached out to the bright patch—tugged himself along its rays of luminescence—and it gradually grew sharper. There was an ache behind his eyes as his brain struggled to resolve the picture, to match it with patterns contained in its own database. He used the focusing system of his eye muscles as another analogy, felt the lenses of his eyes change shape, and with the lethargy of a new awakening, lines and patterns began to emerge.

At last, an image snapped into place. The television set.

He raised his fingers to his own eyes to confirm that the lids were still closed. Then he slowly dropped his hands and took a long, deep breath.

It was one of those sycophantic celebrity TV shows—the kind Valerie liked.

He was seeing through the eyes of another human being.

8

April 18, 2040

Project: Minotaur
File: Janus 1
Progress report: The unauthorized test of projected imagery has had more serious consequences than originally anticipated, prompting the subject Leiter to draw other test subjects together into a social network. This was never part of the plan and will certainly alter results, especially since he has begun to teach them skills that will impede our information gathering. Our legal department is also alert to potential lawsuits resulting from the test.
Alternate transmission frequencies are still available and, so far, undiscovered. But new factors such as possible mental resistance will have to be accounted for. There have been signs of such resistance from subjects Robbins and Parrish, however West has proven to be

encouragingly pliable. We must expect that Leiter will share his own effective resistance techniques with his new group of implanteees.

It has been suggested that exceptional measures might be needed regarding Leiter, especially if he continues to probe projection marketing casualties; however, I advise against any precipitate action in that regard. Leiter continues to develop wholly unforeseen capacities within the wet brain-computer interface that could provide exactly the breakthrough we need.

H. Reinhardt Janus

Image: *Skin: smooth, unblemished; gentle outlines of cellular borders, pores, fine hairs; between cells: slick surfaces and viscous liquid, ruddy epidermis, coils of sweat glands and dark phallic-looking nerve endings; along the nerve, like a twisting, writhing snake tunnelling through pink flesh until it reaches grey matter, then dividing, branching into tendrils whose ends meld into star-shaped cells: neurons flashing with sparks of thought.*

How can you tell someone about the things you've seen in her mind?

Valerie beat him to it. "You saw my visit to my parent's place, on the lake, didn't you? Last September. As I was watching TV that memory just popped into my head. And then...a date, a dinner date—is that what you saw?"

Damon was surprised. "I guess it's less like hacking and more like controlling a computer with a remote framebuffer protocol. Program windows pop up on the host computer as well as the controlling machine."

"That's good, right? It means people can't just hack into our heads without us knowing about it."

"I can't say for sure. I've gotten into other people's commercial BCID's before—Neuros and Corticos—without them knowing. But I only accessed data files—devices like that don't record memories the way ours can. Not yet, anyway."

"You've hacked people's augments? I didn't know that."

"Just for kicks—in college. I guess I wanted to prove that mine was still better than theirs. Anyway, this date of yours...."

"Mark Phelps. He works at the Taggart Clinic."

"I know."

"Well, we went out a few times, but we didn't click. He's an okay guy, but very focused on his research work and hardly anything else. Almost no outside interests." She laughed. "Nothing below the surface. Nothing worth digging for."

"Not like me."

"True."

Damon let the subject drop. With Valerie's awareness of what he'd accessed, he was doubly glad he hadn't probed for any real secrets. If he really loved her, he owed her that much.

Even so, he was sure there'd be a way to block that awareness, and he knew he wouldn't be content until he'd found that way. What she'd said about every implant holding the key to its own access codes—did that mean they could all be penetrated? The idea was both reprehensible and irresistible at the same time.

He did a lot of experimenting after that, linking with Valerie's implant from time to time when they were together, careful to not be too invasive. He only wanted to get the lay of the land, to see what he could learn about the process. There was a lot to learn.

Taggart implants defaulted to Bluetooth connections when distance permitted, to decrease power consumption. But the data rate was too slow for him to experience her augment synesthetically. So, he used wifi. He tried making a connection through the internet while she was at work, but couldn't. That was probably because her implant didn't maintain a constant link to the internet—it only connected when requested. If he made the attempt sometime when she was using wifi on her own, he'd likely be able to slip through the open door. He'd get around to trying that sooner or later.

She'd never said anything about him seeing through her eyes—presumably she hadn't sensed it—so he didn't mention it either, for now. It might creep her out. He remembered the reaction of Naya and Helayne at the thought of the Taggart Clinic seeing what they saw. Something like that could destroy any sense of privacy. He promised himself he wouldn't spy on Valerie that way. There had to be better uses for that kind of sensory immersion.

He was with Con when one of those 'better uses' occurred to him.

"I can't believe you'd have something like this," he said to his roommate, using only finger and thumb to hold up a series of thick, fleshy, suggestively-shaped pads connected by wires to a wifi box. "Don't you get enough from real women?"

"What? You've never had *'net sex*?" Con asked. "Man, you don't know what you're missing. It's amazing the number of chicks who'll let you screw 'em as long as there's no body contact involved. I've been able to get it on with women from China, India, South America. Language isn't even a barrier—you should see all the sites dedicated to making anonymous sex connections. It's making the world a better place, my friend."

"You're kidding."

"No way, man. It's better'n porn. Real time. No inhibitions. Try it out—I've even made a few custom tweaks of my own to really give a guy a ride."

"I don't think so." The thought of where the gadget's haptic pads had been made him drop the contraption in a hurry. "But what about the software? How does it work?"

"Brain-computer interface—you put the BCI cap on and it reads EEG. Knows when and where your fancy is being tickled. And the two consenting parties—or more—swap the signals. Kind of like biofeedback, except mix and match. She visualizes your body and what she wants to be doing to it, the signal comes over the 'net, and then the pads respond in the right way. And man, that's what I call Good Vibrations."

Damon laughed. "The perfect solution for a lonely geek. Except you've never had a problem getting women."

"Nope. But maybe I'm getting lazier these days. It's easier to skip dinner and a movie and get straight to the main event."

They both laughed this time, but Damon couldn't help wondering if he was witnessing a major shift in human relationships.

"I bet it'll be standard equipment in the next generation of augments," Con said, as if reading his thoughts. "I'd invest in the company myself except the software's too easy to pirate."

"In that case you won't mind giving me a copy," Damon said. "I have a feeling it could be useful in a lot of ways."

"You and your lady hitting the one-year doldrums?"

"It hasn't been a year yet; and no, we're.... Never mind. Let's just say I'm a curious kind of guy."

"Well one curious cat is about to get into the cream."

#

Con had already tinkered with the program's code and created his own interface, but the main thing

Damon wanted from it was precise correlations between tactile sensations in specific parts of the body and the neural processing those sensations triggered. That required analysing the code and some other reverse engineering—he would need Con's help with that. He'd expected the list of monitored nerve clusters would be limited to the genitals and little else, but he was wrong. The haptic pads could be placed in a wide variety of erogenous zones, each linked to a specific cluster of brain cells that had been identified. Earlobes, eyelids, the nape of the neck, backs of knees...the most sensitive patches of skin were included—Con had paid for the very best.

The other key feature was a detection and analysis subroutine that measured brainwaves associated with pleasure centres. The original interface included a visual representation of frequency and amplitude that reminded Damon of the volume unit meters used in audio recording software: colored columns danced as a bar graph as the sex partners' pleasure increased, providing the means to refine the user's technique. Con suggested converting the readout to an audio tone, but a noise in the head like a Doppler-shifted siren would be a major sexual buzzkill. Provisionally, Damon settled on a visual analog of changing color: a calm delta or theta brain-wave would tint the user's vision with the blue end of the spectrum, while readings rising through beta to gamma would make his view increasingly red. Red light for sexual excitement seemed appropriate.

Then he had to figure out how to tap into the existing neural feeds to Valerie's implant, sort them according to their point of origin, and analyze their frequency range.

Once the program had been adapted to the specialized operating system that Taggart implants used, he installed the resulting hybrid in his own BCID. Con watched the process, jokingly holding a fire extinguisher in case of short circuits, but the installation went without a hitch. After that, Damon spent more than a week surreptitiously keeping track of neuron impulses produced whenever objects—furniture, utensils, cushions—touched specific places on Valerie's body. Sometimes he supplied the touching, too.

He didn't tell her what he was up to—he wanted it to be a surprise.

Finally, on a Friday night after a bottle of wine, he satisfied her curiosity—and much more.

"My God. Where did you learn how to do that?" she panted, sweat filming her skin.

Damon grinned like the Cheshire cat. "Just a little technology to tell me how I'm doing."

"I'd say you did brilliantly. You could make a fortune as a gigolo. But don't, OK?"

"Purely designed for *your* pleasure, ma'am." He laughed.

"Now teach me how I can give you a good time like that."

He was more than willing. The process took another couple of weeks, but the practice sessions were highly motivational. They didn't see very much of their friends for a while.

There were times when Damon wondered if this latest pursuit had become a sex obsession. That wasn't like him. There was more to life than sex, and it certainly wasn't the most important part of his relationship with Valerie. But he was convinced that what they were exploring was a key to unlocking potentially limitless other personal interactions that augment-to-augment connections might enable. His imagination had only touched on the possibilities, he was sure. His gut told him that this could be a watershed moment in human neurology.

And it wasn't as if the research was a chore.

AUGMENT NATION

Con insisted there was a fortune to be made if they could adapt the program to the commercial implants, but Damon felt the job was only half done. His creation could make a couple into the most empathetic lovers ever, but its exclusively mental approach didn't have any parallel to the limited physical system of the haptic pads. So even though they had immediate feedback about their partner's level of arousal for every change in technique, each participant still had to do the best they could with their original physical equipment. What if they weren't limited by that? What if the technology could *give* as well as *receive*?

BCIDs did provide two-way communication—they sent text and other visuals to the optic nerve, and audio was translated into impulses along the cochlear nerve. They wouldn't have been much use without that. But could the system be adapted to the brain's haptic network? For all Damon had learned about the capabilities of his two implants, he knew very little about their inner workings. Taggart implants provided direct neural contact, but did the same electrodes deliver current as well as detecting it? An internet search told him that the newest generation of electrodes was capable of it, so he took that as a provisional yes. But it still wouldn't be as simple as just sending current back down the line.

An electrode could sense signals from many nearby neurons. There wasn't a one-to-one ratio of electrodes to neuron clusters; and, as far as he knew, none of the micro-electrode arrays implanted in his head had been placed in direct proximity to the tactile centres of his brain. There had been no reason to do that. He'd have to create an analog to the way his BCID communicated with his visual cortex. In *neurospeak*, he'd have to decipher the signals from the somatosensory areas of the post central gyrus—unlock the code his parietal lobe used to pass sensory information to the rest of the brain—then send false signals of his own. Was his implant capable of that? It would probably depend on the similarity of the body's own code for tactile signals, to the visual and aural signals the BCID was designed to decode and use.

All he could do was try. Except, even coming up with a way to make the attempt stumped him for days. It was like an itch he couldn't scratch.

Which was exactly the metaphor he needed.

He chose an itch in the small of his back. There weren't a lot of nerves there, so it ought to be a good test. Closing his eyes, he focused on the physical sensations of the itch—really tried to bring it to the center of his mind. Then he visualized his hand scratching the itchy spot, and what that would feel like. It required a state of near-hypnotic concentration, and after a half-hour or more he thought he felt something: a pressure. A light scrape. But it was too inconsistent. Maybe the problem was that he was visualizing the hand—using his visual cortex. That extra step might be gumming up the works.

Instead, he tried to really *feel* what it was like to have the skin scratched by fingernails, to feel a succession of nerve endings triggered as phantom fingers moved over them. After such a long time with such intense focus, he couldn't be certain whether he'd actually felt something or just imagined it. There was a newer itch on his forearm. He concentrated on that, and finally evoked a sensation strong enough to make him open his eyes and look at the spot. Nothing was physically touching it. His mind was being tricked into believing the nerve endings had fired.

He tried other places, where there was no itch. It took a lot of practice to pinpoint an exact location without first receiving a sensory impulse from it. That shouldn't be a problem during sex—there'd be plenty of input—but he was determined to do more.

Valerie jokingly asked if he'd taken up transcendental meditation. He answered cryptically that the meditation he was working on would corrupt the most devout ascetic.

When he thought he'd become reliably proficient, he tried using the technique to masturbate without any physical contact. He didn't climax, but the feeling was good enough that he maintained a state of high stimulation for a long time. The testing ground that counted would be inside Valerie's head, not his, but he didn't want to spoil the surprise with trial runs. He decided his first test should be under real conditions. That wouldn't be easy. Valerie had adopted his other methods with such enthusiasm that it would take all of his mental strength to concentrate on something else while she worked her magic.

The opportunity came the next night. She was ready and willing but puzzled at what she took to be his lack of attention. He made an offhand comment and put more effort into his rhythm, but she soon made a quip about his distractedness and rolled on top, vowing to take control. A minute later she straightened like a shot and twisted around to look behind her.

"What the hell?"

"What is it?"

"It felt like somebody nipped my *ass*."

"Was it good for you?"

She stared at him, trying to read the enigmatic sparkle in his eyes.

"What's that supposed to mean? You're not saying...?"

He laughed at the shock in her face.

"I told you I had a meditation technique the monks would love."

"Ooh, baby. I don't know how you're doing it, but don't stop."

He toyed with her, teased her, gave her simultaneous stimulation that wasn't physically possible for a single partner to perform. When she climaxed, it lasted so long he became afraid he'd done some real psychological damage. Instead, she just smiled lasciviously, sweating and sated, her eyelids low.

"OK," she said, out of breath, "I've got a lot of catching up to do. Give me a minute and I'm willing to take a shot. Just promise me you'll never leave."

Over the next weeks they confirmed that her implant was capable of reciprocating. In spades.

Lying post-coitus one night, Damon felt vindicated for his recent obsessiveness. As he'd hoped, they'd achieved an incredible breakthrough in human interaction. That one human being could not only directly experience the physical sensations of another, but even reciprocate those sensory impressions—the implications were mind-blowing. It was no surprise that, as with so many breakthroughs, sex had been the motivator.

He tried to stay awake, thinking about many other possibilities, but the rush of sleep-inducing endorphins through his system made that impossible.

#

Image: *Facial expressions in every variety: surprise, incredulity, rapt interest. Amusement, intrigue, then...uncertainty, concern. Even fear?*

Damon had opened a gateway to let Valerie into his implant for sex. Now he gave her more access. Her own act of faith had restored his.

Evenings they often left the TV off and sat together holding hands, exchanging memories like the trading cards of schoolyard collectors. Damon created an avatar of himself for the purpose, then taught her how. Then her avatar would lead him, as if by the hand, through her museum of recorded memories, and he would return the favor. She was particularly interested in his early recollections of adjusting to his first implant, and the ordeals of high school. He didn't enjoy that, though the years had provided some objectivity. He was often surprised at the triviality of his juvenile crises—the emotional weight they bore was far out of proportion—but some had legitimately been life-altering. She said they explained a lot, but refused to elaborate.

He occasionally asked about her work, but she maintained that it wasn't something she wanted to waste their private time on. She also steered him away from memories of Ron, the sugar daddy. Damon only caught accidental glimpses of him, he thought: impressions much as he'd expected of a bulky build and well-trained greying hair.

Valerie witnessed Damon's abortive attempt to return to hockey when he was fifteen, in a pick-up game at a small outdoor rink, very much without his mother's knowledge. He'd been taken hard into the boards and spent a week in terrible fear that he'd damaged his implant.

A memory of another unlucky romantic interlude in Valerie's past gave Damon a rueful smile: it was a blind date—the man a muscular specimen with smooth good looks and little else going for him. The guy had gotten drunk—on the first date! —and had become far too aggressive once the cab had returned them to Valerie's street. When her attempts to discourage his groping hands failed, she'd had to resort to a swift knee to the balls. The frozen expression on the man's face had been captured in faithful detail by her implant.

There was the high school dance Damon's mother had pushed him to attend: a writhing hell of pounding music and intimidating scowls from both sexes, compounded by the unfortunate fact of adolescent life that the girls were all two inches taller than he was. Even so, a pretty girl with braces had finally given him a look that he'd interpreted as an invitation, and they'd taken to the floor just as a nice, safe up-tempo number was replaced by a slow dance. He'd done his best, but then, as they'd passed a dishevelled boy with a vacant look and unruly hair, there was a rude bodily noise that wasn't faked. Damon had quickly looked at his partner's face with its wrinkled nose and accusation in her eyes. His pleas of innocence went unheard, and she'd returned stiffly to her coterie of friends, ending his dreams of romance for years to come.

As Damon encountered one of Valerie's most vivid memories, he could have sworn he felt her body temperature drop. She was in a hospital gown in a sterile room with lights too bright to permit any self-deception. Waiting for surgery: a breast lump. The implant hadn't recorded her vital signs—it didn't need to. The rapid rise and fall of the front of her gown was evidence enough. The helpless surrender to the attendants, an endless journey along corridors, the ambush by a throng of masked strangers wielding instruments of dissection, the lowering shroud of darkness and finality produced by anesthetic: all of those images were so familiar to Damon, yet more terrifying when seen through Valerie's mind as she anticipated death. Yet, after all, the lump had been benign and the ordeal had left behind only scars, on her skin and on her psyche.

When Damon had first met Mud the dog, he'd been reluctant to let his guard down and make friends with the animal. He'd never told Valerie why. The answer was in a teenaged memory of his neighbor's big, friendly mutt who'd latched onto Damon because its owners were neglectful and often cruel. Damon's mother had used his implant as an excuse yet again, and forbidden him to pay attention to the dog, an edict Damon had never considered obeying. One day in the bitter heart of winter, he'd played with the dog for an hour in the snow, rough-housing and throwing snowballs in a vain attempt to teach it to fetch. When his mother had returned from an appointment and he'd gone home for the night, he'd had no idea of the tragedy he'd sowed. Not until he left for school the next morning and found the dog's frozen body, curled stiffly on their front step.

Shared experience of that melancholy episode led Valerie to recall of one of the lowest points in her life. It had happened after a love affair had ended badly—Damon wondered if it might have been Ron, but Valerie wouldn't say more, and Damon did not snoop. Instead, her avatar led him to a cramped university office lined with books and folders meticulously shelved, yet still giving the appearance of disorder because of the indiscriminate variety of their sizes and shapes. It was the office of a woman, a very attractive brunette, perhaps a few years older than Valerie and slimmer, with neatly trimmed hair and perfect makeup. To Damon's surprise, the woman stepped close and brushed Valerie's lips with her own. He could sense the memory-Valerie begin to respond, but then there were soft murmurs in her ear: something about *reward* and higher grades. The next words were as clear as cut ice, as Valerie told the woman to go to hell and stalked from the room. The aftermath of that shared recollection was a long, uncomfortable silence, finally broken by a sheepish laugh from Valerie, and a bruising hug.

"You probably thought you were in for some hot girl-on-girl action there," she said, blushing.

"I'm not sorry that it wasn't," he said. "But apparently the university environment does include some surprising methods of education."

Her next laugh was full and liberating.

Their discovery of each other wasn't confined to the past. When Damon finally revealed that he'd been able to see through her eyes in real time, the idea astonished and delighted her. She couldn't wait to try it, but they quickly learned the drawbacks when Valerie walked into a lamp post while remote viewing through Damon. Even though he saw the collision coming at the last moment, he couldn't control her muscles to avoid it. They both felt the pain of the collision, and a bruised nose motivated them to establish some rules. Like warning labels on medication: *not to be used while operating machinery*. They tacitly agreed to respect each other's privacy in bathrooms and other sensitive situations. Valerie suggested they should get permission before eavesdropping with the other's eyes or ears. A quick message would suffice—instant messaging between them came to be nearly as automatic and unremarkable as thought.

Damon had found it hard to believe that Valerie liked to do her shopping in person, despite the inconvenience of travelling to one of the high-rise shopping centres and carrying merchandise around. Now it was one of the quirks he loved about her, and even shopping trips were welcome diversions. The fun was in the sharing. There was no need for them to stay side-by-side: with a quick mental call, Damon could be looking at a dress in Valerie's hands two floors away—or across town, although they still preferred to go places together.

With her permission, he tried to experience her thoughts as she wrote her poetry, but true thought remained elusive. Instead, he discovered that he could see flashes of the imagery she pictured while writing. It made sense—the visual cortex was used for imagined images as well as real ones. He'd stumbled onto that connection as a kid when he pictured Ashley Good's face on a naked picture from the internet. The new knowledge led to Valerie imagining scenarios for his amusement, and sometimes to arouse him. It worked brilliantly.

In that way, and only that way, he finally came to see some of her wet memories, the actual stored memories of her living brain. If she deliberately recalled them with full visualization, he was able to see them, too; but they were vastly different from the implant recordings. Where the computer recorded data files and stored them using sophisticated compression algorithms, live brain memories were amorphous, with no clearly defined borders: one moment flowed into any contiguous moment. He was convinced that they were continually rewritten even as they were remembered. They were never sharp—the most he could grasp were fleeting impressions, blurred by motion and emotion, perhaps even by time.

He hoped that the encoding systems of all human brains would be similar enough that one would eventually be able to interpret the signals of another, like learning a foreign language. He thought he could detect an improvement over time, but he wasn't certain. It might only have been wishful thinking.

He'd already been closer to Valerie than he'd ever been to another living soul. Their new experiences went far beyond that—a quantum shift into a whole new territory for human relationships. He was ecstatically happy. If only all people could experience what they had. The John Lennon song "Imagine" popped into his head and made him smile at its naiveté, and his own. Still, the next time he and Valerie got together with the other Taggart implantees over dinner, he couldn't wait to share the news.

It was an eclectic group: the show-biz couple, Naya and Jace Robbins; the surgeon, Rosa Ferraro; Helayne West, the midwife; and history teacher, Ebon Parrish.

The restaurant had been recommended by the newest members of their circle, Kenzo and Shiori Shabata from Tokyo. Kenzo's export business occasionally brought them to North America, but they'd made a special trip three years earlier to get a Taggart implant for Shiori to correct a neurological disorder. She'd had serious misgivings, so Kenzo had promised to get an implant too, and he'd followed through. By then, the Taggart team had been glad to have an implantee whose brain had no pre-existing handicap. Damon had found their names in the D-M file and had contacted them, even though their distance from the city had spared them from the projected advertising debacle that had cost others their lives.

The Shabatas' English was excellent, but Helayne tried out some halting Japanese. Several of the midwives she worked with were from Japan, and she'd picked up a few phrases. Shiori Shabata complemented her on her accent, and also on a sparkling ruby and diamond ring on her right hand. Helayne flashed her ring around. It couldn't have been an impulse buy for someone in her income bracket; and at their first meeting, she'd seemed as firmly opposed to ostentatious consumerism as she was to eating meat or burning fossil fuels. As he thought about that, Damon noticed Valerie checking out Helayne's jacket. It was obviously new and looked like a product from an expensive designer. To each her own.

"Imagine what it could be like for international relations." Damon continued what he'd been saying before the waitress had interrupted with their trays of sushi. "So many problems are caused because the two sides don't know how far they can trust each other. If their representatives could link mind-to-mind there'd be no hiding, and no misunderstanding. Clear, honest, open communication...it could be the key to everything."

"That's a lot to hope for," Jace said, reaching to pour sake for the rest. "Nations will always want to hide things from each other."

"Only because they don't trust each other," Damon insisted, "and they don't know how the other side will react to whatever they find out. But if those doubts didn't enter into the equation because everyone was equally open, there'd be no need for barriers."

"I'm afraid I have to agree with Jace." Kenzo gave a respectful nod to remove offence from his words. "It is certainly a result to be wished for, but it might be too much to expect from human nature."

"Honest, open communication has to begin with individuals." Damon's eyes gleamed as he told them about the experiences he and Valerie were enjoying. She winced when he mentioned sex, so he didn't go into detail. "But it's an incredible feeling," he said. "We can't quite read each other's thoughts, but sometimes we're pretty close to it. You could do it, too. The couples who both have implants, anyway. We can teach you."

Their reaction disappointed him. Jace and Kenzo were interested. "She can read me like a book anyway," Jace said with a laugh. But Naya and Shiori were much more reluctant. Helayne and Rosa seemed glad to be forcibly excluded by their lack of a partner, while Ebon made a mock pout.

"Damn shame to miss out on sex like that," he said. "I don't suppose any of you guys want to share? Or maybe do a group thing." His face was serious, but when he saw the expressions of the women, he roared with a laugh that turned every head in the restaurant.

"It could probably be done," Damon said with a chuckle, then caught Valerie shaking her head at him. "Or maybe not. Anyway, give the other idea some thought—talk it over between you and let us know if you're interested. The sex program was only the doorway to find the connections, but the rest is mainly a mind-set and lots of practice. I'm sure anyone with a recent Taggart implant could do it. I'm going to try to figure out how to adapt it to the commercial augments, too, so we can really see how much it will benefit people." He gave a half-smile. "Besides, my roommate, Con, is *begging* me to."

They laughed, but most of them still looked uncomfortable.

Their shared "otherness" made the group a natural social club, and they began to meet every few weeks. It was impossible to ignore Damon and Valerie's devotion to each other, nor the enthusiasm in their voices as they talked about their adventures in mutual discovery. Eventually the reluctant were won over, though it turned out that none of them could get the hang of the process on their own. They had to allow Damon access to their implants so he could use his avatar to lead them to the knowledge they needed; but he assured them that once he'd finished, they only needed to change their permission codes and passwords to lock him out again, *and* their partners, if desired.

The married couples soon wore smiles of wonder as they began to discover each other in an all-new way. Ebon and Rosa agreed to pair up, only for the sake of learning the techniques. Rosa looked after her elderly mother and an aunt who lived with her. Both mother and aunt suffered from dementia. She hoped the skills developed for augments might someday lead to a way to peer through the dark veils gathered over the old women's minds. Damon couldn't say it was impossible, and didn't want to.

Helayne remained the lone holdout. She gave an uncomfortable smile when asked and proclaimed that she'd never want to inflict her mind on anyone else.

Once Damon had taught the others what they needed, he was surprised to find that his access to their BCIDs remained intact. When his friends changed their implants' passwords, his own simply recorded the change, and he couldn't make it erase the knowledge. It might be possible to get around that by having them change their passwords while he voluntarily shut off his implant's wifi and Bluetooth, but to admit a glitch like that could also ruin some of their new-found camaraderie by making them suspicious.

He was badly distracted for the rest of their evening together.

He'd been given the combination to the cupboard that held the keys.

He elected not to mention it.

August 14, 2040

Project: Minotaur
File: Janus 1
Progress report: Due to "philosophical differences" Mark Phelps has been dismissed from the Taggart clinic, and Ram Khouri has been reprimanded for incompetence. Because of them, the Damon Leiter situation has gotten out of hand. In addition, the predictions of Leiter's skill development with his BCIDs were unacceptably deficient, and his tendencies toward anarchic behavior went unreported. Leiter's roommate, Conway, is thought to have had an unfortunate influence on Leiter's attitudes and conduct, and steps are being taken to mitigate that influence, but likely too late. As described in Attachment A, Leiter has begun to train other implantees, awaken their suspicions, and

AUGMENT NATION

potentially make them equally difficult to control. These actions threaten our entire project.

The situation is complicated by Leiter's usefulness, some of it according to plan, but much clearly unintentional and unexpected. It is impossible to predict which of his damaging actions might also provide unwitting benefits to the project; and so, to decide when, how, or even *if* Leiter should be stopped. I strongly counsel against drastic measures that have been proposed by some agents of our primary client.

Unfortunately, our best source of information about Leiter shows evidence of him becoming unreliable. Therefore, technological surveillance of Leiter himself becomes more important than ever.

H. Reinhardt Janus

Image: *A cartoonish Flash rendition of birthday cake, glossy brown with occasional colored sparkles from the icing. A single, fat red candle juts up from the exact center with an animated flame that shrinks and stretches in predictable rhythm. Glowing white script letters paint themselves across the cake, saying, "Click Here."*

"So that's your idea?" Ram Khouri looked like he'd eaten something disagreeable.

"Well...yeah. We can't just stuff unwanted advertising into people's augments—that has to be illegal, or it soon would be." Damon watched his boss's eyes carefully for any betrayal of guilt, but there was none. "So instead, we get them to *ask* for it. They walk by a billboard or a place of business and we send a little pop-up into their heads for a few seconds—something small. Brief enough not to irritate them, but intriguing. They mentally select the icon, and *we're in*. After that, we can stream as much as we want until they say stop—it's an implied relationship at that point. Gets us around legalities and defuses a lot of the potential resistance from rights groups."

"ACLU will still bitch," Greg Welsh muttered.

"Not if the augment manufacturers provide a firmware update that lets users block *all* pop-ups if they want to."

"*Block all*...what the hell good is *this* then?" Khouri's scowl looked more threatening.

"They'll be *able* to block them, but how many really will?" Damon asked. "When social network websites were forced to let members opt out of advertising, less than three per cent actually did. In the old days of paper flyers, you could just throw them into recycling without looking at them, but most people still read them. People *want* to be pitched to—you just have to stir their appetite the right way with an attractive approach."

"A flat, cartoon birthday cake wouldn't do it for me." Layla Goring was sitting in on the session, even though most of her job involved handling focus groups and surveys.

"I'm not a graphic artist, OK?" Damon shrugged. "D-M's art department can come up with something irresistible, I'm sure."

There was more discussion about minor points, and then technical aspects of implementation, but Damon left the room confident his scheme would be accepted. The real question was whether consumers would even *notice* the projected icons amid the astonishing number of distractions they already faced, mostly by choice. Damon believed in the importance of marketing, and truly thought his idea could provide a service people would want. But it was also the only way he could think of to steer Dyna-Mantech BCI away from the kind of blundering approach that had cost some implant users their lives.

That had to count for something.

#

Image: *An Abercrombie & Fitch suit on a physique that was once fit but now betrayed a legacy of indulgent living. Perfectly trained hair, fashionably short and greying with distinction. A strong, square face. The essence of personality is in the eyes: the color of battleships and made of the same cold steel.*

Damon was astonished when he opened his door. His befuddled mind thought: *Ron?* just as his implant supplied the name [*Emery Rueld Taggart, MD*]. It was never wrong, yet he was still unsure.

"May I come in, David? Or, of course, I should call you Damon now."

"*Doctor Taggart?*"

"A part of you remembers me, I see. I can guess which part. May I come in? Your neighbors will start to think I'm a salesman."

Damon stood aside but couldn't think of anything at all to say. Taggart brushed past him with the air of a British lord. He surveyed the living space Damon shared with Con, its comfortable chaos suddenly transformed into wretched squalor. There were three chairs available, but Taggart hesitated, looking among the three as if performing mental triage. He turned back to Damon.

"I have to talk with you. I think it's overdue. Is there somewhere we can go?"

Equally eager to escape the place, Damon coughed. "Well, the campus is just a couple of minutes away if we walk. There's a faculty lounge—I'm allowed to use it, and at this time of night there's nobody around. Usually some decent bottles of wine stashed in a cupboard, too."

"Perfect."

They said little that mattered as they walked through the night air. Taggart had actually given some lectures on the campus and he made small-talk about the experience. The richness of his voice awakened memories and echoes of memories. Damon shivered, though not from cold.

The faculty lounge was designed to mimic a gentleman's club, with oak on the walls and deeply padded green-leather furniture. Damon felt comically out of place as he settled into an armchair with a glass of dark wine, but Taggart could have been born there, he was so much at ease.

"Did Dyna-Mantech send you?" Damon asked.

"No. Not at all. Its parent company Imaging Capital International funded my clinic, as I suppose you know. But I left the clinic. ImagiCap asks for my services as a consultant occasionally. I comply if I'm interested. Nobody asked me to come here. I came on my own." He drew the wine glass to his nose and swirled the liquid, but didn't drink.

He looked over at Damon. "Why did you change your name? Why Damon?"

"David was a victim. I didn't want to be a victim anymore. I liked the idea of computer *daemons*, working in the background, unnoticed. But you can't drop the British 'a' from the word and call yourself *demon* without people getting the wrong idea. *Damon* was close enough. But tell me about my implants. Tell me why they're capable of so much more than just curing agnosia. Please. Tell me things I don't know about them."

"Did you know that, in mythology, demons handled the tasks the gods couldn't be bothered with?" Taggart took a measured sip of his wine, and an eyebrow rose in appreciation. "From what I've heard, there seems to be very little you don't already know about your implants.

Although it seems you didn't know they were capable of delivering electrical current as well as measuring it."

"Yeah, why is that? And why wasn't I told?"

"There were many things you weren't told in the beginning because you were young, and those facts wouldn't have meant anything to you. Later... well...it was considered *prudent* to hold some information back until the right moment. The distribution of current to the cerebral cortex was intended to stimulate the abilities of certain brain cells—it was discovered that electro-stimulation can actually enhance learning, if only for short periods of time. And the assumption was that more discoveries along that line would be made, so it was better to equip the augments for the future. That is also part of the explanation for the extensive *extra features* of your BCID. Why not build for potential instead of just current need?"

"*Part* of the explanation?"

Taggart smiled. "You were the beginning of a great social experiment, of course. But we'll get to that. I was trying to think of more technical elements. Did you ever wonder how your implants are powered?"

Damon stiffened with the realization that he'd never thought much about it. How was that possible? He'd so thoroughly accepted the mechanisms as parts of his body that he'd given their metabolism no more thought than that of his own cells.

"The original Taggart model," the doctor continued, "used an ingenious *piezoelectric* system. Don't bother to Google it—I'll explain. Some materials, common quartz for example, produce electric current under stress. You don't smoke, but you've seen butane cigarette lighters. A spring-loaded hammer strikes a piezoelectric ceramic and a current is generated that jumps a gap, creating a spark. Well, certain cellular proteins and even the collagen in bone tissue can be convinced to do much the same thing. In your case, though, we used artificial materials sandwiched with silicone. The generator is in your chest. Every breath you take induces a piezoelectric current that powers your BCID. Fitting, don't you think? Almost the same process that powers your own brain."

Damon unconsciously raised a hand to his ribs. Taggart took a swallow of wine and Damon took a larger one.

"The *Taggart Opus* is more sophisticated." Its creator looked nearly smug. "It's powered in much the same way as your own body cells, by metabolizing glucose in the bloodstream. Oxidase enzymes burn glucose with oxygen, and there's plenty of both in the human body. Oh, I can't really take credit for the design, but I'm proud of it, all the same. Our team was years ahead of anyone else in our field."

"Congratulations."

"No need for sarcasm. Has it been such a hardship? No, you're simply offended at the thought of being a guinea pig. You should know by now that there's no such thing as a gift—there's always a price to pay."

"You have no idea of the price I've paid. But I won't say the prize wasn't worth it."

"Of course it was worth it. You're still a young man. The things you'll do in your lifetime!" For the first time, Taggart looked animated. "I'd have given my left nut to have what you have, but there wasn't another surgeon I'd trust to perform the operation on me." He laughed, but Damon knew the truth when he heard it. "Who cuts the barber's hair?"

"I'm surprised my mother agreed to it," he said.

"So am I. I always was. Implantations like that have become much more routine these days—rich people get them just for the novelty. But when you got your first...it was very risky. Even I had never done anything *close* to that many electrode implantations. No-one really knew what the consequences might be. I told your mother about the risks—I didn't hide anything—but she didn't seem to hear me. She only heard opportunity. An unusual woman, in many ways."

"You should never have spied on me. Or let *her* spy on me."

"I told them not to do that. That's when you turned against us, isn't it? When you began to be...difficult."

Damon thought about that. It was true. He'd suddenly known what it meant to have his life exposed to others; and for the first time, the price had felt too high to pay. He gulped the last of his wine, barely tasting it, then poured himself some more. It would cost his beer money for a couple of weeks to replace the bottle. He grudgingly refilled Taggart's glass. The man gave a nod and held the wine up to the light to observe its color.

"Many things stay hidden unless you know how to look at them the right way," he said. Then he straightened. "Everything has a price, and everything is a compromise. I think you should know that the electric stimulation your implant can provide is also a double-edged sword."

"How?"

"It can stimulate the memory-encoding process, and enhance other things, I'm sure. It can also send current where it should, perhaps, not be sent."

"Such as?"

"The pleasure centres of the brain. They're activated by electrical impulses, of course. Imagine what happens when you send an even stronger current directly into those nodes?"

"One hell of a great high."

"Too good, in fact. Lab rats quickly become addicted to that kind of current high to the point that they choose it over food."

"A science fiction writer named Larry Niven predicted current addicts in his stories. I thought it was pretty unlikely. Especially with anti-addiction vaccines."

"Think again," said Taggert. "If you haven't tried it, I suggest you don't. We have no real data on how much current a human can give themselves and still be able to refuse it. How do you refuse instant, pure pleasure, any time you want it? We weren't made to resist something like that."

"*Made*, Doctor? I would have thought you'd be on the side of evolution, not creation."

"Tell that to someone who hasn't spent his career delving into the miracle of the human brain." Taggart took a long drink. "Which reminds me of the other place I was thinking of—where current shouldn't go. Have you ever heard of the 'God spot?' No? There's good evidence that when parts of the temporal lobe of the brain are stimulated with a magnetic field—a way of inducing a current flow—a feeling of a God-like presence is produced. Religious transcendence. Cosmic bliss. How the person interprets the feeling depends on their upbringing; but whether they attribute the presence to God, or Christ, or some other entity, it is a deeply spiritual experience. You can imagine how influential something like that could be."

"You mean, in the wrong hands."

"How could there be any *right* hands for power like that?"

The room went quiet; and after a time, Damon realised that both of them were simply staring out the window.

"Is there anything else I should know? Other risks associated with my implant?"

Taggart's head came around and he rubbed his chin. "Did I ever mention sunspots? Actually, that's too specific. Your *Opus* implant, and every Taggart model from the *Tertius* on, uses much more sensitive, less-intrusive sensors that circumvent the need for physical emplacement of electrodes wherever possible, in fact. However, that does leave them more susceptible to electrical interference. Including, but by no means limited to, sunspots with their high levels of cosmic radiation. There are many ways of producing such interference artificially, and it could *play hell* with your implant's systems."

"Important safety tip," Damon muttered with a nod. He was finding it disconcerting to discover how much he hadn't known about the things in his head.

"Your original implant is much less vulnerable to anything like that. And since the processor itself is like a metal cap within your skull, it provides a fair bit of shielding as well. You're luckier than most. You've got a spare. You won't ever be left on your own."

"Luck. How did I get so lucky, anyway?"

"To get your first one? You had a handicap we could cure, and also met other minor requirements; but it was mostly random chance. And we were all damn lucky that the development of your brain—your child brain—into its adult structure lined up nearly perfectly; so, even as areas of brain function shifted position, nothing got seriously out of alignment. Some sensing even improved. But that was pure luck. Since then...well, that's a different story."

"How do you mean?" Damon leaned forward. Taggart smiled and prolonged the moment by draining his glass. Damon filled it again but didn't pour more for himself.

"Let's just say that your path has been smoother than it might have been." Taggart lowered his eyelids as if to cultivate an air of mystery. "Your clashes with your high-school Vice-Principal, for instance—he wanted to expel you, but that was prevented. Your clumsy hacking into his computer was covered up. And your scholarship to university—didn't you ever wonder how you could get that with your very ordinary grades? Or how you weren't forced to quit when you were caught cheating? Did you think the college admin really couldn't do without you?"

"What are you saying—that someone has been looking out for me all this time? What, some kind of guardian angel?"

Taggart simply inclined his head, and then busied himself trying to pluck a crumb of cork from his tongue.

"And I suppose this same guardian angel got me the job at Dyna-Mantech, too?" He was startled when Taggart laughed.

"Good Lord, that was inevitable. Nearly from the beginning." The doctor saw that Damon was going to press for more and waved him off. "I don't have time to get into all of that right now. Besides, you'll appreciate it more when you dig it up on your own. I'll give you some key codes before I leave that will allow you to access the original progress reports on your case. But don't you think there are more important questions about all this? *Why* instead of *how*?"

"All right. Tell me *why*. What's my implant really all about?"

Taggart's eyes sparkled as he emptied the bottle into his glass and wriggled his body deep into the chair. "The future of humanity, of course. We moderns like to think we're so vastly superior to our ancestors—that we've evolved into a higher form. Nonsense. We haven't changed in any significant way since the time of the Sumerians, or the Trojans. We are just Cro-Magnons in modern dress. Yes, we can travel in space and communicate around the globe, but our flesh-and-blood hardware hasn't changed at all.

"But *you*, Damon Leiter, really are a different animal from the rest of us. It's been inevitable since the invention of the digital computer that humankind would one day incorporate such technology into our own bodies. The question has always been how to do it the right way—but, more importantly, what would happen next. A Canadian professor named Steve Mann experimented for decades, beginning in the 1970s, with ways to incorporate technology into the human experience, sometimes turning himself into a kind of cyborg—except with computing devices that were wearable, not actually implanted into the body. He tried to produce a sort of synthetic synesthesia: a way for electronic sensing instruments to be mapped to our own corporeal senses."

"I *smell* wifi signals," Damon said. "A lot of my implants' tricks have to be controlled by using a physical analog to one of my senses, or to muscular movements."

"Fascinating. Of course, the original interface was designed that way and you've taken it to extraordinary levels. It's a brave new world, isn't it? When I was born, people couldn't have imagined what it's like to have the internet, to carry a mobile phone at all times, or even to know with certainty where you are, thanks to GPS. And you, Damon, have dozens of other capabilities my parents couldn't even have understood."

"But isn't that like what you were saying about the Sumerians? Isn't it just that I have fancier toys?"

"If Alexander the Great had been given those capabilities, how do you think the course of history might have gone? But it's more than that. Much more. What about your connectedness to my other patients via the implants. You've said it yourself: conflicts so often arise because of misunderstanding, but where there is such clarity of communication and understanding, do we not dare, finally, to dream of peace?"

"How did you know about...?"

"That isn't important. What *is* important is that you're not only the next true step in human advancement—the marriage of the best of flesh and machine—but you also arrive at a time when human beings are rapidly becoming estranged from one another. In some respects, people communicate more than ever, but they do so by Jabber, or texting, or other means that are cold and impersonal. They spend their time with television and the internet instead of socializing face to face. They entrust their children's moral education to Hollywood and Fox News, to violent screen games. And they allow themselves to become isolated—and even *work* at it, in fact. But you and your friends...you can be closer than brothers, closer than twins. You can show the way to bring humanity back into connectedness. Perhaps even into true global unity."

The man's eyes were lit with a fire that Damon began to fear might be the fires of fanaticism. Taggart's strong hands were clenched as if they sought to grasp truth from the air.

"But all of that," Damon rocked his head, confused. "Are you saying that's why ImagiCap has arranged...?"

"No, *no*. Not them!" Taggart spat. "Consumerism is the only drug they're interested in dispensing. Listen to me, Damon." He leaned forward, and his hands that had been grasping only air stretched forward almost pleadingly. "You won't be able to resist everything they want you to do, but you have to try. Make your own path. Lead them on, but then leave them in the dust. However, you'll have to be careful. They already see you as a threat—you'll have to defuse that somehow. The best way will be for you to appear to go along with them, then weaken their foundation from within.

"That's why I'm going to give you the keys to the kingdom."

10

August 15, 2040

Project: Minotaur
File: Janus 1
Progress report: Damon Leiter is on track to provide the breakthrough our project requires—there is no question in my mind. In areas of security penetration, stealth surveillance, data search and retrieval, and others, he has developed methods that completely elude our own technical staff. We are still unable to gain access to these methods directly from Leiter, although that will not be an impediment much longer, since he continues to teach his discoveries to his companions who are much more tractable. The best solution would be to recruit Leiter into our fold. Unfortunately, early mishandling of his case soured that opportunity; and now Dr. Emery Taggart himself has met with

Leiter. Taggart has shown himself to be a proverbial 'loose cannon', and he is considered likely to have increased Leiter's antipathy to our efforts.

In light of this development, I suggest strengthening corporate network-security even more, and advising our clients to do the same, but not taking direct action. Damon Leiter must be considered a threat, but he must also be acknowledged as our most vital prospect.

H. Reinhardt Janus

Image: *Nested cubes: one inside another inside another, stretching to infinity. Padlocks, passwords, puzzles. Unknowns containing secrets concealing mysteries hiding cyphers disguising more unknowns. Truth a half-remembered shadow beyond a wall of obfuscation.*

Damon felt like celebrating after the visit from Taggart; and when Valerie came home from work the next day, he was waiting at her apartment to cook dinner for her. As he dabbled with pesto and artichoke hearts in the kitchen, and she prepared the dining area in the next room, he told her about Taggart. He could hear surprise in her voice, but he didn't give her the chance to say much as he talked non-stop about Taggart's revelations and his own plans to use the access Taggert had gifted him. Valerie gave her attention to the food, proclaiming it excellent when she could get a word in. Afterward, he was puzzled to find her holding some pictures of the two of them that she kept on a sideboard: a cross-country ski outing, a New Year's Eve party, and a picture from one of their first dinner dates. Her face was melancholy until she saw him watching, and then she forced a smile.

That night she made love with a passion that caught him off guard. He responded with equal enthusiasm. He felt energized and re-motivated, as if making a new beginning. Maybe that was what she was feeling, too.

The next day, Con returned from a gaming convention out of town. Damon expected him to be stoked about the prospect of some major-league computer infiltration, but he was wrong. After getting Damon started with the protocols and passwords Taggart had given, Con pulled up short.

"Hey, man. A lot of this isn't just Deep Web stuff, it's *Dark* Web. OK, I get that. I go there all the time. But some of these links lead to government sites even I won't touch. They involve some serious shit, and the security measures are insane. If the average firewall is like a barbed wire fence, *these* suckers throw buzz-saws at you. And they don't stop. If your penetration techniques aren't foolproof, you'd better have a goddamned good escape route planned, 'cause you'll be in the crosshairs from then on."

"It's OK if you don't want to be involved," Damon said.

"No, man. I couldn't let you go into a shitstorm like this on your own. The Dark Web stuff, you'll probably be OK with the new TOR upgrade. Good anonymity. But the Deep Web government sites? Give me a day to set up a bunch of dead ends and ghost trails and false identities. Better use some bots, too. If guys in black suits are gonna bust in somebody's door, let it be some unsuspecting schlep in Idaho instead of you and me."

Damon agreed, but then Con asked for another day, and another. On the fourth day Damon's impatience bulled through one last pacing, fidgeting attempt by Con to change his mind, and the strategy was set into motion.

"But I'm not gonna watch, man. There are some secrets I don't wanna know." His face was lined with concern Damon had never seen there before.

"Don't worry. I'm not out to bring down the government. I probably won't even go to those sites. The fish I'm after are Dyna-Mantech and ImagiCap."

"Big fish, man. Sharks more like. And don't think that only going after ImagiCap will keep you clean with the feds. Are you sure you'll know where one ends and the other begins?" With that, Con left, looking ashamed but resolute. Damon's confidence was badly shaken. He should cancel the hunt. But he couldn't.

As Damon began his quest, his misgivings were quickly swept aside by the discovery of a series of progress reports about his own case. Some doctor named Klug had written them. Damon didn't remember the guy, but the observations were first-hand and detailed. And revealing. They included the ill-fated decision to allow his mother access to his implant's surveillance feed. More alarming were speculations about ImagiCap's involvement in the project, and the implications of it.

He quickly read all the reports. Then he got quietly drunk.

He'd known that he was a human guinea pig for the implant procedures. It was the price he paid for the benefits of the technology. But he'd never suspected how far the experiment had gone. The chinotto drinks—ImagiCap had conditioned him to like them. Programmed him. Salted licorice, too. How many more of his tastes and preferences had been planted by subliminal suggestion? Even his decision to go into marketing as a career. Especially that. No wonder Taggart had laughed.

He was struck by wrenching nausea. This was a violation far worse than that horrible adolescence-defining trauma of when his mother had burst through his bedroom door. Now he realized that his very personality had been a toy for others to play with.

He needed Valerie, but she was working, and her wifi connection was turned off. Maybe that was for the best—he had no right to burden the one he loved with this kind of pain. Instead, he wallowed in misery and bourbon, until consciousness mercifully relinquished its spark for a time.

He awoke nauseated in the dark. The middle of the night. Con was sleeping. Valerie, too, though she'd left several worried messages. He sent a reply, telling her only that he was OK, then went to the bathroom to empty his writhing stomach. When its spasms finally subsided, he returned to his computer and began the search again, filled with cold fury.

Without knowing what he was looking for, it was hard to know how to proceed; but after hours of reading random documents, some pieces began to knit together. Taggart had begun his specialization in implants with pure motives, and probably hadn't even noticed at first when ImagiCap dollars had begun to flow into his bank account. But once established, the funding, and the threat of its withdrawal, was made very clear. Taggart was hooked—he couldn't refuse ImagiCap's meddling without giving up his precious project and starting all over again. Even so, there was little evidence that Taggart had lost any sleep over the corporate machinations—he was too focused on the prize: a technological breakthrough with his name on it. Damon wasn't an innocent life in his care, but only a means to an end.

There were extensive files on each of the Taggart BCID recipients, but Damon resisted the temptation to pry into his friends' lives. They were already victims of a gross invasion of privacy.

More surprising, there were thousands of files on other people, that included a staggering amount of private detail. At first, he thought the individuals in the records must be owners of commercial implants and D-

M had found a way to scour its competitors' databases. But he found files on a number of public figures who were outspoken against implants—their lives had been thoroughly scrutinized. Such information must have been gathered through more conventional means to use as blackmail or for some other form of manipulation. What that said about ImagiCap's resources was frightening.

It no longer came as a shock to learn that ImagiCap was one of the world's worst spammers. An obscure folder in one set of files had been incongruously named "Monty Python." In it he found links that outlined the structure of a spam network that spanned the globe and relocated its central hub every few days. Its revenue was enormous, but carefully disguised to look legitimate. Many of the clients wouldn't even know where their advertising dollars were being spent. Or could easily turn a blind eye.

He used a custom program of Con's to search for his own name, and one of the tantalizing results was a reference to a project called "Minotaur." His implants supplied the story of a mythical monster, half man and half bull, imprisoned in a labyrinth. The Wikipedia entry offered even more about the myth, but such general information was of no help in cracking the file's security. The most he could determine was that there was hard copy on the project in a secret file repository somewhere in the city, but he could find no reference to the archive's location.

As the hours went by, he encountered more and more locked files that Taggart's incantations couldn't penetrate. There were teasing references to subliminal suggestion, the "God spot," and stimulating the pleasure centers of the brain. Growing angry, Damon cast aside his caution about the risky government sites and sent probes in their direction.

AUGMENT NATION

It quickly became clear that the US government was one of ImagiCap's most important customers. There were dozens of links between the two, though the only project he could learn much about was a product called *Dynamic Vision Systems* produced by a west-coast division of Dyna-Mantech BCI: an enhanced targeting system for foot soldiers that used facial recognition techniques to identify likely enemies in a crowd. The sparse description made it sound distastefully racist, but that wasn't his problem. The fact that the project wasn't protected behind an impenetrable wall of security probably meant that it wasn't very significant.

His net came up empty of other D-M or ImagiCap projects for the government. The passwords and tricks Taggart had given him were of little use except to find file directories with intriguing but non-descriptive names, yet even the merest touch of a search program drew warnings so dire that Damon began to understand Con's fear. And the main worry: Con's cryptic comment that it might be impossible to tell where ImagiCap ended and capital-g Government began.

Although it was the equivalent of leaving fingerprints all over a crime scene, he ran one more search for his own name and looked for related references with a high number of occurrences. One of them was "Minotaur." Another was a man's name: H. Reinhardt Janus, listed as ImagiCap's "Director of Strategic Responses", whatever that meant. There'd been a fleeting mention in one of the progress reports from the Taggart clinic when Janus had visited the place to see Damon for himself. Did that make him an enemy, or a friend? Or just an anonymous corporate suit? There was something about the name that made Damon's nose twitch.

#

When Con got up just after eleven, Damon was waiting outside his bedroom door.

"I need your help."

"Shit, man. You didn't stomp your way through a hornet's nest, did you? Don't expect me to help you stick your head up so they know where to find you." Con snapped open a Red Bull and downed it with barely a breath. Breakfast—too early for beer.

Damon didn't mention searching for his own name.

"The files I could access were just the tip of the iceberg. The real stuff is supposed to be in hard copy, in a physical archive. A real room somewhere. I need you to see if there's some way to find it."

Con rubbed his face and gave a long look at a bottle of vodka in the corner of the counter. "I...I don't think so. Man, you're walking the plank with your eyes blindfolded, hoping there's land on the other side. That ain't the way it is." He held Damon's gaze. After a pause, he said, "Suppose we did find this archive? What are you gonna do? Just waltz into the building and pick the lock? Security in a place like that ain't electrons and flashing lights. We're talking big, mean bastards with guns. Dogs. Places to hide bodies."

"I think you've been watching too much TV."

"And I think those computers in your head have made you think you're invincible. You're not." Con grabbed the vodka bottle and walked sullenly over to the apartment's only window, where he took a big swallow, then slouched against the frame staring down toward the street.

"Look, this isn't a game for me," Damon said softly. "I found out that ImagiCap has been using me. For years. A test case. A toy. They planted things in my head. They arranged my goddamned *life*—my university degrees, my job...who knows what else? They made me like *Italian sodas*, for shit's sake! Just because they could. Can you even imagine how that feels?" His voice took on a steel edge. "They think they own me. And they're going to find out they're wrong."

Con raised the bottle toward his mouth again, then stopped and stepped back from the window. He put the cap back on.

"OK, OK. Show me what you got."

RECOVERY AND REHABILITATION October 13, 2040
Memorial Hospital Inpatient Rehabilitation Unit—Eighth Floor:

Damon looked though the hospital window at the setting sun and his attention was caught by the flashing lights of a helicopter landing on the pad just visible to his far left. A new arrival—someone else at a crossroad in their life.

Confinement to a soulless little cube decorated in shades of bland conformity had done nothing good for his state of mind over his past month and more in the hospital. He was frustrated that the search of his long-term digital memory hadn't revealed a killer, only some strong suspects. What it had done by accident, though, was to uncover scraps of data from just before the attack, preserved in a moment of transition while his dual mind assessed them for longer storage. Broken pieces only, but any supplement to the more impressionistic recall of his human memory was welcome.

Much as he chafed at its inactivity, his convalescence had provided some healing of mind as well as body. The mental blockage caused by the trauma of the attempt on his life had been whittled away. Now he could *remember* those last hours before his brush with death, albeit in a form more defined by emotion than fact. Those impressions, stretched over the frame of the newly retrieved hard data, should let him reconstruct the events with accuracy.

In a perfect world, an Agatha Christie detective avatar in his mind would point out the guilty party from a roomful of suspects using only his 'little grey cells.'

A bit much to hope for, but he turned away from the window, sat in a chair, closed his eyes to bring the memories into focus again, and took a deep breath.

It wasn't easy facing your death, even the second time around.

11

September 3, 2040

Project: Minotaur
File: Janus 1

Our most recent discussions are further evidence that differing opinions must be set aside in the interest of a united goal, and that drastic actions must require unanimous approval.

That Damon Leiter has learned about core elements of our project was not unexpected. It may have been inevitable. However, it is in no sense disastrous. He is one man with a handful of followers, no special platform or access to either popular media or our political opponents. He still has potential to benefit our goals, but can do very little to thwart them.

We might do well to learn a lesson from literature: it was Viktor Frankenstein's efforts to deny and thereby destroy the

monster he had created that brought about his own doom.
 H. Reinhardt Janus

Image: A long tunnel. Squared walls. Girders connected at right angles, gridlike, one after another away into the distance. Straight lines slung taut in mid-air toward a single vanishing-point. Glaring lights. Rectangles cut in the walls like split doors. Doors?

The perspective shifts ninety degrees and the tunnel becomes a yawning pit.

The archive turned out to be in the city's tallest office tower, Mori 2, but on a floor rented by Dyna-Mantech BCI. It had taken another week and a satchel of money for Con to arrange for a very special fake security-badge based on Damon's own D-M ID, except with a picture that would offer electronic scanners a different face from the one it showed to human eyes. A badge with far higher security clearance than Damon's own.

Now Damon gave another silent thank you to Con as he followed an anonymous hallway with a frustrating number of offshoots and corners. Without Con's map, he would have been lost within thirty seconds. His stomach was queasy, but he didn't know if it was because of needing to pass three sets of guards, or from the rocket-fast elevator.

The building was disturbingly quiet, distant office sounds muted by the hiss of air conditioning or deliberate white noise. There was very little traffic—for that he was grateful. He was also surprised at an apparent lack of security cameras along the halls. Either they were well-hidden, or they were completely absent. No cameras could mean nothing worth stealing. It could also mean the activities that took place there were the kind no-one wanted recorded.

He'd estimated that it should take him four minutes from the last guard station to the archive room. After six minutes, he realised that he must have missed it. Cautiously, he doubled back, checking each room against the map. The door numbers were embossed, but in the same institutional grey as the doors themselves. He came to the place marked for the archive room.

There was nothing there.

Quickly he went up and down the hall, fifteen meters in each direction, verifying room numbers again. There was no mistake. Where the room should have been there was only a blank wall.

Wait. That would be better protection than an armed guard. Damon pulled out his security card and began to slide it along the surface of the wall, first at waist height, then slightly higher. There was an audible click and a small rectangle illuminated: a nine-digit touch pad. His implants supplied the code Con had given him, and he punched it in.

With a light chuff of air, the outline of a door appeared in the grey paint. Damon gave it a gentle push and the left side swung inward until he could enter. A light came on overhead and revealed that he was in a shallow alcove. He quietly guided the door closed behind him, first making sure there was a regular handle on the inner side. There was another keypad on the far wall. He entered a second string of numbers—God only knew where Con had come up with them—and another door swung back. Damon shoved and waited for the room to brighten.

It was a small room, only about four meters square.

And it was completely empty.

He slumped against the door frame, stunned. That couldn't be. Empty? No longer in use? He didn't believe it. One document that had mentioned it was only weeks old.

Could they have known he was coming? No. They wouldn't have moved the documents—they would simply have stopped him. Unless they believed he'd bring the police. But that would have required a search warrant, and a company like D-M would have enough lawyers to stall a search for months.

It must be another trick, another disguise.

He went around the room gently tapping the walls. They often produced a hollow sound, but no different from most offices, and no secret panels appeared. He tried waving his pass card over the surface, but to no effect. As he looked more closely for any sign of seams, he noticed subtle differences in the paint, but not from hidden cubbyholes. More like the shadowy outlines of where filing cabinets had once stood and prevented the paint from fading.

He straightened and released his breath in a long sigh. The files had been there. Now they were gone.

The reason didn't matter much. He was too late. He'd risked so much for nothing, and still faced a gauntlet of guards to get out of the building. He could only hope that his entry into the safe room hadn't put them all on alert.

He made it out of the room, and through the security checkpoint at the entrance of the D-M offices, then tried to walk casually toward the bank of elevators, dreading the fast ride down from the seventy-third floor. The call button was between the inner two of four elevators in a line. He waved a hand over it and took a step back, glad to be alone.

No, not alone. There was another man he hadn't noticed at first. Big. Like a third wall but standing completely still a couple of meters farther back, as if not wanting to commit to any particular elevator. Why hadn't he triggered the call signal? He had to be waiting for something else.

Waiting for him?

As the thought became a certainty, Damon heard the chime of an arriving car and took a reflexive step toward it.

The door slid open—onto an empty pit.

His brain had barely registered the fact when a silver blur shot past, hurtling down the shaft with a banshee howl. The powerful wind of its passage first pushed him back, but when the car passed its trailing vacuum yanked him forward, off balance. His outflung arm found only space, a toe caught his other heel, knees buckled, head cracked against the edge of the opening... and suddenly there was a gaping void beneath him. Even if the air hadn't been sucked from his lungs, he had no time to yell. Only to fall.

Flashes of pale concrete; bursts of piercing white lamplight; a barrage of implacable grey beams with razor edges: microsecond impressions spun in a blender and linked by writhing black pythons.

Death as a nebulous concept about to become real.

He slammed into a hard surface—fireworks filled his brain and made nerve endings dance in agony. The rag doll of his flesh bounced... bounced and rolled and then jerked to a stop.   The universe went black.

BOOK TWO

12

November 12, 2040

"Is there a cost when people share thoughts? Will they become too much alike: mental twins, or a nation of robots? Better to ask the cost when people do *not* share their thoughts: misunderstandings, lies, betrayals. It is of these that human history is made."
                The Speeches of Damon Leiter
                Collected by V.A. Klug

Damon's two-month recovery had provided a lot of time for him to figure out why he wasn't dead.

The data he'd needed for that had come from second-hand sources, though: extrapolated, not known with any certainty. His digital memory of the actual critical moment was gone forever.

The 'net provided plenty of information about the Mori 2 Tower. Elevators were controlled by a central computer—how else could someone have overridden the door safeties? Four twelve-person high-speed elevators, bullet-nosed top and bottom, travelling at a downward speed of 36 km/h—ten meters per second. That was an important part of the equation. One second or less for Damon to be sucked into the shaft. How many seconds to fall? Three? Four? Somewhere in between. That meant he'd hit the descending elevator at about 54 km/h, his body's roll down the curved roof taking just enough force away from the impact that his bones fractured but didn't shatter. Then came the sudden stop.

His leather jacket. It had caught on something and torn, but had kept him from going over the side.

They'd found him draped over the elevator roof when someone was sent to investigate the god-almighty bang.

Someone had known he was coming. Let him get past security. Moved the files. Arranged for elevator doors to open without an elevator present and for a flunky to push Damon into the empty elevator shaft. Except that a push hadn't been needed—the passing elevator had done the trick, even as it had saved him from a fatal fall. His survival wasn't part of the plan.

Now what? Would they try again? Or decide that his death wasn't necessary because he had nothing that could hurt them?

He'd probably never know that answer until it was too late.

He'd sent Con a warning from the hospital, but his friend had worried more about Damon's welfare than his own. He tried to take the blame for the trap, but Damon had been the careless one, the impulsive one, the one who'd refused to listen to Con's advice.

Had he learned his lesson?

He still didn't know who wanted him dead. The strongest evidence certainly seemed to point to Dyna-Mantech itself, or at least someone within their corporate structure. Would they risk killing him on the same floor as their own offices? Why not? His presence there would easily be explained; and it was, after all, a tragic accident.

When he was finally allowed to leave the hospital, he took a cab to work and walked into the ostentatious lobby leaning heavily on a cane. As the elevator dispensed him on the lab level, Ram Khouri was waiting for him.

"The prodigal returns. You picked a strange way to goof off."

"Do I still have a job?"

"If it had been up to me, no. But someone overruled me. So, I live with it and will find another cubicle to store the bathroom supplies."

Layla Goring walked up as Khouri turned back to his d-scroll and waddled away.

"Ram has a strange sense of humor," she said. "It's good to have you back. Nice timing, too. We're missing something in the setup language for the voluntary overrides, and it's just not working." She started to move down the hall, obviously expecting Damon to follow. He shrugged and fell into step behind her.

His first few days back were surreal. Was he truly working for his enemy? Yet Dyna-Mantech was only a mindless corporation. If he could find a less harmful way to accomplish its marketing goals, it would embrace whatever produced the greatest profits. Right? All the better to avoid expensive lawsuits and regulatory penalties.

That's what he told himself. He didn't absolutely need the job—he could live off his inheritance for a time. But maybe he could accomplish some good from the inside. And it was such a relief to be doing something useful again.

He'd just have to watch his back, that's all.

#

Damon's bubble of self-deception faded after a few days. He'd hoped to pull on the fabric of his former existence like a comfortable old coat. But to his dismay, it no longer fit.

The secret document archive still obsessed him. It couldn't only have been bait for a trap—the trail was far too elaborate. Even the random fragments he'd uncovered had serious implications for society; but if records still existed, he'd never find them. Hard-copy files had likely been destroyed as too much of a risk.

Con was a changed man: distracted and wary. His contagious laugh was now rare—his smile shrunken and fleeting. He'd developed a habit of rubbing his fingertips with his thumb, as if rolling a smoke or testing the texture of a five-dollar bill. And when anyone invited him out to the pub or a ball game, he made excuses and stayed home alone. Damon knew the blame was his own. He had suffocated his friend's joy and replaced it with fear.

Valerie had changed, too. At times she clung to him as if in desperation. At other times she became distant and melancholy. He didn't know how to ask her about it, and she didn't volunteer anything. She still loved him; he was sure. But sometimes he felt a chill in his gut when he looked into her eyes.

They arranged a get-together with their implantee friends. Damon was eager to tell them what he'd learned, but they cut him short, preferring not to know too much. Instead of the camaraderie he'd looked forward to, the mood was strangely formal and cold. The couples acted in turns petulant with each other, then indifferent. What could have happened during the months he was in recovery?

He jokingly asked if everyone had been practicing their skills.

Their skills were fine, they said.

"Too good," Naya added in a near whisper.

The conversation shifted back to trivial subjects. Damon hesitated, then gently probed into each of their implants. He found images of conflict and anger, taunts, and tears, but the cause of their coolness wasn't evident.

The gathering broke up after less than an hour.

"Did you really expect everything would be all sweetness and light?" Con asked him that evening. "Didn't it occur to you that people aren't meant to communicate at that level? That maybe we have to have our masks and secrets?"

"But Valerie and I...."

"You what? You have no secrets from each other? Brother, you're not nearly as smart as I thought you were."

"What's that supposed to mean?"

"Nothing."

And Con wouldn't elaborate, no matter how often Damon asked.

#

A week later, Dyna-Mantech launched its new commercial BCID, the *Vanquish*.

The marketing material promised it would eliminate all the frustrating delays of modern life. Finding information, shopping, making calls for business or pleasure—and very much more—all were available at the speed of thought.

Surprisingly, it was the first time Damon had been given access to one. The Vanquish was produced by the west-coast division of D-M, and they'd guarded its secrets even within the company. He was gratified to learn that it included his system permitting users to enable or disable intrusive advertising, but he wasn't convinced the protocols were solid enough. He tapped into some of the source code and looked it over. From what he could tell, once a user gave permission to receive messages five times, the BCID would bypass the permission protocol completely from then on and simply allow the connection. Every time.

That couldn't be right. Maybe it was an oversight. He'd have to find out who was in charge and contact them. He couldn't count on Khouri to pass along a message, he knew that.

Opening sales for the Vanquish broke records. They offered far more features than the Neuro and the Cortico, and a price tag within a few dollars of their now-obsolete competitors. Damon suspected the company must be losing money at that price, but it was their money to lose. He bought a couple for himself, just to take them apart and learn their secrets. An inner voice told him that it might be important.

A couple of weeks later he was walking past a shopping concourse when he got a flash of an ad for Old Navy in the corner of his eye. Nothing like that should have been able to get through his shielding, so he stopped to make some adjustments. It took a few minutes—he had to probe for the incoming signal, then adjust a filter patch to block it out.

A growing noise made him turn around.

The sidewalk behind him had suddenly filled. Cars were honking as their way was blocked by bodies. Like locusts, people swarmed toward a building he'd just passed, merging into a ragged, bloated line only because passage through the doors necessitated it. Damon's eyes lifted to the sign above.

Old Navy.

He slumped against the nearby wall, then probed again for the signal he'd just blocked. It was an ad for a seventy-five per cent off sale that would only last a half-hour. Obviously, a test, the first test of the real capabilities of the Vanquish.

An overwhelming success. Too good—people would be trampled. Damon tried to think of something he could do, but knew that a mob like that wouldn't listen to him. The police should have been forewarned. Most likely the effectiveness of their venture had taken even the D-M masters by surprise.

Quickly creating a false comm ID, he made a 911 call and described the danger. Irate drivers might be doing the same—but it was going to be damned hard for cop cars to get through.

There would be a backlash, with Dyna-Mantech on the receiving end. But they'd rally and adjust their strategy.

It was only a test. Only the beginning.

#

A few weeks later, Jace Robbins contacted Damon and conferenced in the others. They agreed to meet at a dingy bowling alley for its noise and anonymity. Kenzo Shabata found an excuse to make the trip and brought Shiori. Only Helayne stayed away. This time they were eager to hear Damon outline what he knew and what he expected.

"It's crazy, man," Jace said. "All but three of the other families on our block have bought a new car in the past month. Furniture store vans block the street once or twice a day. Where is everybody getting the money?"

"They're not. It's all credit." Ebon shook his head. "Or sometimes they're able to sell their old stuff, but not too often. People want new things, not old. A friend of mine—another teacher—he took a second job, working evenings just to buy stuff. A third car. A fifth TV. There's only his wife and him—they don't have any kids." He forced a laugh and said, "Hell, I'm weakening myself. Some of those new cars are pretty tempting, you know?" Then he looked at Damon. "Help me resist them.

Fight them. This is about more than just blocking pretty pictures in our heads, isn't it?"

"I think so. I know that ImagiCap had subliminal directives built right into my implant that preempted even my choice of career. I can't tell which of my tastes and ideas are my own and which are from their tinkering." Damon's eyes glazed over. "Unfortunately, there's no reason to think they didn't do the same thing to the rest of you. It was their great experiment, and we were their guinea pigs. Still are."

"Now they've turned it loose on everybody else," Jace said. "Everybody with a Vanquish BCID. Shit, probably the other augments too, by now. Right?"

"How can we fight something like that?" Rosa looked scared.

"Someone must," Kenzo said, jaw rigid.

"We fight it by getting our own implants under control, and then teaching how we did that to the people with commercial augments." Damon's eyes sparked. "There must be some who realize what's happening, even if they don't know how to stop it. And there will be more, as they see their lives get out of control."

There was a loud crash and a raucous cheer. Someone had bowled a strike.

Naya looked toward the noise, then brought her gaze back to the table. "Once people see how they're being influenced, won't they just give up their augments? Turn them off?"

"Could you give up phone calls? Television? Texting, GPS, and the internet all at once? That's what it would be like." Damon gave a slow shake of his head. "Once the genie is out of the bottle, it's nearly impossible to stuff it back in."

"You must have come up with some tricks by now," Jace insisted.

"A few."

"So, teach us."

"There's no way to just explain how it works, or even lead you through the steps with my avatar in your implant. I'll going to have to try to transfer the knowledge directly into each augment's memory. Individually. And I'll need full access because I have to go in deep." He wanted to make very clear what was involved, and how very much they would need to trust him. "I won't snoop around," he promised, "but I will see things. I don't know how to prevent that."

Rosa looked unhappy. Naya was scared. Jace memorized the skin of his knuckles. The Shabatas looked at each other, their facial expressions changing in subtle ways.

Ebon slapped the table. "I'll go first."

#

They rented a hotel room. Damon had no idea how long the information transfer would take, and the noise of a bowling alley was good for confounding eavesdroppers, but bad for concentration.

Valerie had kept her skills up to date—as Damon had learned a new technique, he'd taught it to her. She'd even improved on some of them, but she hadn't achieved the ability to pass those techniques on to others. She wasn't sure she wanted that responsibility, though Damon insisted she should try. If anything was to happen to him, he wanted to be sure the knowledge would survive and spread.

He and Ebon lay side by side on the bed in the hotel room while the others sat, or stood, or quietly paced. Silent minutes hung in the air like fog, heavy and cold, but Damon improved with practice, so the process took a little less time with each partner. Each success provided some reassurance too, but Naya and Rosa were still dry-mouthed and jittery when their turns came.

The effort bathed Damon in sweat. Passage through the hidden gateways of the implants had become second nature—his BCID supplied required passwords and protocols without conscious thought. But the regions of memory themselves were like corridors of a fortress: long, labyrinthine, and devoid of signposts, replete with the mental equivalents of dead ends, staircases, secret passages, catwalks, and pits. Damon had to navigate them all, carrying a precious cargo of information and depositing pieces of it in the right places and in the proper order.

Along the way were displays of life events, like open galleries and murals he couldn't avoid seeing. Scenes acted out that he couldn't help hearing. Wet memory was still inaccessible, but he was disturbed to find how much the present bore the scars of past trauma, and how many of those scars were revealed in insults and arguments between partners. In diaries, journals, and photo albums. From lips loosened with alcohol while among friends.

The past cast long shadows.

From his first foray into Ebon Parrish's mind, Damon began to wonder if the man was a sex addict: the passage through his memories was like flipping through a porn magazine. But he was unattached, and none of the liaisons appeared to be forced. A few of his sex partners looked pretty young, but Damon couldn't be sure they were students of his. On the other hand, there were also scenes that clearly showed Ebon working with stressed-out students of both sexes outside school hours—tutoring them, coaching them, trying to fan the fragile flames of their self-respect.

Jace Robbins was a serial adulterer—he'd had at least two affairs with female singers he'd represented, and his smooth approach with them indicated lots of practice. An unlikely number of the amorphous set pieces Damon saw featured hotel rooms with iced champagne and carpets dotted with filmy underthings.

And when it was Naya's turn, Damon saw that although Jace didn't know it, Naya had found out about at least one of his affairs, and meek little Naya had ruined the woman's career by leaking details to the media about abortions and children abandoned as the singer had slept her way to the verge of success.

Jace's cheating extended to his taxes, too; but within the music circles he travelled, it was a matter of status to boast about the creative ways hard-earned income was kept from finding its way into Uncle Sam's ungrateful hands.

Probing the minds of the Shabatas was exotic and often puzzling, with cultural nuances as foreign to Damon as the landscapes. With no understanding of the language, he had a hard time distinguishing between acts of friendly one-upmanship, and salvos between stoic enemies. But one scene in Kenzo's mind unfolded like a spread fan: vignettes of Kenzo and his business partner meeting with a coldly malicious gangster-type surrounded by burly henchmen, and then a succession of financial readouts displaying many zeroes. Damon didn't encounter any images of the partner after that. A sacrifice had been made and Kenzo had been spared.

It was clear even from Shiori's implant memories that Kenzo's mother had been firmly set against the marriage—Shiori was an orphan, raised in poverty, who'd managed to earn enough to put herself through art school. But, in her mother-in-law's assessment, she had squandered even that talent, using it mainly to teach art free of charge to other orphans.

Even so, Shiori was no victim. Damon witnessed a scene with all the ritual of a tea ceremony: Shiori and the mother-in-law. Flowers arranged with the care accorded deadly weapons. Bits of elegant notepaper laid out like landmines. Dagger-sharp glances, and honeyed words that seeped like poison. The confrontation had been over the choice of school for the Shabata's children.

The children excelled, Kenzo was proud, Shiori was elevated, and the mother-in-law lost much face. Yet most surprising was the way Shiori had put the vicious contest of wills behind her and treated her new mother-in-law with perfect respect thereafter.

Rosa Ferraro was an outstanding surgeon, but only infallible in her own mind. She had made mistakes, people had suffered and died, but she was never at fault. If there was any doubt, she found ways to remove it, even deflecting blame onto a hapless technician one time when an outcome was particularly gruesome. Damon deeply hoped he would be able to forget the images of splayed viscera and fountaining blood.

Rosa had no strong need for a man in her life, but she could make use of men if the occasion arose. The Chief Surgeon of the hospital in his sumptuous office reappeared in another mind-image as a pasty naked form between Rosa's sheets. There were no sounds of true passion attached. But in a hallway scene Damon heard a frustrated colleague questioning why Rosa's patients never seemed to wait as long for their scheduled surgeries as his own clientele.

When Damon finally finished with Rosa, he stumbled to the washroom sink to splash the sweat off his face with cold water. He was exhausted, but pleased, convinced that they were erecting an effective firewall against Dyna-Mantech and its operatives. The company was too cocksure. It needed to realise that there were now other forces in play. He'd learned things about his friends that he wished he could unlearn, but their secrets were safe with him, so there was no real harm done.

The group went their separate ways, but on an impulse Damon and Valerie went to see Helayne. She appeared glad to see them but was flatly opposed to learning more from Damon's mind. She wouldn't explain her reluctance, either, but she was more than willing to give them a tour of her new loft apartment, if only to show off the appliances she'd bought to go with it and some new window appointments by a designer whose name made Valerie blanche. Damon took a quick glance into the bedroom and noticed a man's tie draped over a chair. He'd been sure that Helayne was a lesbian.

He and Valerie said little on the way home, but Damon was still feeling buoyant.

The only thing that spoiled his mood was the memory of something Kenzo Shabata had said. When Damon had thanked the others for their commitment to carrying on the fight if anything happened to him, Kenzo had subtly taken him aside and said, "Watch with your mind and not your heart. ImagiCap is very powerful and very experienced. Your enemies will be closer than friends."

#

As summer took hold of the city, Valerie had cause to celebrate. A small but dynamic publisher put out a collection of her poems, and very soon reviews of the book began to appear on respected poetry websites and in some online journals. All were favorable—some were effusive, proclaiming Valerie the "next major talent." She didn't quite know how to react to that, but Damon was delighted to see her smile again. It had been far too long. They went out to an expensive restaurant to mark each milestone of her book in sales or promotion, but soon didn't need to because the milestones began to have their own parties attached. A contract with a bigger distributor. A nomination for the Agnes Lynch

Starrett prize. Then—nearly unheard of with poetry—a trial deal with a giant retail outlet.

The promotional commitments that followed meant that Damon and Valerie didn't see a lot of each other for a while, but Damon kept himself busy. He enlisted the help of Con and Rosa to figure out the dirty secrets of the Vanquish BCID, and let Valerie enjoy her time in the spotlight without the distraction of what turned out to be disturbing revelations.

The Vanquish was equipped to provide *one-thought shopping*, allowing a user to mentally approve a transaction and transfer an account code to a special reader. It was even easier than using the NFC chip in a handheld phone, and it caught on nearly overnight. Not surprisingly, since its appeal had been given an artificial boost.

As Taggart had hinted, Dyna-Mantech's new offering included a magnetic field generator with an amazingly precise focus that could electrically stimulate the pleasure centers of the user. The effect was mild but undeniable, initially triggered when the user gave permission to accept incoming ad messages. That made them feel pretty good. The next trigger was the purchase transaction itself. When the account information was transferred, the BCID provided its owner with a warm glow of satisfaction.

Damon found indications of other triggers installed, but without seeing them in action, he couldn't determine what would activate them.

Rosa was sickened. She feared that if the electro-stimulation also affected the brain's "God spot" it might transform the consumption of goods into a mystical experience, but they couldn't find any hard evidence of that.

To Con, their quest was like a drug: He was terrified by what they were doing, but he couldn't leave it alone.

It was Con who discovered the Vanquish's toolbox for creating buzz.

He explained that buzz originally referred to people talking about a commodity on their own, either to recommend it to their friends, or to experience shared anticipation of an event like the premiere of a movie or the launch of a new product. Buzz was more powerful than any other form of promotion, but it was elusive. Billions of dollars had been spent over decades to figure out what generated such talk. Most of it was wasted. But buzz now included all forms of electronic communication, too, and that's where the makers of the Vanquish had found the key to the candy store.

People hooked on Jabber and JoinSpace had come to rely on their networks of friends to make an extraordinary number of day-to-day choices: what restaurant to go to, what movies to see, music to buy, jeans to wear. Few made any major purchase without consulting their networks. The Vanquish had that covered.

One of its most popular apps kept track of all personal purchases and encouraged a rating system for each one. By default, the list was made available to the user's selected peer group. That usually ran into dozens of contacts, each regularly able to check their friends' preferences and shopping experiences.

When an ad message was received, the Vanquish immediately canvassed the peer group for related entries, and then enhanced the ad message with assurances that "all your friends love this." If all the user's friends *didn't* love the advertised product or service, the Vanquish fudged the information with the confidence that few users would ever check. Almost none would confront a virtual friend with a difference of opinion. Instead, if they were dissatisfied with something recommended by their peers, they'd blame themselves—if your friends loved it, and you didn't, there had to be something wrong with *you*.

It was monstrous. And completely brilliant.

Damon had asked for Rosa's help because of her knowledge of brain anatomy, but that knowledge wasn't all that useful. Knowing which areas of the brain were targeted didn't enable the mind to create specific defences. The inbuilt functions of the Vanquish had to be disabled, or at least circumvented. With the help of a nano-engineer friend of Con's, they stripped a Vanquish down to its component parts looking for a physical fix: a circuit or series of them that could be switched off or bypassed. But the D-M engineers had thought of that. All management of the BCID's functions was routed through its permission circuits. If any of those became inactive, the whole device refused to function. Similarly, the power supply of the Vanquish was designed around the same electromagnetic generator that delivered the pleasure current. An EM generator put out of commission rendered the BCID no more than a dead chunk of graphene and plastic.

The only avenue left seemed to be for Damon to figure out a neural solution, but it wasn't that simple. He'd had every waking moment of ten years to investigate his own BCID, and many of his techniques had been discovered by accident. He couldn't devote that kind of time to the Vanquish. And anyway, that option wasn't open to him. Because he already had two brain augments, he couldn't use a third—he'd tried and it didn't work. No matter what he did, the signals to and from the Vanquish were jammed by his other implants.

Rosa tried too, with the same results. Con simply refused. He'd owned a Vanquish from the moment they came on the market despite Damon's misgivings, and he was disturbed by what they'd learned. But he refused to let Damon, or anyone else, probe his mind.

They had to find another volunteer.

Their answer came in the form of a young grad student named Camillo Ricci who had been in a couple of Damon's undergrad classes in his university days. Damon had caught Camillo in some minor cheating as a freshman, but the young guy was so naïve and so sincerely remorseful that Damon hadn't reported it. Pathetically grateful, Camillo had latched on to his benefactor like a puppy.

For all his innocence, he was sharp, and followed direction to the letter. Above all, he would be loyal.

Damon needed all the loyalty he could get.

13

June 11, 2041

"Must love depend on trust? Most would consider that a given. Then the harder question is, must trust forever depend on ignorance? Or, put another way, where there is true and full knowledge, can there ever again be love?"
                        The Speeches of Damon Leiter
                        Collected by V.A. Klug

With Camillo's help they were able to learn most of the Vanquish systems and how they operated. Damon couldn't use the Vanquish directly, but he could access Camillo's through wifi and Bluetooth, and explore it that way. Once inside, he saw that many of the BCID's features had been adapted from Taggart technology. That was a big break—it gave Damon a running start deciphering the various functions and how they related to each other.

Damon's remote presence in the augment wasn't nearly as strong as with Taggart implants. Though he could see through Camillo's eyes, with a lot of effort, the definition was so poor it wasn't worth the trouble. Other sense-related data was similarly degraded. So, it was critical to have Camillo actually tell them his impressions and relate, from his own perspective, how the things they tried affected the augment.

The permission module couldn't be physically bypassed; and although it was possible to command the device to refuse all messages, that command was time-limited. After three days it had to be reset, and the process was tedious by BCI standards. Dyna-Mantech wanted to discourage users from blocking ads. Damon found a way to redirect the message-processing pathway so that each incoming ad reset the message denial command to refuse the next ad in an endless procession. But the drawback was that people might *want* to receive some advertising; and as soon as they opened the door a crack, the whole firewall collapsed.

Another strategy also turned out to have an unfortunate side-effect. Con's engineer friend found that the Vanquish's electromagnetic output was limited by law, so a special circuit kept it below a certain threshold. It was a relief to know that someone in the legislative hierarchy was keeping an eye on this new technology. But when Damon finally succeeded in disabling the automatic triggers that sent pleasure signals related to purchases, the EM field limiter was disabled, too. If they encouraged people to alter their BCIDs that way, they'd be flouting the law. It was a bizarre situation, but Damon decided that it was the least of their worries.

Gradually they built up a series of procedures that would defeat most of Dyna-Mantech's subliminal traps while still allowing a Vanquish owner to use its features. Camillo was ecstatic. Con was deeply apprehensive. Especially when Damon asked him for help to set up an anonymous website. The site would use text and video to describe the simpler techniques they'd discovered and webinars for the more complicated procedures. Damon would need some sophisticated programs to alter his voice and appearance to keep D-M from identifying him. Con wanted no part of it, and when Damon got the site up and running with the help of another tech-head friend, he couldn't even persuade Con to take a look.

"Congratulations," Con said, "you've just made yourself Public Enemy Number One."

"Come on, don't be so melodramatic."

"Listen, bro, this may be a game to you, but to ImagiCap and their clients it means big money. The biggest money there is. You've just slit a big hole in the bottom of their money bag, and you're still waving the knife. You don't think they're going to come after you?"

"They've already come after me. I'm more careful now."

"For what you're doing, no amount of *careful* will be enough." Con stepped close and looked into Damon's eyes. "Take the site down, man. Before it's too late. Otherwise...I won't be able to help you."

"Then don't help. No hard feelings, Con. Honest. I don't want you involved in something that bothers you that much. But I can't stop. This is something that has to be done. And no-one else knows how to do it."

"That's exactly what they'll be thinking, too."

#

Before twenty-four hours had passed, Damon's site was crashed by denial-of-service attacks, and was buried so deep that the ISP refused to host it any longer. Damon switched servers, but the same thing happened within an hour. Then his domain registration was revoked.

Furious, he called in favors from every tech-head he knew to flesh out a rough solution he'd conceived, enlisting each of them to provide one small piece of the pie without anyone seeing the whole. By the end of another week, he'd set up a rotating array of dozens of web domains on different servers in a randomly scheduled series of source/replica relationships that would provide the page and its components for only minutes at a time. He especially relished the fact that he'd drawn the techniques from ImagiCap's own bag of tricks, used by the company's clandestine spamming division.

It worked. For now. The site stayed up. And Damon hadn't yet lost his job.

Within another week his webinars were drawing thousands of hits.

Con was grudgingly impressed, but still fearful.

"Don't get cocky," he said. "And how come you don't have any way to raise money?"

"Money? I can't take money from people while I'm teaching them how to keep someone from taking their money."

"You got to have funds, man. You think Dyna-Mantech won't figure out who you are? You'll be on the run for the rest of your life. Better be flush with cash before that happens." He slid into place at the keyboard. "I hope I'm not just raising money for your funeral."

Although Damon worried that donors would make targets of themselves by contributing, Con made the payment section of the site as secure and anonymous as his own web presence, then produced some false identities and corresponding bank accounts to give Damon access to the donated dollars without leaving an electronic trail.

After only four days, the site had raised more than a hundred thousand dollars.

"Unbelievable," Camillo Ricci responded when Damon told him. "What are you going to do with the money?"

"I don't know yet. Maybe I'll buy some ads on social media directing people to my site."

"Are you sure you shouldn't be a little more...I don't know. Subtle?" Camillo asked, with a worried grin.

"This is the best way to protect myself," Damon replied. "Once the cat is well and truly out of the bag, there'll be no reason to shut me up. It'll be too late."

He was wrong about that.

#

Valerie had become the toast of the literary circuit, to everyone's surprise. Established wisdom insisted that poetry just didn't sell enough to make money from it. The idea of a poetry tour was ludicrous. But her publisher was a risk-taker, and Valerie had an edge that let her defy the odds. Talent was the product, but the Taggart implant was the gimmick.

After Damon and Valerie had refined their ability to see through each other's eyes, Damon had searched for a way to disseminate such a view to a broader audience using BCIDs linked by wifi and white-fi. Then he'd forgotten about it, busy with other things. But Valerie hadn't forgotten.

When her first reading outside the city drew only a handful of die-hards, she was determined that the evening wouldn't be a waste of time. Even for users of older commercial augments, it was easy to forward messages and brief video clips to their circle of friends—people did it all the time. Valerie quickly taught her small audience how to distribute a streaming view in much the same way. She encouraged them to alert their friends and family, and then to offer a sampling of the reading as they were seeing it. She even found a way to include her own views of both audience and text from time to time. Such new converts weren't skilled, and the quality of the transmission was poor, but within minutes more people began coming through the doors of the hall. They wanted to be part of the show, to be *seen* by others.

They were starved for shared experiences.

The event turned into a flash mob. The flash mob phenomenon had almost entirely died out once most reasons to gather spontaneously had been exhausted. But suddenly there was a new reason, and people responded in droves.

Skeptics predicted that distributing the performance in such a way removed any need for people to attend in person; but, paradoxically, the distribution gave a huge boost to live attendance, and Valerie's poetry venues filled to overflowing. It was an organic experience, far beyond simple webcasting. She was a *hit*—her tour was extended, and then extended again.

Damon was genuinely thrilled for her, though he couldn't deny some jealousy that others were now seeing through her eyes, as he alone once had done. But as he thought about it, he realised that, with some adjustments to protect his identity, he could use the same technique to spread his methods for defusing the Vanquish BCIDs. If his website went down for good, the knowledge would still spread, person to person.

He and Valerie were a consummate team, even when they weren't together.

#

Their ability to link mentally went a long way to ease the pain of separation. In Valerie's idle hours in anonymous hotel rooms, they would soak in each other's mental presence and shut out the world for a time. Yet things had changed. Perversely, as Valerie shared more of her tour experiences with her fans, Damon was less willing to take part in them. Something intimate had been lost, and he wasn't sure how to get it back.

He missed her physically, more than he could have imagined. In a strange way, Mud the dog came to represent their connection in tangible form. The big dog needed lots of exercise, lots of food, and lots of affection; but Con had a mild allergy to animal fur, so Damon spent most of his off time at Valerie's. He told himself he did it for Mud, not to satisfy his senses with the smells and other nebulous traces of his absent lover.

One Friday after work, as he poured dried dog kibble into a big metal bowl, a flashing light caught his eye. He'd forgotten that Valerie's apartment had an actual landline phone—it was part of a group package her landlord paid for, so she'd never bothered to have it disconnected. Some of the labels on the buttons were too worn to be easily read, but the one close to the flashing light had seen little use. It said "voicemail."

His finger hesitated over the button, but he reasoned that it might be something important. The kind of person who'd leave a message by something as insecure as voicemail would likely be a cop, or a medical laboratory tech—people for whom privacy was a foreign concept.

He pressed the button.

"Doctor Klug? Thought you were back today. Sorry for calling you at home. There's just a question that needs answering at the clinic. Guess it can wait 'till Monday. Have a good one."

The message ended, and Damon shook his head. A wrong number on such an archaic system wasn't surprising. He reached out to delete the message.

Then his world came crashing in.

#

Sunday night he was waiting in the big armchair facing the door when Valerie came through it. By then he felt nothing but numbness—his emotions had been wrung out, like blood from a carcass.

His blank face stopped her approach.

"I tried to reach you," she said softly. "All weekend. You didn't respond."

His neck tensed, as if preparing to nod, but the impulse stalled. He cleared his throat, unsure if the organs of speech would make intelligible sounds.

"There's a voicemail message for you. A message from work...Doctor Klug."

Valerie crumpled into the frame chair behind her: a straw scarecrow draped over a pyre of wood.

"I knew you'd find out. Sometime."

"A perfect reason not to tell me yourself."

"How could I tell you something like that? And throw away whatever time we had left together? I *wanted* what we've had this past year. I couldn't...I couldn't just kill it."

"Right. Because things like honesty, and trust—what have they got to do with love?"

"I gave you my trust. I let you inside my head, as far as I could, knowing that you might discover who I was at any time. I suppose part of me even wanted you to find out, so at least I wouldn't have to keep the secret anymore. But I just couldn't find a way to tell you."

"It feels like I've heard that excuse before. How about, 'Hey, lover. By the way, I'm really Dr. V.A. Klug who wrote all those progress reports about you at the Taggart Clinic'." He saw a smouldering deep in her eyes, but she didn't reply. "Valerie *Wise*—that's what you tell everyone. You even publish your poetry under that name."

"Klug is German. It means..."

"Wise. Yeah, I got that. How the hell did you keep me from ever seeing your real name, anyway? Hypnosis?"

"You never looked—it didn't occur to you to look. The clues were there, but they never caught your attention." Her voice had shrivelled into a dry, discarded corn husk rattling along pavement in the wind.

He thought about clues that he must have missed. If he'd seen any scraps of memory from her workplace, he hadn't recognized it. She didn't receive email under the name Klug, and no paper mail at all. Like everyone, she paid bills online. He'd never witnessed her signing any legal documents. So, if someone regularly used a pseudonym, how often would their real name actually appear in a digital record? Apparently, not often. There were no labels in the archives of her implant saying, "These are the memories of Valerie Klug."

"You watched me for years. Studied me. Psychologically dissected me. Why don't I remember you from the clinic?"

"Doctor Taggart made me observe from behind one-way glass. You...reacted...to seeing me once, when you were a teenager. After that he felt my presence might have a disruptive influence."

He took a sharp breath. "A dark-haired woman. Thin. Big breasts." He ran a quick search through his old implant and found the image, buried deep. But he still couldn't make a match in his mind. Wait. The eyes?

"My Romani days. My father had the blood in him, and I was looking for an identity, so I dyed my hair black...did a few other things. Same boobs though. But I was skinnier then, I guess."

"All this time, you must have thought I was an idiot not to figure it out. Probably had a good laugh over it with the girls at work."

"*No. Never.* None of them even know about us. Only Emery knew. At the clinic." She tried to hold his eyes, but he looked away. "You have to understand, I didn't mean for it to happen. Once I fell in love with you, I was trapped. The moment you found out, it would be over—I knew that. That's why I didn't tell you about my implant, either, because you might have been suspicious of the coincidence."

"Love? How can you even call it that? Lovers don't hide who they are. Have you been honest with me about anything? Really honest?" He gave a slow shake of his head. "I'm surprised Taggart didn't tell me himself, if only to gloat. Or maybe giving me access to your reports was a coward's way of doing it, figuring I'd put two and two together."

"Yes. That would be like him." Her voice was almost too soft to hear. "But you're wrong. I did love you. I *do* love you."

"Sounds like you've been deluding yourself as much as me." He pushed out of the chair and walked unsteadily toward the door, his face waxy.

Valerie's head snapped up, angry tears spilling from her eyes.

"OK, have it your way. You're right. I was never really in love. But you weren't, either. It's all been a trick."

Damon turned his head at the door. "What are you talking about?"

"Emery told me a month ago, probably just to be cruel. That day we met...in the bookstore? Reinhardt Janus was there. An ImagiCap executive." She waited for Damon's puzzled nod. "He zapped us. Gave us a shot of pure juice in the pleasure centres of our brains. He made us *think* we were in love."

Damon felt his balance go and grabbed at the door frame for support. "Whaa...Why?"

"So I'd be close to you. Influence you. Spy on you. *I don't know.* But he engineered it all. You think my love has been a lie? Well, if mine has been a lie, yours has, too."

Then her voice failed her, and he could hear nothing but gasping sobs as his legs carried him down the stairs and out of her life.

14

July 8, 2041

"Nature made the human mind a fortress. Now, corporations drop siege ladders against our walls, and no-one pushes them away. Hard-won personal sanctity, embedded in canon and constitution, surrendered so readily for a handful of bright baubles."

The Speeches of Damon Leiter
Collected by V.A. Klug

"She's going to be your death, man."

"What? Why do you say that?" Damon was more than half-pissed. Con had been paid for a big programming job and had brought a case of double-strength beer from Quebec to celebrate.

"Up to now, D-M hasn't known who you are, who's running the website. But now? Maybe it'll be revenge, or maybe just crying on some colleague's shoulder, but she'll spill it. She'll have to, and they'll know."

"Valerie would never do that. Even if she twists it around in her head that our breakup was my fault, she knows other people will get hurt if she talks. Anyway, she believes in what we're doing."

"Believes in it? She's spent all her adult life working for the other side!"

Damon started to reply, but instead cracked open another beer and downed half of it on one breath.

"Even if Valerie doesn't squawk," Con continued in a gentler voice, "you brought in what? A dozen other programmers? More? Sure, they may not have known what you were up to, but D-M will be pushing hard—offering big money to anybody who knows anything, or even thinks they do. Somebody will put the pieces together. You gotta shut down the site, man. In fact, you really should leave…leave town." He dropped his eyes and dejectedly reached for another beer. He'd had at least as many as Damon, but he was still wired.

Leave town? Damon thought about that. Valerie had lied to him, and lied, and lied again, yet he refused to believe that she'd betray him, possibly to be killed. But the others…? Yeah. Maybe it was time to hide—except he'd lose his insider status at Dyna-Mantech. Without that, he might never be able to confirm the ulterior motives he suspected behind the design of the Vanquish. Or learn why the *Dynamic Vision Systems* program warranted inclusion in the secret archive.

He needed to find that archive, in physical or digital form. Whatever. He had no doubt that their own work in Research Lab C was part of ImagiCap's greater plan, and in that connection might lie a back-door entrance to the vault with secrets.

"OK, bro." He gave Con a half-smile. "Say you're right. Where would I go? Any suggestions?"

"Southeast Asia," Con said without hesitation. "A guy could disappear there, no problem. Or maybe Hong Kong. Shanghai? Except you'd stand out as a white guy." He took a hefty swallow and sank back into his favorite overstuffed chair to give the problem serious attention. Damon slouched, too, and closed his eyes, picturing in his mind landscapes that ranged from steaming jungles to squalid streets between sun-blotting high-rises.

A few minutes later Con snapped forward and waved an arm.

"Goddamn. Look at this, man. On the news nets." He reached for Damon's digiscroll on the side table between them. Con never linked with Damon implant-to-augment anymore. "Here it is."

Damon tried to follow the images the slim rectangle was flashing. A protest somewhere—it looked like Europe. France? Yes, there was the Eiffel tower far in the background, lit by the setting sun. Lots of bodies waved flags made from white sheets, and banners with hand-sprayed letters like white-collar graffiti.

"It's a protest against Dyna-Mantech," Con said. "Holy shit! Look—they're using some of *your* phrases from the website!"

Just then Damon saw a banner in English that read, "Keep Your Head", and another with, "Your Mind Is Your Own." He burst into a smile.

"That's fantastic!"

"The shit's hit the fan now, for sure." Con looked even paler than before. "You should book your flight tonight."

"To go there?"

"*No!* To disappear. Geez! You think I'm just talking out my ass?"

"No. No, I don't. But I can't leave town yet. There are things I have to find out. This is big, Con. Really big. It could be a make-or-break moment."

"Bro, look at yourself in the mirror. Your eyes. Like a fanatic—a fucking terrorist!" Con tossed his empty beer bottle toward the kitchen, but it bounced on the edge of the carpet and didn't smash. "I need some air."

He slammed the door, leaving Damon stunned.

Terrorist?

That was ridiculous. If anything, Damon was a freedom fighter. A man who found himself at a key moment in history, with the fate of a generation in his hands. He couldn't back down now. He couldn't.

He closed his eyes and called up the news reports with his implant. The images of people marching and jostling and shouting were hypnotic. He couldn't understand many of the words, his translator having trouble with overlapping voices pitched high in anger, but it was clear that the protestors were driven by righteous fervor ignited by his website.

And Damon realized that if they'd known who he was, they'd have been shouting his name.

#

The Paris protest continued late into the night, but then changed to rioting and looting, and hundreds were arrested. Damon fell asleep at some point but checked news feeds again when dawn's light streamed in through the window he'd forgotten to darken. By then another gathering had formed, but in Rome this time. D-M only had a small office there in an anonymous building of reddish-brown brick, but the protestors had found it. They filled a half-dozen of the surrounding streets, then marched to the nearest major thoroughfare and blocked it for an hour before riot police dispersed them. Damon didn't know what blocking a street was supposed to achieve, but maybe it was a regular tactic. It certainly got attention.

The next day brought news of a protest in Tokyo. Since the Shinjuku riot of 1968, the Japanese weren't often given to demonstrations of any kind—but they were crazy about their tech; and privacy, respect, and personal dignity were keystones of their culture. D-M's intrusiveness would be an affront to all of those.

Night had just fallen. Thousands filled the Ginza district, completely clogging the intersection of Chuo-Dori and Harumi-dori. Damon knew the Café Doutor was on the ground floor of the San-ai Building, but he could barely see its sign above the swarms of bodies. The giant neon Ricoh sign that topped the glass tower was like a beacon, a marshalling point. No-one would be getting into the Dior or Georgio Armani buildings nearby. Before long, the amorphous mob extended a pseudopod along Chuo-Dori, and flowed into it like an amoeba in motion, surging inexorably over the three blocks to where Dyna-Mantech had taken over a storefront between Lanvin and H & M. Police had arrived but couldn't get through the crowd.

Just then Shiori Shabata contacted him. She activated audio and Damon allowed the reception.

"It's horrible, Damon. I was just window shopping at Prada when I heard the roar. I managed to get across the street, but now I'm trapped. No one can get anywhere."

"I'm watching the news feeds, Shiori. But can you let me see? Through you?"

He heard her hesitate. He hadn't really needed to ask—he could do it without her permission or knowledge. Maybe she knew that.

"OK. Sure." She opened her implant to him. Within seconds he was staring at an alien creature made up of human bodies. Shiori was pressed back against a store—probably Abercrombie & Fitch—and as she looked south, he could see the name Yamaha across the top of one of the taller buildings. That would be just past the D-M store. The street looked like a river of bubbling tar

223

with spikes of flotsam sticking up at every angle, carried along with the flow. There were bright sparks beginning to appear above the heads. Had people brought flashlights? Handheld phones, maybe? Shit, they weren't lighting torches, were they? He had a memory flash of an ancient clip from a Frankenstein movie.

"Good God, Shiori. Can you get inside?"

"No, all of the businesses have barred their doors." He could tell she was badly frightened, but she was maintaining control. Then Kenzo joined the conversation. He was in his office, kilometers away—there was nothing he could do physically to help his wife.

"Shiori, Damon…I've just learned that one of the organizers of the protest is a woman I know. I have a contact address for her Vanquish."

"Fantastic," Damon said. "Send it to me. I hope she speaks English."

She was an activist lawyer named Tamao Kagami, who specialized in privacy law. She had helped to organize the rally, but she wasn't there in person.

"Kagami-san, I'm the man who discovered what the D-M people were up to. I run the 'Vanquish the Vanquish' web site. I'm gratified to see that citizens of Tokyo are protesting, but has anyone got any control over that mob? Shiori Shabata is trapped in it."

"I'm very sorry to hear that, Mr. ….?"

"Call me Damon, but please don't give my name to anyone else. As you can appreciate, I've remained anonymous for good reason."

"I'm sure. As for control, does anyone control a mob once they've formed? We organized a corps of a thousand protestors who were set to follow a plan, but they're outnumbered ten to one by now. Two of our speakers tried to address the crowd, but Tokyo police have an anti-protest device that records such sounds and plays them back a fraction of a second later, disorienting the brain. People become unable to speak at all within its influence. The crowd became very angry when that was used. Since then, our people have only been able to go along with the mob to try to keep their focus. Three of our core group are right in the thick of it, in front of Van Cleef and Arpels. But I can't promise they can do anything to help."

"If you can direct me to their BCIDs, they just might. I have an idea."

Acknowledging a debt to Valerie, he quickly contacted Kagami's three protest leaders, who were indeed willing to help, and they linked in every acquaintance they knew in the crowd. Each of those began to enlist the strangers next to them. Within twenty-five minutes, Damon was connected to nearly seventy per cent of the throng. He kept his message visual and repeated the sequence of images over and over. Amateur hackers in the mob caught on first and helped to link in the rest of the protestors.

They bombarded the Dyna-Mantech store's networks with access requests, transmitting every possible username and password combination. In another seventeen minutes they were into the D-M system, stealing codes and spreading outward to other D-M installations. Five minutes after that, all Tokyo operations of Dyna-Mantech and ImagiCap were deliberately cut off from the internet and all other direct network connections.

That was the end of the attack, but the protestors had made their point. Without net access, the two corporations' offices in Tokyo ground to a halt.

Damon felt on fire and knew that now he needed to speak to the massed protestors, to calm them down. Many would understand English. Online translators could do the rest.

"You have done what you came to do," he said, his words making thousands of heads lift in unison, like a wave over the sea of black. Since there was no external sound, the feedback device of the Tokyo police could have no effect. "Together, we have forced Dyna-Mantech to pay attention. They can no longer ignore us. They know that we can renew our attack at any time. But there is no longer any need to do so with physical force. It is time to disperse. So far, you have hurt no-one. You have done nothing, left no evidence, that police can respond to. Please go back to your homes in peace and think about the new force you have brought into the world tonight. You've struck your blow. You are victorious!"

There was a deafening cheer. He heard it through countless ears and could swear he *felt* it in his bones. And then the crowd began to disperse.

It took a long time for the streets to clear, and some hooligans smashed a few windows; but the police sought them out and mostly left the other protestors alone. As Damon had said, there was no evidence with which to lay charges.

Shiori wasn't hurt. She and Kenzo were effusively grateful to Damon for his intervention. Before he broke contact, Damon promised Tamao Kagami that he'd keep in touch. He was riding high, euphoric in a way he hadn't experienced since the early days of sex with Valerie. His mind boiled with the ramifications of what had just been done.

Late that evening, when he went out to get some beer, he was taken.

#

First, they beat the shit out of him.

He couldn't understand why they did that when they were going to kill him anyway. To make sure he wouldn't put up a fight? Or just for revenge?

He didn't even feel the blows after the first two. Only one single bloom of pain that moved from place to place around his body, billowing like a flame that finds new pockets of oxygen. The flare in his face was fierce and hot, melting his nose and upper lip together into one molten stream that ran into his mouth tasting like iron and ash.

His boyhood defence mechanism asserted itself and he held his arms over his head to protect his implants. Without them, he might as well be dead. One man grabbed his feet and another his arms. His elbows cracked hard against unyielding metal edges, and he landed heavily on a rigid shape that nearly broke his spine. There came a slamming noise, and a sensation like a strong puff of wind. All sound became muted, except for whimpering that might have come from an injured puppy. It couldn't have come from him, could it?

His back roared its outrage. He swallowed his fear and shifted to another position that provided a little relief. His injuries throbbed with the rhythm of his pulse, as if he had another seven or eight hearts. Gingerly, he reached out a hand to probe the extent of his surroundings. At the same moment, his cage jerked, and he was rolled against a sharp object that dug into his forehead. He pushed away and felt something warm and wet run into his right eye.

The trunk of a car. A fairly big one, thankfully. The kind driven by old, retired people, or by gangsters who retired people. It didn't mesh with his image of Dyna-Mantech, or even the government. Wouldn't their hit squads drive big black SUVs, like on television?

If this was a hit, why go to the trouble of kidnapping him? A single bullet in the middle of the street would have been adequate. Or a nice long drop down an elevator shaft. Maybe that was it: they'd been thwarted by a fluke on the first attempt and didn't want to take any chances this time. Needed him good and dead. Or maybe they thought he had a whole organization and wanted to get all the names of his lieutenants before they killed him. That was conceivable, especially given what had happened in Tokyo. They wouldn't want to believe that so much disruption could simply be improvised.

The car lurched at random, and he couldn't brace himself with just his knees and his chin to keep from rolling against the trunk's metal protrusions. The car was electric and wasn't old—he could tell that by the smells that managed to get through the one nostril not plugged with clotting blood. Chemical and plastic smells that weren't unpleasant, plus some grease and glue smells that were. Maybe some of the last sensations that he would ever know.

What would it be like to die? Would it be slow or quick? Would he have three deaths, as first one implant, then the next, and finally his meat brain gave up the spark that made them aware? His second implant should last the longest because it was fuelled by glucose, with capacitor-like circuits that would slow the final power drain into a prolonged, weary fade to black. Would it be like a robot without a master, left without initiative or motivation for its last confused moments?

I remember, but I don't think, therefore I am...not?

A wild idea came to him. What if the essence of him could escape over the 'net? If he could send out data parcels: his mind reduced to ones and zeroes, to be saved and stored like obsolete documents or teen-romance tunes with the sparkle compressed out of them? White-fi might be accessible from a moving car, if he were still in the city. All of him wouldn't fit in just one person's implant, though. Part of him would have to go to

Valerie, part to the Robbins, a few odds and ends to the Shabatas.

Valerie. If he could speak to her one last time, what would he say?

Wait. There *was* white-fi—he could sense it. They were probably traveling one of the main routes where thousands of commuters needed to trust their cars to autopilot while they conducted important business. There were nodes everywhere. His brain must've been seriously rattled not to have noticed them. He could reach Valerie! Tell her to call the police. In fact, he could do better than just call for help.

He didn't think he could triangulate his position from the white-fi nodes, but his BCIDs would have kept unconscious track of every movement of the car: every stop, every turn to the right or left. He could estimate speeds and look for a match in Google Neighborhood.

There were three possible route matches right away, depending on the car's speed and the number of green traffic lights that had let them through. He brought up Street View for the route he thought most likely.

There. A big jolt accompanied by a clanging thump, just as Street View showed him the entry to a bridge. That was it—that was the route they were on.

Part of him yearned to contact Valerie—it might be the last time he ever would—but it made more sense to alert 911 directly. Then, just as the link was made, he felt the car jerk to a stop. He sent a quick burst of information: he was injured, assume the kidnappers were armed, the approximate Google address, somewhere on the docks.

A bright light stabbed into his only open eye. Rough hands clutched him. His reflex was to resist, but there was no point. One of the hands cuffed him hard across the face as if to confirm that.

It was like a scene from any hoary old police drama. Dim overhead lights struggled to illuminate a space between dark buildings that looked abandoned. There was a soft sound of water lapping, and city lights from far away reflected on the nearly calm surface of the river. Underfoot might have been asphalt once, but was now covered with uncounted decades of grit, decayed memories of cargoes come and gone. The faceless, hulking thugs that pulled him out of the trunk stood him upright on his own feet, but his left leg collapsed, his knee too badly abused. They hauled him up again, and he dangled there, limply awaiting what was to come.

He half expected to see the face of H. Reinhardt Janus emerge into a patch of light. He'd only ever found an old corporate photo of the man online. But it looked nothing like the figure approaching him. This man was tall, with thick grey hair that sucked up the light, leaving his face a featureless pool of black. He wore dark clothes, too, and gloves. Certainly not for warmth—the night air was muggy, thick with the odor of fish and sweat. In one gloved hand was a gun-like shape, but not quite right. The angles were different.

A riot prod. It produced enough voltage to kill, if set that way. Or it could merely be a source of excruciating pain. Damon tried to connect with a signal—any signal—and scream for help.

"You dickheads." The rasping voice was a shock, as if the darkness itself had spoken. "He's *awake*. Didn't I warn you to bring him here unconscious?" The prod hand darted forward and Damon spasmed right out of his captors' hands, to land writhing in the dirt. His lungs couldn't draw air. He was certain his implants must be shooting sparks because he could see them, like fireworks ricocheting around his skull. He'd never felt so much pain in his life.

"Computer...head...cops by now." The voice wavered in and out like a mistuned radio signal. The prod descended again.

As Damon bucked helplessly on the ground, his teeth clacking together, he dimly heard a repeating noise like an electronic alarm.

"Cops...scatter.... No, leave him. ...his friends...won't matter anyway."

The world contracted into a whining buzz in his ears. An unknowable span of time later he became aware of blue and red light washing over the nearby walls, and the scraping crunch of tires on grit. White light impaled his eye, forcing it closed. He felt himself touched. There were sounds almost like voices. Then the darkness of the river rolled up and over him like a wave.

#

He awakened in a hospital room.

Not again! Were hospital rooms fated to be the pattern of his life?

A greenish-white ceiling filled his view, so he twisted his head to the right to see the room. His last impression before unconsciousness was that his head had sheared off and rolled across the hard floor.

The next time he awoke, Valerie was there. She quickly rested a hand on his forehead to keep him still. He didn't fight it. Her skin was wonderfully cool.

"Can you hear me?" she asked.

He was afraid to nod, so he blinked. Both eyes participated—someone must have washed the blood away. Even so he must look god-awful. The wet sheen of Valerie's eyes was evidence of that.

"Looks like your fate is to wake up in hospital rooms," she said with a tentative smile, echoing his very thoughts. "There are policemen stationed at the door. For your protection, I think."

Her slight qualification agreed with his own thoughts. It was just as likely that the police wanted some time with him of their own. Maybe to help track his abductors. Maybe on behalf of a higher authority.

"Would you like a drink?"

He tried to answer, but no sound came out. She brought a small carafe and a straw close to his mouth, but he couldn't get the right angle. He refused to be an invalid—he couldn't afford to be helpless. So, he forced his body upward, grateful that his muscles' screams of protest weren't escaping from his mouth. With Valerie's help, he finally managed to sit up, but it was one of the longest minutes of his life.

"You shouldn't be moving. There's no need." Her voice was thick with concern.

He took a deep pull from the straw in the small carafe she had picked up again.

"There's every need," he rasped, then gave a choking cough. He took another drink. "I can't stay here."

"Of course you're going to stay here. It'll take you weeks to recover from the beating they gave you. You should see yourself!"

"I'll deny myself that pleasure. It might weaken my resolve." His attempt at a laugh was more like a hack. "If I stay here, I'm a dead man. The police won't stop it—either won't be able to or won't try. ImagiCap probably owns people in the police service. The last time they tried to kill me, I was only a snoop, a nuisance. But now I've gone too far."

"Then what can you do?" Her face had paled to the color of the walls.

He tried to give a brave smile, but those muscles wouldn't cooperate. "I've got to disappear," he said simply.

"How? Where will you go?"

"I...can't tell you that."

"Because you don't trust me. Right? So, I'm like the ex-girlfriend who only gets drunken booty calls at two in the morning. Except *my* calls will only be when you're at death's door. No thanks." She turned away, putting the water carafe on the bedside table, her body rigid.

"There's nothing left between us," Damon declared to her, and to himself. "But I still think you believe in what I've been trying to do. I hope you won't abandon that. Neuroethics still needs you."

"Gee, that makes me feel so much better."

"I hate to have to point this out, but you should disappear too. Janus put us together, so everyone will know about it. They'll believe you betrayed them by helping me."

"I'm not about to give up my life and live on the run, like an animal. I haven't done anything wrong." Her eyes burned with anger, but the welling of tears threatened to put the fires out.

"Goodbye, Valerie." he said, and closed his eyes.

When she was gone, he just lay on the bed for a few moments, then tested out each of his limbs. His injured left knee would give him trouble. That couldn't be helped. Maybe he could steal a crutch.

Just after midnight, the head nurse on the floor was startled by a pair of police officers hurrying past her to the elevators. Her screen read only that a room had become available because the previous patient had been transferred to St. Vincent's. It must have happened at the shift change, while she was distracted with patient updates.

Twenty minutes later the same officers came racing back along the hallway. An intruder alert sent everyone scrambling. But no intruder was found. No one at all.

15

July 25, 2041

"No longer must you dream alone. No longer invoke bright fireworks of imagination, then resort to dead cinders of words to describe them. Even the loneliest flight of fantasy now has room for two."
The Speeches of Damon Leiter
Collected by V.A. Klug

Damon watched his apartment for an hour before going in. The police had quickly discovered that he was missing from the hospital. His home was the last place he should go. At least, he hoped that was how they thought.

He found Con naked, slouched in his favorite chair, eyes glazed. Damon thought he was dead—that the kidnappers had ensured his friend's silence. A smell of urine came from Con's chair.

Then Con's eyes moved, back and forth, as if watching something. They weren't tracking Damon, weren't focused on him, weren't even aware of his presence. Hot rage boiled up.

"*Con!*" he yelled. The figure in the chair started violently, and the arms fluttered; but it took a long time for the head to lift and the eyes to really see. Bloodshot orbs slid loosely in their sockets, trying to focus, then finally locked onto Damon. The harsh intake of air was loud in the still room.

"Yeah, Con, I'm still alive. Sorry to disappoint you."

"No, man, no. God, I'm glad. I'm...I never meant...."

"Never meant for me to get hurt? What did you think they were going to do?"

"I tried to warn you. Tried.... You wouldn't listen." Con was drunk, but his terror made him coherent. More or less.

"What did they use on you? To make you betray me?"

Con was shaking like a fever victim, but he tried to steady his left hand with his right and reached up to his augment. There was a faint click, then he held out his hand, palm up. In it was a tiny sliver of plastic. Damon held it up to the light. It was opaque, and featureless, about the size of the dimes he remembered from when he was a kid. Or the sim cards used by handheld phones back then—it was like one of those cut in half and rounded at the corners.

"A sim disc," Con said, "but sim as in simulation. It's better than online, better than 3-D. It's *real*, man. So real." He shuddered.

"This is *porn*?"

Con swallowed and gave a slight nod. "More than that."

"I've never seen an augment that took discs. Why would they need it?"

"Not trackable." Con bobbed his head. "Only work in altered BCIDs. Bootlegs. Like mine."

"Your Vanquish? It's black market?" Damon's legs were weakening, especially his left knee. He needed to sit, but he didn't want to give up his position of dominance.

"That's what the black-market thinks. They're actually made by D-M itself, but without the EM limiters. Illegal."

"And given to you as a reward," Damon spat. Con hung his head.

"You don't understand," he wheezed. "They target the pleasure centers. Straight in. Full-on ecstasy on demand. It's better than real, man. *Better* than real!"

"And more addictive than crack," Damon breathed, feeling sick. His hurt knee gave out and he collapsed into his armchair. "Wait. You've had it for weeks. Which means if it was a reward for services rendered...." He gasped. "*You*. You helped them lay the trap for me at the Mori 2 tower. And then you tried to make me suspect Valerie!"

Arms wrapped around himself, Con was rocking back and forth in the chair. Tears leaked from his eyes, spittle from his mouth. His words were hard to understand.

"You can kill me, man. Go ahead. Please, kill me. They were going to do worse." His eyes opened wide with new fear. "They had a...thing, a gun. Huge. Said it fired an electromagnetic pulse. Would burn out my augment in a second and *take my brain with it*. God...they tried it on a low setting, enough to scramble but not fry—just to give me a taste of Hell...." He twisted to the side and dry retched over the arm of the chair.

Taggart had told Damon that sunspots and other radiation could destroy an augment. Certainly, an EMP could wreck circuitry, though he'd never heard of a way to produce one with a device small enough to be portable. It sounded like something the government would desperately want as a weapon, which meant that a company like ImagiCap would bend over backwards to supply it.

"Kill me," Con breathed, barely audible. "Please, man. Kill me, wouldja? Please?"

#

Damon sat staring at his best friend, frothing with more emotions than his mind could assimilate, all at once. Disgust, shame...pity. Every possible shade of regret. After a long time, he lurched to the bathroom and flushed the sim disc down the toilet. Con would have more, but there wasn't much he could do about that.

He stopped for a moment to look into his own room, but took nothing. None of it seemed to belong to him anymore. Kenzo Shabata could probably help him move his money quickly, before the police could freeze his accounts. That would be the first order of business, if it wasn't already too late. Then, false identities, false documents—a supply of them. He'd met a guy at university: a cheat and a washout, but a genius with graphics. Best to use the IDs of real people—Damon could hack into lots of databases to come up with those, fully fleshed out and credible.

He shuffled painfully down the hall toward the door. Con was curled into a fetal position, his pale, naked flesh seeming even more obscene with its suggestion of innocence.

A faint sound followed Damon as he left: "I tried to warn you. Tried to warn you. Tried...."

#

He stayed in hotels. Not good ones—not the kind that required fingerprints, or even RFID from his augment. Taggart implants didn't have such a chip, though maybe

Damon could create a fake signal. He'd have to work on that. In the meantime, his body resided in dingy spaces with loosely-woven window coverings of green and purple patterns to match cheap cotton coverlets, bargain-basement furniture, and bulk-discount wall appointments—you couldn't call them art. Visible stains were disingenuously hidden by the placement of throw cushions or wastebaskets. From a small philately shop, he bought a cheap ultraviolet lamp to shine over the bedding. After that, he carried his own sleeping bag and thin pillow and slept on top of the bedclothes.

He sealed his BCID to everyone except Camillo Ricci. The rest had to leave the equivalent of a text message or email at a sub-level of his website, and then he'd contact them if he chose to. Camillo could reach him directly but would never know where he was. Camillo was loyal, but neither he nor Damon thought he could stand up to determined interrogation.

The kid was like a big puppy. Modest height, with dark features, profuse black curls, and a lot more smarts than required to graduate with an undergraduate degree. Camillo's family was old school Italian, so smotheringly conventional that the young man was desperate for any outlet that offered the promise of adventure and personal achievement. Maybe he hoped that a touch of mystery might make him attractive to women. A James Bond. If that were true, Damon saw no sign of it. But there was still more to Camillo's commitment, as if the man had replaced his parent's Catholicism with a new ideology.

Frantic about Damon's kidnapping, he hinted at 'family connections' that could provide protection, but Damon refused. He suspected that Camillo's family was no more connected to organized crime than his own; but even if they were, a gangster entanglement would just add another layer of trouble he didn't need.

There were more international protests against Dyna-Mantech, but they were small and not very effective. Damon wished he could be on scene to provide guidance and inspiration, but they were in places where he knew no-one and therefore couldn't connect. It would have helped if protest planners put contact information on his website, but doing so would have made them instant targets. They were putting themselves at enough risk already. The protests made the news services, but Dyna-Mantech BCI remained resolutely silent.

Whenever he felt secure enough, or foolish enough, Damon led live webinars instructing thousands of users at a time how to bypass the objectionable traits of the Vanquish, and then encouraged them to pass the knowledge on.

It was inevitable that D-M would come up with a firmware upgrade. Absolutely no-one accepted it, so D-M sweetened the offer: the revised upgrade included an app that provided large automatic discounts for ten major product brands, good for five purchases of each brand over a period of thirty days.

Demand rose, until someone blogged that to take advantage of all the discounts, a consumer would have to spend five thousand dollars. D-M was vilified all over again. At that point, executives of the company must have decided they had nothing to lose.

They pushed through the upgrade without permission on every Vanquish that made an electronic purchase or communicated through Jabber—there were rumors that ImagiCap had bought the social network site. The forced upgrade violated the laws of most developed countries, and a dozen of them quickly announced court action, including the United States and Canada. But Damon and everyone else knew that the cases would take years to get through the courts. Dyna-Mantech had won that round.

Damon had to get his hands on an upgraded Vanquish and start over.

The upgrade was a strange mix of rearranged functionality. By then everyone knew that the Vanquish allowed ad-permission circuits to be switched off, but they would reactivate every three days. After the upgrade, the circuit wouldn't reactivate until after fifty purchases, but then could no longer be switched off.

People were mollified—fifty purchases seemed like a lot. Even more disturbing, however, Dyna-Mantech had altered the electromagnetic field generator controls to allow the user to *choose* whether or not they wanted the BCID to give them a pleasurable shot of current when they made a purchase. Those who'd used Damon's methods to bypass the pleasure trigger found that the upgrade restored its function, though *the EM limiter remained disabled.* The new developments provoked an outcry, with a few members of Congress proclaiming that D-M might as well be offering free cocaine. But surveys quickly found that most Vanquish owners did indeed choose the current.

Dyna-Mantech pointed out that there were no studies showing such a low voltage to be harmful. In fact, there were no studies about it at all. As always, safety regulators and legislators were far behind the curve, the same lethargy that had protected cigarette manufacturers for decades.

Damon remembered his last view of Con and vowed to keep up the fight. But for the first time, demand for his services dropped off.

#

He was proud of one achievement during that period. With an adaptation borrowed from his website, he was able to give BCIDs randomly rotating passwords and usernames. That made them far more secure against direct infiltration. But he held back a key command line for himself, so he alone could defeat the system and access even newly protected devices. He needed an ace in the hole. He'd learned his lesson.

He offered the new application to the world, and once again his site burned with activity.

Then came a shock that left him staggered.

It began with a cryptic message left on his website. The header was the word Klug. After that followed a series of numbers in three columns. The numbers in the left-hand column went no higher than twelve, the numbers in the right no higher than twenty, but the middle column had the number 32 in it. That seemed to rule out a simple alphabetical code. He found some code-breaking apps online and ran it through those but couldn't come up with anything intelligible. The message was all numbers except for the header and the last character, which was the letter T.

A signature? Surely not Taggart?

The name Klug was guaranteed to get his attention, but he was sure the message wasn't from Valerie. She would have identified herself with something more personal.

What if it was Taggart? Could he be referring to the progress reports Valerie had written as V.A. Klug?

A *book* code? Get two parties with the same book, then use numbers to point to a certain page, line of text, and word in that line. With enough numbers you could spell out a message, word by word, of almost any length.

Damon didn't even have to hack into the ImagiCap files again. Copies of the progress reports were stored in his second implant. He quickly searched the documents by report number, line number, and word number, following the columns of the message. The result wasn't a coherent sentence. The first part looked like a possible web address. After that, some directions, or maybe passwords.

He went online using every stealth measure he knew. After forty-five minutes of trial and error, and some close brushes with high-level security alarms, the result was well worth it.

The trail led to a US military intelligence site, though it didn't seem to be specific to any of the three military departments or the five branches of service. The address provided by Taggart—if it was him—pointed to a document about BCIDs. Plenty of text, graphs, and diagrams. As Damon read, his throat went dry.

The military had contracted with Dyna-Mantech to provide all of its service personnel with versions of the Vanquish BCID.

It was an enormous contract, easily making the US government D-M's biggest customer. The distribution would take place in stages, partly because of the logistics of supplying such a large number of devices, but more significantly because these would be no ordinary augments. The commercial Vanquish was purely external, but the modified version ordered by the government was different. Its design involved one implanted microelectrode array, entering the skull through a single small burr hole that could be produced by something about the size of a fat needle. Maybe not much different from the needles used for lumbar punctures. Most of the array would remain at a shallow depth not far beneath the dura and the arachnoid mater—obviously to bypass the shielding of the skull while also gaining some protection from it. But a couple of electrodes would go deep. Damon was sure there was a significance to that, and probably to their specific placement, but it eluded him.

He could see the advantage to a soldier of an implanted connection that would be less vulnerable to interference, but it also meant that the soldier would have no recourse if he changed his mind, or his principles. There was no way to safely remove such a device on your own.

The timetable of the rollout was another shock. The members of the top command level, generals and admirals, *already had the new BCIDs installed.* The next tier of officers was in process, and each subsequent descending level in the chain of command would be fitted as product could be supplied and implant operations arranged. Dyna-Mantech committed to deliver all the devices currently required within six months and would provide more as needed to equip new recruits.

It was outrageous, yet not a word of the transaction had leaked to the media. Or the media had somehow been muzzled. Augments were now so ubiquitous that the idea of providing soldiers with them would provoke no alarm on its own. It was the implications of the modifications that were terrifying. Especially since Dyna-Mantech and ImagiCap were involved.

As a final touch of mystery, there'd been several mentions of the way the new military Vanquish would seamlessly integrate with the *Dynamic Vision Systems*, also to be provided by Dyna-Mantech. It left a sour taste in Damon's mouth every time he encountered that name. One day he would understand. He only hoped it wouldn't be too late.

#

Soon afterward, he contacted Kenzo Shabata to learn how the aftermath of the attack on Dyna-Mantech Tokyo had played out. There'd been huge debate about it in the National Diet, Japan's parliament, with arguments for and against D-M almost evenly split. That meant that no official action would be forthcoming anytime soon. More persuasion was necessary, and the organizers of the first protest were already brainstorming about that.

Damon had come to count on Kenzo as a solid ally, with a keen mind, uncanny business intuition honed by experience, and a nearly unflappable personality. So, it was unsettling to hear fatigue in his friend's voice.

"It is the implants," Kenzo finally admitted. "At first, I was most pleased to be in constant touch with Shiori. But now...she consults me over everything to do with the household. Every decision. Every detail of the children's schooling, the work of the gardener, the planning of social events. This is not the Japanese way, Damon. She does not *need* to—she does it because she *can*."

It wouldn't have been easy for a man like Kenzo to make such a revelation. It had to be his way of asking for help. Except Damon had no help to offer.

"Your implant can be set to keep her out," he said, "but...."

"But that would not be...appropriate for our marriage. I know. Such a door once opened, cannot easily be closed." Because feelings would be caught in it like fingers.

Clearly eager to shift the discussion away from such a personal topic, Kenzo reported that he had stayed in touch with Tamao Kagami, even meeting with her in person. The lawyer was well-connected in some surprising ways. One of her American acquaintances was an ex-CIA operative with time on his hands. The man had been a navy frogman and helicopter pilot before his CIA stint, and had extensive weapons experience, too. Such skills would make him a perfect choice as a personal security trainer. Damon had now made powerful enemies and needed to know how to stay free of them.

Kenzo promised to arrange an interview through Kagami.

When Damon finally met the ex-CIA agent, the man introduced himself as Gordon James—probably one of dozens of pseudonyms. He already had one of the most secure brain augments Damon had ever encountered—totally isolated, wifi turned off except while needed—but Damon believed he could make it nearly impenetrable and offered to do so.

James gave a wary smile and said, "Why don't we get to know each other better first?"

It was a good answer. The right answer. Damon laughed and began to explain about his unique situation and needs.

The man was tall, but otherwise average-looking in every way, and he cultivated that look from his sandy hair and light freckles, to his Sears clothing, to eyes that somehow were brown, but sometimes golden. Loose-fitting clothes hid a well-muscled physique, and apparently an assortment of weapons, too.

In two exhausting weeks James trained Damon to spot and elude surveillance, both physical and electronic. To change his appearance and all other aspects of his identity. To scout locations for ambush potential, and also to make multiple plans for ingress and egress. Without his implants Damon would have been overwhelmed by such a torrent of information.

James also wanted Damon to be able to handle vehicles like a professional getaway driver, but there wasn't enough time to reach that level of ability since Damon had never even learned to drive a car. They practiced on a deserted stretch of road, and he did manage to pick up the basic skills. If his only means of escape involved a car or powercycle, he would at least have a chance.

The ex-operative looked over Damon's false documents, proclaimed them good but not good enough, and put him in touch with a true artist in the craft, who had a ready supply. James even taught him how to use knife and pistol, though Damon insisted he would never carry either.

#

The first opportunity to use his new tradecraft arrived unexpectedly a couple of weeks later when a tearful Naya Robbins left him a message.

Damon wasn't entirely surprised to learn that Gordon James' car was well-equipped with anti-electronics measures, some of which were more suited to offense than defense. A drive along the Robbins' street revealed vid-cams on a couple of neighboring buildings aimed at Jace and Naya's home. After parking out of sight around a corner, James was able to tap into the cameras' wifi signals. Their views confirmed that the Robbins' house was being watched, not only by cameras, but also by anonymous men and women who paraded past their door one-at-a-time at irregular intervals—easy to pick out once you knew what to look for, even though they changed clothes after each pass. Damon was sure this was all new. There'd been no reason for that kind of surveillance before. D-M must be expecting Damon to show up.

He didn't oblige them. Instead, he instructed Naya to meet him at an obscure café a few kilometers away. She set out by getting aboard an eastbound trolley outside her door but got off only a block later and descended to the subway to double back, while her 'shadow' was still getting into his car. Two blocks later, Naya returned to the surface and boarded the westbound trolley. Damon was sure she wasn't followed. He was sitting five seats behind her. A kilometer later he tapped her shoulder and led her off the trolley to a nearby hamburger joint.

"This isn't where we were supposed to meet," she said, as they slid into a booth at the back.

"I didn't want to take a chance that you'd inadvertently left behind a clue about where you were going."

"You mean, like a message for Jace. No fear of that." The tears welled in her eyes. "He left me, Damon. He's gone." She began to tear at a paper napkin. He reached across to take her hands in his.

"God, Naya. Why?"

"It's not his fault. I've been a bitch lately. It's these *goddamned implants!*" Her eyes shot flame at him. "If you hadn't...if we just.... We should never have done it, that's all. Never. People shouldn't know everything about one another—not even husbands and wives." Her voice turned flat and listless. "Some secrets need to be kept."

She pulled her hands away as the waitress arrived, and they ordered coffee. Then she tentatively reached for his touch again. He squeezed her fingers, trying to give her strength.

"You don't have to tell me what it was about. Just tell me if there's any way I can help."

"You'll probably find out as soon as I'm gone, anyway. Maybe you have already, probing with that thing in your head. Don't tell me you can't."

"I haven't. I never would."

She gave a half nod but didn't say anything until the server brought their coffee and left. She wrapped her hands around the ceramic mug as if it were a precious thing that might escape, and then looked for her answers in the dark liquid.

"Jace is a good man," she began quietly. "Honest...mostly honest. But you can't be completely truthful in the music business. Sometimes he's lied to save my feelings. I could understand that. I could even almost understand it when...when he cheated on me. The temptation. The need to feel he was still young, like those girls, and his other clients. Sure. But I couldn't leave it alone. I can be a bitch, Damon—you don't know." She took a half-hearted sip of her coffee. It was wretched stuff, but she didn't notice.

"Sometimes he'd want me with him when he talked to a client. Maybe he had to deliver bad news and figured they were less likely to blow up with me in the room. Or maybe his pitch was more convincing if we looked like a partnership. I don't know.

"But I did know when he was lying to them. Not just the signs on his face—any wife can do that. I knew the truth of what he was lying about. I knew the financial numbers, the contacts he'd made and didn't make, the secret deals he'd made with certain clients at the expense of others. Thanks to you, his implant was an open book to me. And I called him on it. Couldn't help myself. It was nasty. He'd tell a lie and I'd contradict him, right to the client's face. Sometimes I'd just make him look like a fool. Other times make him out a liar. He didn't invite me to meetings after that."

"Why? Why sabotage your own husband?"

Her eyes spat fire again. "To get back at him for being able to see inside *my* head. Even though it was really you I wanted to hurt. I hated knowing that I could never have a private thought of my own anymore."

"That's not true, Naya. Your thoughts are still your own. No-one can read them—not even me. Sure, the things that happen to you, the actions you take...those are stored by your implant. But not your thoughts."

"What else *are* thoughts except a bridge between the things we know and the actions we take because of them? Don't take a genius to figure out B when you know A and C. A couple of times, he complained that he'd even seen parts of my dreams. *My dreams*, for Christ's sake!" Her lips had pulled thin. Damon was shocked.

"That shouldn't have happened," he breathed. "Dreams are...well, they're strong visualizations, sure, but your brain shouldn't have activated your implant while you slept. Same reason we don't cry out in our sleep, because our speech centres are temporarily switched off. Unless you're a sleeptalker or a sleepwalker." He left the question in the air, but she didn't seem to have heard. "Never mind. Go on."

Her head slumped and she slowly rocked it from side to side. "Anyway, by hitting back at him for something he hadn't even done, I pushed him into doing it. He dug into my head. Deep. Trying to find out why I was acting like that, probably. And he found it. And then he left."

Damon sat back and waved for the waitress to bring more coffee, even though he could barely drink it and Naya had hardly touched hers. They needed a moment, an interruption.

When they again refused the waitress's offer of food, she shot them a dirty look. Damon grew suddenly angry. He stared at her hairline as she walked away—it was pulled back tightly on both sides, giving him a good view behind her ears. No augment. She was immune to him. He snapped his head back to face his companion, his hands clenched.

"Look, Naya, I'm your friend. You can talk to me about anything. But this isn't the kind of thing I can help with. Maybe some professional counselling...."

"No. I want you to know what you've done." The words were hard, with sharp edges. "Jace and I've known each other since we were teenagers. He knew my family. Worshipped my dad, long before Jace and I started dating. Dad coached a basketball team in the neighborhood, for kids who didn't get picked for the school team. Did other things too—he was a local hero. Jace looked up to him, wanted to *be* him.

"I knew he was no hero. But I didn't ever tell Jace. I couldn't ever let him find out...."

"That your father abused you." Damon felt the blood drain from his face, replaced by a nauseating chill.

"*You knew that?* You *stole* that outta my head?" She was nearly screaming. Faces turned toward them.

"No. No, I didn't. Keep your voice down. It wasn't hard to guess. Your face...."

"Never mind. Makes no difference. Yeah, my dad abused me, right up until I was sixteen. Then I think he figured some boyfriend might find out and come after him, so he stopped. In front of Jace, he was the perfect father, and Jace never suspected a thing—never would have, if it weren't for you."

"But...sixteen. Those memories couldn't have been in your implant."

She stared at the table. He could hear her breathing. "I found a news article. About some woman who sued her father for abusing her as a child. I...I made a copy of it and sent it to my dad, along with a note. To put the fear of God into him, for revenge—I'd never have taken him to court. But that note was burned into my brain, *and* my implant. Jace found it there.

"I wish you'd seen his face." She looked up, her pretty mouth contorted into a snarl. "Look into my head. *Look into it and see his face, goddamn you!*"

Was it true? Was it his fault? Certainly, he'd provided the means. Did that make him responsible? He hadn't accounted for human weakness—that was his mistake.

"He left. Just walked out," Naya said quietly, all strength gone from her voice. "A little over a week ago. I haven't heard from him. *Too late*, he broke the connection between our implants. Now you say people are watching *me*—seeing every single goddamned pathetic moment. My life's not even my own. Because of you."

"I could find him. Contact him."

"And do what?" Her disgust was thick, but he wasn't sure if it was aimed at him or herself. Finally, she said,

"Yeah, find him. Let me know if he's alive. That's all I want to know. If he's alive."

She struggled to her feet and walked out without looking at him again, leaving him to sit there facing the shredded remains of a napkin and two lives.

16

August 16, 2041

"To seek to influence others for our own benefit is surely a survival trait as much as it is a policy for profit. Marketing has been around as long as the so-called oldest profession. Marketing is neither inherently good nor evil. Can the puppeteer be called a villain if the puppet hands him its strings?"
                The Speeches of Damon Leiter
                Collected by V.A. Klug

No matter where Damon went, he couldn't hide from the news: Dyna-Mantech BCI had been the top performer on world stock exchanges for weeks. And its rising tide had floated all boats—especially boats tied to the D-M juggernaut. The two dozen prime clients that had ridden the Vanquish bandwagon from the beginning were swamped with orders, awash in a rain of every major currency. The company continued to offer outrageous time-limited discounts on the most in-demand Vanquish models, so no-one was willing to do without one, even though only a small percentage of users could ever avail themselves of the super-sales within the time restrictions. That element of chance was part of the attraction, like a lottery; and to win a lottery you had to have a ticket.

The best-known brands in the world sought to gain even more stature by their association with the hottest sales device in history. Every major business was clamoring to get into the club; but in that regard, D-M played the economics of scarcity. Only very few new brand-partners were admitted, and they soon began paying for the privilege in stock instead of money. Rumor had it that ImagiCap was secretly buying actual banks. Damon believed it. That would be a necessary part of their strategy. Rampant purchasing required ready credit.

Damon now jokingly called his implant friends his *cabinet*. For their next meeting the arrangements were Byzantine, as each participant had to shake off surveillance and get to a safe location, a run-down bar, within more or less the same timeframe. Damon had managed to contact Jace and told Naya, as promised, but they both stayed away from the gathering. Helayne didn't even respond. The Shabatas couldn't come in person, but they made audio connection with everyone; and Damon enabled them to remote-view securely through him, much as Valerie had done for her poetry fans. Damon could now provide such a channel at will with all his own secrets locked up tight.

For a time, Damon thought Valerie wasn't going to come, but then she made a quiet entrance and sat as far away from him as she could, while they both tried to make it look natural. He told himself that their breakup would have no effect on the work they had to do.

AUGMENT NATION

Rosa was the last to arrive at the hole-in-the-wall tavern, pleading a particularly persistent "tail." She was clearly bewildered by such an experience, uncertain how she'd come to such a state of affairs.

Damon filled them all in on the latest facts he'd learned. About the banking. About the military contract, and about the reference to Dynamic Vision Systems. About Con's betrayal, and the addiction risk of bootleg augments that weren't bootleg at all. And how the popularity of augments continued to grow, despite their group's efforts.

"We've seen this before," Ebon said. "Think about our personal health monitors, the PHMs. First, they were just apps for smartphones. Everybody wanted them—kept track of all your vital signs and health data: blood sugar, blood pressure, alcohol and nicotine levels. All it took was the kind of sensor that advanced blood-sugar monitors had introduced, and the sucker was under your skin and with you for life. Why not? Then the insurance companies caught on and offered big discounts on premiums for people who'd let them monitor their PHM's. Privacy? Hell, no. But people couldn't resist the deal. Now look what we've got: PHM's are mandatory, and the new Better Health Act will make you ineligible for some tax credits if they judge that your lifestyle and personal habits 'adversely affect your health.'"

"On the other hand," Rosa countered, "if you have a sudden critical health emergency the PHM calls for help and an ambulance is on the way before you hit the ground."

"Sure, and if the piece of junk decides that your behaviour is erratic, it can just as easily dispatch psych wardens to drag you to the nuthouse." Ebon had a beer in each hand and nearly baptized the table as he made his point. "How long before the PHM *predicts* that you might be on the verge of committing an antisocial act and the police come for you?"

Damon nodded. "For a smart species, we can be damned slow learners. A few senators and congressmen have made noises about anti-trust legislation against D-M, which is a little like when they jailed Al Capone for tax evasion.

"What worries me more is that some of the people we convinced to alter their augments have begun to reverse the fix. We're losing the fight," he said. "And I don't know what more we can do."

"In Japan, Dyna-Mantech sales are still low," Kenzo said. "Our people were a little quicker to see through the phony offers and many realise the other discounts are a kind of fraud."

"So are lotteries," Ebon declared. "And people know it. But they still buy the goddamn tickets." This time he nearly slopped beer on Rosa as he waved the glass around. "Of course we're losing the fight. People like being tricked. They want to be suckers. You can't save people from themselves."

"From their own demons, or their own greed, maybe not," Damon said. "But this is more than that. It's a conspiracy of the very wealthy and powerful."

"And that's news to you?" Ebon replied. "Man, I'm a history teacher. The wealthy and powerful have *always* conspired to subjugate the common people. This is just a different form of subjugation, and it's probably going to be the most successful one ever, because this one *feels so good!*"

"It only feels good for now," Valerie said, sitting forward, "because the time hasn't yet come to pay the piper. But once everyone's debt comes due...."

"They'll have dug themselves a hole and will have to lie in it. Yes." Beer foam flecked Ebon's lips. "But you think you can make them see that before the piper is at the door looking for his pay? Good luck with that. Aesop wrote a fable about an ant and a grasshopper. No matter how much the ant tried to warn the grasshopper that he'd starve if he didn't store up food for winter, no way that grasshopper would believe it. And Aesop wrote that twenty-six-hundred years ago. Nothing changes." He finished one beer and waved to the waitress.

Damon pulled a peanut from a basket in the middle of the table, but he didn't crack the shell, he just turned it over again and again between his fingers.

"There has to be some way to wake people up."

"Can we find a way to tie government to the conspiracy?" Rosa asked. "I mean tie them to the advertising shit, not just the military contract. People love to hate government."

"Is there any indication that Dyna-Mantech is doing all this on orders from your government, Damon?" Kenzo asked. "If so, that would create a very big backlash throughout the world."

"No, not that I've seen," Damon answered. "And ImagiCap isn't forcing the government to do anything either. Undue control of either one by the other would provoke a huge outcry; but from all I can tell, it's more like a partnership. And that doesn't seem to bother anybody." He looked at Rosa. "As for hating the government...the economy is on fire. Just the kind of thing that gets governments re-elected."

The waitress arrived with another round of drinks. It was an opportunity to change a subject that wasn't getting anywhere. Ebon slapped a hand on the table.

"So how come Jace and Naya ain't here? And how come you and Valerie ain't sittin' together? No more lovey dovey?" He gave a drunken smile, waving his hand back and forth as if the others couldn't see that Damon and Valerie were at opposite ends of the table.

"Jace and Naya...have split up," Damon said quietly. "One of those things."

"*One of those things* that happens when your implants spill all your secrets like a bag of jellybeans with a hole in it?" Rosa looked at him coolly. "And what about you two. Same thing?"

Damon shrugged but said nothing and didn't look at Valerie. Even Ebon left his beer on the table, waiting expectantly. Finally, Valerie lifted her head and spread both hands across the tabletop.

"You all should know. You have a right to know. I...never worked at a bookstore. I work at the Taggart clinic." She watched their reactions. "None of you saw me because Doctor Taggart wanted it that way. I observed patients from behind glass. I think that was more or less accidental at first, but then became part of the plan. Especially when ImagiCap came into the picture." She stopped, made an effort to continue, but had to take a drink. "A top executive from ImagiCap...arranged for Damon and me to meet. That seems to have been part of their plan, too."

"*Goddamn.*" Ebon blew beer fumes at the ceiling. "And Damon found out you'd been spying...."

"I wasn't spying! I wasn't *spying* on any of you. I...reported some observations about Damon's implant, of course. That was still part of my job. It was important data for the research. We knew that we were creating a medical breakthrough—maybe much more than that. I'm a scientist. I even had an implant of my own installed so I could understand..." Her voice broke, and she covered her mouth with a hand. She'd been talking to all of them, but she'd been looking at Damon. He hadn't looked up.

Valerie brushed her fingers under her eyes, then stood and walked quickly toward the restrooms.

"Y'know, I got to be somewhere else," Ebon said, and stood up unsteadily. "I won't say it hasn't been fun." His tab automatically paid by his implant, with a mock salute, he staggered away.

"We also are expected elsewhere," Shiori said. Kenzo grunted, as Damon felt their audio link disconnect.

"Jesus," Rosa said, and looked into Damon's eyes. "That explains a lot. And leaves a lot unexplained, too. So, you two are quits, huh?"

"How can I trust her? And without that...."

"Yeah, love is supposed to be all about trust and honesty and support. And it's goddamn amazing how often none of that has absolutely anything to do with it."

They sat in silence for a couple of minutes. Then Rosa tapped his hand.

"Tell you one thing. Whether the two of you are in love or not, you can't push her out of the circle. I've watched her—I *still* trust her to put the cause of neuroethics first. She doesn't have to be your lover, but she's still the best lieutenant you've got." She pushed to her feet, gave a small nod, and walked away.

Damon stared at the place she'd been, not noticing when Valerie returned until she slid into the center of his vision.

"Well, I guess that was a conversation killer," she said, with an attempt at a smile.

"They all had to be somewhere."

"Somewhere else, you mean. I don't blame them." She hesitated. "Listen, if you've got a minute, there's something I want to show you."

"There's nothing that's going to..."

"It's not about us. It's about Helayne." She stood up and moved to his side of the table. He slid over to make room, and she pulled her digiscroll from her purse.

"I found this yesterday," she said. The small screen came to life with jerky images of shapes in flesh tones and a gaudy background with lots of red. It took him a moment to recognize the shapes as human bodies writhing against each other.

"*Porn?*" Did she think that would put him in the mood? Then he choked on what he'd been about to say, as he recognized one of the faces.

"*Good God. It's her!*" Helayne was the center of attention for two men and one woman, all energetically engaged. In most ways it was no different from porn he'd sometimes watched with Con, except the faces of both men and the other woman were digitally blanked out. To see his friend Helayne involved made him feel sick.

"I checked out the site. She makes her partners pay for the privilege, actually charging them a premium to be on the webcast. Of course, people pay to watch, too." Valerie's voice was soft and sad. "She's also on YouTube."

"Not like...."

"No. Showing off her home décor. At first, I thought she'd moved again, but she hasn't. It's the same loft apartment, except it's been renovated. More than once, I'd say. And her kitchen—I'd swear it's into its fifth reno. You should see her face gleaming with pride."

"She loved being a midwife." Damon's voice sagged along with his face.

"Well, this time the delivery is an ugly one."

#

All the information he had about the US government's purchase of Vanquish augments went up on Damon's website. He speculated that the modifications to the soldiers' BCIDs must have a sinister purpose, but he couldn't say what it was and admitted that he had no proof. Radical news outlets picked it up, but the military didn't deny the purchase—it was too easy to confirm by other means. They simply maintained that it was incumbent on military chiefs of staff to provide all service personnel with the best equipment to "do their jobs to the high standards expected of all American forces."

Damon wondered if ImagiCap provided speechwriting along with their other services.

Damon knew his campaign was losing ground in the United States—there was no denying it. Dyna-Mantech had found a legal loophole and used it to create a lottery with mammoth prizes valued in millions. Every purchase a user made with their BCID gave that user a chance to win. They could also obtain even more entries by opening their augments to consumer surveys. Damon was certain the surveys must be camouflage for more insidious firmware alterations. He wasn't willing to risk Camillo's augment to find out. So, he infiltrated the Vanquish of a female desk clerk at a third-rate hotel.

And he was right. Once a user opened their BCID to the survey, D-M installed newly written protocols that could give an outside operator full control of the augment, including its electromagnetic field generator. In augments that used Damon's program of randomly changing passwords, the D-M malware turned the password protection off, but left a false readout that made the user believe it was still on.

Damon felt sick. He would put his new findings on his website, and he'd try to create yet another fix, but D-M had the best programming resources money could buy. He was only one man. How could he keep ahead of them? How could he even keep up?

There was only one small hope in his new discoveries. Dyna-Mantech had accomplished something that had eluded him: full outside control of a BCID without the user's cooperation.

He could use that.

#

With North America willingly surrendering to a new tide of augment-driven consumerism, and protests in most other countries losing momentum, Japan appeared to be Damon's best hope. He accepted Tamao Kagami's invitation to come to Tokyo to offer his help to their resistance in person.

The JAL supersonic flight took a tiresome seven hours, but it gave him time to think. More than that, it gave him a taste of something he hadn't experienced for many years. During the aircraft's great-circle route, its transit over the arctic prevented any connection to the internet. Satellites or ground stations could have provided it, but the demand wasn't high enough to justify the expense. To Damon it was unnerving. He'd been connected to something beyond himself for every hour of ten years. It was as if he'd lost control of a limb, or suddenly gone deaf. What if something ever *really* disabled his implants? Would he still be able to function?

Would he still be Damon Leiter?

He was enormously relieved at the first stuttering dribbles of data as the plane passed over the Kamchatka peninsula, and then the return of a stable flow, like fresh oxygen, over northern Japan.

Kenzo was supposed to meet him outside Customs at Narita airport, but Damon didn't make it that far.

He was only mildly concerned when he was pulled aside for a random inspection—he knew he wasn't carrying any contraband. In the examination booth, he was told he could put his shoes back on; but as he bent over, he heard a sound like the puff of an aerosol and smelled something bitter. He snapped straight and found he'd overcompensated, stumbling into a desk. Flinging out his hand for support didn't help. It missed, and he was headed face-first for the floor when he felt arms under his own. That was the last thing he remembered.

#

He first became aware of sharp pains from his hands and hips. A powerful throb came from his neck. Flashes of bright light stabbed deeply as his eyelids fluttered. Gradually, he was able to keep them open longer.

Grey...all he saw was bright grey. Something wet splashed into his left eye. He blinked it open again. Clouds—grey rain clouds; he was on his back looking up at a gloomy sky dropping fat tears on him. But why? There was a dark line across the upper part of his peripheral vision—he lifted his head to see it better. The movement brought a painful jolt from his neck—it was draped over some kind of protrusion, hard and cold. The straight line was topped by something mesh-like. He had to reorient it in his mind. *A fence, seen upside-down.* He tried to sit up, gasped at the pain, quickly lay back down. But not for long. The effort had let him see more; and as the scraps of vision coalesced, he knew he was on train tracks, lying with his neck over one rail and his thighs over the other.

A very bad place to be.

He jack-knifed upward, shuddering from the agony, and grabbed clumsily at the far rail to pull himself into a sitting position. Then he rolled to the side and got to his knees, pushed awkwardly away from a railroad tie and the cold steel rail itself, and staggered to his feet. He nearly fell again, ferociously dizzy. He had no choice but to hang, bent over, vomiting, then lean on his knees to take deep, rasping breaths until the worst of the dizziness passed. Then he cautiously raised his head again and looked around.

Twin tracks lay in front and behind him, separated by only a few meters. He stood unsteadily in the middle, facing one of the fences that guarded the tracks from any interference, human or animal. He turned his head to the right with a wince, then to the left. There was little to see in either direction except the tracks themselves, narrowing in the perspective of distance. Countryside beyond the fences on both sides was untended pasture stretching a hundred meters or so to low cinderblock buildings that looked industrial. Too far away for anyone to hear a yell for help. He must be well outside Tokyo, but in which direction it was impossible to tell. Near Narita? If so, he had a vague recollection that the trains would be normal commuter trains. But if he'd been taken somewhere to the south or east....

Shinkansen. The famous Japanese bullet trains that travelled at up to three hundred kilometers an hour.

He lurched toward the fence. It was strong wire mesh, maybe three meters high, but fairly typical until you saw the top. Barbed wire was what he'd expected. What he found was worse. The cap wire was strung with metal pieces that made him think of ninja stars: multi-bladed with points he was certain would be sharp, meant to rotate but otherwise not move. They gleamed with wet menace. There was no space between them to grip the wire. Nowhere to drag a belly over without it being sliced open. Regular rail routes wouldn't need such nasty protection.

He had to contact Kenzo. There was some weak white-fi around—he might get a signal through—but any rescue would take time. He didn't even know where to tell them to look. And the bullet trains ran every fifteen minutes or so. Whoever had captured him, there was no sign of them now, so it was a good bet they'd dropped him on the track ten minutes earlier or more. A train would be due any minute.

Even if he stood with his back to the fence, he couldn't be sure that the passage of air from a hurtling locomotive wouldn't pull him to his death. Reconstructed memories of the Mori 2 elevator still gave him nightmares. If he'd been wearing a belt, he could have looped that through the mesh to anchor him. His short-sleeved shirt wasn't long enough for that. Maybe his pants?

He looked down the track. Fear gripped him as he saw the distant bright light of an approaching train. It would be on him in seconds. He didn't know whether they travelled on the left track or the right and wouldn't be able to tell until the train was very close. Too close. Should he stay where he was, or take a gamble and cross to the other track? He turned his head the other way.

A second bright light, even closer.

He was out of options.

With a roar of fury at the world, he clambered up the fence, impaled his hands on sharp blades, and gave an adrenaline-fuelled kick that raised him high enough to lock his elbows into his sides and flip his body over the wire without disembowelling himself. He'd tried to get enough momentum to carry him fully over and land on his feet. Instead, his heels hit the ground first, collapsing his knees and slamming his back into the fence. Gasping for breath, head ringing, he toppled sideways, dimly registering the arrival of the first train with a sound like an army of winged demons. Even through the fence, a fist of air knocked him over, and he lay face down in dirt and weeds, listening to the roar and scrape and clatter of steel that vibrated his teeth. The cacophony rose in volume—probably the second train—and then finally diminished, leaving him shaking, the panting of his lungs raising small clouds of plant fluff.

He was alive. He'd cheated death again.

Or had he? There was no way to know if his captors had left the area. More likely they were nearby, watching, to make sure their plan succeeded. In that case, they would have seen him escape, and they'd already be on their way to do something about it. He should run—run for the buildings. Hide until help could arrive.

He tried to get to his feet but couldn't. His left knee hadn't fully recovered from the last kidnapping attempt, and it refused to obey. The best he could manage was to raise himself onto his right knee and crawl. Myriad lacerations all over his torso pulled open with every movement of his skin. His clothing was torn and bloody. The pain from his pierced hands and battered leg made him shake, but it also kept him from passing out again as he scrabbled through the scrub. The plants were too sparse to hide him. He could only hope that his enemies had overestimated how far they should withdraw to observe his fate. A frightened animal part of him wanted to stop and listen for sounds of pursuit, but there was no point. Instead, he pushed what he could spare of his will into his implants and made a cry for help.

#

"Why didn't they just kill me? Make sure this time?"

Damon felt like hell and was sure he looked it, but the Japanese customers were too polite to stare at him. They were sitting in a Starbucks, at the table farthest from the windows. Kenzo was paying much more attention to the door than to Damon as they sipped their coffee. He'd come to the rescue without the police, but it had taken him more than an hour. Damon had passed that hour propped just inside the entrance of an obscure warehouse building, expecting at any moment to be confronted by men with guns. Maybe he'd picked a good hiding place. Maybe they hadn't stayed after dropping him on the tracks. With no way to know, he'd spent the whole drive into Tokyo staring fearfully out the back window of Kenzo's car.

"They don't just want you dead," Kenzo said. "They want to send a message. Most of the people would just hear a news story about some foreigner who decided to commit suicide by *shinkansen*. It happens. But people involved in the protest movement would learn otherwise, and everyone would know that Dyna-Mantech was behind it. The warning would be clear."

"How did they know I was coming here? I didn't tell anyone—even Camillo only knew I was going away for a while. I'd bet they even knew what flight I was on. Did Tamao Kagami and her people know that?"

"She knew you were expected today. It wouldn't be hard to guess which flight you were most likely to be on. But she's very careful. Are you sure there's no other way?"

"D-M couldn't have surveillance on me back in the States or they'd have stopped me by now. I didn't think they'd be as well organized here. That was a stupid mistake."

"Looks like that's what they were hoping, though."

"Yeah, but I should have known that the strength of Japanese resistance would make the company double down on its investment here."

Damon raised his hand to rub his eyes, then remembered he had gloves on. Kenzo had used a spare shirt in his car for bandages, and then put gloves on Damon's cut-up hands to hide them, even though gloves looked ridiculous in the heat of a Tokyo summer. A thin trickle of blood ran down Damon's wrist, and he quickly lowered his hand.

"Can we go to your house?" he asked. "Maybe Shiori can do a better job of first aid on these hands." His attempt at a smile was stillborn as he saw Kenzo's face.

"I...have a friend who's a doctor. He'll do me a favour without telling the police." He looked into Damon's eyes. "Shiori has gone home to her parents' house."

"For a visit?"

"No, to stay." He closed his eyes tightly, then opened them and stared out the window, raising his coffee cup to drink. "It was too much. These implants. Do you remember I told you it was hard for me, being connected every moment?" Damon nodded. "It was worse for her. At first, she thought she was doing the right thing, involving me in our children's lives, in running the household. Then she realised it left her with no purpose. She no longer had to run everything—she was no longer needed.

"Even harder was the loss of privacy. You must know that privacy is difficult for us here in Japan. There are so many of us, and we live so close together, with small rooms separated by thin dividers. We must find our own privacy, within our minds—we create spaces of our own where we can retreat from others when we need to."

"The implants took away that retreat," Damon said quietly. Kenzo nodded.

"Her last refuge. Her last private space. Gone. Even a husband and wife must have time alone, without the other. Time to reconsider all the petty grievances and irritations of living together in the light of mutual love for one another. Without it, such wounds can only fester."

"Why didn't you just agree to close your implants to one another?"

"We did. But by then too much had been said, too much revealed. Real separation became necessary."

"Do you think she might come back?"

"I don't know." Kenzo sighed. "Perhaps if we stay apart, one day we will once again remember each other with love. And that will have to be enough." He gulped down the last of his coffee and put the mug down on the table with a loud thud. "For now, we've got work to do. Last time we gave Dyna-Mantech a bloody nose. This time let's see if we can't knock out a few teeth."

17

September 10, 2041

"The subjugation of one mind by another is considered the worst kind of violation. But do parents seek anything less than that with their young children? Where is the line between domination and direction, between governance and guidance? Within the answer to that question lies the difference between being a citizen or a powerless ward of the state."
      The Speeches of Damon Leiter
      Collected by V.A. Klug

For the first time, Damon allowed his face to be seen on his website—it wasn't as if his enemies didn't know who he was. Kagami's people filmed him delivering a communiqué to the troops, raising bandaged hands to show what Dyna-Mantech had tried to do. He was photographed at some of the famous sites in Tokyo, and even standing in front of the D-M storefront under repair on Chuo-Dori. All to send a message of his own.

He made no speeches in public—the Japanese police still had their feedback device to cancel the voices of protesters—but his presence gave a big boost to the credibility of the Japan group. Even though he couldn't speak Japanese, and a lot of passion was probably lost in translation, Kagami told him he had great presence, with the authoritative voice of a true leader. The assessment came as a surprise to him. Being a leader had never been his ambition. He'd assumed the lead in the efforts against ImagiCap only because he was better equipped than anyone else. And the battle was a very personal one.

More personal with every new thing he learned.

It was purely by accident that he came across the name of the rewards program that had bankrupted his mother. An early ImagiCap subsidiary. Whether they'd sold her ID information to someone else, or actually stolen her money themselves didn't really matter much. They'd probably never even made the connection to David Leiter, but they were the architects of his childhood poverty—and, through the Taggart Clinic, had made him a teenaged freak. Yes, they'd given him a gift, of sorts, but solely for their own benefit.

Now he was repaying the favour.

He was glad to have allies, but he didn't consider himself their leader. He pushed people as much as he pulled them and was grateful when they followed his direction, but if they didn't, he simply went on without them. His way. All that counted was the result.

Japanese protests spread beyond Tokyo to other cities and began to target other companies that operated under the ImagiCap banner. Sales of the Vanquish and other implants plummeted in Japan, an unheard-of turn of events among the gadget-loving Japanese.

The unrest began to influence other Asian markets in Seoul and Shanghai, even Hong Kong. Outside the US, D-M would be starting to feel the pain. But to Damon his primary battleground was still the United States, the engine of consumerism.

He contacted Camillo, then Valerie, and made careful plans to return home. Kagami provided four fake Damons, lookalike actors who made appearances at Narita, Haneda, and Kansai airports, while the real Damon flew from Chubu airport to Hong Kong before heading to the States. It might have felt vaguely silly to take such precautions if it weren't for the throbs of pain from his still-healing hands.

#

Camillo met him at the airport stateside. After the incident in Tokyo, the young assistant was more determined than ever not to let Damon out of his sight. Damon was in the mood for company anyway and booked adjacent rooms for them at a reasonably good hotel. Gordon James, now a good friend as well as his security advisor, had given him a clip-on button that fit the top of his ear, under his hair, and sent out a false RFID signal that was totally configurable via Bluetooth. The hotel front-desk computer was convinced by it.

Damon and Camillo shared a chateaubriand in the hotel restaurant, and then sat for an hour in the bar lounge drinking Glenfiddich. Kenzo Shabata had introduced Damon to the pleasures of single-malt whiskey, as an alternative to his usual bourbon. Camillo was a novice scotch drinker but put on a brave front.

"I learned something else in Japan," Damon said, after a few minutes of bar talk. "Even with internet everywhere, it's still not a substitute for personal contact. Being right there in the same city, so people can feel a part of what you're doing. It inspires them in a way that just can't be done with long distance video." He took an appreciative sip of golden liquid. "I wouldn't have believed that. We're so used to being in constant communication with each other that we think any form of communication is the same as any other. But there's a reason generals make appearances at the front lines. It's worth the risk in improved morale and motivation. That's what I need to do."

"To go to the front lines?" Camillo drank and then cleared his throat. "If you aren't on the front lines, somebody should tell those D-M guys who tried to kill you. Again."

"I still don't know they were from D-M. I must be hurting some of their clients almost as much as the company itself. But what I'm saying is that I need to appear for the troops *where they live*. I need to take our show on the road."

#

He swallowed his pride and asked Valerie for advice.

"Are you sure this is a good idea?" she asked. "Travelling around will actually make you easier to find. Tokyo should have proved that."

"I…just didn't expect it there. They probably counted on that. They were smarter, I'll admit. I won't make the same mistake again. It'll be harder to pin me down if I avoid planes and trains. We'll go by car, renting them under false names and switching them at each city. Maybe even more often."

"*We?*"

"Sorry, I didn't mean you and me. Camillo will go. I need another driver, at the very least. But we can't hit everywhere. The reason I'm calling is to get your opinion about what cities we should go to. Where we'd make the biggest impact. On your poetry tour, maybe you noticed some places where the people are a little more likely to stand up for themselves."

"That's what people everywhere like to think about themselves. Only you can't skip the major cities: Chicago, Boston, Detroit...all the hot spots on the eastern seaboard. Then the west coast: L.A., of course, and San Francisco, but also Phoenix and Las Vegas."

"Vegas?"

"Brother, if you can influence people in Vegas away from high-tech gadgets and the almighty buck, you'll know you've got your message down to perfection."

#

Damon and Camillo spent September and October on endless stretches of asphalt and in an interminable succession of saggy beds. Damon had developed a list of potential contacts by digging deep into the traffic data of his website. Some of its visitors were too careful even for him to track, but he got in touch with a lot of others, and discovered that, in spite of his pessimism, there were grassroots resistance-movements against the new augments almost everywhere. Just one contact could get the ball rolling with a bit of warning, though Damon didn't dare give much advance notice.

Especially after Chicago.

He had made a habit of contacting local agitators an hour before his planned appearance. But as soon as he stood up in front of Buckingham Fountain in Chicago's Grant Park, his miniature loudspeaker unit went dead, and his localized 'netcast, too, powerful interference scrambling the wifi signal. Men in suits started closing in on him. A cry for help over Bluetooth and white-fi drew a cordon of local supporters around Damon and Camillo like a giant football huddle until they could shuffle together out onto South Columbus Drive and force a cab to stop. Damon had never felt so horribly exposed—the park surroundings offered no place to hide and no ready escape-route. With the help of a traffic light, the cab driver was able to lose the pursuing vehicles just long enough for Damon and Camillo to jump out and vanish into the Roosevelt subway station.

Seeing the look on Camillo's face as they waited for a train, Damon had to fight back a nervous laugh. He pulled his friend over to look at an information screen on the wall.

"What? It's just some safety messages. Is that important?"

"No," Damon said. "What's important is keeping your face hidden until you can drop that deer-in-the-headlights look. It'll be a dead giveaway on the security cameras."

"What *was* that in the park? I felt like Public Enemy Number One!"

"I...never expected them to come for us so quickly in a crowd like that." His eyes flicked toward the nearest camera. "Maybe the subway isn't such a good idea after all. If they check these camera feeds, they could just wait for us at the next stop. Come on."

A train arrived just then, but instead of boarding, they merged into the departing crowd and returned to the street. It took a major effort of will not to break into a run. They took a zigzag path for a few blocks and ducked into a small restaurant for sandwiches that neither was able to finish, then killed some more time in a couple of different coffee shops before they dared to return to their rented car hours later. The downtown core still bristled with police vehicles, and they expected to be stopped at any moment, but it didn't happen.

With the car windows rolled up, the skunky odor of fear sweat hung in the air. Camillo tuned in a news station on the radio. Chicago PD claimed they'd been informed of a bomb threat and a pair of suspects fleeing from Grant Park. Damon tried to ignore the news report, instead using his augment to sample a couple of streaming local phone-in shows.

"There's some good news." He slouched in the seat and let out a long breath.

"What is?"

"People are already phoning in to call bullshit on what the cops are saying. They're posting videos online and insisting it was a peaceful protest." He couldn't help but grin.

"You think this is funny?"

"No! But people are on our side. That's what I'm happy about."

"On our side right now. Tomorrow? Who knows what side they'll be on? They don't."

Damon couldn't bring himself to argue. He didn't blame Camillo for being prickly. Maybe he'd thought the city-to-city campaign would be a lark, but now he'd seen just what a serious turn it could take.

Before the end of the day, an alderman had issued a release questioning whether the police might have been placed at the service of corporate interests, and the heat on Damon and Camillo began to die down. They switched cars and changed their appearances anyway, then backtracked east and then north.

A shorter-than-ideal impromptu rally in Detroit didn't garner much attention from anyone, but since they were already so close to the border, they crossed into Canada, hoping to cool pursuit even further. In general, Canadians were more concerned than most Americans about the privacy issues the Vanquish and its competitors represented, and Camillo thought that Damon's message would find a warm reception there. So, they drove as far as Toronto and initiated a rally in Nathan Phillips Square, in front of City Hall. Again, Damon felt grievously exposed, especially so close to the heart of the country's financial sector on nearby Bay St., but his fears were unfounded. A demonstration was quickly realised, peaceful but energetic; and although the private media networks were apparently cowed by fear of their advertising clients, the Canadian Broadcasting Corporation gave the event generous coverage. Their reporters only seemed bemused that Damon, the only recognizable figure, disappeared so quickly after the event.

He and Camillo were already on their way to Niagara Falls, equally confused by such a different Canadian approach to their anti-Big Tech campaign, and uncertain how far they could trust it. They knew there was no point trying to compete with the consumerism that held sway on both sides of the border in Niagara Falls, so they didn't stop there.

Without the donated money from his website, their journey would have been short-lived. Before leaving home, they'd set up a series of DollarTrans cards under fake names using the strongest possible encryption and hidden IP addresses at every step. On the road, they paid every expense, from a room rental to a package of chewing gum, with a randomly selected card, and changed their DollarTrans address with each transaction. But even with peer-to-peer payment like that, their method wasn't foolproof. By knowing where Damon and Camillo had been and when, it would eventually be possible for government and corporate computers to pin down the fake DollarTrans IDs and set alerts for them. That would require a lot of personpower at a national level, and Damon didn't think the tour had stirred up quite enough shit for that yet.

They chose roadside motels with human attendants instead of multi-factor ID screening booths, and checked in late hoping to find the front desk people lazy and sleepy. But it meant the accommodations were not the best. One motel room was old enough to have a landline phone. The sight disturbed Damon somehow, and though he couldn't think of how it might pose a threat to them, he unplugged it anyway.

As Damon tried in vain to fluff his pillow that night, Camillo sat up in his own bed clasping his arms around his knees.

"Do you think we're doing the right thing?" he asked.

"Of course, we are. Why would you ask that? Don't you think people need to know when their way of life is threatened, and what they can do about it?"

"Sure, but who are we to judge the best way of life for everyone? I mean, for centuries lifestyles hardly changed at all, but now the things our society prioritizes seem to change every generation. Maybe more often than that. And if new technology has its dangers, well...you're not exactly a poster boy for caution." Camillo's eyes darted to Damon's face and away.

Damon bit back an angry denial. Then he sighed.

"You're scared. I can understand that."

"*Of course, I'm scared!*" Camillo kicked his legs straight and flopped back on the bed. "I'm always scared these days. Scared of D-M, scared of the cops, scared that the people who are cheering us on now will turn on us. I used to think that I could trust the police and the government to look out for me. Now who can we trust? Why isn't there anybody left that we *can* trust?"

Damon spoke softly. "I trust you. I'd hoped that you could trust me."

Camillo said nothing, his face turned to the wall. After a moment, Damon reached up and turned off the light.

For the rest of their junket, Damon and Camillo were careful to the point of paranoia. Damon provided no more than a half-hour of advance notice before an appearance—often less, if he had any premonition of trouble. They chose prominent sites, but only those with several possible escape routes into crowded transit hubs or shopping concourses. And they planted an escape vehicle early in the day, so the car they used to get to the venue could be left behind. Soon, Damon knew, their opponents would notice a pattern of abandoned rental cars, and he'd have to change identities with each new city, or risk being caught at a car-rental office.

In the meantime, he perfected his messaging and honed his speaking skills. There were certain key words that provoked the reaction he was looking for: catchphrases like *freedom* and *human rights, repression* and *invasion of privacy*. He conjured images of slavery; of Communist brainwashing during the Cold War, and of US waterboarding; of the greedy corporate opportunists who'd brought about Black Monday in 1987, and especially the worldwide financial crisis of 2008. None of those references was a particularly good analogy for the ImagiCap conspiracy, but that didn't matter. They stirred powerful emotions, and Damon had learned that such strong emotions were the only effective antidote to the siren call of consumerism. Not a sure thing, but the best weapon he could muster.

His second-best weapon was something he discovered by accident. In Dallas, Texas, he mentioned the two attempts on his life, and even showed the scars on the palms of his hands. The response was immediate and forceful. America loved martyrs.

He ruefully vowed not to become one.

#

Opposition to D-M and the Vanquish finally began to take root. It was like the evils of oil pollution and climate change in past decades: many people had been concerned, but not enough to give up their precious toys. Still, once a certain level of *buzz* was achieved, the controversy over brain augments became part of the national conversation. There were cross-country phone-in radio shows, and jokes from late-night TV hosts. The movement just needed a focal point: an event that would really make it gel.

It was inevitable—Damon would have to go to Washington.

He consulted ten of the major contacts he'd made nationwide, along with his original Taggart implant comrades. For the first time Damon alerted the media, and did so an unprecedented twelve hours in advance. They didn't announce the location of Damon's appearance—he deliberately left selection of the location to the last possible moment, though he assured the others that the wide publicity of the event would, itself, prevent Dyna-Mantech or its partners from taking any drastic action.

That's what he tried to tell himself, too.

Washington offered a long list of prominent sites, but his friends argued that all of them were too obvious, and therefore risky. Camillo insisted that none of them provided ready escape routes. Damon tried to reach Gordon James for advice, but the former CIA man had his implant's wifi turned off, as usual. With luck, James would hear about the event and contact them.

"OK, so let's try a process of elimination," Damon said. "Does it have to be somewhere along the National Mall?"

The head contact for the DC protest was a man named Jon Pak who had reached out to Damon after the controversial police involvement at the Chicago rally stirred up strong disapproval on social media.

"Do you want national attention? Do you want media coverage?" Pak asked. "Most big marches go to the Capitol building, but it's a huge space that regularly gets hundreds of thousands of people. If we can't match that we'll look like pikers."

"Is Camillo right, though? How could we make a quick getaway if unfriendly agents come calling?"

"They'll be there, guaranteed," said Ebon Parrish. "But you can bet you won't see all of them. So how you going to pick an escape route when you could just as easily be running toward the enemy?"

"Mr. Parrish is right," Pak said. "Corporate and government agents may dress in suits in other cities, but in DC infiltrating a crowd is almost an everyday occurrence. So, they'll look like everybody else. If you really think you'll need a quick getaway, then you should probably skip Washington. Think about it: if this thing succeeds at all, how do you figure to get through the crowd to a waiting car or bus anyway? You won't be able to move. The good side is, nobody will be able to kidnap you either."

"Not so sure about a gunshot, though," Camillo mumbled.

Damon pretended not to hear. "We need the attention. So, the National Mall is where we've got to be. But not at the Capitol. What about at the Smithsonian? Henry Park? If we're successful, this could be a watershed moment in the history of science."

The suggestion wasn't greeted with any real enthusiasm, but none of the counter proposals garnered majority approval either. So, in the end, Damon got his way.

Before they called an end to the conference, the other Washington rep, Jody Hecht spoke in a tentative voice. "Sorry to bring this up, but...has anybody contacted the National Park Service to get permits?"

The question surprised nearly everyone, but Pak confirmed it was a valid concern. "What can I say? It's DC. Things are done differently here."

"There's no time to get permits," Damon replied. "But don't think of this as an official protest. More like a flash mob. Our release to the media said I would make a public appearance, and concerned citizens were welcome to show their support. So, we're about to see how many of the good citizens of Washington are actually concerned."

He was right about that. He was also about to learn what Dynamic Vision Systems could do.

18

October 5, 2041

> "To deceive the senses is to control the mind. Even the strongest will is at the mercy of its sources of information."
> *The Speeches of Damon Leiter*
> Collected by V.A. Klug

Even in hindsight, it was impossible to pinpoint where the Washington protest began to go wrong.

The first dozen troops arrived before most of the demonstrators, pouring out of two giant Pave Hawk helicopters that landed in Henry Park. Many more arrived soon after, on foot. Was that because there'd been a leak? Or had they just assumed that he would pick a place in the National Mall and were ready? Certainly, the public had made that assumption. A crowd had begun to gather in front of the Capitol building early in the day; and when word spread about his arrival, they quickly swarmed the sidewalks along Maryland Avenue and then Jefferson Drive, hurrying to the Smithsonian Institution. Damon had planned to speak from the steps of the Smithsonian, but the troops beat him to it. He was forced to commandeer a small table from a refreshment stand on the other side of the road and speak with his back to the menacing helicopters.

"This isn't right," Jon Pak told him. "They never bring in helicopters to a place like this."

"At least the media are here, too." Jody Hecht waved an arm at five news trucks that were unloading or looking for space on Jefferson, and another few across the park on Madison. "The soldiers won't dare do anything with that much coverage."

"But why a military presence in the first place?" Pak asked. "There's never been any violence at your other appearances. Why would they expect it this time?"

"Unless they're planning to start it themselves," Camillo said.

"That's not the way it works," Hecht admonished. "We live in a democracy, for God's sake."

Damon tried to ignore the conversation. He was concentrating on gathering the people, forging core network links, expanding his reach, spreading the word farther and farther. The space around him was filling rapidly. He urged people not to block traffic on Jefferson Drive. The authorities mustn't be given any excuse to interfere.

He was taken aback by the number of uniforms he saw, in a stunning variety. Apart from the military, the largest number were obviously Washington Metro cops, but he didn't recognize the rest.

"US Park Police and US Capitol Police," Pak said. "Probably some Secret Service mixed in—they'll be in uniform for an event like this. Given your national profile, I'd be surprised if there aren't a good number of FBI agents, too. There—over there. See?"

"Good God," said Camillo. "You'd think Damon was on the UN's Most Wanted list." His face showed that he wasn't trying to make a joke. "Boss, I think this is a bad idea. We should get out while we still can. Fight another day." He kept running his fingers through his dark hair, but only succeeded in pushing his curls into greater disarray.

"To pull out now could set us back months, maybe enough to kill our momentum completely." Damon shook his head. "We have to go on. Jody's right—the soldiers won't try anything with the eyes of the world on them." As he scanned the audience with his own eyes, he felt a surge of joy from the sight of a familiar face. Jace Robbins was only about ten meters away and slowly working his way closer. He gave a sheepish shrug as Damon caught his eye. Damon returned a warm smile. He turned to Pak. "Is the crowd respectable yet? Should we get started and give those news teams something to look at?"

Pak nodded, and Damon climbed onto the table while his friends steadied it. Pak's people had supplied a powerful portable PA system. It supplied the inevitable squeal of feedback as it was switched on.

A roar went up as his voice was heard, and heads turned in unison toward the figure mounting the commandeered table, rising above the throng. Damon felt a fierce surge of adrenaline and vindication, a crackling charge of energy from the surrounding bodies. An intoxicating sense of godhead.

There was no need to vary much from his usual message—he'd refined the raw material of his convictions into a purer ore of divine purpose. Each phrase, each word was solemnly weighted with ambitious design and forceful significance. He could feel his audience begin to surrender to his spell.

After forty-seven seconds, the wifi and white-fi signals went down. It was like shutters being closed in his head. A ripple of motion ran through the startled crowd.

The news trucks were still transmitting back to their headquarters—could he tap into that signal? Not easily, there were too many different frequencies; and if he couldn't do it, there was no chance that the people surrounding him could. He had no choice but to rely on the PA alone.

Within another minute he noticed that his words had gained a strange echo, then it became distorted and garbled. He stopped talking.

His voice continued.

Someone had hijacked his PA system. With a dead ringer for his own voice. He hurriedly motioned for Pak to shut it down, but the sound didn't stop. Whoever it was had provided their own sound gear, and the increasingly strident tones of the false Damon rang throughout the park and bounced back from the walls of the Smithsonian. He strained to hear the words, but only a few made it into his numbed brain. Words like *kill, overthrow, war.*

Jihad.

He awkwardly reached for Camillo's shoulder and dropped down from the table. Maybe if people saw that, they'd realise it wasn't the real him talking, but the odds weren't good. Camillo tried to make an opening in the swarm of bodies.

Just then came the thunder of an explosion from the direction of the Smithsonian. They couldn't see what had happened. A ball of smoke and flame roiled into the air.

That's when the shooting started.

Within seconds there was sporadic gunfire from multiple directions. The crowd instinctively tried to crouch, but they were too closely packed together. Camillo shoved harder and tugged at Damon's sleeve. Suddenly Jace was next to them, shouldering the nearest bystanders aside and beckoning Damon on. Damon ducked at the crack of a bullet, followed instantly by another, and felt Jace yank violently at his arm. Turning his head, he saw his friend go down hard with a bloom of red sprouting on his upper chest.

"Jace is hit!" Damon screamed, and dropped to Jace's side, feeling utterly helpless. Camillo, Pak and the others struggled to provide some space in the now-panicking crowd.

Why, in God's name, were the soldiers shooting?

He cast his mind out to link with one that was close enough for Bluetooth, and forcefully took over the man's vision. What he saw shocked him to the core.

Overlaid onto the soldier's view was a graphic target tracking system, rapidly seeking out faces, highlighting them with red circles, popping up names, numbers, and other information. Then a green circle would move across the field to overlap one of the red circles: a direct link from the soldier's weapon sights. He saw the view buck as the soldier fired and the target toppled.

D-M's *Dynamic Vision System*—it had to be.

But it didn't explain *why* the soldiers had chosen to fire on innocent civilians. He searched the man's implant for an answer, but a momentary flicker in the view caught his attention. Something had changed, but he couldn't tell what. He focused on the faces of the people in the middle of the man's target zone. It was a spot very close to where Damon was kneeling. He cautiously stood, switched his concentration to his own eyes and found the location, then tried to match the soldier's view with his own.

The faces weren't the same.

Where Damon saw panicked faces, their eyes wide in fear, the soldier saw masks, black eyes, and malicious smiles.

The soldiers were reacting to terrorists because they were *seeing* terrorists!

Their Vanquish implants were imposing false images onto their field of vision—not only isolating targets, but providing those very targets, and a compelling motivation to kill them.

"Everyone down!" he yelled. "Flat on the ground. The soldiers think we're terrorists! Lie flat—don't give them an excuse to shoot!" He tried to send the command out on Bluetooth and every other frequency he could, and kept sending it. Whether from that, or a sudden common understanding, people everywhere began to fling themselves to the grass.

Damon dropped too, and scrambled back to Jace. Valerie appeared from somewhere, and dropped down beside him. She leaned over their friend and frantically stripped his shirt back to examine the wound. It seemed to be just below the base of his neck. There was a lot of blood.

"His health monitor will have alerted EMS."

"They'll never be able to get through the crowd in time," she said.

"What can we do?"

"Rosa," Valerie gasped. "I need Rosa."

Wireless frequencies were still being jammed, but the source of the jamming had to be nearby. Damon swung his head around and spotted a truck only ten meters away, with a small dish antenna on its roof. Its driver was standing beside it. He closed his eyes and reached for the man. Too far for Bluetooth. He scanned up and down the white-fi spectrum. *There.* An unscrambled frequency: it was the one the soldiers were using to communicate.

Two could play the imposter game.

He set his implant to quickly scan the troop augments and match elements of their visual fields. Within thirty seconds he'd found the driver and pushed through an urgent command into the man's BCID. The uniformed figure hesitated for a moment, then clambered into the truck. A few seconds later Damon felt the jamming collapse.

"We've got wifi back," he gasped to Valerie. "But I don't know for how long. Find Rosa."

The next minutes were like something from a dream: random cracks of gunfire, screams of pain and fear, a blurry shadow of body shapes swaying chaotically or writhing on the ground. Over wifi, Damon reinforced his command for everyone to lie flat and still, and then showed them what the soldiers were seeing. It caused confusion at first—people thought there were real terrorists among them, and a few tried to flee. But others understood Damon's message and passed it to their circle of contacts. Gradually it spread. He didn't know what else to do. At any instant he expected the soldiers to come for him, but for the moment they seemed content to wave their guns back and forth, waiting for further orders or further provocation.

Maybe their augments hadn't been programmed to show *him* as a terrorist. Many of them would know what he looked like, and balk if shown a different face.

He hoped the media crews had been transmitting everything, but the odds were against it. If D-M had provided the government with such control over the minds of their own troops, they would have found a way to disrupt or alter the feeds of commercial news networks. Unless they were sure that their false Damon's words, carried by the broadcast media, would provide enough justification for the gunfire. He didn't know.

He turned back to Valerie and leaned forward in amazement. She deftly wielded a small knife and some tiny scissors smeared with red as she tried to stop the blood coming from Jace. Was she even *sewing* something?

"She's channelling Rosa," Camillo said. "But this goes way beyond just seeing. Rosa's visualizing Valerie's hands doing the work as if they were her own hands, and Valerie's somehow letting her muscles be guided directly by those visual impulses. There's got to be some haptic data sharing too—sensing how much pressure to use. It was a little jerky at first, but...."

Yes, Damon could see the occasional hesitation, as if Valerie sometimes had trouble parsing the two sets of visual data her brain was receiving. But she got the job done. He watched her pour bottled water over the wound, then cover it with a wad of gauze-like material. It was amazing what women carried in their purses.

Valerie's head jerked oddly, then she rolled it slightly to loosen the muscles and turned to Damon. "I can take it from here with Rosa just giving advice. But Jace has lost a lot of blood. He could still die if we don't get him to hospital. Fast."

"No chance of that." Jon Pak had used a commando crawl to get close to them. "Those soldiers still have their fingers on their triggers, and we're surrounded by a couple of thousand people. We can't even move."

"Could we just raise our hands and plead with the soldiers to help our wounded?" Hecht asked.

"They're not seeing the real world," Damon said. "Who knows what they'd think was happening? They'd already be moving to help the wounded if something wasn't stopping them. Don't make yourself a target." He raised his head slightly to scan the vicinity. The helicopters and their armed crews were only thirty meters away or so. He thrust his mind out onto the 'net and nearly whooped with satisfaction as he sensed the presence of Gordon James.

"I have an idea," he told the man. "You're going to hate it."

#

The others were fearful when the small contingent of soldiers began picking their way through the prostrate bodies toward them, even more so when they stopped and lifted Jace from the ground. But the fear turned to alarm when Damon stood and followed.

He signalled his friends to stay where they were—he refused to have them implicated in what he was about to do. He walked with the soldiers to the nearest helicopter and waited while they pulled out a stretcher, strapped Jace onto it, and loaded him aboard. Then, suddenly the crews of both 'copters straightened up as one and began running across the park toward 4th Street. All the soldiers close by joined in the unexplained charge. Damon swiftly climbed into the cockpit of the Pave Hawk, settled into the pilot's seat, pulled its door closed, and within moments the overhead rotor began to turn.

"This is insane," Gordon James told him through his implant. The ex-CIA man couldn't have picked a better time to check in.

"I've just seen a woman perform surgery like she was trained for it. All I'm asking you to do is get me to the nearest hospital roof. How hard can it be?"

"Says the guy who can barely drive a car."

"Probably the best bet is Washington Hospital Center—what do you think?"

"You get anywhere close to the White House, and they'll shoot you down. They might anyway, once they realise who's flying that thing."

"No time to argue. Can you see OK? All right, then. Let's do this together, Mr. James."

Damon willed his muscles to relax, but they tensed up again as he realized how difficult it was to act on information from another mind. He couldn't close his eyes—James had to see everything as if he were there in person. Damon would have to try to enter a trance-like state. Give himself to the will of the other: a puppet responding precisely to the motions of the puppet master, but without strings. He watched a vision of his legs moving, his feet flexing, then felt them make the actual motions an instant later. The tail rotor of the Pave Hawk responded, and the craft tried to torque a little. He'd already placed his hands on the collective lever and the cyclic control. James pictured Damon's fingers pulling together into a loose grip, Damon's head swivelling to scan the instruments and controls. The body complied. The number of switches and readouts was terrifying. Most wouldn't be needed. They wouldn't be going into combat.

At least he hoped not.

The big helicopter lifted and dropped, lifted and dropped, each time skidding a couple of meters closer to the trees.

"Stop anticipating me, *goddammit!*" James said. "And keep your fucking eyes open. I have to see!"

The aircraft lifted off again and kept rising. Damon had a vague impression of bodies rushing in to fill the space it had vacated. Then he was above the treetops, still facing the Smithsonian. His right foot pressed down, and the late afternoon sun temporarily blinded him through the windscreen as the Pave Hawk swung around toward the north. James wasn't about to try anything fancy and waited for the helicopter to stabilize again before having Damon push the cyclic forward to get underway. A slow increase in throttle gave them more altitude.

Damon was amazed at the view, but he didn't dare look around or even move his eyes. He focused every scrap of will into keeping his body relaxed and attuned to the other force that was leading it, a dreamlike state that reminded him of the disconnected feeling in the moments before he succumbed to anesthetic.

He wondered whether any pursuit was underway. He'd sent a last quick order to the other air crews to stand down, but that wouldn't last once their real commanding officer began to tear a strip off them. Would they guess where he was headed? Probably not.

They'd be expecting him to fly straight out of the city to make his escape, so they wouldn't feel the need to risk approaching him too closely, too soon. Not over a densely populated area.

The radio began to chatter angrily, but he tuned it out, listening instead to Gordon James, who talked to himself as he led Damon through each action.

"The other chopper can't be far away," James said. "Maybe they've got more in the air by now. So, I can't give them enough time to react. I'll have to bring you in fast and dirty. Which means it's going to be rough."

Damon had a powerful urge to tighten his safety belt and glance at Jace's, but he resisted. He swallowed hard and tried not to think about what would happen if the trailing helicopter had a radio jammer.

James was true to his word. As the Pave Hawk passed over a small reservoir it began to drop sharply toward the nearest structures of a large complex ahead. At the last minute, Damon saw they were heading toward a white cross on the roof of a rectangular building. Seconds later there was a jarring bang, and they were down. He flicked some switches, and then James eased out of the connection with some forceful noises Damon didn't try to make out.

He gave Jace a quick check and a squeeze of the hand. His friend was unconscious, but still breathing. Clambering from the cockpit, he sprinted across the helipad to the door. The hospital would be alerted to the landing by now.

Taking some stairs, he came out near a nursing station and found a lab coat draped over a chair. It was too big and might not be the same as the hospital's doctors wore, but it had to do. At least no-one saw him take it. To get out, he had to navigate a bewildering series of hallways, trying not to be caught looking for signs. Finally, a window showed him a street below with heavy traffic. There was an elevator not far from him—doctors probably didn't take stairs.

On the ground floor, he found that his white garb stood out, so he tossed it behind an array of potted plants. Most of the people around him were in regular clothes: families, from the look of it. Probably a children's hospital. But someone would get Jace to the care he needed, he was sure of that.

He walked as calmly as he could through the exit doors and blinked in the bright sunlight. He also flinched at the hospital lockdown alarm just behind him.

19

October 7, 2041

"You will say that people communicate more than ever before, with messages exchanged over electronic pathways by the billions. I say that these are only cold, orphan words, without the defining human cues of vocal nuance, facial expression, body language, or touch. Such words are no more than confetti thrown upon the wind. Some will land, few will stick, none will penetrate."
      The Speeches of Damon Leiter
       Collected by V.A. Klug

The Washington Metro police held Valerie, Camillo, Jon Pak and Jody Hecht for a few hours, but there was ample video in the hands of the TV outlets to show that they'd done nothing except dodge bullets. The cops kept a guard on Jace Robbins for the better part of two weeks, so Damon couldn't visit him in person—he was officially wanted for the theft of the helicopter. Instead, he linked in by implant when the rest of their group went to the hospital. Naya was inseparable from her husband, though equal parts proud and angry. Rosa couldn't stop talking about what Valerie had done, though she herself had provided the skill. Jace would survive and heal.

It didn't need to be said that a corner had been turned, and the machinations of Dyna-Mantech and its partners, including the government itself, had reached a new level of malice.

The aftermath of the protest was demoralizing, its impact indecisive. Although nearly eighty people had been injured and nine killed, many of the injuries had been the result of trampling during the first panicked stampede. The blast on the steps of the Smithsonian had accounted for five of the deaths and twenty-eight injuries. Government releases to the media blamed it on the protestors. Jon Pak proclaimed in his media releases that the explosion had been a ploy by the military to justify their subsequent gunfire, and pointed to the fact that only civilians had been hurt, not soldiers. Government sources insisted that the anti-augment movement had now become a core of terrorists intending to accomplish their goals through violence, and they claimed intelligence that revealed the crowd that day had been infiltrated by more than a dozen suicide-bombers.

Media footage showed nothing of the kind, but several soldiers who were allowed to be interviewed under controlled conditions all swore they only fired their guns when they saw clear indications of terrorist activity.

In the face of cleverly manufactured deep-fake news, the public didn't know what to think. The event was unprecedented, and corporate media outlets had little taste for further investigation. Damon's website provided a detailed account from his perspective, including side-by-side images recorded by his implants of what he'd seen versus what the soldiers' equipment had shown them. It was a devastating indictment, but the concept was too frightening, and his evidence could be faked too easily.

One thing was all too clear: a strong precedent had been set. There were soon reports of similar protests against D-M meeting with similar violent military response in Cairo, Calcutta, Cape Town, Berlin, and Rome. Planned protests in London and Paris were cancelled. Formative plans for demonstrations in various parts of the United States lost their momentum and died. An overeager bureaucrat with the US Department of Commerce announced that an investigation into the augments was being considered; but when reporters tried to follow up on the story, the bureaucrat could no longer be found.

Dyna-Mantech itself made no announcements whatsoever about the protest movement or its accusations, refusing to be drawn into questions by the media. Instead, they offered ever more irresistible discounts and increased the prizes in the Vanquish lottery. Damon's followers looked for a response from him; but for once, he was silent.

A few weeks later, Valerie reached out to him, but he couldn't bring himself to respond. Over several days, she left messages in every possible form, including cryptic clues on his web site. Finally, late one evening, he returned her contact.

"What's the urgency?" he asked. He'd allowed an audio connection only, and her intake of breath meant that she was steeling herself for something.

"Con is dead," she said. "He killed himself. A combination of prescription pain killers and a powerful current into his brain."

Damon didn't respond for nearly half a minute. "Is there any chance it wasn't a suicide?"

"He left a note. His handwriting and fingerprints were authenticated. It just said, 'Hell is getting what you wish for, in the worst possible way'."

"That sounds like Con." After another long silence he asked, "Is there going to be a funeral?"

"There already was a cremation service. I couldn't reach you. I went. Only about a dozen other people, though."

"Not much to show for a whole lifetime."

"Is that all you've got to say? No regrets?"

"Con had…a lot of demons. I wish I could have helped him. I didn't know how."

She waited for him to say more but heard only silence.

#

In early October, US government statistics showed that the economy was like a locomotive at full throttle. The unemployment rate was 2.8%, a low not seen since the 1950s. Businesses were thriving, many announcing record quarterly profits. The Prime Rate jumped to 14.5%, as the Fed insisted it was necessary to head off serious inflation. But many bank rates were four per cent higher, and credit rates had climbed far beyond that.

Valerie reached out to Damon again, but Cancun's finest tequila had him in its grip for a few days, until he accidentally sobered up one morning.

"What do you want?"

"Nice to talk to you, too. Someone wants to see you."

"Someone wants…. Who?"

"Mark Phelps. Taggart's assistant?"

"I know who Phelps is. What does he have to do with me?"

"A lot, according to him. And don't ask me to give you a summary. He told me enough to convince me to contact you, but...he can explain it much better than I can. Damon, it *is* important—you'll want to hear him out. Mark is with the Department of Brain and Cognitive Sciences at MIT now."

"Unbelievable."

"Not every genius needs artificial help."

"Phelps is a genius now?"

She sighed. "Please tell me jealousy isn't going to come into this. Are you going to see him, or not?"

There was a long pause. "Tell me how to contact him."

"He doesn't have an implant. Not even an augment. You'll have to meet him in person. Get Gordon James to set it up—that should be secure enough for you. Mark knows your situation. He's willing to jump through hoops. Whatever will satisfy you."

"We'll see about that. OK, I'll have Gordon contact you. Was there anything else you wanted to say?"

She hesitated. "I've just put out another book. I'm going on another tour."

"That's great. I'm happy for you."

He was sincere, but judging from the way she broke the connection, she didn't believe him.

#

Phelps met him at a sports bar in Orlando's airport. They both wore casual clothes, suitable for travelling, but Damon didn't have any luggage with him. The noise from the surrounding food court was distracting, as swarms of Disneyized families dragged over-stimulated children toward McDonald's and Nathan's Famous Hot Dogs. But there wasn't much chance of an armed confrontation in such a location, either. It was a slow point in the day, and the bar was nearly empty.

"Congratulations on your professorship," Damon said. "At MIT, no less. You're pretty young for that."

"Some faculty members retired much earlier than expected. To give them time to enjoy their toys, they said." His expression seemed to ask whether Damon had caught the significance of that.

"This whole situation with brain augments is bigger than you think," Phelps continued.

"How do you know what I think?"

"OK, it's bigger than Valerie thinks. And a few other followers of yours that I've been able to speak to."

"Followers. You make me sound like some kind of guru, or wannabe prophet. I'm not. I didn't want any of this."

"No-one would want this, once you've heard what I have to say." Phelps gave his head a shake. "Mind if I order us beer?" There were no servers on duty. He waved to the bartender, then walked over to pick up two mugs of draft. When he returned, he took a long drink. As he set his mug down, he paused, as if still uncertain where to begin.

"The reason I say it's bigger is because I'm talking about the long-term implications of these augments, and not just whatever manipulation Dyna-Mantech has been up to. How much do you know about human consciousness?"

"I think, therefore I am."

"Decartes' benchmark for our sense of our own existence in a real universe. But I mean how consciousness operates."

"I didn't think anybody knew. Isn't that still one of the great mysteries of philosophy *and* neuroscience?"

"Yeah, it is. But there's growing agreement that our consciousness doesn't reside in one special place in the brain, or in some undetectable energy field separate from the body—what some people call a soul. It's an ongoing process of information reception, processing and editing that's very fluid and hard to pin down. The old analogy of a 'stream of consciousness' doesn't even go far enough. And that streaming process is very susceptible to outside influence, even after the fact."

"After the fact?"

"I mean, once our senses have perceived something, even a subtle interference or substitution immediately afterward will cause that first perception to change in our awareness, or even be edited out of our awareness entirely."

"So we might see something, but then not realise we've seen it, or think we saw something else."

"Exactly. And the new augments are so closely tied to the sensory processing centers of the brain that I think they might well have the capability to insert that kind of false information. Even more so with someone who has actual implanted electrodes, like you and Valerie."

Damon sat back. "You think Valerie and I have experienced hallucinations engineered by someone?"

"I'm not saying you have. I'm saying I think the technology is capable of it. Even on a mass scale with those Vanquish things."

"It might already have been done," Damon said. He told Phelps about the soldiers in Washington and the false images created by their Dynamic Vision Systems.

"That's something similar, yes, except I assume the soldiers have custom implants with a very particular software connection to the visual cortex. I don't think that will be required much longer. With a few more hardware and firmware upgrades, I believe almost every commercial augment will be able to insert false data, and not just into vision centers. We might begin to hear, feel, smell, and taste what Dyna-Mantech wants us to taste. And if our eyes inadvertently see something the augment is programmed to prevent us from seeing...zap, the data signal is altered, and we didn't see a thing."

Damon fell silent. Phelps's warning was horrifying; but based on what he already knew, it wasn't far-fetched.

"I'm doing everything I can to throw a monkey wrench into their machinery," Damon said. "To give people the means to deactivate the implants' subliminal functions."

"I know that, and I have to ask you to stop."

"*What?*"

"Maybe I should say to modify your techniques. You're creating a problem that could end up doing as much damage as what D-M is doing."

"That's a hell of an accusation from a guy who's sitting on the sidelines while some of us are in the middle of a war." Damon straightened and felt a powerful urge to just keep rising and walk away.

"Wait, wait. I didn't mean to accuse! You didn't know." Phelps raised his hands in apology. "It's the way people are deactivating their augments' permission circuits. When they do that, it also disables the voltage limiters governing the current the devices can deliver to the brain."

"I know. It can't be helped."

"Well, you've got to find a way. People are getting hooked on the current. You're unwittingly providing a new version of Prozac and OxyContin combined. And the timing couldn't be worse."

"What do you mean?"

"I don't suppose you read medical journals, but how about the pop headline news stuff online? Remember any mentions of clinical depression? Yeah, well, official channels are keeping their mouths shut, but depression is reaching epidemic proportions in the US. I'm not just talking about a case of the blues, I'm talking about ongoing, crippling black-dog depression. It's a looming crisis all on its own. And guess where people are turning for relief?"

"Their BCIDs."

"You got it. Our society buries people under an avalanche of choices—decisions to be made every minute of every day—and the rise in consumerism has just made it worse. We've got to keep up with our peer group; we've got to have the most prestigious brands. And in the back of our minds is the constant fear that we try to ignore: that the flow of credit will be turned off like a tap. All those little stressors accumulate into a mountain." Phelps nearly knocked over his beer as he thrust himself forward over the table. "People have tried to buy happiness for ages, especially since the advent of advertising. Then their augments began to give them little electric shots of pure pleasure when they bought something. You freed them from that, but the black market is now giving those people their own control over the current."

"It's not the black market."

"What?"

"My friend was an addict. He found out that his bootleg current modification was actually made by Dyna-Mantech themselves, in secret. Why, I don't know. Maybe just another revenue stream. Though they wouldn't want their advertising clients to find out."

"God help us!" Phelps sat back in dismay. "But that makes it even more urgent that you find a way—*some way!*— to defeat the BCIDs' subliminal controls without disabling the limiters. Direct current into the brain is just too seductive—we can't resist it."

"Dr. Taggart told me the same thing."

"I never knew you spoke to him. How much did he tell you? That probably explains his death."

"Taggart is dead?"

"Just last week. They said it was a fishing accident. No way to prove otherwise." He picked at his fingernails. "Valerie's pretty upset."

Damon gave him a puzzled look. "I need some air," he said, after a long pause. "Let's go up on the observation deck and watch some planes."

"Can't. I read a brochure. Nowadays, you have to fill out a form just to watch from the top of the terminal. That means an ID check. Photos."

"And they call *me* a terrorist. All right. Let's just wander around the parking garage and see what we can see."

Damon paid their bill with cash. The young bartender raised an eyebrow and looked confused about making change, so Damon told him to keep it. They walked without speaking to the nearest elevator, and then strode deliberately through the rows of parked cars toward the edge of the building. Security cameras might eventually bring guards to check out two men who looked suspiciously idle.

"You might wish you'd stayed for another beer," Phelps said. "'Cause I haven't even got to the main thing I wanted to talk to you about. That's a longer story. Still interested?"

"We both came a long way to get here."

"OK. Well, it comes back to the question of human consciousness, and how it works. You see, back in the 1970s a psychologist and philosopher named Julian Jaynes published a theory that claimed humans weren't truly conscious for most of our species' history. Not until sometime in the last few centuries BCE—maybe between the stories of *The Iliad* and *The Odyssey*."

"Are you serious? What about the ancient civilizations of Mesopotamia and Egypt? Besides, *The Iliad* and *The Odyssey* were both written during the same lifetime, by Homer."

"Both books are *attributed* to Homer, but most researchers don't think they were actually written by the same guy. Anyway, Jaynes claimed that ancient man had no concept of individual consciousness—no real sense of the self: of 'me' as a separate being from 'you.' No sense of extended time either. Kind of like dogs, we lived entirely in the moment, with no understanding of yesterday or tomorrow."

"That's ridiculous."

"His theory's still very influential. There's no evidence to refute it yet."

"How could farmers plan their crops? Why would they? Never mind building pyramids."

"According to Jaynes, the right hemisphere of our brains literally told us what to do. Neuroscientists have never thought the right hemisphere had much involvement in our day-to-day decision making, but Jaynes asserted that, until the last millennium BCE, it was actually running the show. When ancient man faced a decision, the right brain assessed past experience and provided an *auditory hallucination* that the man perceived as a real voice: the voice of his chieftain or of a god telling him what to do. He heard it. He obeyed that voice without question—it didn't occur to him not to. And there was no moral ambiguity involved—if the god voice said to plant, he planted; if it said kill, he killed."

"That's hard to swallow."

"Probably because I'm explaining it too quickly and too badly. But my point is, the transition to consciousness only began to happen when the humans who'd been living in fairly small, insular communities, began to interact with large numbers of strangers who were migrating over great distances at that point in history. And strangers were *different*—they didn't even answer to the same gods—and from that mingling was born the first real conception of *the other*: someone distinct from yourself, with different experiences, opinions, and feelings. Which required the first actual sense of self-awareness, and the beginning of true consciousness."

Damon turned his face away, wishing a breeze would stir the stifling air.

"What does any of that have to do with brain augments?"

Phelps nodded to himself, as if comfortable spouting other people's theories, but less certain of his own. He looked at his hands and rubbed the palms slowly together.

"In our society we like to think we're in touch with our friends all the time. Communicating all the time, with things like JoinSpace and Jabber, even email. I gather people with augments use them constantly for that. But it's all impersonal. We interact *in person* less and less every day. Instead of social activities, we spend increasing amounts of time passively soaking up entertainment or interacting with a computer. We raise our kids that way, too. And it can only get worse, thanks now to computers linked to our brains.

"I'm afraid...." He hesitated and then looked directly into Damon's eyes. "I'm afraid that we could be seeing the beginning of the *end* of human consciousness."

"Wait a minute. You think that our sense of self—our internal awareness—depends on people interacting socially, face-to-face. And as that disappears, our individual consciousness will...what? Atrophy?"

"A perfect word for it, yes. I have no proof, obviously, but that's what I'm afraid of. The human race regressing into mindless...sheep, with no individual volition. It might take generations to get that bad, but Dyna-Mantech is bringing it about faster than ever before. They—or their partners in government—may even be doing it deliberately. Probably are, in fact."

"Deliberately? Why on Earth would Dyna-Mantech—or anyone—want to cripple human consciousness."

"If Jaynes' theory was right, and individual consciousness fails, what do we fall back on?" His voice dropped to a throaty rasp.

"The voice of God, telling us what to do."

20

November 4, 2041

"I'm not a saint. Neither am I a prophet nor a savior. I'm a conduit; I'm a bridge. Maybe I'm a catalyst of sorts. One thing I am emphatically *not*, is a poster-boy for a life well-lived."
      The Speeches of Damon Leiter
       Collected by V.A. Klug

Damon was holed up in a small hotel in Little Rock, Arkansas when he read the news about Valerie.

He'd been working far too many hours, barely sleeping, trying to achieve Mark Phelps' urgent directive. He'd finally found a way to disable the subliminal functions of the Vanquish and other implants without deactivating their voltage limiters, but it was complicated. Not something he could teach an average person by video. He'd need to train people to do it, a few at a time. That wouldn't be much help to stem the epidemic Phelps feared. More like trying to empty the ocean with a spoon.

When he simply couldn't work any longer without a break, he scanned the news streams for word of Valerie's poetry tour.

Critical reviews of her second book had been even better than for her first, and it had reached bestseller lists within weeks of its release, confounding the industry a second time. When she went out on tour, there was no need to bolster attendance; but she still provided the remote viewing she'd done before, and impromptu networks of linked individuals sprang into existence with surprising speed. Valerie was far better at that than he was, and he became determined to learn how she did it. In the meantime, he linked in to occasional performances himself, just to hear her voice and see the world through her eyes and her words, trying to ignore the fact that thousands of others were experiencing it with him.

He sent a congratulatory message, but she didn't reply. Even after so much time apart, it required a conscious effort not to make more intimate contact with her. When he wasn't paying attention, the partnership of his flesh and digital brains would fall into old pathways and he'd begin to sense Valerie at the edges of his awareness. He suspected she could probably sense him, too, and he felt it was a show of weakness he was powerless to stop.

A month after the book release, the scaffold that sustained her success came crashing down.

She'd become a minor celebrity, but the first revelation didn't come from a celeb gossip site. A relatively small New England literary journal proclaimed that half a stanza from one of Valerie's new poems had been taken word-for-word from a poem by Emily Dickinson, without any attribution given. The splash was small, at first, but ripples spread. A prominent columnist did a careful comparison and found two more cases of "borrowed" verse, both, this time, from Elizabeth Barrett Browning. A poetry class at Brown University produced another two examples of evident plagiarism, including one from a poem by Maya Angelou, one of Valerie's favorites, Damon knew. That was the last that was uncovered, but it was more than enough.

In pop art and music, "sampling" of other artists' work was routine, but the literary establishment still steadfastly rejected the concept. The blogosphere burned. The rest of the tour was cancelled. Valerie's publisher was forced to issue apologies—denials weren't possible.

Damon knew that Valerie couldn't have committed plagiarism knowingly—he understood what had happened. It was like his university days after his second implant: he was no longer able to tell which information was being supplied by his biological brain and which from his electronic one. A mere thought commanded both brains to act, and the answer was supplied. Simple as that.

Except it wasn't so simple if the goal was *original* thought. The implants had access to the whole of human knowledge available online, and their use had become so automatic that attributions of sources weren't provided without a specific directive to do so.

Valerie simply hadn't known when her brain supplied her with words that were not her own.

It had happened to other writers before her— unintentional plagiarism was a particularly common trap in songwriting—but it was now easier than ever to avoid. Valerie could and should have used her implant to run comparisons of her verses with every recorded poem in the online databases. But she'd missed that step for a handful of her new poems, likely in the publisher's rush to get the new book to press while her star still shone brightly. The reason didn't matter.

As soon as he found out, Damon tried to reach her, but she'd sealed herself off from any contact whatsoever. She must have turned off the transceiver in her implant. Even her publisher didn't know where she was to be found.

The thought of what she must be going through made his chest ache. He tried to dismiss those feelings and summon the old anger, but it had grown faded and feeble. His only relief was to lose himself even more deeply in his work.

As hard as he tried, he couldn't come up with any way to simplify his new method of sabotaging the Vanquish. Some online forums claimed there were people who had the willpower to give up their BCIDs—clearly the best option of all—but they were very few. The augments offered so much that renouncing them was almost like voluntarily returning to a pre-technology lifestyle no living person remembered. And even though unofficial web surveys showed that most people accepted Damon's accusations of malfeasance, the charges didn't change anything. Startling admissions of wrongdoing by the tobacco industry hadn't been enough to eliminate smoking. Years of evidence about climate change had been ignored. Recent history provided dozens of similar examples.

No-one had yet made a safe cigarette. Could Damon hope to produce a safe brain augment? Especially from the raw material he had to work with, deliberately corrupted and booby-trapped?

He could only try. And if he couldn't make the process simple enough for people to do for themselves, he'd just have to get more help.

The breakthrough came after another failed attempt to reach Valerie. It made him think about their network of friends, and whether their combined efforts might somehow break through her shell of pain.

Network. Combined effort.

He leapt from his chair and paced the hotel room, cursing.

Valerie was the answer. She held the key. He had to find her.

And suddenly he realized where she'd be.

#

The lake was exactly the way he'd seen it in her mind: white birches and a chalet-style cottage that was too sophisticated for the term. Her mother was the same, too: slim, fashionably pale, with hair a brighter red than Valerie's, probably due more to her hairdresser than genetics. As she faced Damon, there were deep lines at her eyes and mouth matched by severe frown lines on her forehead.

"Mrs. Klug? I'm..."

"I know who you are. Why should I let a *terrorist* anywhere near my daughter?"

"I'm sure Valerie's told you I'm no terrorist. You don't trust your daughter's judgment?"

"Hasn't served her very well lately."

"I'll see him, Mom," Valerie called from the steps of the chalet. She looked more fragile than Damon could ever remember. Terrible. And wonderful.

Mrs. Klug refused to move until Valerie stood defiantly, inches from her face.

"Go, Mom. This isn't about you. Don't worry—I can handle myself around terrorists."

Even her faint hint of a smile made a weight lift from Damon's heart. He didn't say anything until her mother had gone inside.

"I'm so sorry about what happened," Damon said. "It wasn't your fault."

"It was my fault. You know that, or you wouldn't have felt the need to say it."

She turned and began to walk toward the lake. He fell into step behind her.

"Is there anything I can do to help?"

"Not unless you have a time machine."

"I've tried to reach you."

"There wasn't any point."

She stopped beside a birch at the water's edge and rested her hand on it, her touch more of a caress than a need for support. Her eyes caught some of the blue-grey of the choppy lake under an uncertain sky. Damon licked his lips, trying the air to see if it tasted of her.

"What do you want? What is it you need from me?"

"You're so sure I didn't just want to comfort a friend?"

Her mouth twitched. "You said it yourself, Damon—there's nothing left between us. I'm a soldier for the cause of neuroethics, nothing more. Why pretend otherwise? There's something you *need*, and you came a long way to get it—so just tell me." She turned to face him matter-of-factly and sat on the grass with her back against the birch. Damon folded his knees and sat nearby, leaning on an arm.

"I talked to Phelps. You were right—it is important." He told her about the meeting in Orlando, and what he'd been doing since.

"Except I need help to do the mods. A lot of help. I thought about you. About channelling, and networking. You do both of those things better than I do—you've obviously figured out some refinements of your own. I need them. I need to learn your techniques."

She let him look deep into her eyes. "You know I gave you full access to my implant once. I've never taken it away. I've just shut off my wifi and white-fi transceivers for a while. But you're close enough now for Bluetooth. Go ahead—take it. Take what you want."

"That's not what..."

"Well, what, then? You expect me to just welcome you in like nothing's changed? I can't do that."

Damon broke eye contact and stared at the ground.

"Then...then come into *my* head. I'll let you in. Give me what you think I need and no more. Whatever you decide."

"Wow. You really must be desperate. It means that much?"

"If Phelps is right, yeah, it might mean everything."

He shut down his own wifi and white-fi, and lay back on the cold grass. Then, for the first time in more than a dozen years, he let his defences down.

#

The Gallivan Center, downtown Salt Lake City's open-air 'people space' hub, was filling quickly when Damon appeared. He'd given a little more notice than usual, and he didn't know how motivated the Salt Lake City police would be to arrest a helicopter thief from faraway Washington, DC. He'd been called a terrorist in media interviews, but he'd never officially been branded with that status in law-enforcement databases. That would have required some legitimate justification. Even so, he left Camillo circling the block in a nondescript Ford sedan in case a quick getaway was needed.

As he faced north toward East 200 Street, he watched the bodies surge toward him around the empty ice-skating rink, and he began to speak—not by PA system, but over wifi, first to a young man in worn leathers, then to a girl who looked about thirteen; a man with a faded grey trench coat and black oxfords; an elderly Asian man in a loose brown grocery store uniform; an attractive black woman in spike heels. They were his prime nodes, but his words were instantly relayed from each of them to a dozen others, each of those to a dozen more. Heads turned; faces became attentive. Within seconds, everyone in the crowd was listening to him.

Damon called upon them to change their lives. He called upon them to regain their freedom and independence. He called upon them to open their minds to have the technological demons within exorcised and cast out. One by one they accepted his invitation, and their response built into a vast wave that swept across the crowd and back again. He cast his mind into the few with whom he'd begun the process and worked his cures; and as each step proceeded, it triggered identical processes in the next series of augments, and the next.

Physical touch wasn't necessary, but the would-be converts drifted dazedly toward him—he raised his hands to fend them off, touching the first ones on the hearts, then others at arm's length on the tops of their heads. Once touched, they moved away and made room for others. The crowd flowed around him like molten rock, in currents both powerful and patient. A thrum of sound began—from throats or from the friction of bodies, he didn't know. It pulsed rhythmically, hypnotically.

The first, police uniforms appeared on the fringes of the crowd; but they made no move to penetrate it. They couldn't, without giving up their own freedom of mobility. They waited.

After a half-hour, the massive current had slowed. The murmur had grown into a low roar. Then the police sensed their moment and began to thrust their way through the crush of bodies.

Damon bent to waist height and began to move, too. A quick request over wifi opened a narrow path for him to South State Street just as Camillo pulled over and flung open the car door. The police on the scene didn't even see it happen. By the time police had been informed by Surveillance Central and were able to extricate themselves from the throng, Damon and

Camillo had abandoned the car, navigated a series of restaurants and shops, and boarded the TRAX on East 400 South. As he'd often done before, Damon bent over a sink in a public washroom to spray his face and hands with a skin darkener and put on a dread cap for the sake of roadside cameras.

They got away clean.

With a new rental car, they headed south on I-15 toward Provo. Damon slouched in the seat and closed his eyes to get some rest.

"Were you able to test the altered BCIDs to see if the modification worked?" Camillo asked.

"I ran a quick test on a couple, yeah. There wasn't time for more than that. The limiters were still functioning—not just a false reading, but the real thing. I couldn't test the permission systems fully, but I'm sure the mods will work. Why? Are you suddenly having doubts?"

"To do this, you basically had control of hundreds of augments? I mean real control."

"In a progressive network, yeah. Each tier triggered actions in another tier and so on."

"Isn't that kind of...scary?"

"What do you mean? Like...dangerous? Subversive? Are you wondering if I could have made five hundred people *goose-step* around downtown Salt Lake City? It doesn't work that way."

"How do you know? Have you tried?"

"*No!* But I'm just ordering the augments to make internal changes. A BCID isn't designed to be more than a glorified information processor. It's not equipped to send impulses to the central nervous system and out to the muscles, like some kind of robot controller."

"But it might be able to interfere with the processing and editing of our stream of consciousness?"

"That's what Phelps thinks."

Camillo looked at him. His face had a slight flush, but his jaw was firm. "So, it could be possible to trick someone into doing something you wanted by altering their perceptions—like those soldiers who saw us with the faces of terrorists. Except you could even make them think they were squirting a water pistol when they were actually firing a gun. Or encourage them to step off a bridge by convincing them they were just going down stairs."

"Jesus, Camillo. I'm sure it's not that simple. I certainly don't have that kind of control."

"But somebody will, someday. And you've just figured out how to do it with hundreds of people at one time."

There was a long silence in the car after that.

#

Damon's website roved as much as he did, and just managed to keep ahead of those who sought to shut it down. Its following kept growing, and member postings became Damon's most important source of information about the so-called New Freedom of Mind movement. A few of the posts were off the wall, but most were intelligent and earnest. The news was disturbing. There were rumors of experiments in obscure parts of Africa and southeast Asia by the corporate establishment: supposed tests of countermeasures against augments protected by Damon's defensive procedures. Taggart had told him that augments were vulnerable to interference from sunspots and other radiation. A handful of postings told of augments becoming non-functional in proximity to mysterious black boxes carried by soldiers. Some augments had been permanently damaged, and one rumor claimed that the crash of the augments caused flesh brains to suffer serious collateral injury. Apparently, the scare tactics used on Con hadn't been idle threats.

Dyna-Mantech and its partners had brought a new weapon into the fray.

Damon and Camillo covered a bewildering amount of territory, stopping in large cities and smaller towns in as unpredictable a pattern as they possibly could. They took to spinning a pointer on a card to decide which direction to go next and stopped wherever Damon felt the need. It was wasteful in time and fuel, but local police forces showed no signs of having expected them. In a few cities they even appeared in one place, made their getaway, then popped up across the same town while the police were occupied at the first site. But they didn't dare do that too often.

Once in a while, in smaller centers, Camillo was able to park the car and watch the proceedings. The normal flow of pedestrian traffic would suddenly slow and fracture, with a small number of people sourly pushing ahead to keep on their original course, but the far larger number turning, almost as one, and drifting toward Damon.

Then it was no longer just pedestrians. Drivers began to heed the call. Vehicles pulled over to curbs, and when there was no more room there, they stopped in the middle of the street. Some drivers even got out of their cars and stalked away from them, like zombies answering a mystical command. Streets became gridlocked almost instantly; and on reflex, Camillo honked the horn to get Damon's attention. But that only started other horns honking, from drivers not in the loop, and Camillo had to run to Damon and pull him away before it was too late. One time, only a white-knuckle race along sidewalks and across a public park enabled them to escape a closing police net.

After that, they made sure to map out at least five potential escape routes from each site, by car, transit, or on foot.

Damon was especially exhilarated after one huge, electric gathering in New Orleans that numbered into the thousands.

"What did you think?" he asked, panting after another narrow escape.

"You just need a choir, a really expensive suit, and some plastic hair."

"What the hell is that supposed to mean?"

"Sorry. I guess lack of sleep is getting to me." Camillo rubbed his face, then tightened his grip on the wheel, blinking. "It's just that...this whole thing isn't what I expected."

"In what way?"

"I thought it would be about...*empowering* the people. Like going around the country lighting fires: we'd provide the spark and get little pockets of flame going here and there, and then the flames would spread out on their own until the whole country was on fire."

"Right. And?"

"Except it's turning out to be all about *you*."

Damon crossed his arms. "We've reached millions by now. Maybe tens of millions. The pockets you mention are spreading."

"But not fast, and not for long. When we went to Wichita the second time, a week after the first, there was no sign that the modifications had spread very far." He looked at Damon. "You need to pick *leaders* each time we stop. Maybe those 'prime nodes' of yours—maybe somebody else, but there has to be a presence left behind to keep things going."

"That would put them at risk."

"Well, you can bet a lot of those people have been picked up and questioned by police anyway. Closed circuit cameras would show who responded to you first, and the cops will want to know why. So, they're already suspects. And maybe there are people willing to *take* that risk, for the sake of what we're doing. We don't have a monopoly on sacrifice."

"You mean *I* don't. That's what you're saying, isn't it?"

Camillo didn't answer.

"I'll think about it," Damon sighed, and closed his eyes.

Camillo had made some very valid points, but what disturbed Damon just as much was the bitterness in the man's voice. How had he not heard that before? He'd been so focused on their mission that he'd only ever seen Camillo as the naïvely eager recruit he'd once been. If the man's unquestioning loyalty was weakening, it probably was Damon's fault, but he had no idea what to do about it. Maybe he was going to have to find a replacement. It was yet another task added to a growing list.

#

They were in Seattle when they saw Ebon Parrish's face on a newsfeed. Ebon was leading a demonstration in Brooklyn, a big one that was getting lots of coverage. He was giving a speech, backed by thousands of chanting protesters. Damon was surprised, and proud of him.

"Throughout history," Ebon was saying, "governments with corrupt agendas dealt with their people in two ways: they oppressed them, or they distracted them. Robespierre gave the people a steady supply of sacrifices to the guillotine. Hitler invented a conspiracy of Jews. Our governments today encourage far more congenial distractions. Consumerism has now become the opiate of the masses, and it is self-perpetuating. We must not let ourselves fall under its sway."

A roar from the crowd brought a look of satisfaction to Ebon's face. Then the camera shifted to a line of soldiers slowly approaching. They'd made their way to within less than ten meters of where Ebon stood. Damon clutched the arm of his chair.

Two of the soldiers were carrying a cylindrical black box about the size of a guitar case.

The cameras didn't show Ebon's collapse, but they swung around in time to find him limp on the ground, and other protestors nearby staggering into each other. There was a scream, and then more, and the crowd began to back away in frightened confusion. The news feed became chaotic: little more than flashes of stumbling feet, thrusting arms, terrified faces, scraps of cloudy sky, then more jumbled bodies jostling and slipping, seen mostly from behind and off-kilter. After that the screen went blank, and an anchorperson appeared, floundering for something to say.

Damon and Camillo looked at each other, appalled. They began to throw clothes into suitcases.

They risked a flight back to New York. Valerie knew what hospital Ebon had been taken to, and met them there, but all three were well-disguised and entered separately. When they got to Ebon's room Rosa was already on hand, dressed in scrubs.

"Did you...?" Damon began.

"No, I didn't operate on him," Rosa said. "I only do general surgery, but these clothes get me through the door. And access to his charts, as long as nobody's watching too closely." She tried to smile, but tears welled in her eyes instead. "It's bad, Damon. It's very bad."

"Is he dying?"

"No." She snatched a Kleenex from a small table and dabbed her eyes. "Death might be better."

As Damon stepped toward the bed, he was shocked to find Ebon's eyes open. They were unfocused and wandering, but after a moment they discovered Damon's face, and the limp mouth twitched as if trying to smile. Ebon made a guttural sound in his throat, but if it was a word, Damon didn't recognize it.

"Is he trying to talk? What's he saying?"

"I think...," Rosa began. "I think he's trying to say *Nirvana*."

"Nirvana? Why would he...?"

Rosa beckoned him away from the bed, and the four visitors gathered in the far corner of the room. It wouldn't prevent Ebon from hearing them, but it was easier than looking at the unsettling expression on his face.

"I've talked to the doctors treating him," Rosa said quietly. "I've even seen some brain scans. His implant is fried—completely non-functional. But...." She took a ragged breath. "It took the left hemisphere of his brain with it."

Valerie flung her hand to her mouth. Camillo gagged and turned away, breathing hard.

Damon closed his eyes and pushed a knuckle hard under his nose. After a long moment he looked up at Rosa. "Why would he try to say *Nirvana*?"

"I'm really only guessing, but as I'm sure you know, the right hemisphere of our brains operates separately from the left, and in a very different way. Some compare it to a parallel processor, in computer terms. In essence, it lives only in the present moment: a continual processing of incoming data with no restriction of linear time. Some people who've recovered from severe left-brain damage have said that they couldn't distinguish the boundaries of their bodies. Couldn't separate their own molecules from the molecules of their surroundings. Or from some pervasive flow of energy outside *and inside* themselves."

"At one with the universe," Valerie said.

"That's right. They existed in a universal 'here and now', at one with everything around them. And at peace."

"Nirvana," Damon breathed.

"That doesn't sound so terrible," Camillo said.

Rosa looked at him. "The left hemisphere is where our logical thought happens. Our concept of self. Our sense of time, space, organization, *purpose*. It's also where our language centers are. Without them we not only can't speak or write, we can't understand speech or writing. That left brain is where the person you know as Ebon Parrish lives. Without that, what's really left behind?" Her eyes teared up again.

"But you said people have recovered." Valerie rested a hand on Rosa's arm. "I remember hearing about a woman, a neurologist or something, who recovered enough to lecture about it."

"Yes, but Dr. Bolte Taylor's injury wasn't as pervasive as Ebon's." Rosa rubbed a hand down her face. "There's still activity in many parts of his left hemisphere, but right now those places can't talk to each other. Could he recover? God, I hope so. But it will take a hell of a long time, and he may never completely heal. I'm afraid...we've lost our friend." Her voice choked off with a sob, and she turned into Valerie's waiting arms. Damon was shaken to see a woman of such strength so wrenchingly heartbroken. He hadn't realised that she and Ebon had connected so deeply. He should have.

He stepped toward the window and gripped the vinyl frame, not noticing when it snapped.

"We didn't lose him," his voice rumbled. "He was taken from us."

21

January 8, 2042

"Have you experienced the smell of rust and ozone that is wifi? The acrid taste of corrupted data? The tentative touch of another's mental presence? Strong network connections spark bright colors; signal interference is gratingly loud. All of these are new tricks from old sensory apparatus. Don't try to tell me that the human animal no longer evolves."
The Speeches of Damon Leiter
Collected by V.A. Klug

Ebon Parrish's mindless face tormented Damon when he tried to sleep.

Ebon was a martyr for neuroethics—another sacrifice. How many more sacrifices would be demanded? And would it be worth it? Did the people of the world even care about the battle that was being fought on their behalf? Almost certainly not. As Ebon himself had said, governments had chosen the most congenial of distractions: shiny baubles to enthral hapless victims until quicksand rose over their heads. "Bread and circuses," as the Roman Juvenal put it.

Damon had not been spared. He'd sacrificed all semblance of a normal life. He faced constant danger, and was willing to take even greater risks, if needed. But not what had been done to Ebon. That was a fate he couldn't face.

Valerie was stunned to see him at her door.

"What are you doing here? Don't you know I must be watched?"

"I'm packing new hardware—I can stir up some hefty interference of my own, now."

"A gun?"

"No, I mean interference. Electrical interference." Damon opened his jacket to show a strap-on packet. "Makes surveillance systems loop back on themselves, replaying random lengths of footage. Believe me, nobody saw me come in."

She stepped out of the way to let him enter the apartment, then hurriedly shut the door and faced him.

"You still didn't say why you're here."

"I want you to come away with me."

"*What?* Where?"

"Underground. Deep cover. Mostly in other countries—the US is getting just too hot."

"Why would I do that? Why do you want me to?"

"For your own safety."

Her shoulders slumped and she turned away. "Not a good enough reason."

"Valerie, I'm not joking. You saw what they did to Ebon. And they got away with it. They claimed it was a cerebral hemorrhage, and the other victims were on drugs—and *people believed them!* The news channels dropped it like…"

"I know that, Damon. The major news outlets are all corporately owned, and the small ones have taken the hint. They're willing to risk having their knuckles rapped, but not having their brains fried."

"Exactly. Our popularity doesn't mean squat."

"It's notoriety not popularity, Damon. *Your* notoriety. I'm only notorious for being a poetry thief."

"Even worse. Dyna-Mantech and their allies could make you disappear, and no-one would ever connect it to them."

"I'm not going on the run with you. If they saw me as any kind of threat, they'd have dealt with me already. Clearly, they don't. And they're right. I'm not the leader of the forces against them—I never could be. All they could want from me is information about you, and they haven't managed that either. That's a bad sign. I'm not sure what it means."

"Be thankful. But they could still take you—kidnap you to draw me out."

"They could have done that anytime, too, but they haven't. So, they won't."

"You don't know that. It could just be a card they're holding in reserve; and by staying vulnerable, you let them hang on to that card to use whenever they want."

"Or they may just prefer to leave me where I am, figuring you'll do something stupid like showing up at my apartment. You'd better go."

"Valerie." He started to reach out a hand but stopped himself. "I'm...just thinking about what happened to Ebon. That changes everything."

She looked at his hand, then at the floor. "You're not doing him any good here. You need to be out there, finding a way to *stop* them! By all means, hide somewhere deep undercover—but escalate the fight! Take the gloves off! I'll stay here to let them think...nothing's changed." She turned her head. He followed the look and saw a picture on an end table: the two of them sitting on a rock beside the ocean. "Don't even tell me where you are," she said. "You can't trust me not to tell them."

"But I do trust you. With my life."

"You just don't trust me with your heart. Goodbye, Damon."

#

From his window on the sixth floor of the Ipanema Plaza Hotel, Damon looked north toward the Corcovado and the statue of Christ the Redeemer. It was a sweltering forty-two degrees Celsius on the other side of the glass, and the air conditioning struggled to keep up. He felt a powerful urge to join all the tourists that filled the hotel and simply walk down to the beach to find oblivion in sun, salt-water, and sangria. Maybe later.

He should probably have picked a more obscure hotel—there was a chance that one of the American guests might recognize his face from news feeds. On the other hand, he didn't stand out among the many foreigners in the place. He'd also acquired a bleached crew-cut and a three-week-old mustache. With wire-rimmed John Lennon dark glasses, that ought to be enough to provide anonymity.

There was lots of wifi and white-fi around, but what he really wanted was powerful broadband, and with Rio's infrastructure having been thoroughly upgraded ten years earlier, it would do.

There was no point delaying. He lay down on the bed and made himself comfortable. Then he began to cast his mind far afield.

First, he reached out for the VeriSign root servers in Brasilia. It took a few minutes—not too hard to find. He memorized their texture, and a faint lemony tang at the back of the throat. Then he tasted again, seeking similar flavors. Toronto. Edinburgh.

London—that's what he wanted.

He allowed his tight focus to unravel a little, and immediately he was nearly overwhelmed by the traffic. A chaotic ocean of sensations. His brain fought to categorize the bombardment of signals, organize them into smells and tastes and mouth textures, from acid sour to a floral delicacy. Burnt coffee. Bleu cheese. Sardine oil. Lavender.

He knew he'd recognize the distinctive character of a Vanquish augment, but it was like facing into a wind filled with grains of spices, raising and lowering his nose, first riding waves of sensation, then letting them break over his face.

There. He found one. More.

He concentrated on the initial contact and assessed its status. Still fully compliant to Dyna-Mantech—not protected or modified. As he'd expected—he hadn't made many inroads into the UK, which was why he chose London for his experiment.

He didn't want to use language since that would limit him to English-speaking countries. So, with a series of images, sound tones, and brief examples of what he wanted to do, he requested permission to make modifications. The connection stuttered—a manifestation of extreme anxiety, probably a rejection. That was hardly surprising. He was a sudden, unexpected, and unknown presence on the fringe of the mind. A mental spectre. He eased out, and tried someone else, but the reaction was the same. Anxiety, then outright fear.

Had he been foolish to expect anything else? The changes he offered were radical, and invasive. Almost everyone in developed nations would have heard rumblings about subterfuge involving the augments, but most would be in denial, unwilling to risk the loss of so much convenience and wonder. His mass modification events had involved people who knew about him, who'd already made the decision to seek his intervention. Strangers would have none of the same trust, and a whole lot of healthy fear.

What could he do? Show them a picture of himself? A resume? The link to his Wikipedia page?

Camillo had been right. He needed a local coordinator in each area. He'd begun to do that in the States, but then Ebon's injury had derailed the program. Could he find an ally in London that other Londoners would trust?

One of Tamao Kagami's associates had moved back to England. A lord. No, an earl. Damon's implant remembered the ID of the man's Vanquish, and connected instantly.

The earl was a distant member of the royal family, but with a good public profile because of his charity endeavors. He was willing to help. Damon upgraded the man's augment to the latest protected status with its voltage limiter restored, then guided him as they sent out probing fingers together.

A contact. Another. Three more. Another five.

Damon's new net spread quickly, each recruit learning the drill and recruiting more. London turned out to have been a good choice because many of the people were well-informed. They knew of Damon, and they knew that his promise of protection without loss of functionality had been verified throughout the US.

When Damon judged that a critical mass had been reached, he left the earl and his new network to carry on and then slumped into an exhausted sleep.

That night he tried it again in Brazil. He knew a prominent priest in Sao Paulo whom he could trust, and who trusted him. And the strategy was successful again.

Next, he followed the course of the sunset, making contact with a magazine photographer in Bolivia and a ship's captain in port in Peru. He rested until morning, then went to work again. During breaks, he made changes to his website to alert his supporters to expect his presence with them at any time, and invited them to volunteer their help if they could do so without compromising their own safety. He created a multi-level electronic persona of himself that was infused through each connection: a signature and stamp of approval all in one, instantly identifiable by its digital DNA.

Within weeks, the impact of his quiet efforts was becoming evident throughout the world. Smaller governments issued warnings to their people, but the larger countries didn't bother. They knew it was pointless. Damon tapped into Dyna-Mantech's internal communications, but the company stayed stubbornly quiet. Their executives were surely discussing the situation, but they were doing so in person, with their own augments virtually locked down.

Damon was jubilant. He took a day off to spend on the beach and was rewarded with a bad sunburn and a cracker of a hangover.

Now it was time for the next step.

#

He'd initiated a network of millions: a kind of unregulated human internet. And in doing so, he'd gathered the ID signatures of all of those augments. Each of them had unused computing capacity. Wasted work cycles. He needed those—his own implants could only do so much. So, he took a page from the SETI@home project, the famous initiative that had persuaded supporters to donate surplus processing capacity on their home computers to help analyse radio signals in the search for extraterrestrial intelligence. Damon began to recruit surplus brainpower. He didn't need permission to tap individual augments, but he sent out a mass request for compliance anyway, then was too impatient to wait and went ahead with his plans.

A sense of urgency he couldn't explain made him feel as if his life's work was building to a climax; and now, timing was critical. He had few qualms left about personal privacy. The need was too great. He built his networks anew and tapped into hundreds of thousands of nearly idle augments, then ultimately millions, all just waiting to be given a command.

He gave it. ImagiCap's servers were still securely protected, and Damon intended to change that.

Although he was only in direct control of a couple of dozen BCIDs, he immediately sensed the cumulative power of the rest, surging like liquid fire through his veins one moment, crackling like a skin of lightning the next. Breaching ImagiCap's security protocols was child's play. He gave a clarion call on his cybernetic trumpet, and the corporate servers came crashing down like the walls of Jericho.

In the full force of his exultation, he felt a new element that made him sit bolt upright in the bed.

It was...*consent*. Approval. Some of the users of the conscripted augments were becoming aware of his presence and wanted to know more. He embraced their manifestation, and folded them into the mass of activity, welcomed others, and still more, so many more. He wrapped them together, spun them into a larger entity. An all-consuming curiosity. A nebulous whole that struggled for cohesion.

He stretched out his mind. He was in Hamburg, and Hanoi. Bangkok, Brisbane, and Bombay. He braved night-time darkness and basked in fierce sunlight. He was asleep, awake, shovelling dirt, and making love. He was everywhere, and he was not himself.

He was....

Something else. Something entirely *new*!

#

It was only after a night's rest that he could begin to define what had happened. In machine terms, although he'd begun with what would have been called distributed computing, it had become much more. After all, these computers were linked directly to human brains. No silicon or graphene or even RNA computer had yet come close to a consciousness of its own. But the latest generation of BCIDs were so closely integrated with human consciousness, that even Damon couldn't be certain where one left off and the other began.

He kept shaking his head, his rational mind trying to reject the direction his logic was leading. It was impossible to deny that he had interlinked millions of computers in concerted function in real time. And those computational links had brought with them a spillover of consciousness: elusive, transitory fragments, yes—but undeniably *consciousness*. Which meant that they, too, had been linked. Didn't it? A vast cloud: droplets of human awareness piggybacking on a net of electrons. Or looked at the other way: a cold framework of ones and zeroes overlaid with a warm skin of who, what, where, when, and why.

Of what else is a mind made?

For those brief moments, the global network he had forged had carried on its back a global awareness.

A group *mind*. A *global* mind.

He was numbed. Awestruck. At a loss about what to do.

Except to try it again.

For a long time, he was too agitated to concentrate, unable to ignore the distractions of samba music coming through the floor, the snorting and wheezing of the air conditioning, and sand grating between his toes. But years of practice took hold, and he entered a trancelike state. He felt for the invisible data pipeline carried on the air, tapped the pulse of its electric veins and arteries, and poured his mind into its labyrinthine channels. The digital network coalesced and spread like crystals in time-lapse video. He gave it a task to do. Then he held his mental breath and listened for the whisper of other voices.

They came. By ones. By twos. Then dozens, and scores. Exclamations and queries, puzzled mutterings and extemporaneous music. Voices that swelled and waned, prismed into harmonic and cacophonic layers, then blended slowly, slowly, slowly into a homogeneous whole as Damon moulded and sculpted this new consciousness with mental fingers until it hummed with life and vibrant expectancy.

He asked it a question:

What is the antidote to consumerism?

Answers floated to the surface like bubbles:

Love. Purpose. Fulfillment.

There were others, but they perished before they could be grasped, thin foam on the sea of thought.

He revelled in the euphoria of the moment, a headier joy than the previous day's revenge upon his enemies. He yearned to ask questions of cosmic dimensions. Instead, he came to understand a profound truth: that this new entity was not for his use, but for its own.

Look at yourself, he said to it, *and know that you **are**.*

#

He awoke not knowing where he was, not entirely certain *who* he was. The practical mechanisms of his implants came instantly to his service and re-established factual reality, but his heart raced as if he'd just stepped back from a precipice.

That way lay madness. That way lay loss of identity.

If he weren't careful, he could end up like Ebon Parrish. The awareness he had cultivated, the mind to which he had helped give birth, was not a toy. It was not his to do with as he would. It was probably the greatest threat he had yet faced. The greatest temptation.

Master or monster?

He remembered Nietzsche: *"And if you gaze long enough into an abyss, the abyss will gaze back into you."*

He had almost lost himself in it. He dared not flirt with it again without much greater wisdom than he now possessed.

There must be those in the world who would know how to deal with such an entity. Priests? Brahmas? The Dalai Lama, or the Pope? Probably not even them, but someone. He would search, for as long as it took.

But first he had to tell Valerie and the others.

He reached out for her over the 'net and was surprised to find her implant waiting open to him.

"Valerie...."

"Damon, were you responsible for the crash of ImagiCap's servers yesterday? All around the world? You did it, didn't you?"

"Yes, but I..."

"But what? It's a little late for remorse, isn't it?"

"Remorse? What do you mean?"

"Did you think ImagiCap existed in isolation? You wanted revenge for Ebon—I get that. But you must have known how many other companies would crash with it. The chaos in the global stock markets."

She must have sensed his confusion and suppressed some of her anger. "If you really didn't think about that, think now. Countries around the world will be forced to *bail them out*, after all the harm they've done. Taxpayers' money used to save those bastards. Money that should have gone to health care and education. It's either that, or risk letting national economies go down the toilet. You've resurrected ghosts of every financial crash since the invention of capitalism. You may have surpassed them all."

"God, Valerie, I..."

"Don't make excuses. When you play with that kind of power there are realities you need to face, goddamnit!"

"But you told me to escalate. To take the gloves off!"

Her long silence was followed by a sigh like a sob. "I had no idea.... I don't think even you know what you're capable of."

Their connection was still so strong that Damon's body was suffused with heat, and he didn't know if it was her anger or his own shame.

He wanted to tell her about his discovery, but the taste of triumph had turned to ash.

After another long silence, she cleared her throat and said, "Speaking of things you need to face, one of those is waiting for you now."

"What do you mean?"

"Reinhardt Janus was just here."

"*Just there?* In your apartment?"

"He left you a message. He said, tell Damon: *I am the archive he's been hunting for.*"

22

January 25, 2042

"Power has always belonged to those with the most currency. The first currency was food. Then came money. The new currency is the control of information. And now, more than ever, the world is divided into those who have, and those who have *not*."

The Speeches of Damon Leiter
Collected by V.A. Klug

"I hear you're a little short on money. I think I can spare five bucks."

Damon stepped out from behind a steel beam, with his hands in his pockets.

H. Reinhardt Janus looked up quickly from a digiscroll in his hand. He was a small man, but impeccably dressed in a navy-blue suit. His full head of dark hair had random patches of grey. His smile was broad and seemed genuine.

"Very good, Mr. Leiter. Not your attempt at humor, but your success at getting through our building security. I counted on it—I even arranged for some...weak spots in our network, shall we say. But still, an impressive feat. Of course, without walls on these upper floors yet, there aren't any cameras either."

"You need government bailouts, but you're still going ahead with new headquarters?"

"Oh, your mischief might slow the project down a little, but not for long. I was just making a few adjustments to the plans. For the office of the Director of Strategic Responses." He flashed another smile. "Which is me."

"I'm sorry. I thought you were Director of the Ministry of Truth."

"Ah, Mr. Leiter—or should I call you Damon? Or David perhaps, wielding his sling on the battlefield? Orwell got many things wrong. And many right. People do want to be coddled and duped. *Ignorance Is Strength*—he was definitely right about that. But there is no Big Brother oligarchical government, and there won't be. Russia tried that, and look where they wound up. Business and government partnering together—that's the way of the future. The way of the present, for that matter. Why does that bother you so much?"

"A small thing called personal freedom."

Janus laughed. There was a simple plastic chair nearby. He sat in it, put his d-scroll on the floor, and crossed his legs. "Most people don't know what to *do* with freedom, Damon. They think it means freedom to buy things—bigger and better *things*—and we've given them that."

"What about integrity of self? Freedom of privacy?"

"Do you really think you're the one to lecture me about that?"

Damon looked at him. There was no other place to sit, so he slouched against the beam behind him.

Standing should have given him a psychological advantage, but Janus acted as if it was the other way around.

"Your message said you're the archive."

"And so I am. There are no paper records of what you're looking for. Certainly not in one place. That was a ruse. Bait. Digital records are very carefully distributed among many secure sites, where they are unlikely to be connected to each other even if they are discovered. The only place they are all gathered together is right here." He tapped a finger to his head.

"No man could remember that much detail."

"You do."

"Because of my..." Damon's eyes widened. "Ah. You have an implant."

"Yes. But before you try to bludgeon your way into it, I should tell you that mine has no outside connections. No wifi, no white-fi, no Bluetooth. It can only be accessed with a physical connection, and there is none of the necessary hardware in this building." His smile was forced this time. "Or do you think you might just kill me and cut me open? You could. And your reward would be a completely inert lump of exotic metals and rare earths."

"You're...quite a piece of work."

"A megalomaniac. Isn't that what you wanted to say? Except I'm not. I'm a family man. I have a wife, and a son. He's almost the same age as you, as a matter of fact." He lightly rubbed the bridge of his nose, as if he'd once worn glasses.

"Yeah, I was surprised to find out about that. But not surprised to find that he hates your guts. That he ran away to South America to get away from you."

Janus's grey eyes sparked. "Wilhelm had the bad luck to be born into wealth, with a father who was extravagantly successful. It sometimes takes radical measures to forge your own identity with a background like that. Much easier for a child of parents who never amounted to anything."

Damon didn't rise to the bait. "And I'm sure Mrs. Janus is a good Stepford wife and diligent consumer, perfectly happy as long as she gets a new string of pearls every second week. Does she know what you really do?"

"My wife chairs two charitable boards: one of them helps children with AIDS, the other provides housing for single mothers with chronic health problems. She spends much of her week visiting young people in hospital."

"So the answer is no."

Janus had become upright in his chair. Now he relaxed again.

"You remind me of my son in some ways, Damon. That's part of the reason you're still alive."

"The other part is because your operatives were incompetent."

"You're quite wrong. We weren't involved in any of the attempts on your life. In fact, we've tried very hard to keep you alive. Just as we worked to smooth your path all your life. You were quite an investment—why would we want to destroy that?"

"You expect me to take your word for it?"

"Those...farcical acts of violence were the work of rogue elements in government. Perhaps even different ones each time—I honestly don't know. I told them again and again that we needed you *alive*; but it really is true: the right hand doesn't know what the left hand's doing." He seemed genuinely annoyed. Damon was at a loss.

"Why would you want me alive, and the government want me dead?"

"Only some elements in the government. The men at the top, they understand our work and know better. Come, now. You're a smart man. Who do you think needs all of those 'extra features' in the Vanquish? ImagiCap?" He shook his head. "Come *on!* We're a business. We can make all the money we could ever want just by influencing people to buy things. Which we did, very effectively. Why would we need more than that? *Controlling* people isn't our line—it's counter-productive and way too labor-intensive. Not worth doing. Unless some very rich clients want it done."

"The government."

"You think only the US government could have such motives? You really are naïve. No big government can resist a temptation like that—they can justify it to themselves any number of ways. That's the easy part."

"So the government came after me. Why? Because I knew about *Dynamic Vision Systems*—tricking soldiers into seeing innocent citizens as terrorists?"

"Oh, it goes far beyond that. They were afraid of you. Afraid you'd find out things. Afraid that you could read minds."

"I can't read minds. I can only read augments."

"Which would have a record of all orders issued and about to be issued. A record of all logistical information required for a soldier to carry out those orders. Whether or not you could tell if a captain lusted for his colonel's secretary is of no importance. But if secret orders were to be compromised...." Janus was smiling again, but it was almost regretful. And there was no mistaking the condescension in his voice. "They were afraid you would learn how to *divert* their soldiers' carefully-constructed loyalty, and eventually control the soldiers themselves."

"That's ridiculous. I'd never be able to control a human body. I've...*channeled* actions with my body that were directed by others, but they didn't control it against my will. Augments aren't made to work that way."

"But if they were altered to *have* that capability, you would learn how to use it. Of that I have no doubt."

Damon pushed lightly away from the support beam and began to walk the rough, unfinished floor. The scuffle of his footsteps echoed indistinct sibilants, like whispers, from distant surfaces.

"Good God. Dynamic Visions Systems isn't enough—the government wants direct control. And what do you mean by *constructed loyalty*?"

"You've heard of the brain's 'God spot'—I know you have. It's actually quite easy to stimulate, once you know how. Just think of the advantage of having soldiers..."

"...who think their commanders are gods."

"Or at least godlike in their wisdom. Of course, a soldier's rational mind would never parse it that way. But the subconscious...."

"Then why not do that to everyone? The whole voting population? A governing party would never be defeated."

"Orwell again. Believe me, there are simpler ways to control sheep. Oh, I suppose some might try it. Our Russian friends, perhaps. But the real danger of being too Machiavellian is that you can never be sure when you'll suddenly go from being the oppressor to the oppressed."

Damon rubbed his forehead and paced. He felt like he was in a nightmare. As if his implant had been short-circuited and was spewing forth his worst fears.

Janus sat beneath a harsh fluorescent light, but Damon felt as if he was the one under interrogation.

"None of that explains why you've decided to kill me now." He saw the reaction in Janus's eyes. "Of course, you've lured me here to kill me, haven't you? You know you can't recruit me, and somehow I have the feeling it's not about getting information from me, either."

"We don't need it."

"But you couldn't have thought I'd come here defenseless. Every word we're saying right now is being spread along the network from my implants. To thousands. Millions. Will you kill me in front of all of them?"

"Check your network feed a little deeper, Damon. Test a few sample connections." Janus's smile was exultant. "That's right. Your signals aren't going anywhere. They're being caught in an electronic net around this building, the very one you thought you could use to amplify your transmission. But we aren't as blind as all that. What's coming back to you are only simulations. Do you see it? Spoofing. False data handshakes. Shallow user profiles. Anyone paying attention would quickly sense the duplicates and inconsistencies. Except you weren't paying attention to it. Only to me."

Damon felt the pounding of his heart reverberate amongst the girders. He had gambled against Death so many times, but this time he had lost. He was alone after all. Standing again on the edge of a bottomless shaft, powerless to stop his fall.

"Then why kill me? Because I finally hurt ImagiCap too badly, by crashing your servers?"

"You're *still* not seeing the big picture. Your friend Ebon Parrish was right: consumerism *is* the new opiate of the masses. It's how ImagiCap makes money. It's good for governments, too, because it keeps the economy stimulated and distracts the people from seeing what's going on around them. But there are antidotes. A sense of purpose. Meaningful work. Deep religious faith. And most of all, human social interaction. *That*'s where you've been doing your damage.

"All on their own, the people of the world have been isolating themselves from each other for decades. Choosing solitary pursuits. Moving all over the place so they sever themselves from any support group they had. All of those things create a breeding ground for consumerism like sugar in a petri dish of bacteria. We gave a few little pushes, but they were hardly necessary." Janus sat forward. "But you threaten to undo it all and enable people to find fulfillment in each other, with your extraordinary mental intimacy, and now even your *group mind*, or whatever you've labelled it."

Damon couldn't stifle a gasp. "How did you know about that? I haven't told anyone."

The expression on Janus's face was unmistakable: a snake approaching a frog. "Did you really think you'd shut down all of our surveillance signals from your implant? That's your greatest weakness, Damon. Overconfidence. We've been receiving information all along. I'll grant you that it was a mistake not to include a GPS, or some way to track you. But we always knew what you were doing."

Damon felt his face grow warm. "But not what I was planning to do. Or you would have caught me as I travelled the country. Stopped me from crashing your servers."

Janus acknowledged the point with a tilt of his head.

"Then you know what Mark Phelps believes," Damon continued. "That this same isolation you're talking about could threaten the very consciousness of the human race. And *you're OK with that?*" He was disconcerted to hear his voice crack.

"Mr. Phelps is a hysterical alarmist. And *you*—you would create a *group mind*, a global consciousness spanning the Earth. Like a next step in evolution! Which of us is really the greater threat to the future of humanity?"

Damon's shoulders sagged. He felt drained of energy, wearier than he had ever felt before.

"If you saw all the things I was doing, you could also see where it was going," he said softly. "Why didn't you kill me before now? It wasn't because I remind you of your son."

"This is the best part. It's because you were doing our work *for* us." Janus's eyes gleamed.

"No."

"Of course you were. You found elegant ways to infiltrate augments, reliably and surreptitiously. You deactivated the voltage limiters that the government had to legislate for the sake of appearances."

"I reversed that. Among millions."

Janus shrugged. "Too late. Your reversal modifications can also be reversed, now that we know how they're done. It was you who pioneered all the breakthroughs of remote viewing, stimulating the pleasure centres, every basic process behind the Dynamic Vision System, and much more. You achieved more than a whole division of Dyna-Mantech had done. You and your lover." Janus laughed. "And then the biggest gift: the means to network thousands of augments together. *And control them.*" His voice dropped to a deep hiss. "I was the one who convinced Taggart to make you the way you are, Damon. You could say I created you. But even I had no idea how useful you would turn out to be."

A wave of nausea made Damon turn away and he nearly retched. The aftermath left him shaking. Finally, he turned a ghostly face back to Janus.

"So what now?" he rasped. "I've outlived my usefulness? You're going to what? Shoot me?"

"You've become too powerful. And unpredictable. I can't justify the risk any longer. But I'm not going to kill you." He took a phone from his pocket and pressed the screen. "Someone else wants that pleasure."

The sound of a door made Damon turn. A figure was stepping into the open about ten meters away.

Camillo Ricci.

He was wearing a tented mesh loosely over his clothing. It looked metallic.

And he was carrying a black box.

23

January 25, 2042

"Prometheus stole fire from the gods and was punished with unending evisceration. Icarus dared to fly too close to the sun and was cast back down to Earth. What punishment awaits those with the hubris to gather the collected wisdom of a whole world?"
The Speeches of Damon Leiter
Collected by V.A. Klug

"Camillo. Please God, not you."
"You betrayed us, Damon. *Demon.* You betrayed all of us." Camillo's face was ashen, and his hands trembled, but as he stepped slowly forward, black box held in a firm grip. "You've been doing ImagiCap's work all along. You've belonged to them ever since you were a kid."

Damon's legs wouldn't support him any longer. He collapsed to his knees.

"I didn't.... I didn't know. God help me. I didn't know." Tears welled in his eyes and a rivulet spilled down his left cheek.

"I tried to tell you it was too dangerous. Too much access. Too much control. *I tried to tell you!*" Camillo shook with rage and fear. He wiped a hand under his nose, breathing heavily, and took another deliberate step. "But you wouldn't listen. You had to play God. You had to *be* God. There's only one God, Damon. And it's not you." He raised the box.

"*No, Camillo*. Think about what you're doing. If you fire that thing, you're dead."

"No, I'm not. The weapon is highly directional; but even if it wasn't, this mesh is a Faraday cage. It'll protect me from the EMP. The soldiers have augments that are specially shielded, but this will work even better."

"That's not what I mean. Once you've done what ImagiCap wants, you'll be a liability. They won't let you live. They can't."

Camillo looked at Janus, who said nothing.

"I'm not as stupid as you've always thought, Damon. I know they can kill me any time. They always could. I'd never be able to run far enough, hide well enough. I've accepted that. What matters is that this time we agree on something." His voice began to crack, as he fought to keep back tears. "You're too dangerous, Damon. You have to be stopped. Goodbye, my friend."

He raised the weapon and triggered it, his tears splashing on its black surface.

Damon had opened his mouth to cry out, but in mid-motion he twitched hard in a grotesque spasm. His body vibrated. The air around him crackled. Then he slumped heavily and toppled to the floor.

"*Damon!*"

The shriek came from the far end of the room still obscured in shadow. Valerie ran into the light, tried to stop as she saw the body, and collapsed awkwardly onto her knees.

"*No!* she wailed. "No, no. Please God, no." Her body became racked with sobs as she dragged herself to Damon's side. His mouth and eyes were open. But he didn't see.

"It's very unfortunate that you're here, Ms. Klug," Janus said, his mouth tight. "There was no need for you to witness this. Perhaps I'm to blame. I should have reactivated our building's security net once Damon was inside. You somehow planted a tracker on him? I was not informed that you had such skills." The look he gave her crackled with suspicion. "No matter. How you got here is not important."

He turned his gaze to Camillo. "What *is* important is that *you*, Mr. Ricci, now have a problem. You also have the weapon with which to solve it."

Camillo's mouth hung open.

"No. Not Valerie! I can't...it was different with Damon. Damon had to be stopped." His red face glistened with tears and saliva. The EMP box hung limply from his hand.

"Damon was wrong. ImagiCap isn't going to kill you, Camillo. We need you to tell the rest of your people about how Damon betrayed your movement. How he's not the *martyr* they will try to make him out to be. A warning to others who might follow him, or try to replace him. But Dr. Klug? She knows what you've done. You won't be able to...*select* the things you tell. The world will only see you as an assassin."

Camillo gave a wrenching sob, then gripped the black box with his other hand and slowly raised it.

The sound of a suppressed gun barely made an echo in the huge room. The clatter of the EMP weapon falling on the concrete was far louder. And then a thud as Camillo's head hit the floor.

Janus leapt from his chair, looking for the source of the shot. He turned a shocked face to Valerie.

He tried to run, but hadn't taken three steps when two more chuffs of gunfire sounded. His lifeless body skidded and lay still.

Gordon James stepped from the shadows.

"I'm so sorry, Valerie. Damon told me the two of you no longer had a mental connection. So when you said he was coming here, I just didn't understand. And then I thought it was too obvious to be a trap." His voice caught, but he forced out the words. "If not for that, we might have made it here in time."

He knelt beside Camillo to confirm the man was dead. "I trusted Camillo, too. Maybe it's time to turn in my *spook* badge."

"It's not your fault," she said. "Without you, I wouldn't have got in. And these bastards would have walked away scot-free." She dabbed her eyes with the sleeve of her blouse and leaned over Damon. His face was unlined, as if at peace for the first time. Blood pulsed through his veins, but there was no spark of life in his eyes.

"He's gone," she breathed. "Give me your gun."

"You don't have to do that. He might recover."

She shook her head. "He won't. I know."

"I suppose you would." James hesitated, then handed her the butt of the gun. It was heavier than she expected, the weight of the suppressor pulling the barrel down. With her hands shaking she moved it toward Damon's head.

"On his *right* side," James said gently. "If you hit his implant, it could stop the bullet. And...he's right-handed. The cops just might accept it as a murder-suicide."

Shocked at the suggestion, she looked in confusion at Camillo's crumpled form and then at Janus. They were in a rough line from Damon. Weakly, she shifted to Damon's right, but as she tried to lift the gun, a sob full of all the heartache of the world erupted from her lungs.

James took the gun from her and supported her arm to pull her away.

There was a silence, as at the end of all things.

The muffled crack that shattered it was the thunder of her personal Armageddon.

24

December 21, 2042

"We ask, are there other minds like ours in the universe? Then ask, are they also handicapped by the same individual isolation? For surely minds that can transcend such crippling confinement are minds that could span the stars."
The Speeches of Damon Leiter
Collected by V.A. Klug

The smell of vegetation was soothing: earthy undertones of forest loam with a straw-like duskiness of drying grass, and resinous accents carried gently down the mountainside from evergreen trees higher up. Valerie stood at the edge of the village, enjoying the birdsong, but listening for something else. At first, she'd tried to make the time productive, gathering grasses for a broom, but now she just stood, waiting.

She heard the party coming ten minutes before she saw flashes of clothing through branches. Tam Bya pha was in the lead. Two other guides accompanied him. The fourth figure was clearly a white man. In another five minutes Gordon James came around a tree trunk and stopped in front of her, his face a mixture of sweat and surprise.

"I guess I was expected," he said.

"I heard you coming."

"I'd be amazed if you didn't *smell* me coming. But in my defence, more than half of the stench is elephant. I'm just glad I was the only foreigner in the group, so they let me ride on the neck. Being tossed around in one of those tourist baskets would've made me puke."

Valerie laughed and took the duffle bag from his hand, then led him toward the center of the village.

"How do you live out here?" he asked. "I thought Wiang Nuea was the end of the Earth, but then from there to here...."

"I warned you it would take a few days. Even longer when the rainy season keeps us from using the river. Anyway, it's wonderful living here. Its isolation is the point—I don't have to tell you that."

"I know. I nearly didn't get out of the US. Detained at the airport. I had to fake a call from the Department of Homeland Security." He gave a nod and a smile to two elderly women who were using an oversized mortar and pestle to pound an unseen substance.

"Grinding chillies for dinner," Valerie said.

"Is there something special going on? Those ornamented headdresses...."

"No, they wear those all the time. They think the silver beads and bangles bring them long life."

"Maybe I should get one." He bobbed his head and was rewarded with a flash of white teeth from a younger woman, winnowing, tossing grain into the air from a tray. Probably rice. "I'm glad you picked higher ground. It was stifling down in the tropical undergrowth."

Valerie nodded. "The village was already here. We just built our compound on the far side of it."

"And everybody's still here? Nobody got cabin fever and hightailed it back to civilization?"

She returned his smile. "The Robbins, the Shamatas...although they don't live together as couples. Quite a few people from Tamao's organization. Even the Washington guys. Ebon Parrish...well, there was no point in moving him, and Rosa won't come without him. So I hope ImagiCap will leave them alone."

"There's a good chance of that," James said. "Have you followed the news?"

"Of course. We've got very efficient power generators—both solar and water—and our satellite uplink is surprisingly reliable. *And* secure—don't worry."

"Then you know that ImagiCap has its hands full, just like every other company around the world. More than most, because they invested heavily into banking just before the whole house of cards began to wobble. They've got more important things on their minds than chasing after any of us. It's the paranoia of the governments that nearly got me caught."

"Is it really as bad as they say?" Valerie stopped at a pair of carts on the street and haggled fluently in Thai with two women over some vegetables. James waited until she'd finished and they started walking again before answering. Even then, the words came reluctantly.

"Yeah, it is. And there's worse to come. Companies can cope with some decline in productivity, but drops of forty and fifty percent because of the goddamn augments...nobody's paying attention to their work anymore. The business failures. Well, we've seen those all too many times before, but governments rushed in to bail out the big companies. This time they can't afford to. And the personal bankruptcies. I just don't know what will happen." They stopped walking and he looked into her eyes. "Ordinary people who've had their credit cut off...they're stealing because they need the high they get from *acquiring* things!"

"God." It was hard to imagine. But then she thought of Helayne West.

"There've always been people who spent beyond their means," he continued. "But now...it's like a sickness. And by the time the banks realised how far everyone's debts exceeded their assets—and I mean *everyone*'s—it was like a train whose locomotive has already gone over the cliff. There's just no way to push it back." They began to walk again, but were silent for a time. They'd left most of the wooden and bamboo shacks behind, and even the forest birds had gone quiet. Valerie looked at James and he gave a slow shake of his head.

"Whole economies are going to collapse this time. Maybe all of them. That'll be reason enough for you to hide out here in the middle of nowhere."

"Thailand won't be immune, then," she said. "No tourism. There won't be anything left but the drug trade." She was surprised to see James smile.

"Sorry," he said. "That just reminded me of one of the small villages on the way here. They tried to tell me that the village pusher's place was actually a *museum* to the opium trade."

"We all need our opium...of one kind or another," she said quietly.

Then they were at the compound. It was like a smaller version of the Lisu village, carefully designed that way to fool satellite surveillance. The main difference was the color of the faces: Whites, Blacks, Asians, Latinos, native Americans—the world in microcosm. Some still wore western-style clothing that showed heavy wear, but most had adopted the loose garments of the local people. Valerie watched her companion's face. He was clearly surprised at their number.

"More come almost every day," she said. "God knows how they all find us. I almost think...." Then she gave an apologetic shrug. "Never mind. That explanation can wait. I'll show you a place you can shower. A rain barrel with a spigot."

His laugh was good to hear.

#

It hadn't been easy, forging a community in the jungle, but most of the logistical problems were now behind them. Without any overt direction from her, people in the compound had begun to link their minds through their augments via bluetooth to speed the process of making decisions. Instead of requiring long verbal presentations, the facts of any issue could be shared instantly, without any misinterpretation, mind-to-mind. And a general consensus always became apparent, even without formalized vote-counting. It was democracy in its most basic form; and though Valerie feared for its fragility, it gave her a warm hope that buoyed her above the day-to-day challenges.

She called for a special feast, and then gathered the community together around a huge bonfire. She had never sought the leadership of their collective. Everyone simply deferred to her in a way she still couldn't explain. That night she sensed that they needed to hear from her. Words hadn't lost their importance, and probably never would. They were the foundation of human history, culture, and intellectual progress. And a lifetime of spoken language was a habit that couldn't be dismissed or replaced. She would need the help of the augments to translate her words into the many languages and dialects represented in their little model of a global village. But the human voice with its complex sounds was still a better conduit of emotional and spiritual matters than digital appliances could yet provide.

The things she had to say would be hard to hear.

"Our friend Gordon James has come to us," she began, "bringing word from the outside. We've all seen the newsfeeds. Gordon confirms them. The civilization we've so utterly taken for granted is on the verge of collapse. It is impossible to predict the outcome. Civilizations have collapsed before, and the human race has carried on. But it is also impossible to deny that twilight has come, and in all likelihood, a long night is ahead of us." She allowed the soft echoes of her words to quiet, while she looked into faces she knew so well.

"It is one thing to leave behind our homes, and in many cases our families, to sequester ourselves in this remote place. It's quite another to know that those families are in danger. That there may soon be no homes to return to. And I cannot tell you what to do. Each of you will have to make your own decision. Should you go back to those you left, and face their fate with them? Or should you stay here, and try to build a better future: a society able to rise above the remains of the last? One that will ultimately provide rescue and hope to those who can weather the coming storm?

"There *is* hope amidst the gloom. The hardships of economic collapse do not only pit people against people, they also force those same people to come together to help one another. Strangers must extend the hand of assistance and friendship and must seek it in return.

"A colleague of mine in neuro-research believed that human consciousness was on the brink of a precipice much more dangerous than an economic one. In many ways, individuals who make up our society had become isolated to a far greater degree than those of us here, in the jungle of Thailand. In the hard times to come, that kind of isolation will no longer be possible. And from that harsh truth springs great hope."

The emotions in the clearing were as palpable as the forest scents. Fear, regret, deep inner turmoil. But also, the first stirrings of encouragement and optimistic determination.

"The hope that comes from dissolving isolation is strange and tenuous," Valerie resumed. The low buzz of voices stilled once again. "This new hope involves us all. Envelops us all, here and out there.

"*A new consciousness has arisen.*"

#

Valerie had been thunderstruck when she learned of the global mind Damon had discovered. And her first efforts to access it were a failure. She had tried to reconstruct it, but finally realised that it already existed on its own and she had only to find it. To reawaken it.

That first connection, when it came, overwhelmed her—she came back to awareness afterward to find herself lying awkwardly on the rough floor of her hut. But gradually she had found her footing amid the mental maelstrom and cast forth a steady beacon of calm until chaos resolved into order, like the discordant tuning of a full orchestra brought together by the maestro into one single powerful, throbbing note.

If the economies of the world were truly about to collapse, the internet and the systems that powered it would not survive. Yet humanity would find ways to produce electricity, as her compatriots in the compound had, and the technologies of communication, especially the human internet, would not be abandoned except in the last extremity. The global mind had been raised to self-sustaining life, and it would not now relinquish that spark.

She sang back to it reassuringly, like a lullaby. She coddled, coaxed, and comforted, and it responded. It was both awesomely powerful, and heartbreakingly vulnerable; knowledgeable beyond reckoning, yet still innocent.

She showed it pictures of its father. And then introduced them.

For Damon was still with her.

#

After the fire had burned down, and the thrum of voices and minds had subsided into a restless murmur, she returned to her hut and began to undress. She ran a hand through her hair to the oblong plate at the back of her head: the most advanced solid-state data-storage unit available. Falsifying a requisition to have it installed had been her consummate act of defiance against the Taggart Clinic. Her actual departure, weeks later, had only been a formality.

Her plan had been to go to Damon. To show him that he needed her. To be at his side, where she belonged, even though she knew it would take a long time before he would acknowledge that he still loved her.

But time ran out on them.

She'd known where to find him—she had always known where he was, just one of many skills she had developed on her own and which he had never suspected. He'd had a native genius with his implants that she did not, but she had become his equal and even his superior in many of the devices' capabilities. She'd found applications of their power that hadn't yet occurred to him, and had occasionally let him believe that a new function she'd discovered had come to him on its own. And the crowning achievement was the doorway between their minds that he'd permitted at their last meeting, at her parents' place. She'd kept it wedged open, even after he had set his skills to sealing it shut.

Then she'd set about saving his life.

There was nothing that could be done to save the physical man known as Damon Leiter—somehow, she'd known that for months. It was as if he'd deliberately focused the evil of the world upon himself, and his flesh and blood would have to be sacrificed. But his mind...there might be a way to keep *that* from oblivion. Her hope was that Damon had invested so much of himself into his implants for so long that there would be almost nothing of the being that inhabited his flesh brain that was not duplicated in the plexus of graphene circuits.

And she'd set about copying every byte of data from his implants into her new storage device.

Every spark; every gesture. Every pixel; every fond memory. Every string of ones and zeroes; every conviction and commitment. Bit by bit, day by day, she had coaxed the data stream across the ether, expending her greatest energy to keep it secure and inviolate. He'd flowed into her with a digital purity unequalled. And soon after the transference was complete, Damon Leiter had been caught and killed.

In the throes of despair, she had fled to that refuge grafted onto her body *and had found him there*. Wrapped herself in him. Retreated from the world for a long span of stark, unfeeling days. Then, on a day of sunshine and a promise of spring, *they* had emerged, like a butterfly from a cocoon. Outwardly, still with the skin of Valerie Anne Klug. But inwardly...?

Even she was not sure. Were they Siamese twins, joined at the psyche? Or was it even closer than that: one mind, she the *ego*, he the *id*?

Her friends treated her differently—that much she could see. But they had no suspicion of the truth. Perhaps one day she would reveal it.

She'd only been looking for a way to cling to the warmth of his memories, and to preserve his intellect. The reality was unforeseeable and breathtaking. Had the true, essential flame of his existence—his identity, his *soul*—somehow transported itself from his dying body into a new home?

That was beyond her understanding.

She only knew that he was with her when she needed him. Which was always, and forever. She was no longer certain which thoughts were his and which her own.

The way it was meant to be.

And in that realization, she saw the face of a new age.

Acknowledgments

Writing a book can be a solitary pursuit: one mind and one pair of hands. But there can't be many books that don't owe *anything* to someone other than their primary creator. Support comes in many forms and at many levels, and it is all appreciated.

My wife Terry-Lynne patiently listens to me chatter about my ideas and characters, then reads the first polished draft. She doesn't say much (though it's always worthwhile when she does) but she is *never* discouraging, and that means so much.

My first readers for *Augment Nation* were David Carnes, Judy Blanchard, Matthew Del Papa, and Ben Reitzel, who took a chance on an untested story and give me their views. Most importantly, they confirmed that I'd produced a viable novel and not just a bunch of fancy words on a page.

For *Augment Nation* I also owe a debt of thanks to my agent at the time, Justin Bell, for his efforts to place the manuscript, and for support and helpful suggestions. And especially Eleanor Wood, who called *Augment Nation* a "powerful novel". From someone who has represented SF giants like Robert A. Heinlein, Larry Niven, Spider Robinson, Jack Williamson, and so many others who fueled my lifelong love of science fiction, that assessment gave me a much-appreciated boost of confidence. (I can do this—Eleanor said so!)

I've read the works of so many great writers, and benefited from their generous assistance and teaching, but no one more so than "Canada's dean of science fiction" Robert J. Sawyer. One of the most valuable things Rob has taught me is that science fiction should be *about something important*. I try to live by that mantra. Thanks, Rob!

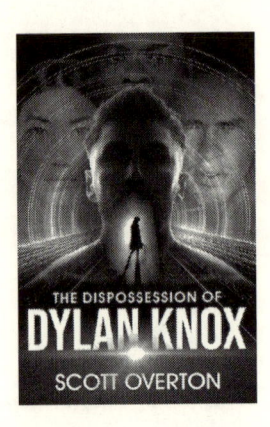

THE DISPOSSESSION OF DYLAN KNOX

Dylan Knox is not the man he was. He may be like no man who ever existed.
How do you *feel* if an old lover doesn't remember you?
What do you *say* if they act like a different person each time you meet?
What should you *do* if they might be an impostor? Mentally unstable. A threat to the very security of your country.
Dylan's tale of a bold space mission, and a tragic accident is utter fantasy. Unless it's too crazy *not* to be true.
Brooke Chappelle has two choices: trust, or betrayal. And falling in love is the last thing she needs.

" The futuristic and technological elements combine seamlessly with political issues to create a plot that is timely and thought-provoking…will appeal to any reader who values the enduring human story of love and trust."
Renny deGroot—author of *Torn Asunder*

Buy yours: https://books2read.com/Dispossession

NAÏDA

The glowing structure at the bottom of a lonely northern lake is clearly not of this Earth, but scuba diver Michael Hart can't stay away. What it offers will change him forever, leaving him with astonishing abilities and a destiny he would never have imagined. Except it might be a destiny he no longer controls.

The actions Michael takes will make him a hero, or the greatest traitor the world has ever known.

Because he is no longer alone, not even in his own body.

There is another.

Naïda.

Readers say:

"A deep dive into the best parts of science fiction—thrilling and thought-provoking! *Naïda* is Overton's best book yet. I buy him on sight and never regret the choice."

"I COULD NOT PUT IT DOWN. ... Extraordinary. Enjoy."

Buy your copy: https://books2read.com/Naida

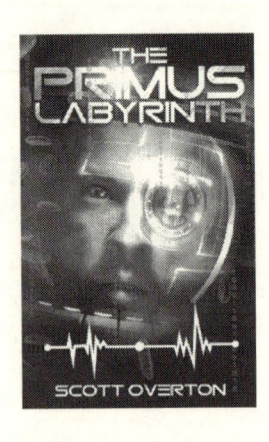

THE PRIMUS LABYRINTH

    A woman's bloodstream has been seeded with destruction.

    Curran Hunter almost died at the bottom of the ocean. Now an innocent victim will die unless Hunter can purge her body of deadly devices by piloting the *Primus*, a prototype submersible the size of a virus. Its control system uses *Virtual Reality*—its creators assure Hunter there can be no danger.

    They are utterly wrong.

    "Loved it! I give this book an enthusiastic four stars for its political intrigue, discussion of moral dilemmas, exciting action scenes, and fully fleshed characters..." Charlotte Graham—Reedsy Discovery reviewer

Buy yours: https://books2read.com/PrimusLabyrinth

BEYOND: Stories Beyond Time, Technology, and the Stars

Ride a bright flame of imagination across time and space with fifteen mind-stretching stories beyond time, beyond technology, and even beyond the stars.

A man who can walk through walls.

Agents who repair the mistakes of the past.

An invasion from beneath our feet.

A man who learns his replacement body was previously owned and died mysteriously.

A disastrous experiment to harness the awesome power of a hurricane.

Don't be afraid to go BEYOND.

"Scott Overton is a storyteller of boundless skill...a writer to watch." —Mark Leslie, author of *Haunted Hamilton* and *I, Death*

Buy yours: https://books2read.com/rl/scottovertonSFF

DEAD AIR

It's a hard thing to accept that someone wants you dead. It forces you to decide if you have anything worth living for.

When radio morning man Lee Garrett finds a death threat on his control console, he shrugs it off as a sick prank—until minor harassment turns into undeniable attempts on his life. When the deadliest assault yet claims an innocent victim, Garrett knows he has to force a confrontation.

"A gripping, insightful debut from a veteran radio personality and gifted wordsmith." —Sean Costello, author of *Here After*

Find out how to add these compelling reads to your own collection at www.scottoverton.ca .

Or https://books2read.com/DeadAir

ABOUT THE AUTHOR

A radio broadcaster for more than thirty years, Scott Overton described that world in his first novel, the mystery/thriller Dead Air, published by Scrivener Press. Dead Air was shortlisted for a Northern Lit Award in Ontario, Canada. But the rest of his writing is science fiction and fantasy, including his 2020 science fiction/thriller The Primus Labyrinth, the 2021 SF adventure Naïda, and 2022's SF/psychological thriller The Dispossession of Dylan Knox. His short fiction has been published in numerous magazines and anthologies, many of those stories brought together in his BEYOND collections.

Now a freelance author and voice talent, Scott works from his home on a lake in Northern Ontario. His distractions from writing include scuba diving and a vintage sports car.

You can learn more and read free stories at Scott's website www.scottoverton.ca .

A Word to the Reader.

Authors cherish their readers and readers can become devoted to their favorite authors. We always hope so!

If you enjoyed this book please consider leaving an honest review wherever you bought it, or with any reading communities you participate in. After buying our books, that's the absolute best way you can help us continue doing what we do and bringing you the stories you want to read. Just a few lines will do, and I'd truly appreciate it.

Thanks, and I hope you'll look for my other books too.

Scott

Manufactured by Amazon.ca
Bolton, ON